Killer in the Shadows

Trip Hazard Book 1

JANNINE MILLAR

ISBN: 979-8-4664-9957-5

DEDICATION

To my parents,
for their undying belief that I could achieve anything
and make my dreams come true.

And to my brother,
I miss you every day and wish you were here to be a part
of this. I hope you have access to Amazon up there.

CONTENTS

Acknowledgments   i

Prologue   1

Part One   3

Chapter 1   5

Chapter 2   10

Chapter 3   17

Chapter 4   30

Chapter 5   34

Chapter 6   42

Chapter 7   50

Chapter 8   57

Chapter 9   62

Chapter 10   69

Chapter 11   77

Chapter 12   80

Chapter 13   90

Chapter 14   94

Chapter 15   107

Chapter 16	109
Part Two	111
Chapter 17	113
Chapter 18	117
Chapter 19	127
Chapter 20	136
Chapter 21	146
Chapter 22	149
Chapter 23	154
Chapter 24	157
Chapter 25	161
Chapter 26	164
Chapter 27	171
Chapter 28	179
Chapter 29	187
Chapter 30	195
Chapter 31	200
Chapter 32	207
Chapter 33	211
Chapter 34	217

Chapter 35	221
Chapter 36	231
Chapter 37	235
Chapter 38	240
Chapter 39	245
Chapter 40	248
Chapter 41	253
Chapter 42	260
Chapter 43	262
Chapter 44	272
Chapter 45	276
Chapter 46	279
Chapter 47	282
Chapter 48	284
Chapter 49	288
Chapter 50	300
Chapter 51	314
Chapter 52	317
Chapter 53	324
Chapter 54	326

Chapter 55   333

Epilogue   345

A Bit About Me   351

Book 2 Taster   353

Trip Hazard News   355

ACKNOWLEDGMENTS

Firstly, thank you again to my parents, for the infinite hours of support and enthusiasm in editing, reading and discussing – this wouldn't be happening without you. Mum, thanks for the endless cups of tea and arbitration when dad and I couldn't agree on a comma. Dad, thanks for the road trips to potential murder scenes and your worrying knowledge on all things covert. Trip Hazard has completely consumed their lives, almost as much as mine.

To a missed family member, who sadly will never get to read this. Karen, I hope Ross would have liked seeing his name in print.

Thanks also to my friends and clients, for listening to my anxious ramblings about the books and for boosting my confidence to proceed.

And finally, to any potential TV or film producers out there – please audition my father for a role (any role will do) or I won't hear the last of it.

Killer in the Shadows

Trip Hazard Book 1

PROLOGUE

North Devon - Twenty Years Earlier

She stood at the top of the cliff and for the first time in her life, truly appreciated the stunning beauty of The Valley of The Rocks. It's craggy, harsh stone faces bled down into the calm dark waters below, gently pulsing against their foundations. It was silent except for the light breeze catching loose tendrils of her dark hair, whipping them forward to wrap across her face like inky ribbons. Earlier, there had been endless tears, but they had long since dried into dirty streaks down her pale skin. Her blouse, once white and crisp, now hung torn and dirty.

Her long skirt was ripped and damp against her body and she shivered, but felt no cold. She felt nothing now as she stared into the darkness below. For a brief moment, she wondered how many souls were hidden in those deep waters and felt as though they were beckoning her to join them. So, unblinking, she stepped forward and disappeared from sight. Silently, she fell towards the rock-strewn cold waters below, where the troubled souls beneath the surface welcomed her into their murky world.

Moments later, a young boy on a bicycle, skidded to a stop a few feet from where the woman had disappeared. He fell to his knees and hesitantly crawled towards the rocky edge.

'MUM!' he screamed.

Tears streamed down his face as he looked over the edge of the cliff, his eyes settling upon the twisted, lifeless body. The ragged rocks below had become her final resting place, her dark hair now moving like ghostly fingers in the sea breeze.

The boy was unable to pull his eyes away from the motionless shape that was once his mother, the image now burned indelibly into his conscious mind and would continue to haunt him forevermore.

PART ONE

KILLER IN THE SHADOWS

CHAPTER 1

West Bay, Dorset - Present Day

On the dark horizon, a mile from shore, the Royal Navy frigate HMS Portland loomed ominously as a blackened silhouette. It was 2am and the sea mist hung heavily in the still air, calm waters lapping gently against the vessel. In the silence of the night, a RIB was lowered into the sea with three crew and a passenger onboard the small powered boat. It made its way slowly through the shallow waters until it was only a few metres from the sandy shoreline. The passenger, dressed in a wetsuit, jumped overboard and waded onto the beach, as the RIB turned and disappeared into the gloom, heading back towards the ship.

The passenger walked along the sand and shingle towards a stony embankment, leading up to a car park. There was only one vehicle parked there, a man slumped behind the wheel.

The figure crept up to the driver's window and lightly tapped the glass. The man didn't move. Trying the handle and realising it was locked, the gentle tapping quickly became a loud hammering. The man's body jolted and as he turned towards the side window, his elbow rested on the horn – the noise blasting out into the silent stillness.

'What the hell!' he said as he opened his car door.

'Bloody hell Trip, I told you to be stealth like! You've just woken up the entire population of West Bay,' the woman tutted.

'Just get in the damn Jeep Pippa, while I recover from my heart attack.'

As she got into the passenger seat, she immediately leant over towards the indicator stick.

'What are you doing?' he said as she flashed the headlights of the car towards the horizon.

'Just telling them I'm safe.'

'Who?' he looked around, 'we're the only ones stupid enough to be out at this time of night.'

'HMS Portland.'

'Huh?'

'Here,' she said passing him a pair of night vision goggles.

He looked towards the horizon. 'There's a big boat there!'

'It's a frigate - HMS Portland,' and she rolled her eyes.

He watched as the small boat was hoisted back onboard the ship, then the Aldis lamp on the main deck flashed a number of times.

Trip looked across at Pippa. 'What did they just flash back?'

'L-A-T-E-R-S,' she smiled. 'Come on then, we need to make two stops before we go home.'

He turned towards her. 'What? It's the middle of the night for god's sake! Where the hell do you need to go at 2am in a wetsuit?'

'Rampisham, near Maiden Newton.'

'The old BBC radio transmission site?' he asked confused.

'Yes.'

He started the ignition, having learnt over the years that the world which Pippa lived in, was far from normal. He'd known her for many years, having met her initially through his friend Tooga Davis. No one knew her exact age, but Trip would have guessed she was in her late fifties, although he knew better than suggesting that to her. She was slim and of average height - but that's where the averageness of Pippa ended. She was a complete enigma. The image she portrayed to the majority, hid a chequered and colourful past of which Trip was pretty sure he hadn't even scratched the surface of yet.

Just over twenty minutes later, they approached Rampisham.

'Park in front of the metal gate there,' she pointed.

'I thought this place was decommissioned in 2011?' he said, pulling over.

'That's what you're meant to think,' she winked and got out the vehicle. 'I'll be five minutes,' and slammed the car door.

He watched as she talked into a small intercom, then seconds later, the gate slowly slid open and she disappeared inside the compound. As she approached one of the derelict-looking buildings, a door swung open and two men stepped forward. After a brief discussion, she followed them inside and the door closed.

Trip glanced around. Five minutes ago, he assumed he was alone, but now felt as though there were many eyes watching him.

His mobile rang, startling him.

'Trip Hazard,' he said looking around for cameras.

'It's me you idiot – you OK?'

'Jeez Tooga, bad timing mate.'

'Why, what you up to?'

'Half an hour ago, I was picking up a hitchhiker wading out the sea in a wetsuit at West Bay, who'd cadged a lift with HMS Portland. The same person nearly gave me a heart attack banging on the car door. Now I'm currently sitting outside an alleged decommissioned radio transmission site, having just watched the wetsuit-clad hitchhiker disappear inside with two men dressed in black – and feel as if I'm being watched from every angle.'

'So, just a normal night in sleepy Dorset with Pippa then!' Tooga laughed.

'Yep exactly. Anyway, what did you want at this time of night – everything OK?'

'I knew you'd be awake, with it being the anniversary of Gabby's death. Just wanted to make sure you weren't wallowing in misery and needing your arse pulled out the quagmire.'

'Your kind words are very touching mate! Seriously though, I think this is why Pippa decided to drag me into her covert weirdness tonight to be honest. The distraction is good though and I'm doing OK, generally.'

For the previous three days leading up to this date, he'd tried to not slip back into the miserable state Tooga now referred to.

'Good to hear – come up to Birmingham and stay at my club soon. OK?'

'Yep, will do. Thanks for calling mate – appreciate it.'

'Say hello to Pippa – and tell her she owes me a crate of Aberfeldy!' and Tooga hung up laughing.

Suddenly, the door in the building opened and Pippa reappeared. As she retraced her steps back to the gate, it automatically slid open and she walked through, heading towards the Jeep.

'Home?' he asked.

'Not quite – one more stop,' and she clicked on her seatbelt. 'Head towards Poundbury and I'll direct you when we get closer.'

He started the ignition and pulled out on to the road.

'Tooga phoned – he said you owe him a crate of whisky.'

'Bloody hell that man forgets nothing!' she laughed.

As they approached Dorchester forty minutes later,

Pippa pointed across the road. 'Pull in there.'

'The petrol station?'

'Yes.'

He turned off the ignition and she jumped out, walking up to the kiosk window, still in her wetsuit.

A few minutes later, she got back in the Jeep.

'Seriously?' he said as she closed the door.

'What?' she said innocently, 'I was hungry.'

He shook his head. 'Now can we go home?'

'We can.'

CHAPTER 2

Roni Porter shivered slightly as the cool sea breeze wrapped itself around her like a damp cloak. There was no one else around, but that's how she preferred it – the peace and tranquillity of the early morning hours. Zipping up her jacket, she pulled out her cigarettes as she walked along the coastal path towards Portland Bill Lighthouse - her adopted stray dog Bear, trotting beside her. She sat down on a bench, lit a cigarette and looked out across the water. Within moments, her mind began flickering back to her early childhood in North Devon. The memories, as usual, began to resurface and as much as she tried to suppress them, they persisted.

Her father had been an alcoholic who was in the pub more than he was ever at home. Her mother had worked three jobs, just to earn enough money to put food on the table for Roni and her younger brother, William. There was never anything left for new clothes or toys - cheap cast offs from the local charity shop were all that could ever be afforded. And yet her father had always managed to stagger home drunk with a belly full of beer and whisky.

When Roni was 8 years old, her mother had been killed

10

in front of her by a hit and run driver. The Skoda had come speeding around the corner, driven by a teenager swigging from a beer can, music blasting from the speakers. He hadn't seen the woman crossing the road. The noise of the impact was chilling as her mother's body was tossed into the air like a frisbee, falling back to the ground in slow motion, crumpled and lifeless. The driver never stopped, racing off into the night, eventually abandoning the stolen vehicle. Every night in bed, Roni could still see her mother's bent and bloodied body, lying like discarded litter, her soulless eyes blindly staring into the night sky unable to see anything now.

Her father couldn't, or wouldn't, cope on his own with two young children. Only a few weeks after her mother's death, they'd been taken into care by Social Services. She'd never seen her father again. Six months later, he'd been found dead behind a pub.

From then on, a life of foster homes had commenced. She was labelled a 'problem child' after foster home number two. The father had insisted they had to leave the bathroom door open – after she refused, he smacked her, so she stamped on his foot and punched him. And so, appeared foster home number three…and then four…

This pattern continued until Roni was 13 years old, when the final straw came. Her latest foster parents had believed their own unpleasant son, when he said she'd pushed him down the stairs. The reality was, she'd caught him throwing stones at her brother and chased him inside, where the boy slipped on the stairs, banging his head. She, of course, was blamed and after a scolding from her foster parents, packed her rucksack with the few belongings they owned. She told William they were going to find their own place to live, but as they were escaping through the window, the foster father managed to grab William. That was the last time she would ever see her brother.

The next morning, after a cold and uncomfortable night's sleep in bushes, she'd watched as the son walked off to school - alone. Later that morning, she overheard the mother tell a neighbour, '....*my husband insisted Social Services remove both of the children as he thought the girl was beyond salvation...*'

With no means to find where William was taken, she ran away, eventually getting on a bus to Plymouth, completely broken hearted. The years between thirteen to twenty-two had been blocked from her mind, those memories firmly locked away. On the eve of her twenty-third birthday, she was stabbed as a warning by the local drug dealer she owed money to. That nearly cost Roni her life, for what it was worth. After leaving hospital two weeks later, she got on a train to Weymouth, then a bus onto Portland. Over the next six months, she got herself clean and a job in the local Co-op shop, eventually being able to afford to rent a one-bedroom flat - her first ever proper home.

Now at thirty-eight, she had no real friends, except Bear and her neighbour Finn. He owned the local fish and chip shop and occasionally brought her back some leftover chips.

She blinked away a tear, not realising she'd been crying. Bear nudged her hand and she rubbed his dark head, hugging him close to her body.

***

The man had been sitting in his vehicle, watching the woman with the long dark hair. He'd first seen her walk along the coastal path when he'd driven past early one morning. This was now the fourth time he'd watched her - and the dog. The animal was going to be a problem, he knew that. But when he saw her dark hair dancing in the wind, the rage that burned in his mind would make the dog a minor inconvenience.

He watched her get up from the bench and walk towards him, the dog by her side. Quickly looking around, he put on some thick glasses and pulled his baseball cap down over his eyes. After getting out of his vehicle, he walked towards the rear and opened the boot, pretending to look for something. As the woman walked in his direction, he glanced up.

'Excuse me, do you know where The Admiralty Hotel is on South Way? I was supposed to check in by 10pm, but there was a bad accident on the motorway near Exeter, my battery is dead on my mobile and I've borrowed a friend's car that hasn't got SatNav. I can't tell you how glad I am that someone else is awake at this time of night – I was just about to get my coat out and sleep in the car tonight!' he smiled.

She looked up, surprised to see someone else around. 'Oh, errm yes actually – I…' Before she could finish her sentence, the man punched her hard in the stomach. She fell against him, her body folding over, completely winded and gasping for breath. He grabbed the dog by its collar and with effort threw it into the boot, quickly slamming it closed. The dog was growling and barking, scratching at the inside as he grabbed the woman by the hair, pulling her sharply upwards. His hand lashed out, hitting her viciously across the face and her body collapsed towards him once more. Holding her, he pulled open the rear door of the vehicle, roughly pushing her onto the back seat, face down. Her legs hung limply out of the car and he picked them up, sliding her further inside, before slamming the door shut.

He climbed into the driver's seat and grabbed one of the wads of material lying next to him, then leaning over into the back, shoved it into her gaping mouth. Her split lip glistened with fresh blood as it trickled down her chin. Next, he snatched up a small hessian sack and pulled it over her head, tying some string tightly around her neck to keep the hood in place. Finally, he bound her wrists behind her back and reached down to tie the laces together in her boots, preventing her feet from being able to kick out at him.

Satisfied she was well restrained, he started the vehicle

and reversed out of the secluded car park. The dog was still frantically scratching and barking inside the boot, so he turned on the radio to drown out the maddening noise as he drove along Portland Bill Road, towards the lighthouse.

Roni's breath was slowly returning to normal as her eyes flickered open. She tried to recall what had happened in those minutes before blacking out, but all she could remember was someone asking for directions…

With a jolt, her brain clicked into motion. A man had punched her hard in the stomach – but where is she now? She could see nothing, but could feel rough, dank smelling material scratching at her face and something wedged in her mouth. Her head jerked to the left, causing a tightness around her neck and she became aware of her arms painfully pulled back behind her, hands bound together. She tried kicking out with her feet, but had too little movement to help in any way. Instinct made her scream out for help, but all that escaped her lips was a muffled noise.

Suddenly, she heard the scratching and barking nearby – 'Bear!' she tried to shout, but again no words came out.

She was in a vehicle, that much was obvious – but why?

Then the movement stopped and the humming of the engine ceased.

He pulled into the car park by the lighthouse, making sure no one was around and turned off the ignition. Reaching towards the back seat, he roughly jabbed her body with his finger.

'If you make even the slightest noise or struggle in any way or try to escape, I will cut your dog's throat open in front of you. Stay quiet and I'll let your dog live,' the man snarled, then got out of the vehicle and opened the rear door.

Fear made her body tremble uncontrollably - sniffing, snivelling noises coming from inside the makeshift hood. He twisted her feet and untied the laces in her boots, then forcibly grabbed her jacket, pulling her out of the car. She stumbled, her foot twisting at an awkward angle making her fall to the ground. Grabbing her jacket again, he yanked her upright and pushed her forward.

Every few steps she would stop, completely unaware of where she was, but his hand kept ramming into her back, urging her forward. She couldn't make any sense of what was happening to her and what the stranger wanted.

She was stumbling more now – not sure whether it was the shaking in her body - or the fact that the ground was getting stonier and more uneven with each step she blindly took.

The man could see wisps of her dark hair snaking out from under the sack – the breeze catching them and making them dance provocatively in front of his eyes. Anger and hatred coursed through his veins like dark poison, for which there was no antidote. He tensed, wanting to wrap her hair around his hand and snap her neck like a twig, but he needed to contain his anger. Nothing could spoil that final moment for him.

The air had dropped in temperature and she could only now hear blood pounding in her ears. Suddenly, her arm was pulled backwards forcing her to stop. She instinctively went to turn but both shoulders were seized to prevent it. She stood motionless – frozen with fear. The string around the hood was untied and a sudden gust of wind whipped the sack off, carrying it into the air. It vanished from sight and the man cursed. She quickly turned around and saw his face, dark callous eyes glaring back at her. His cap and glasses were now gone and he looked completely different.

She tried to say something through the gag, but he spun her around, untying the cloth wrapped around her wrists.

'And I looked…' he said from behind her.

Blinking, she saw her surroundings for the first time. She was standing at the edge of a cliff face.

'... *and behold a pale horse...,*' he continued, '*...and his name that sat on him was Death...*'

He pulled the gag from her mouth and with one heavy push, she lunged forward over the edge of the cliff. '*...and Hell followed with him.*'

As the final words left his sneering lips, the man leaned over, looking down to the rocks below. Satisfied she was gone, he turned and walked away into the darkness, smiling.

As he neared the vehicle, he could hear the dog still scratching and barking in the boot. He opened it to grab the animal, intending to throw it over the rocks to join the woman. But the dog was too quick and it leapt out and ran off barking into the darkness.

Cursing, the man quickly got back into his vehicle and started the ignition.

The sun would start to come up in a few hours - it was going to be a beautiful day he smiled to himself.

CHAPTER 3

Her body was trying to move, but something warm was across her face, trying to stifle and smother her. Confused images of a dream were still flashing in her mind….an intruder breaking into her house, creeping up the stairs; a knife in his hand twisting, ready to plunge or lash out. The dark figure was large and imposing, casting a dark menacing shadow against the wall of her bedroom. A loud banging began on the door…

Felicity woke up with a start. Something warm *was* in fact across her face and she blinked her eyes trying to focus; beads of sweat clinging to her neck and chest. One of her Ragdoll cats, Wurzel, was sitting on her pillow, his fluffy ginger tail swishing across her face. She scooted him off and her two small dogs, Dusty and Pickle, looked up from the bottom of the bed, eyes blinking at the sudden disruption to their night's sleep.

She picked up her phone to check the time. It was 3am. Yawning, she slumped back down onto her pillow and stared up at the ceiling. She didn't like this time of the morning because her mind would start wandering down a road she preferred not to travel, towards a past she kept locked away.

Suddenly the banging noise from her nightmare resumed - except this time, she was awake. She sat bolt upright, looking around in the gloom, her brain trying to rationalise the sound.

Someone was pounding on her front door.

Felicity lived in a Coach House - a detached building consisting of garages on the ground floor and her living accommodation above. A long staircase led directly from the front door up to a landing, where a stairgate prevented her menagerie of animals from escaping outside. The property was located in a quiet courtyard, consisting of three other coach houses and two detached houses. Considering it was the early hours of the morning, it was particularly worrying and very unusual for anyone to be awake.

The banging began again and panicking now, she peered between her bedroom curtains. Her panic was quickly replaced with irritation and she closed her eyes, counting to ten. Against her better judgement, she stomped downstairs in her pyjamas, unlocked the front door and frustratedly pulled it open.

'Mrs Brumby, what can I do for you at THREE in the morning?'

'It's Mrs Goober – she's stuck up a tree,' Agnes Brumby said. 'She's been up there for ages - I've thrown a wedge of Edam cheese at her hoping it would entice her down, but it hasn't.'

'I'm not sure what you want me to do about it?' Felicity said, stifling a yawn.

'Get her down of course! I've tried the other neighbours, but no one answered – except you.'

Yes - and more fool me, she thought.

Agnes Brumby lived in the coach house at the top of the courtyard. She was eighty-years old, forgetful, nosey, rude and insensitive – and she always wore a tea cosy on her head. No one has ever got to the bottom of her choice of fashion accessory, but Felicity had always just assumed it was because she thought it was a woolly hat – and she wasn't going to be the one to break the news to her that it wasn't.

'So how did your friend get stuck up a tree Mrs Brumby?' she said, humouring the confused old woman.

'Well, I have no doubt she was chasing Mr. Darcy around the neighbourhood again. He probably legged it up the tree to escape, but the old girl clearly followed him hoping for some night time shenanigans. Not that you'd know what that was about, deary,' she said harshly.

She was surprised it had taken Mrs Brumby this long to insult her.

'Well, I'm sure she'll make her way down when she's finished her date,' Felicity smiled, through gritted teeth.

'Not at her age she won't! Her arthritis is terrible now – and if she managed to pounce on Mr Darcy, she'll be worn out, poor old thing.'

'So why did you think throwing a lump of Edam cheese would help the situation?'

'It's her favourite food of course.'

'Of course,' Felicity sighed, wishing she'd ignored the banging on her front door, as all of her other neighbours had.

'So, are you going to help or not?' Mrs Brumby asked impatiently.

'As I said, I'm not sure what I can do to help,' she shrugged, no longer trying to stifle her yawns.

'You can climb up and poke her. You're only a strip of a girl, you'll be able to shimmy up that tree in no time. Come on, follow me….,' and disappearing up the courtyard, she shouted back, '…and I'll get a kipper.'

As much as she wanted to tell the rude old woman to sod off, Felicity knew her conscience wouldn't let her, so instead she pulled some trainers on, grabbed a torch and followed Mrs Brumby outside into the night.

She caught up with the old lady who was now standing near a large tree, staring up into the darkness, tea cosy on her head and waving a kipper around. Felicity wondered if there was an out-of-hours number she could call for a psychiatric evaluation.

Felicity shone the torch up into the tree, to keep Mrs Brumby happy and just as she was about to say goodnight and go home, the beam of torch light reflected off two small orange eyes staring down at her.

'There's a cat up there.'

'Well of course there is – it's Mrs Goober!' Mrs Brumby said looking up at the cat.

'Mrs Goober is a cat?'

'Yes! Oh, keep up deary!' the old woman mocked.

'So, who is Mr Darcy then?'

'The local tom cat of course. I always thought you had a modicum of intelligence my dear, but you're really letting yourself down tonight.'

Count to ten Felicity and don't hit an old lady.

'Right, you wait here Mrs Brumby, while I get some cat treats to coax her down – seeing as the wedge of Edam didn't work,' and nodded towards a 500g block of cheese on the ground, still shrink-wrapped in plastic.

Returning home, she stomped back upstairs to her kitchen and grabbed a packet of cat treats and her mobile phone, then walked back out, towards the tree. Noisily, she shook the bag of treats. Nothing. She scattered a couple of biscuits on the ground. Still nothing. Finding no other option and most definitely not prepared to abandon Mrs Goober, she phoned 999 and was put through to Fire and Rescue.

Having explained the problem, the Fire crew, who were currently out on another call, said they would swing by on their way back to the station - which was located just across the road from the courtyard.

Felicity *being Felicity*, stubborn and impulsive, decided to take matters into her own hands. She placed her mobile safely on top of a wall next to the tree, not trusting Mrs Brumby to hold it, shoved the treats in the small pocket in her pyjama top and put the torch in her mouth. Then, tucking her pyjama trousers into her bed socks, she began to climb.

First, she pulled herself onto the wall surrounding the tree, then shone the torch towards the cat, whose small orange eyes stared down at her. The tree was sturdy with heavy thick branches and she hoped her childhood adventures as a tomboy clambering up trees with her brother, would now come in useful.

She grabbed the first branch and heaved herself up, but as she swung her leg across to go higher, became suspended at a dangerous angle. Worried she would not be able to hold the torch in her mouth for much longer, she tucked it in the waistband of her pyjama trousers. Reaching up to the next branch, her body felt more balanced and she looked up at the cat - it's eyes fixated on the human trying to save it. Pulling herself up a little higher, she finally drew level with Mrs Goober.

'Hello there,' she said as the cat scrambled up out of reach. 'No, don't go higher!'

Straining her arms, she managed to pull herself up to the next branch and as she did, her waistband snagged, creating a gap for the torch to fall down inside her trousers. It lodged at the bottom of her pyjamas, shining through like a beacon.

Her head was now at the same height as the cat.

'Come here little one,' she said, blowing kissing noises at it.

The cat glared at her as she tried to bend slightly to unhook her trousers, but couldn't reach without releasing her hands. As she tried moving her body to free herself, the bag of cat treats slipped out of her pocket and bounced down the tree, all the way to the ground. She glanced down seeing she was much higher than she thought and a moment of panic swept through her.

As Mrs Brumby tutted at the cat treats bouncing off her tea cosy, Mrs Goober slinked past Felicity's head and proceeded to gracefully glide down the branches effortlessly. It jumped onto the wall, leapt off and began its feast on the treats scattered across the floor.

She stood paralysed on her branch, completely stuck with no means of getting down. Clinging onto the tree, she suddenly wished she wasn't so stubborn and impulsive.

As she watched Mrs Goober scoffing the treats below, another cat appeared around the corner. A few moments later two more joined the party, unable to believe their luck at the unexpected feast laid on for them.

When the cats were satisfied that they'd eaten all the buffet food on offer, they congregated at the bottom of the tree looking up at her, their entertainment sorted for the night.

'Come here, Mrs Goober!' Mrs Brumby said bending down and scooping the cat into her arms. 'You've had quite an adventure tonight haven't you!' and she began walking away towards her home.

'Err, Mrs Brumby!' Felicity shouted after her.

'Yes, yes deary – thanks for your help!' she waved from the distance.

She was speechless as the old lady disappeared inside her house - cat in her arms, tea cosy on her head and kipper in her hand.

A few moments later, Felicity became aware of a vehicle approaching. She looked up the courtyard and saw the milk delivery van slowly driving down, pulling up outside a house. The man got out and walked towards the rear of his van.

'HELLO!' Felicity shouted trying to attract his attention.

The man's head looked from side to side, shrugged and carried on opening the van's back door.

'HELLO!' she shouted again.

The man's head appeared around the van, looking

around once more.

'I'M UP HERE!'

He looked towards the roof of Mrs Brumby's coach house.

'NO – I'M UP THE TREE OVER HERE!'

The man cautiously walked over to the tree and looked up.

'What you do?' he said.

'I'm stuck,' she said, staring in the gloom at the Chinese man below her.

'Yes. Stuck. Why?'

'I climbed up to get a cat!'

'Cat, here,' he said pointing to the congregation of cats still staring up the tree, hoping more treats would fall.

'Yes, I know – this was a different cat.'

'Why you can't have this cat?'

Felicity was quickly losing the will to live.

'Do you think you could use my phone there to call 999 and see if the fire engine is on its way yet?'

'OK,' he said picking up her phone. 'Nice phone. Samsung. Do you like? I got iPhone but don't like. You say this good phone? What it do? Good camera?'

'Well, yes it's fine. But do you think you could make the call, then when I get down, I'll happily give you a full and detailed review of it,' she said gritting her teeth again, for the second time tonight.

'OK,' he said. 'No - no call. It want your finger. I try my finger, it not like.'

Felicity closed her eyes and let out a silent scream in her head.

'Have you got a phone you could use?' she asked.

'I got iPhone, but don't like. Give it to daughter.'

But of course, she thought.

'You should get down – it cold. You get frostbum if not careful.'

'Frostbite,' she sighed wearily having gone way beyond losing the will to live.

'Want yoghurt? Got strawberry or toffee. On house. I throw.'

'Please don't throw a yoghurt at me,' she said wondering if the night could get any worse.

'What name?'

'Felicity.'

'Flippity – nice name. I'm Ivan - the Milkman,' he said waving.

'Ivan?' she asked bewildered, looking down at the Chinese man. 'Are you from Wales?'

'No. China,' he said confused.

She wondered if she should risk the broken limbs by jumping, just to escape this bizarre event happening in her life right now.

Finally, in the distance, she could hear a heavy vehicle approaching. Relief flooded through her as the fire engine pulled into the courtyard.

***

As Trip and Pippa drove into Poundbury, a fire engine pulled out in front of them and turned immediately left into a courtyard.

'Follow it! Let's see what's happening in good old sleepy Poundbury,' Pippa grinned.

'But I just want to go home to sleep,' Trip sighed.

'Yes, yes, in a minute.'

He pulled into the courtyard and saw the fire engine parking beside a milk delivery van, blocking any access through. One of the firemen walked up to the Jeep and Trip buzzed the window down.

'Hey Dan, what's happening?' he said to his friend.

'Hi Trip - some woman's got herself trapped up a tree - although the original call said it was a cat, so I'm not really sure what's going on at the moment.' Dan bent down and looked at the passenger seat. 'I'm guessing you know you've got a woman in a wetsuit eating a meat pasty beside you, right?'

'Yeah, it's been a long night and she was hungry apparently. I think the bloke in the petrol station thought he was about to be robbed by a woman in a wetsuit and looked pretty relieved when he only had to hand over a pasty.'

'I bet he was,' Dan said. 'And the wetsuit is because?'

'Because it was bloody raining earlier!' Pippa said with a mouth full of food. 'Now, any chance of you getting the woman out the tree and shifting that bloody truck anytime soon?'

'You could just reverse and go back the way you came?'

'What and miss all the fun! Just hurry up and save her and for god's sake don't drop her.'

'Yes – I mean, no…errrm…well anyway, we shouldn't be long and you can drive through then,' and to avoid Pippa's impatient glares, he quickly walked away.

Dan looked up into the tree. 'Cat stuck?' he said looking at a woman in Snoopy pyjamas in the tree instead.

She nodded her head towards the crowd of cats below.

'My trousers are caught and I don't think I can free them without falling!' she said embarrassed at her predicament.

'Your trousers falling?'

'No - me falling!'

'She stuck,' said Ivan the Milkman helpfully. 'I offered yoghurt. She said no.'

'OK. Hold on,' Dan said, completely baffled at the scene he found himself in. He went to the truck and spoke to his crew mates, who all piled out to have a look, joining the crowd of cats. The arrival of the fire engine had also meant the neighbours were now spilling out of their houses, their camera flashes temporarily blinding her.

'Right, we're putting a ladder up so I can come up and…errrr…undo your trousers,' he said grinning, 'then you should be OK to climb back down the ladder with me. OK?'

'OK,' she sighed with relief.

The fire crew below stood with their arms folded nudging one another enjoying the show, Ivan the Milkman handing out yoghurts.

'Nice night for a tree climb was it?' Dan smiled as he stepped onto the ladder.

'I was helping an old lady - and saving a deceitful cat who swindled my food off me and left me for dead up a tree,' she smiled weakly.

'Where's the old lady?' he asked.

'Buggered off inside the warmth of her house with her bloody cat!'

'You're having a bad night aren't you!' he laughed.

'You could say that, yes.'

'I'm Dan and you are?'

'Felicity.'

'Well Felicity, let's get you down from here. What do you say?'

'Oh god, yes please.'

He reached behind her, unhooking the trousers from a branch. 'Right, you grab the top of the ladder, then turn around so you're coming down backwards towards me.'

'OK.'

As she began to swing her legs on the top rung of the ladder, Dan noticed a tiny tattoo peeking out above her waistband. He then became aware of the glowing bulge at the bottom of her trousers. She followed his eyes to where he was looking.

'I put the torch in my waistband and it slipped down my leg,' she explained.

'Of course you did,' he smiled.

Moments later, she was back on the ground, to a rousing round of applause from the gathered crowd. Feeling embarrassed, she grabbed her phone with as much dignity as possible, whilst wearing pyjamas with a glowing torch trapped in her trouser bottoms. After thanking the crew and repeatedly apologising, she quickly started to walk back towards her house, Dan insisting on escorting her, to make sure she was OK.

She unlocked her front door, slumped down on the stairs and closed her eyes as she sighed, relieved that her ordeal was finally over.

'Are you OK?' Dan asked.

'Not really – helped an old lady with a tea cosy on her head, waving a kipper around. Rescued a stuck cat that wasn't stuck, but then I became stuck. Was asked for a detailed review of my Samsung phone by a Chinese Milkman called Ivan who also offered to throw a toffee yoghurt at me. So, no, it's not been the best night out to be honest,' she sighed.

A car horn beeped as it drove past Felicity's front door.

'I leave yoghurt and extra milk for hot mug for frostbum,' Ivan the Milkman gestured towards her front door.

She looked down and saw the items.

'Thanks,' she smiled wearily.

'Night Flippity,' he said as he drove away.

'Frostbum?' Dan asked.

'Don't ask,' she sighed. 'Thanks again Dan – I'm going to crawl into a corner and die quietly.'

A black Jeep drove past her doorway and she looked up at the driver. Their eyes locked onto each other for the briefest of moments, until finally, she pulled her eyes away.

'Look after yourself Flippity!' Dan laughed and walked back towards the fire engine.

She locked the front door, dragged herself up the stairs and went straight into the bedroom, where she flopped wearily onto her bed.

***

Having deposited Pippa, her wetsuit and the empty pasty wrapper at her house, Trip headed to his apartment building. As he parked in the car park and got out the Jeep, a voice whispered his name. Looking around, he saw it was his neighbour from the flat below. He knew him only as Gav and always thought he looked as if he'd just done something illegal or stupid - and tonight would prove to be no exception.

'Gav,' Trip said yawning.

'Alright Trip. Need you to do something for me,' he said quietly.

'Whatever it is, the answer's no.'

'I need a favour,' Gav said, furtively looking round the dark car park.

'Definitely a no,' Trip reiterated.

'It's life or death man.'

'Still a no, Gav,' and walked towards the apartment block.

'Here,' Gav said following him and pulled out a small plastic bag from his jeans. 'Keep this somewhere safe for me,' and he dropped it inside Trip's jacket pocket.

He reached inside and took it out, seeing it was a USB stick. 'Do you even know what this is?'

'I found it in a laptop which had come into my possession.'

'And where's the laptop now?'

'I dropped it. But I had time to look at that stick first and there's some interesting stuff on it,' he winked.

'Is this illegal Gav?'

'Nah, promise.'

'Why do you need me to hold it for you then?' he said wearily, losing the will to live by the second.

'Cos you're a decent bloke and if anything happens to me, you'll do the right thing,' and with that, Gav quickly walked away.

Feeling too tired to argue, he shoved it in his jeans pocket and headed towards the apartment building.

'And Gav,' he shouted back, 'make sure your bloody car alarm doesn't go off at 6am LIKE IT DOES EVERY SODDING MORNING!'

'Yeah, 'course,' Gav muttered from the shadows.

He unlocked the door to his apartment, threw his jacket onto the chair and headed straight for the bedroom. Kicking his boots off, he fell onto the bed, massaging his temples trying to ease the headache threatening to start. He scratched at the stubble on his face, that was always present in some form or other and ran his hand through his dark hair.

As he finally closed his eyes to sleep, he had no idea about the day he would be waking up to, in just a few short hours.

CHAPTER 4

Later in the morning, after a few hours of restless sleep and unable to settle after her eventful start to the day, Felicity dragged her tired body to the supermarket in Queen Mother's Square, in the centre of Poundbury, West Dorset.

She walked across the car park laden down with grocery bags, placed her shopping in the boot of her car, got into the driver's seat and started the ignition. She glanced into her rear-view mirror and began to reverse, but had only moved a few feet, when there was a sudden metallic bang and her car jolted to an abrupt stop. Utterly confused, she looked into the mirror again where she saw, pushed up into the rear of her car, a black vehicle. Confusion was quickly replaced with anger and she flew out of her car, looking down at the mangled boot. She stared incredulously at the driver who was getting out of his vehicle, scratching the dark stubble on his chin.

He checked the damage to the front of his car then looked up, straight into the eyes of a wild animal.

'What the hell do you think you're doing!' Felicity roared at him, 'I was half way out of my parking space – where did you even come from?'

'I was pulling out of my parking space and YOU

reversed into me!' he said. 'You really should pay more attention when reversing. Have you thought about investing in a rear-view camera?'

'WHAT?' she shouted, her anger now reaching levels she didn't even realise existed.

'A rear-view camera – really helpful for people who aren't so good at reversing.'

'I know what a rear-view camera is! I have one you idiot!' she said, now understanding how road rage can cause sane people to punch someone in the face.

'Oh,' he said, 'how's that working out for you?'

At this point, Felicity saw red and took a step towards him, sensing he was actually enjoying all of this.

'Just give me your insurance details. I don't have time to hear your excuses as to why you are such a terrible driver! I'll get you a pen and paper,' and she turned back to her car.

'What do you need my insurance details for? You hit me! Look, I know a local man who can repair this on the cheap – I'll give you his number if you like?' he offered.

'Cheap?! Oh, I bet you do! - and YOU HIT ME!'

He hesitated, looking quizzically at her.

'Do I know you?' he said feeling there was something familiar about her.

'Absolutely not!'

'Listen, I've had a long morning already and I'm tired, so if we could….,' he started to say when Felicity interrupted.

'LONG MORNING? TIRED! At 3am I helped an old lady with a tea cosy on her head who was waving a kipper around, throwing blocks of cheese at Mrs Goober, who'd climbed up a tree to have sex with Mr Darcy. I got stuck up the bloody tree trying to help a sex-crazed cat, had to be rescued by a fire engine and a Chinese Milkman called Ivan, who's not from Wales, discussed the merits of a Samsung mobile, at the same time as wanting to throw yoghurts at me! So, I think, as far as being tired goes – I BLOODY WIN!'

Trip stared at the woman screaming in front of him and

a smile began to spread across his face.

'You win,' he winked, realising why he recognised her.

A woman leaving the supermarket bravely walked towards the two combatants. 'Are you OK?' she said as she touched the man's arm. 'I saw you drive out of the space and....'

'Ha!' Felicity said interrupting the woman, 'see I told you it was you who hit me! Thank you, a witness! - can I take your...'

'Sorry,' the woman interrupted, 'I was going to say I saw you both collide at the same moment,' she then looked dreamily into the man's eyes, 'are you OK?'

Felicity stood watching the scene evolve. 'Err excuse me? Sorry to interrupt your speed date, but if you're not going to admit this was your fault, then I'll leave you both to it!' and turning, she flounced off back to her car.

Thanking the woman for intervening, he went up to a now very red-faced Felicity and tapped on her window. She opened it an inch.

'Look, let's just admit it was both of our faults, as it clearly was,' he said, 'and let me at least give you the number of my contact who – '

'No. Thank. You!' she snapped. 'I don't need *any* help from you,' and with that, she pressed the button on the window and it sped up sealing him away from her.

'Oh and move your Jeep so I can go!' she shouted through the closed window, looking into his eyes, then suddenly realising he was the driver she'd seen during her early morning antics.

He smiled and reversed out of her way, casually gesturing to her with a flourish of his hand in acknowledgement. As she started to drive off, the car stalled and he raised his eyebrows and smiled. Felicity gritted her teeth, restarted the car and drove away feeling angry and annoyed, then realised that for some reason, she was looking back at him in her mirror.

He watched as she disappeared, his eyes following the vehicle for longer than he could explain why. Finally pulling his attention away, he picked up his mobile and checked the address in the text message. The Editor of the Dorset Echo had asked him to attend a breaking news story.

Trip started up his Jeep and headed towards Portland Bill Lighthouse.

CHAPTER 5

The huge stack of rocks rose up out of the sea like an intimidating giant, towering over the waters below. It was an imposing presence against the bright blue sky and the large slab of stone leaning at an angle against the stack, resembled an open bible on a pulpit.

Trip parked his Jeep in the lighthouse car park and looked across the rugged headland towards Pulpit Rock. As he opened his door, he briefly closed his eyes, breathing in the salty sea air and listening to the sounds of seagulls and undulating water. He grabbed a notebook and climbed out of his vehicle, immediately walking towards a group of people huddled together. Their shoulders were hunched and heads tilted at angles, talking quietly to one another.

'Hey, what's happening over there?' Trip asked as he joined them.

One of the men looked up. 'Think someone has chucked themselves off the rocks,' he said in a strong Dorset accent.

'There's a body then?'

Another man in the group glanced up. 'Yeah, Mick saw it.' He nodded his headed to the left, 'he's the bloke over there talking to the Policeman.'

A grey-haired bearded man, his head tipped down, was

34

shuffling his feet nervously and talking to the officer. A Policewoman, standing at the edge of the car park, was holding a huge dog on a lead. From where Trip was standing, the ferocious dog looked like he would attack anyone that glanced in its direction.

Trip walked over to the Policewoman.

'Morning officer – has someone lost a dog?'

'Sorry sir,' the Policewoman said, 'I'm going to have to ask you to step away – we're waiting for the Crime Scene Unit to arrive and more officers are due any moment to cordon off the area.'

'Oh right, sorry, hope everything is OK…?' Trip waited for an answer to his question, but none came.

The Policewoman gestured with her head, indicating he should move. 'Sir, please…'

'Yes sure, sorry, leave you to it then,' and he walked back towards the group of men.

'Is your friend OK over there? Mick you said? Think I've seen him around here before, doesn't he work at errrm …,' Trip subtly hesitated.

'Yeah, he does the gardening at the lighthouse. Been doing it for years,' one of the group replied.

'Right,' Trip said, getting the answer he was hoping for. 'Must have been quite a shock for him.'

'When he got 'ere this morning to cut the grass, he saw the dog standing at the end of them rocks over there. Barking like crazy he was, still had its lead on. He looked down to see what the dog was barking at and that's when he saw a body down on the rocks, all bashed up. Poor old Mick, glad it weren't me that found it.'

'Yep, not nice,' Trip sighed. 'Is the café over there open do you know?'

The man looked over at The Lobster Pot Café, 'yeah, should be.'

'Thanks,' and Trip left the group alone once more.

He walked across the car park into the Café, taking a seat

by the window and began making some notes, but after a few sentences, his pen ran out of ink. He walked over to a waitress who was busily wiping down and clearing one of the tables.

'Excuse me, have you got a spare pen I can borrow while I have a coffee?'

The woman tutted and began to turn around, agitated by the sound of a voice disrupting her – no doubt another tourist asking ridiculous questions, she thought. She was feeling tired and irritable already and her shift had only just begun. But the moment she looked up at his face, she slightly tilted her head and nervously tucked a loose strand of hair behind her ear. His deep brown eyes together with the warm friendly smile on the lips of his unshaven face, immediately dissolved her bad mood and she suddenly felt a lot less tired.

'Yes of course – have a seat and I'll go and get you a pen and coffee.'

Trip sat down on the chair nearest the window again and looked out towards the rocks and dark sea beyond. He wondered what made someone feel that they had no alternative but to end their life in such a way. Did they have no one in their life for help or support? Were they simply better off leaving this world? Trip had once known all too well that feeling of desperation, but luckily for him, his friend Tooga had sent a man called Tank in a Bentley to stop him from doing something stupid.

The waitress returned with his coffee, pen and a bacon sandwich. 'On the house – you look like you need one,' she purred.

Trip smiled, thanked her for the kindness and was pleased she'd interrupted the dark thoughts of his past.

She returned his smile and walked away feeling slightly flustered, *oh that smile*, she thought.

Trip took a bite of his sandwich and opened his

notebook, continuing to jot down his notes.

Ten minutes later, the waitress returned, 'another coffee?' she asked.

'Thanks, yes great. Sandwich was just what I needed too. Tell me, do you know anything about what's happened at the rocks today?'

'Not really,' she said, 'when I got here this morning the Police were already here, talking to Mick. Terrible shame though.'

'Do you know who the woman was?'

'I've seen her up here before with her dog, Bear, I think I've heard her call it. Don't know her name though.'

'Do you think she could have slipped and fallen over the rocks?'

'Maybe – must have happened when it was still dark 'cos Mick gets here really early in the morning to do the gardening, especially during the summer. This means he's finished before it gets too warm at lunchtime.'

'Does Mick live nearby?'

'Why all the questions,' the waitress laughed, 'you a journalist or something?'

'Yes, well sort of – I'm a freelance journalist *sometimes*. If a newspaper hasn't got someone to cover a story, they'll ask me. But mainly I write for a local Charitable Foundation newsletter, as I prefer a quieter life these days,' he smiled.

'Ah OK,' she said, 'I know Mick really well – at least my dad does. They're drinking buddies, known each other for years. Hang around here a bit longer and Mick will come for his breakfast - once the Police finish with him of course. When he comes in, I'll introduce you,' she smiled.

'That would be great, thank you errr...,' he stalled, hoping to find out her name.

'Jenny,' she blushed.

'Jenny. I'm Trip – Trip Hazard,' he said smiling his appreciation, keen to get that introduction to Mick later.

'Trip Hazard! Seriously? That's your name?' she

laughed.

'Yeah, I know, my dad had a good sense of humour,' he replied – surprisingly not the first time he'd said that.

Jenny walked away smiling.

Trip began to wonder why the dead woman would walk so close to the edge of the rocks in the dark. Surely she would have known the dangers if she came up here regularly in the daylight?

Twenty minutes later, the door to the café opened and in walked Mick, his head hung low. He sat at a table next to Trip, staring out of the window towards the rocks, his eyes red and bloodshot, his skin sallow and grey.

Jenny came up to his table with a coffee. 'I've put extra sugar in Mick, to help with the shock and all that,' she said, reaching down and lightly squeezing his arm.

'Appreciate it,' rasped Mick, his voice still thick with emotion.

'Mick, this is Trip Hazard,' Jenny said, nodding her head towards him. 'He's a journalist, a nice one. He's got a few questions if you're feeling OK to talk.'

'Yeah sure, better than me sitting here staring into nothing,' Mick said.

'That's good of you Mick. Mind if I sit with you?' Trip asked.

'Yeah, course you can.'

Trip got up and pulled out a chair. 'Thanks Mick - can I get you anything to eat? On me obviously.'

'Nice of yer, yeah sausage sandwich would be good. Seems wrong to eat though, considering…,' he said, glancing out through the window towards the cordoned off area.

The waitress disappeared off, leaving the two men alone.

'You lived around here a long time Mick?'

'Yeah, all me life. Was born in Portland and seventy years later I'm still here. Never wanted to live nowhere else.'

'You been doing the gardens at the lighthouse all that

time then?'

'Last thirty years I have – plus some other folks gardens at the Coastal Cottages. Worked at the Brewery in Weymouth before then, until it shut in the 80's.'

Trip jotted down some notes. 'Live alone Mick?'

'Do now, been ten years since my Tess died, god rest her soul. Cancer it was. Nasty way to go that,' Mick glanced off through the window again, temporarily lost in his memories.

Trip gave him a moment, then said, 'what time did you find her Mick?'

'Start work at seven in the summer, gets too warm for me by lunchtime so I'd rather start early and finish early. When I got here this morning the dog was standing at the edge of the rocks, barking his head off. I shouted over to him to come to me but he wouldn't budge. In the end I went over to him, see what he was stressing over and that's when…,' Mick's voice trailed off, '……that's when I saw her down on the rocks below…,' he gulped, rubbing his old calloused hand across his forehead, '…she was just lying there and her hair was blowing around in the wind. Never will forget the way her body was bent out of shape like that.'

'Sorry to ask you this Mick, but was she face down?'

'Yeah.'

'Did you know the girl?'

'Not really – Roni her name was, quiet girl. Always said hello though when I saw her walking her dog. Poor thing, loved her he did, could tell the way it never left her side. I'd see her sat looking out at the sea, the two of them and they wouldn't move for ages. Only saw her the other morning. Won't see her again now. Sad ain't it, that she felt she had to do that. Poor Roni, wished I'd talked to her more now, maybe I could've helped, you know? What'll happen to the dog?' Mick asked.

'Probably go to a shelter.'

'I'd have it, but I got an old moggy that hates dogs. Hope they find him a good home soon,' Mick said, looking down at his coffee.

'Do you think she could have accidentally fallen, as it sounds like it happened in the dark.'

'Nah, she was up here most days walking her dog – she'd have known not to walk here at night cos of the danger of tripping or falling off the rocks.'

'Don't you think it's strange that if she came up here at night purposely with the aim of ending her life, that she wouldn't have left her dog with someone, rather than bring it with her?' Trip asked.

'Dunno.'

Trip definitely thought it was odd – but until he knew more about Roni, then he wouldn't know what had happened to make her feel that she wanted to end her life so badly - or why she'd brought her dog with her.

'One last question Mick - do you know her last name by any chance?'

'No, only knew her as Roni, sorry.'

'You've been really helpful Mick, thanks for your time today.' Trip reached into his jacket pocket and slid a card across the table. 'Here's my number - if you think of anything else that might be useful, please give me a call. I want to write a nice article for this poor woman, so she just doesn't disappear as if she's been erased.'

'Yeah, that'll be good,' he took the card off Trip, 'thanks I will.'

Trip stood up and squeezed Mick's shoulder, 'take care of yourself and thanks again for your time,' and he walked over to the counter.

'Poor Mick, he's such a nice old fella,' the chef said, who was on his way back into the kitchen.

'Yeah, he seems a nice bloke,' Trip said. 'Did you know the woman who's died?'

'Only to say hello to. She used to sometimes pop in for a cuppa and get her dog some water. She kept herself to herself really,' the chef said.

'Did you ever see her with anyone else – particularly in the last couple of weeks?'

'No, only her dog. Seen her in town a couple of times. She worked at the Co-Op on Weston Road, served me last week when I nipped in for some fags.'

'OK that's great – appreciate your help.'

Trip settled the bills, returned the pen to the waitress and walked back outside. The weather was warming up now and he could see the policewoman still standing with the dog. He went back into the café and a moment later came out with a bowl of water and walked over towards them.

'Thought the dog probably needed a drink,' Trip smiled, placing the bowl on the floor in front of him. 'Seems a nice dog.'

'Yeah, he's a real softie, poor thing,' the officer said.

'What'll happen to him?'

'He'll be going to the shelter in Weymouth, just waiting for the van to collect him now.'

Trip crouched down and the dog warily craned his neck forward, sniffing at his shoes, then looked up into his eyes and nudged his hand.

Trip rubbed his head. 'You'll be OK buddy - they'll find you a nice home.'

The dog stared into his eyes, tilting his head slightly as though trying to understand the human words.

Trip nodded to the policewoman and walked back towards his Jeep. If only he could see what the dog's eyes had seen, he thought.

CHAPTER 6

Trip parked his Jeep in Portland town centre and went into the Co-op on Weston Road. He wandered around the shop, grabbed a few items then took them over to the cashier.

'Going to be a warm day again out there,' Trip said.

'Yeah great – I'm here until 10pm tonight. Was supposed to be done at 3pm, but they're short staffed today,' moaned the young man behind the till.

'Guess that's the problem in the summer with people going off on holidays.'

'Nah it's not that, one of the women who works here killed herself last night apparently.'

'Oh,' Trip said, trying to sound surprised, 'that's terrible. Did you know her?'

'Not really, we never worked the same shifts, but my mate knew her. He lived next door to her.'

'Must be a shock for your mate then. Good friends, were they?'

'Yeah, think so, he used to go round to her flat sometimes with some leftovers from his chippy.'

'Nice, feeling a bit hungry myself. Chippy near here, is it?'

'Yeah, it's just down the road,' and he pointed in the

general direction of the takeaway.

Trip paid for his shopping and headed back out the shop to his Jeep, placing his shopping in the boot. As he walked down towards the chippy, *Fryer Tucks*, he could see that the shop looked closed, so used the time to add to his notes until it reopened for the evening.

A few minutes later though, he saw a man carrying some bags, trying to juggle them in one hand whilst getting the shop keys from his pocket. Struggling, he dropped the keys and most of the bags on the floor.

Trip quickly walked over. 'Let me help you.'

'I'm OK thanks – just not really with it at the moment.'

'You OK?'

'Shit day.'

'Sorry to hear that. Come on, I'll help you with your bags – I was just passing hoping you were open. Your friend in the Co-op recommended your chips,' Trip said.

'Yeah, was supposed to open just before lunchtime today, but had some bad news and couldn't face coming in, but gotta work. Don't work, don't earn. Come on in mate while I get everything switched on. My nephew will be here soon to help out,' he said unlocking the door. 'Have a seat while I get set up.'

Trip followed him inside carrying the bags.

'Thanks. I haven't lived in Dorset long, think this is the first time I've been to Portland. You lived here a long time?' Trip asked.

'Yeah, few years now, originally from Poole. Moved here when me dad died a few years back, to help out with the business. Been here ever since.'

'So why you having a bad day? Staff problems?'

'No, my neighbour died last night. Can't quite get me head around it to be honest. She was OK Roni was - I was only round there a couple of nights ago, had some food left over when I closed up for the night and took her round some chips and a sausage for Bear.'

'Bear…?' Trip asked.

'Her dog. Big black scary looking thing, but soft as anything once he knew you. Shit, wonder what'll happen to him? She loved that dog. I always got the feeling she'd had a crap time of it and was wary of people. It took ages for her to feel she could chat properly with me, do you know what I mean? Like she wasn't sure I was OK... safe like? But she loved that dog and Bear loved her. Glued to her he was. She told me Bear had adopted her by the bins at the back of our flats.'

'Think the dog will probably end up at the rescue shelter in Weymouth,' Trip said.

'I'd have Bear myself, but you know, with the shop I can't. He'd be on his own all evening and it wouldn't be fair on him. I'm gonna miss Roni, was planning on calling round to see her tonight – postman put an envelope through my door this morning instead of hers and now I don't know what to do with it. No point me posting it through her door though....,' he pulled the letter from his trouser pocket and absentmindedly placed it on the counter between him and Trip. 'Don't know what'll happen with her flat now...,' he said, as though talking to himself.

'Didn't she have any family then?' Trip asked, glancing down at the envelope, noting the name and address.

'Not that she ever mentioned, no,' he said and picked up the envelope, shoving it back into his pocket. 'No point being maudlin is there, ain't gonna bring her back.'

'No, sadly not mate.' Trip's mobile started to ring, 'Sorry, just need to take this....,' and he stepped outside to answer the call.

'Hello Trip, Roger here. Just a reminder we need the newsletter ready to go to the printers by lunchtime on Monday.' Roger Barraclough was the Chairman of The Poundbury Charitable Foundation and the bane of Trip's writing life.

'Yep noted Roger, all on schedule for Monday, fear not. Thanks for the reminder, have a good weekend!' and Trip quickly ended the call before Roger could pontificate about his beehive for the next twenty minutes.

Trip stuck his head around the door to the takeaway, 'Sorry, got an emergency call to deal with. Nice meeting you err….?'

'Finn. Yeah, no worries. Here, done you some chips on the house, to say thanks for helping me with the bags earlier.'

'That's very kind of you, thank you and I'm sorry to hear about your friend. Take care of yourself Finn and I'll see you again sometime,' Trip smiled.

He walked back to his Jeep and pulled out his phone, hitting an entry in the contacts' book.

It rang for a moment, then a voice at the other end spoke. 'Yo.'

'Hey Coop. How's it going?'

'Can't complain. How's life in sunny Dorset?'

'Yeah, good so far, nicer pace of life. Listen Coop, need a bit of information please.'

'Shoot,' he said, never one to use more words than were necessary.

'Can you see what you can find out about a woman called Roni Porter,' and Trip gave him the address from the envelope.

'What info do you want?'

'Anything you can find. Got nothing more than she worked in the Co-op on Weston Road in Portland and she had a big black scary looking dog called Bear. Oh, and she killed herself last night.'

'Right. Laters.'

'Wait – before you go, were you on a naval frigate, anchored off West Bay recently by any chance!'

'Can't confirm or deny mate.'

'Of course you can't,' Trip laughed.

And with that, Coop was gone.

Trip couldn't tell you what Coop's real name was, or where he lived - in fact no one could. He'd first dealt with him when he lived in The Midlands and Trip was an investigative journalist for the Birmingham Evening Mail. Needing some information on an article he was writing, regarding alleged corrupt dealings between a construction company and a local town councillor, Trip had asked his dodgiest friend, Tooga Davies, if he knew anyone who could hack in to someone's emails without leaving a trail. Unsurprisingly, Tooga knew just the person required. It also turned out, that Coop and Pippa knew each other too. Many years later, he still only knew the same three things about him - that he was called Coop; his phone number; and there wasn't anything he couldn't hack into.

Thanks to Coop's services, the local town councillor was sacked and the construction company went into liquidation. The company directors went to prison having tried to flee the country on a private jet, but were thankfully located before they had chance to take off, courtesy of information gained once again from Coop.

He also never wanted any payment for helping Trip - he just used to say; *if Tooga says yer alright, then yer alright.*

Trip sat in his Jeep eating the chips, thinking how odd it was to take your dog with you when you were planning to jump off a cliff. Everyone he'd spoken to about Roni had said how much she loved her dog. Would she not, therefore, have left it with someone like Finn? Or even just left him at home on his own, rather than jump to her death right in front of the poor animal, leaving him to go berserk with stress?

He put the chips on the passenger seat and decided to drive to the address seen on the envelope.

Five minutes later, he parked behind the flats and walked over to the entrance, pressing all of the intercom buttons until someone answered. Finally, a voice said through the speaker, 'Gordo, that you?'

'Yeah,' Trip mumbled and the door buzzed open.

He walked over to the stairs, up to the second floor and along the corridor to flat twenty-six. He knocked the door and waited. After a few moments he knocked again, then tried the door handle. Locked. He then went to the flat next door and knocked on that. Nothing. Two doors down the corridor, a man appeared wearing a black Adidas tracksuit. His hair was dark and slicked backed, a thick gold chain around his neck.

'Who are you?' the man asked, 'what ya doing?'

'Looking to see if Finn was in,' Trip replied.

'Be at the chippy won't he - but of course you'd know that if you knew him,' he said, eyeing Trip suspiciously.

'Yes, but I thought after the bad news he's had today, he might be here.'

'Well, he ain't by the looks of it is he, so you'd better be leaving then…,' and the man took a step closer to Trip.

'Did you hear about Roni? – sad news hey.'

'Yeah poor cow – but was always gonna happen one day.'

'Why do you say that?'

'Cos she was bloody miserable that one, never seen her smile once.'

Probably because she lived close to you, Trip thought. 'Right, still makes you wonder though doesn't it…'

'Wonder what?'

'What could be so bad that she wanted it all to be over so permanently.'

'What are you? A journo or something? Stop nosing around my flats and piss off!'

'You the owner then?' Trip smiled.

Before he had time to think, the man's fist collided with his nose. His head snapped back with the force and in fairness to the scrawny man in front of him, Trip thought it was a pretty decent punch.

The door to the man's flat opened and a young woman

stepped out.

'Get back inside,' the man spat towards her.

'I was just seeing what the noise was Daz.'

'Just getting rid of this journo - get back inside ya dozy cow and keep an eye on me dinner – I don't want it bloody burnt again!'

'Daz is it?' Trip interrupted, feeling increasingly annoyed with the way he was speaking to the woman.

He turned around to face him again. 'Yeah and what of it?'

'You need to speak nicer to women Daz. I can see you didn't make it as far as charm school in the education system, but common decency costs nothing.'

'What? You taking the piss?' and he took another step closer. 'Cos if you are, I'll really mess that pretty face of yours up. What will yer missus think of that when ya get home to yer big house and two snotty brats!'

'Daz, I suggest you shut your big mouth *now*.'

'Why? Ya missus gonna be mad? She can always come round to me and I'll make her feel better!'

At that moment, something snapped inside Trip. He'd only experienced a similar emotion once before, many years ago when he'd worked as a trainee reporter in Glasgow.

He grabbed a handful of the tracksuit top and pushed him hard against the wall. 'I told you to shut your mouth.'

'What if I don't?', Daz smirked. 'Ya too chicken shit to hit me. Wifey got you under the thumb I bet.'

And that was it. Trip's left fist powered into Daz's stomach, his body doubling over from the impact. He fell forwards coughing and spluttering as Trip's right fist slammed up hard into his face, catapulting his head backwards.

Daz slowly slid down the wall into a heap on the floor, sniffing up the bloodied snot trickling from his nose.

Trip crouched down beside him. 'I'll be keeping an eye on you – and if I hear or see any suggestion of you not treating your girlfriend better, then I'll be back to finish what I started. Do we understand each other?', he said quietly, inches from Daz's face.

Still sniffing, he didn't reply.

'*I said*, do we understand each other?', Trip repeated.

'Yeah', he muttered.

'Good. Thanks for your help Daz, been a pleasure meeting you,' and he dragged him into a standing position, before pushing him towards his girlfriend, who had remained in the doorway, watching the drama unfold.

'Don't take any shit from this snivelling lowlife,' Trip said. 'You can do far better than him.'

The girl nodded her head in understanding and smiled, then ignoring Daz, walked back inside the flat as Trip walked away.

Out in the car park, he walked over to the communal bins and saw they'd been recently emptied, but as he hated going through rubbish looking for information, he wasn't that upset. He climbed into his Jeep and pulled down the visor mirror to survey the damage. *Had worse* he shrugged, then grabbing some tissues out the glove box, mopped up the blood as best he could in the failing light.

As he started the ignition and pulled away, his mind once again focussed on the angry curly-haired woman from that morning. *It could easily have been two black eyes he was now nursing*, he smiled.

CHAPTER 7

In the distance he could hear music. Slowly, images from a fragmented dream began to fade and his eyes flickered open as his sleepy mind tried to focus. Gradually he realised the music was in fact his mobile ringing beside him and he groggily grabbed it, his body still wanting to be pulled back to sleep.

'Trip,' he mumbled.

'Didn't wake you, did I?' Coop said.

'Arrgghh…!' Trip winced, catching his nose as he swapped his mobile over to the other ear.

'Alright mate?'

'Yeah, my nose got in the way of someone's fist last night,' he said, carefully dabbing it and checking for blood. He glanced down at the phone screen, 'it's 2am Coop!'

'Not where I am! Sorry 'bout that.'

'Yeah, not sounding too sorry there mate. What can I do for you?' Trip yawned.

'That woman you asked me about, Roni or Veronica Porter – I'm not getting much at the moment, but so far I've found out that basically she had a shit childhood, shit teenage years, slightly less-shit adulthood. She was eight when her mum was killed in a hit and run accident. Dad was a drunk. She was taken into care. Dad died a few months later behind a pub. In and out of fosters homes, *lots* of foster homes – but the info on those isn't easy to access, plus the fact we're talking about a time before the internet and digital records. Everything was paper-based back then mate and it was a massive job transferring records onto computers, so things got missed unfortunately. But anyway, she had a few drug problems and was in hospital for a stab wound at twenty-three, nearly fatal it was too. She then popped up in Dorset a few weeks after that. Been in Portland ever since.'

'So not a great life then.'

'Nope. From everything I've found so far, I can see why she'd lob herself off a cliff to be honest,' Coop said, somewhat unsympathetically.

'Appreciate the information. If you come up with anything else, give me a call.'

'Yep, laters,' and with his usual abrupt farewell, Coop was gone.

Trip looked at the notes he'd made during the phone call and as he studied them, thought what a truly tragic life story he was looking at. Everything could be summarised in just a few brief sentences.

***

A few hours later, Trip put his running gear on and decided to go for a short run, via the supermarket to get some milk for his morning coffee. His mind kept thinking about Roni Porter's death in Portland and couldn't shake the feeling that something was amiss. It was that journalistic twitch, some called it. But whatever it was, something was definitely *off* with Roni's death. Everything he'd learned about her, including the background information Coop had obtained, did point to the fact that it was likely to be ruled suicide. The article he'd written for the Echo ended up being such a small piece in the newspaper, as there was so little to say about her.

Completely lost in his thoughts, he jogged up the steps into the supermarket, totally oblivious of the woman he was about to collide with.

The wind left her lungs from the impact and she stumbled backwards, her body starting to tilt precariously towards the ground. Trip instinctively reached out, trying to prevent her from falling and grabbed her arms, pulling them both towards him. Her body quickly righted itself and her eyes shot up at him in stunned bewilderment. Then, as her eyes focussed, the shock was replaced with fiery rage.

'YOU!' she shouted in his face.

Shit, Trip thought.

'YOU have got to be SOME KIND OF SADISTIC MORON!' The words were getting louder and shriller as each one was thrown at him.

'I am so sorry, I just didn't see you,' Trip said.

'CLEARLY!' her voice now thick with fury. 'Do you EVER look where you are going! You obviously can't drive and NOW THIS!'

Trip wanted to say, *actually you reversed and hit my car at the same time as I drove forward and hit your car you snooty, stubborn cow.* But what he actually said was, 'as I said, I'm sorry. Is there something I can do as an apology?'

'YES! You can stay the HELL AWAY FROM ME!' and with that, the woman stormed off down the steps.

He watched her mass of tied back curls bouncing around with the speed at which she was stomping towards her yellow car. *Of all the people I could run into, it had to be her.*

Felicity sat in her car feeling angry and still winded from the impact. *He is without doubt the most annoying man I have ever met! And he clearly thinks he's god's gift to women - well not this woman! Twice I've met this man and twice he's either crashed into my car or crashed into me! And what's with the black eye? - clearly a lothario thug!*

She closed her eyes and counted to ten, trying to get the

image of the man out of her head.

After he'd bought his milk, Trip cautiously exited the supermarket, hoping that the screeching woman who quite clearly had anger management issues, had left.

He jogged back to his apartment and once showered, discovered that although he now had milk, there was nothing else in the fridge. Grabbing his jacket, he headed off to The Potting Shed café, just a few streets away from his apartment. As he walked down the road, his mind again kept thinking about how little an impact Roni had seemed to make on anyone else's life – most of the people he'd spoken to hadn't even known her surname.

He entered the cosy café in the centre of Poundbury, attached to the local garden centre. It had long rustic benches, like mediaeval banqueting tables and large blackboards hung on the wall with the daily specials chalked on them. Trip nodded his greetings to the chef and waitress and took a seat on a long table at the back of the café, then picked up The Daily Telegraph. As he was scanning the headlines, the waitress appeared and a large smile spread across her face as she took his order. There were a few other customers dotted around the cafe and the atmosphere was relaxed and quiet as they read their Sunday newspapers.

Fifteen minutes later, the waitress reappeared with his latte and bacon roll. He opened the newspaper to the crossword and pondered eleven across, '*specific damage done to Robin son's joints, reportedly by Friday…,*' when he became aware of loud voices coming towards him.

'Trip!' said a plummy female voice.

He looked up from his crossword. 'Pippa, good morning. How's everything with you?'

'Yes, yes, all good. Bloody hell, what's happened to your face!' she said seeing his black eye as he looked up at her.

He shrugged. 'My face ran in to someone's fist,' thinking *how can 'bloody hell' sound so posh.*

She rolled her eyes. 'Brenda, this is Trip – he writes the Poundbury Charitable Foundation's newsletter,' and pulled out a chair at his table.

He stood up. 'Hello Brenda, nice to meet you,' and shook her hand.

'Brenda's staying with me for a bit. She's still all nervy and worried about being at her house on her own, because she thinks she heard a noise the other week,' Pippa continued.

Brenda nervously spoke. 'Nice to meet you Trip. Pippa's mentioned you a couple times over the last few months. Sorry, didn't mean to interrupt your breakfast….,' and she glanced down at Pippa, already comfortably seated, reading the specials board.

'Oh, for heaven's sake sit down Brenda, you're making the room look untidy!' and she pulled out a chair for her friend. Brenda took her seat, her eyes looking apologetically at Trip, who just smiled softly at her and winked his understanding.

'You're not interrupting at all – just sitting here struggling on the Telegraph crossword!'

Pippa turned the newspaper around to look at it.

'Shipwrecked!' she laughed and turned to carry on talking to Brenda.

'Ah, yes right,' Trip said, wondering why he bothered doing crosswords when he didn't even understand the answer let alone the clue.

Within minutes, Pippa was knee deep in a one-sided conversation with Brenda, when their pot of Earl Grey Tea and toasted tea cakes arrived. Trip surreptitiously studied the two women. Brenda was a slightly round woman with short, neat grey-hair and wore a long flowing skirt and a yellow blouse, with a delicate gold chain around her neck. He'd estimated she was around seventy years old, although he wasn't overly successful at judging women's ages and had the memories of several embedded handprints on his slapped face to prove it. She seemed quiet and a little on edge, but that could have been because she was currently being bombarded with her friend's opinion on the Telegraph's headlines and couldn't get a word in edgeways. And Pippa liked to talk.

He'd known her for years, but the first time he'd seen her in action in Poundbury was at the PCFNDOG meeting he'd been reluctantly attending. PCFNDOG stood for Poundbury Charitable Foundations Newsletter Discussion and Origination Group. The ridiculous titles groups gave themselves was one of the many reasons he hated being involved in them. Pippa was attending in her role as Secretary, Refreshments Co-ordinator and General Busy Body (Trip had added that third job title himself). Nobody around the meeting table seemed to like Pippa. Many of them rolled their eyes whenever she spoke and the Chairman, Roger, was forever trying to talk over her and cut her criticisms short – not that he ever stood a chance in succeeding.

Throughout the meeting he'd watched her handle herself with the skill of a seasoned professional assassin – she took no nonsense, dealt with the issues promptly and took no prisoners. At one point during the meeting, Roger had made a suggestion on an Agenda item.

Pippa had said, 'no, no, no Roger.'

'Why do you always say 'no' three times!' Roger had asked, clearly trying to make her look petty in front of the other meeting participants. Sadly, for Roger, that ruse had utterly failed.

Pippa had glared and replied, 'because you clearly don't hear me the first two times!'

Since then, Roger had kept his distance and opinions to himself.

As much as no one liked Pippa – she also disliked most people, particularly, but not restricted to - men. From the moment Trip had reached over to the plate of biscuits on the meeting table and nabbed the last Garibaldi a second before Roger's fingers had reached it, Pippa knew she'd made the right decision asking him to write the newsletter. She was also an excellent resource to have in Poundbury too - she knew everyone and everything that was associated with the village and surrounding area.

'Brenda, you must stop twittering about that noise,' Pippa said to her friend, 'honestly you're absolutely fine where you are. No one is going to bash you on the head while you're in your nightie you know!'

'It's OK for you to say that Pippa, but I'm sure I heard something.'

'Excuse me,' Pippa said as the waitress walked past, 'another pot of tea – and a coffee Trip?'

'Err no, I must get on Pippa…'

'Nonsense! It's Sunday! Pot of tea and a coffee please,' Pippa said ignoring him and instructing the waitress.

Trip sighed, conceding. 'Latte, thanks.'

CHAPTER 8

A few weeks later, it was the day of the annual Summer Fundraising Fete in Poundbury. Every August, a stage was erected in Queen Mother Square, with bales of hay positioned as seating and an array of food and craft stalls filling the supermarket car park. The air was filled with a heady mix of local meats sizzling in skillets, sweet-smelling ciders and locally brewed beers, all housed in white tents.

Whilst Trip was buying some locally produced wild boar sausages, a voice called over to him.

'Trip!' Roger shouted over the sound of the singing coming from the stage.

Trip ignored him, pretending he hadn't heard.

Roger shouted louder and people were now beginning to look. 'TRIP!'

He turned around and Roger was now right behind him. 'Oh, hello Roger, how's things?'

'Didn't you hear me shouting? Everyone else did!' he said petulantly.

'No, sorry, too much noise!' Trip lied.

'Hmmm, well, make sure you speak to as many of the stallholders as you can. We'll be producing a bumper edition of the newsletter covering today,' Roger instructed.

'Yes, will do.'

'Good and don't forget to speak to the singers and musicians,' and with that, thankfully, Roger walked away.

Opposite the stage was a stall selling hot bacon rolls and Trip headed towards it.

As he sat down on a bale of hay to eat, someone appeared beside him.

He turned around and saw Pippa and her friend smiling.

'How are you Trip? Nice to see you without a black eye!' Pippa laughed. 'You remember Brenda, she's staying with me again for a couple of days.'

'Hello Brenda – hope you're both enjoying the day.'

'Yes lovely, thank you.'

'Trip, what do you think she should do?' Pippa said.

'About what?' he asked, confused.

'She lost her engagement ring a couple of months ago. Des, her husband, died – what, two years ago now Brenda…?' Pippa looked at Brenda for confirmation and her friend gave a slight nod of her head. 'Anyway, the last time she can remember having it was in her house and she's worried somebody broke in and pinched it.'

'Do you really think someone burgled you Brenda? Was anything else taken?'

'Yes, well maybe, oh, I'm not sure. I get so confused these days and lose things all the time, but my engagement ring means so much to me. It was the same night, I think, that I heard a noise that woke me up and then in the morning when I couldn't find my ring… well, I'm just worried the noise was someone breaking in,' and she looked down at her empty finger.

'Have you phoned the police?' Trip asked.

'No, like I say, I get myself so muddled and I'm sure I've just misplaced it. I do forget to lock my front door sometimes, so it would be own stupid fault if someone did break in and I don't want to waste police time. I'm sorry, I sound so silly I know.'

'You don't at all Brenda and I think it's really worth you

58

phoning the police about the ring.'

'She won't do that,' Pippa interjected, 'she had a bit of confusion with the police last year when she thought the Hermes delivery man had pinched her gnome from outside the front door. Turned out she'd put him in the bath to give him a good scrub.'

'What?', he said surprised.

'The gnome - not the Hermes man!' Pippa said. 'The police made her feel she was a daft old bat, didn't they Brenda? It's put her off speaking to them about this.'

Brenda nodded, looking embarrassed at the memory.

'I told her she needs to get hypnotised!' Pippa laughed.

Brenda looked horrified. 'No! I've told you I'm not doing that!'

'Actually Pippa, maybe that's not such a bad idea. It may help you remember where you put your ring' Trip said.

'Really?' Pippa said, 'Do you think it could help her?'

'Well, Tooga went to a hypnotherapist in Birmingham to help him get over his fear of Pentheraphobia - and it's worked I'd say.'

'Pentheraphobia?' the two women said together.

'Fear of the Mother-in-law. She now lives with him and his wife and he hasn't drowned her in the hot tub yet, so I'd call that a success,' Trip smiled.

'Right, well that settles it then - if it's good enough for Tooga, then it's certainly good enough for you Brenda!'

Brenda now looked even more horrified that this may become a reality. 'Errrr…but…errrr…'

'No complaints! Right let me just…,' Pippa paused. 'Yes!' she suddenly blurted out, giving Brenda a start. 'There's someone in Poundbury…errm…bear with me…one…moment,' and paused to tap away on her mobile. 'Yes!' she shouted again, 'here we go…just…quickly…do…this…bingo! All done!'

'Done what?' Brenda gulped.

'Emailed her, the hypnotherapist, asking for an appointment ASAP!'

Brenda sighed. 'Oh my.'

'This is so exciting isn't it!' Pippa beamed.

'Not really no – I keep telling you I don't want to do this,' and Brenda seemed to be dissolving into a puddle of fear by the second.

'Don't be silly,' Pippa tutted. 'You want to know what happened to your ring don't you? Well, this could sort the matter out one way or the other and then you can relax and stop bloody twittering on about it.'

A few minutes later, Pippa glanced down at her mobile, 'that was quick!' she paused, clearly absorbed reading something on her phone. 'Hmmm not ideal... but...,' and she frantically tapped away on her phone again. 'Done!' she said triumphantly.

Brenda's eyes shot up quickly. 'What's done?'

'All sorted and you're booked in. Right, tomorrow morning at 10am you're going to see the Hypnotherapist for a consultation, completely free, so don't start worrying about that.' She turned to Trip as though Brenda was no longer sitting next to her, 'she worries about everything you know. Now listen Brenda, I can't come as I've got a meeting at Brownsword Hall to do with the HRH visit next week and as I'm a spotter, I can't miss that I'm afraid. But Trip will pick you up from mine at 9.45am Monday morning and go with you. Won't you Trip.'

His head snapped up. 'Wait, no, what? I can't, I've got to go...'

'This is important Trip!' Pippa said with a degree of finality.

'But...,' he tried one last attempt at removing himself from Pippa's plans, but failed miserably when she put her hand up to silence his protestations.

'Right,' he said, '9.45am Monday, Brenda. That's a date it seems!' and feeling exhausted, he headed for the cider tent as he now most definitely needed a drink.

'Excellent, I'll text you the address so you've got it on your phone,' she called after him and he put his hand up in acknowledgement.

Triumphantly, Pippa then strode away with Brenda in tow.

'Pippa, what's a spotter?'

'You know, to protect the shooter and team and I'm the one who shoulders the automatic assault rifle.'

'Er, what…?' Brenda said.

CHAPTER 9

Felicity wandered around the stalls at the Summer Fete, looking at the Dorset produce and quirky crafts. She'd bought some cheese and crusty bread and was looking for the cider tent that was run by one of her clients. Noticing it in the corner, she walked towards the tent.

A voice appeared right in her face. 'Hello there!'

She looked up to see Roger from the Poundbury Charitable Foundation. She had refused his invitation to join the Foundation's committee on numerous occasions, but whenever she saw him, always felt he would try to recruit her again.

'Roger, hello, how are you? Haven't seen you and Hilary for a while.'

'We're both very well thank you. Hilary is hobnobbing over there somewhere…,' and he pointed in the direction of the WI tent. 'How are you my dear? Looking lovely as ever,' and his eyes swept over her.

No, I'm not Roger - I'm wearing a shapeless dress, floppy sunhat and flip flops you creepy old buffoon.

'I'm good thanks Roger. Anyway, must get on, I'm meeting a friend…,' and she scanned the crowd in the hope of seeing someone she knew who could rescue her.

He followed her line of vision as though he was looking with her, 'well I'll carry on chatting until…*she*?' he asked questioningly, '…arrives.'

Damn it, thought Felicity, and looked at him with a withering smile.

'I hope you'll be coming to the annual fundraising Ball in October? It's going to be magnificent this year! We've just put together a Steering Group to plan it – chaired by me of course,' he said, self-importantly.

Of course, Felicity thought.

'And I want you to be part of the Steering Group – and this time I won't take no for an answer.'

'Oh, no – but…,'

'No buts – I am absolutely adamant about this. We need your valuable input my dear,' he grinned, feeling pleased with himself that he'd at last found a reason to have her join the meetings, thus giving him an excuse to ogle her. 'And after the Ball, you will remain on the PCF committee too. No arguments!'

Felicity sighed, resigned to the fact that she could avoid it no longer.

'Also, I'll make sure you're seated on my table at the Ball my dear, so you don't feel alone,' he continued, oblivious to the pained expression on her face.

At that point, she spotted the exasperating man who'd nearly knocked her over in the supermarket doorway. 'Oh, there *he* is!' she said to Roger, emphasising the *he*.

'Err, which err…,' Roger said trying to see who she was referring to.

'Just there…,' she said now frantically waving at him, hoping he would spot her and come to her rescue. As much as she hated the man who kept popping up in her life, she loathed Roger and his wandering eyes far more.

Trip emerged from the tent with a plastic cup filled with cider. Crowds were now increasing as the day wore on and he started weaving through the people standing outside the tent drinking. Suddenly, he became aware of someone in a large floppy hat across from him, waving wildly, standing next to Roger. He quickly turned and walked away in the opposite direction.

Felicity's heart sank as the man walked away. *Oh my god he couldn't just do something nice for once could he and save me from bloody Roger!*

Roger was still unaware of who she'd been waving at. 'I can't…err…see who…,' he said, annoyingly still beside her. He put his arm around her waist, 'shall I walk with you to find errr…,' still hoping Felicity would say a name, rank and position in her life.

She froze at the contact of Roger's arm around her waist and her blood cooled several degrees. She could feel the panic beginning to grow inside, the lid on that box hidden away for so many years in the depths of her mind, was now threatening to open. She tried to breathe slowly and calmly and move away, but her feet seemed to be cemented to the floor.

A child suddenly ran towards them, chasing a balloon, forcing Roger to move a few inches away, allowing the young girl to pass. That was enough for him to momentarily remove the pressure of his arm around her waist and was all she needed to restore the feeling in her legs.

'Got to go Roger…,' she said anxiously, the sweat glistening on her forehead.

'Ah, yes OK! Lovely to see you my dear, don't be a stranger!'

But Felicity hadn't heard him. She'd burst through the crowds to put as much distance as possible between them. Not because Roger had ever overstepped the line, it was *any* man. She would never again want to feel a man's touch, she knew that for certain, as no amount of therapy had been able to erase those past memories.

She continued to zigzag her way through the sea of people in front, trying to find a quiet clearing where she could catch her breath and regain her composure. An elderly gentleman with a stick walked directly into her path and she quickly side stepped, bumping into the back of someone. The person turned around, just as someone knocked his arm, propelling his cup of cider forward.

The chilled cider drenched the front of her dress, taking her breath away as soon as the wet material touched her skin. She looked up to see him standing, open mouthed and staring down at her, the empty cup still tilted forwards.

Neither of them spoke; both stunned into silence.

'Noooooo…,' was the only word to leave her mouth.

'Oh for…,' Trip started to say, only to be cut off by the dripping wet woman in front of him, jabbing her finger towards his chest.

'What have I done?' she asked, looking like she was about to explode.

Trip hadn't been expecting this question at all. 'Errm, done?'

'What have I done to deserve YOU! You crash into my car…'

Trip interrupted, 'actually we crashed into each other's cars…'

She stopped speaking and glared at him.

He quickly realised he should have kept his pedantic observations to himself.

'YOU crash into my car!' she repeated, warning him with her steely eyes not to interrupt again. 'Then YOU nearly kill me running into me outside the supermarket! And now YOU nearly drown me!' and she continued to jab her finger towards his chest.

A small crowd had now formed around them, as they were providing far more entertainment than the man with the banjo on stage.

Trip really, *really*, wanted to point out a few important details to this irritating woman he unfortunately kept having the misfortune of seeing. Lately, it felt like fate was playing a cruel and punishing game with him. But considering the death stare she was now aiming in his direction, he decided to bite his tongue. He'd had enough black eyes over the last couple of months.

'What can I say?' he said simply, shrugging, thinking that was the safest option to go with. In hindsight, he was wrong.

'WHAT – CAN – YOU - SAY? You can say that you will NEVER come anywhere near me EVER again! And if you see me, even if its *waaaay* off in the distance and you aren't even sure if it's me - then you will ERR ON THE BLOODY SIDE OF CAUTION and walk in the OPPOSITE DIRECTION!' she roared at him.

He felt there were some obvious errors is her summary of their three meetings and was finding it almost impossible to keep those observations to himself.

In his head, he could hear three clear voices.

He could hear Tooga saying, *'don't do it mate, keep schtum, always and I mean always, agree with a woman!'*

He could hear his sadly departed father saying, *'always be respectful to a woman, son'.*

And he could hear his neighbour Gav saying, *'don't be such a bloody wuss – tell her to shut up!'*

Thankfully, for the sake of the woman's blood pressure, Trip's nose and to the disappointment of the baying crowd, he simply said, 'I will,' and turning, walked away.

***

That evening Trip arrived home late. After spending several more hours at the Fete talking to stallholders and visitors for the newsletter editorial, he drove down to Pulpit Rock in Portland. He wasn't sure why, but there was still an uneasy feeling sitting heavily in his mind, in relation to Roni Porter's death.

As he pulled in to the car park behind his apartment building, he noticed Gav and his scruffy mate Scooter, lurking in the corner. It was at that moment Trip made yet another bad decision. He picked up his pint of milk from the passenger seat and walked across the car park.

'Alright there fella's?' he asked casually, walking up behind the two men.

Gav span around and instinctively punched Trip in the face. Catching the side of his nose and his right cheek bone, blood splattered across his shirt. He fell to the ground, dropping like sack of potatoes, the plastic milk carton exploding as it hit the floor.

'What the...,' he started to splutter, trying to prop himself up.

'Shit! Sorry Trip, thought you were that scary bloke again. You really shouldn't sneak up on people in dark car parks you know!'

'What scary bloke?' he asked, blood trickling from his nose.

'Big bloke, dressed in black, spider tattooed on his hand. If you see him hanging about, scarper – and phone me.'

'Yeah, whatever,' Trip said, his cheek now pounding from the impact, jeans sodden with milk and gravel digging into his hands.

Gav helped him off the floor. 'Gonna have a right shiner in the morning mate. Hopefully no permanent damage to yer good looks though hey!' he laughed. 'Here, let me go get you another pint of milk to make up for the misunderstanding.'

'You've done enough thanks Gav,' he said, picking the gravel out of his hands. 'I only wanted to know if you want your mysterious USB stick back yet?'

Gav took him to one side and looking around carefully, whispered, 'I need you to hold on to it mate - it's my insurance. Need to know it's safe with someone I trust,' he winked.

Trip wondered why he'd been given the honour of suddenly becoming Gav's best mate, particularly as he made no secret of the fact that he thought he was an idiot - having said that to his face on many occasions.

'Can't your mate over there keep the bloody thing?' he nodded towards Scooter.

'Him? You gotta be kidding me! It's a bonus if he remembers to change his pants let alone where he'd hidden something important like the *you-know-what.*'

'Fine, let me know when you want it back then,' he sighed, 'and Gav?'

'Yeah?'

'Why do I keep getting your mail through my letterbox - and why can't I post it back through yours?'

'Cos I've nailed it shut.'

'Right. Any particular reason?'

'Yeah, cos I don't want nothing shoved through me letterbox, obviously.'

'And how do I give you your post then?' Trip said wearily.

'There ain't nothing I need that comes through the post, so bin it all mate.'

'So, nothing important like bills then?'

'Nah like I said, there ain't nothing I need,' he shrugged and walked back towards his mate.

Trip wiped the blood from his face onto his shirt sleeve and called after him, 'Gav, it's been a pleasure as always.'

'Yeah, sorry again…and don't forget – big scary bloke, spider tattoo. Got it?'

Trip put his hand up in acknowledgement and walked towards the apartment entrance. He could easily have pinned Gav against the wall and thrown a few of his own punches, but he was actually a useful person to know. Trip had learned over the years, that as a journalist, it was always a good idea to have a local thug tucked up your sleeve. Sometimes a bit of brainless muscle was needed in a sticky situation, or just information from one of the many unsavoury characters, Gav no doubt mingled with.

CHAPTER 10

On Monday morning Trip awoke, as usual, courtesy of Gav and his car alarm at 6am. He pulled the duvet up over his head in the futile hope that it would drown out the racket. It didn't. As he threw the covers off, the realisation suddenly dawned on him - he was begrudgingly taking Pippa's friend Brenda to a Hypnotherapist today.

He got out of bed, went into the bathroom and looked in the mirror. His face was looking spectacularly bad and the timing couldn't have been worse - this was not going to make a good impression with the Hypnotherapist.

Ten minutes later, while making his morning coffee, he remembered his milk had been absorbed into the cark park floor the previous evening. His head fell backwards and he closed his eyes, cursing Gav and his fist. It was going to be a long day.

Just before 9.45am, he pulled up outside Pippa's house who only lived a few streets away. He was about to get out the car to knock on the door, when she appeared laden with folders ready for her meeting regarding the impending HRH visit.

'Brenda's just coming…,' she said looking up at Trip

through his open window. 'Bloody hell what's happened to your face now!'

'Case of mistaken identity,' he shrugged.

'Happens to me all the time!' Pippa laughed. 'Brenda's got herself in a right old tizzy over today. Told her she's being ridiculous - she's only going for a chat to see if it could help her foggy old mind. Anyway, can't stop, off to whip Roger into shape!' and with that Pippa bustled off down the road.

Moments later, Brenda appeared and locked the front door behind her. She smiled nervously, walked towards the Jeep and he jumped out to open the door for her.

'Feeling OK Brenda?'

'Oh! Your face!'

'Yep. You should see the other guy though!' he smiled.

'Did you punch someone too?' she asked, almost with a touch of excitement.

He winked at her with his good eye. 'So, all ready for the hypnotherapist then?'

'No, not really. Been up all night worrying and Pippa's no comfort whatsoever.'

'You'll be fine - you're just going to have a chat and see if it can help you remember where you put your engagement ring. I'll be right outside in the Jeep, so don't feel you're all alone,' he reassured her.

'What? No! You have to come in with me Trip! Oh, please don't make me go in there on my own! I'm only doing this to shut Pippa up, but I'm so scared the Hypnotherapist is going to make me do something ridiculous.'

'Like what?'

'Belt out Tina Turner songs when I walk down the vegetable aisle in Tesco!' she said, feeling completely panic stricken.

'Oh, really? Look, don't worry I'll come in with you.'

'Thanks Trip - you're such a nice man,' and relief flooded through her.

He followed the Satnav instructions and pulled up outside the Hypnotherapist's coach house, instantly recognising it from that early morning drama with a fire engine a while back. He had a feeling this was about to be very interesting.

'Ready then?' he asked.

'Not really,' Brenda muttered, 'but let's get this over with or I'll never hear the end of it from Pippa.'

He got out, opened the car door for her and she hesitantly walked towards the house. As she rang the doorbell, a chorus of barking dogs came from inside at the same time as Trip's mobile rang. He turned around to answer it and walked a couple of feet away from the house in the hope it would lessen the noise of barking.

The door opened and a voice said, 'Brenda?'

'Yes, Brenda Talbot – hello.'

'Nice to meet you Brenda – I'm Felicity Marche, Clinical Hypnotherapist. Ignore the dogs, they are my early warning alarm system! They'll shut up as soon as we close the office door,' she smiled.

Brenda returned the smile, feeling a little more relaxed already.

Trip finished his phone call and walked back towards the house. As he put his phone in his pocket, he looked up at the person talking to Brenda in the doorway and their eyes met.

'Hello again,' Trip grinned.

'Please come on in, Brenda,' Felicity said stepping back to allow her room to enter the house.

He took a step forward, as the front door slammed in his face.

She showed Brenda into the ground floor office, and smiling said, 'please, take a seat.'

'Oh errm, can Trip come in too please? He was the man I came with who was on the phone. I'm so nervous and he said he'd stay with me. That's OK, isn't it?' The nerves

71

were quickly beginning to bubble up inside Brenda again.

Felicity swallowed hard and counted to three. 'Yes of course it is Brenda, you just relax and catch your breath while I go and get your -', she cleared her throat, *'friend,'* and smiling through gritted teeth, she left the office.

Once she was out of view of Brenda, she screwed up her fists and looked up at the ceiling for divine intervention. When none came, she opened the front door. Standing the other side of the door in exactly the same position as when she'd shut it in his face, was Trip. The smile still plastered on his face.

'Trip. Trip Hazard,' holding his hand out to shake hers.

Of course you'd have a name like that, she thought. Felicity turned and walked back into the office, expecting him to follow.

As he walked into the house, the two dogs at the top of the stairs started barking at him again. Grateful there was a stairgate at the top, he closed the front door and went into the office.

'Thank you for letting Trip come into the appointment with me Mrs Marche,' Brenda said.

'Please, call me Felicity - all my friends do and it's less of a mouthful!'

Felicity turned to Trip, 'and you can call me Ms Marche...*with an E*,' and she again turned her back on him and walked over to the chair behind the desk to sit down.

He looked at the mass of unruly brown curls being restrained into a ponytail and her lips pulled tightly together in annoyance. 'Nice to see you again, *Ms. Marche, with an E...*,' he said, purposely exaggerating the *E*.

'Oh! Do you two know each other?' Brenda asked.

Felicity said matter-of-factly, 'yes, he's crashed into me on several occasions now, in every way imaginable,' and before Trip could say anything, she continued, 'so, Brenda, how can I help you?'

Smiling, he crossed his leg onto his knee. He had to admit that he was impressed at her professionalism because, right now, this woman must be absolutely seething and the thought that she would be feeling so angry, being this close to the man she explicitly told to stay far, far away from her, gave him a huge degree of satisfaction.

Brenda began to explain. 'Well, I'm not sure you can help really. To be honest I feel a bit silly being here, like I'm wasting your time, but my friend Pippa said you could help. I don't sleep so well since my Des died and I can't find my engagement ring and it means the world to me, but I'm so worried I've lost it. Or worse still that someone broke in and stole it. But the car could so easily have been on a different night. The days just blur from one to another nowadays. Pippa said I should try and get my mind, well…unmuddled.' Brenda finally paused for a breath.

'I'm guessing Des was your husband?' Felicity asked.

'Yes, he passed away two years ago now. We were married forty-eight years,' she said looking down at her lap.

'I'm sorry for your loss,' and Felicity reached over and gently squeezed her hand.

Brenda sniffed back a tear and quietly said, 'thank you.'

Allowing a few moments for the woman to feel calmer, Felicity continued. 'Well, hypnotherapy could definitely help you get your thoughts in order. We would gently take your mind back to when you last remember wearing your ring and then slowly move it forward. A bit like rewinding a film and then pressing play again.'

'Oh, that sounds OK,' Brenda said, 'I thought it would be…well…'

Felicity smiled. 'Like you were going to leave here and burst into Elvis every time you picked up a cucumber in Waitrose?'

'Tina Turner in the vegetable aisle in Tesco actually!' Brenda laughed.

Trip continued to observe Felicity and was begrudgingly impressed at the skill at which she'd quickly put Brenda at ease. She seemed completely different to the wild banshee he'd had the misfortune to run into, literally, on several occasions now.

Felicity was intensely aware of Trip watching her. *Why did it have to be him? And sitting there so arrogantly! I bet he's loving this. And yet another black eye too!*

'So, what happens next?' Brenda asked, breaking the series of negative thoughts in Felicity's head.

'Well, if you think you'd like to try this, then we can book you in for a regression appointment and see how we get on. What do you think?'

'Yes, I think it's worth a try Mrs Marche – thank you.'

'Felicity, please - and it's not Mrs.'

Trip made a noise under his breath and Felicity shot him a look, daring him to explain. He simply smiled *that* smile at her again, *mocking her*, she thought.

'I have a cancellation on Friday at 11am if that's any good for you?'

'11am is fine for me, but do you think Trip could sit in again please? It would make me feel so much more relaxed.'

She inwardly groaned, again. *Oh joy*, she thought, feeling her soul wither away inside.

'If that's what you'd like Brenda, then yes, that's absolutely fine.' Felicity looked at Trip for the first time since he'd sat down and spoke directly to him. 'You will be required to sit in the corner, quietly and not interrupt or disturb the session in any way. Do you think you could manage that?'

'Most definitely,' Trip smiled and winked.

I want to wipe that bloody smile off your face so much right now, she thought, *and give you a matching black eye!*

'11am it is then. Now don't worry about anything Brenda. You'll be sitting in that leather recliner chair in the alcove just there,' Felicity pointed, 'and I will be right here -

and *Mr Hazard* will be sitting *silently* in the corner over there.'

Trip nodded his head slightly in acknowledgement, mainly for Brenda's benefit.

'All you'll need to do is simply sit back, close your eyes and relax. I'll then talk you back through from the time you last remember having your ring. And, don't worry, I can't make you do anything in hypnosis that you don't want to do, so, no Elvis or Tina Turner I promise!'

'Thank you so much Ms. Marche… Felicity. I really appreciate your time today and you've made me feel so much better already.'

'It was lovely to meet you Brenda,' she said, purposely ignoring Trip. 'See you Friday morning.'

They got up and Brenda walked towards the front door, opened it and walked outside.

Trip turned to Felicity, 'see you Friday, *Ms. Marche, with an E*,' and he walked away grinning as the dogs started barking again the moment they saw him.

'Always bark at everyone do they?' he asked.

'Only people they don't like,' she said as she waved a goodbye to Brenda and shut the door in his face - again.

'Oh, wasn't she lovely!' Brenda gushed as she got back into the Jeep with Trip.

'Hmm, *lovely*,' he said sarcastically.

She completely missed his obvious veiled dislike towards Felicity.

'Pippa will be so happy I'm doing this. I won't get any more earache off her now!'

'I must ask Brenda, how on earth do you even know Pippa? You are both so…well…different.'

'We met in the queue backstage at a concert at Weymouth Pavilion, some twenty years ago now.'

'What concert was that then?' he asked, thinking it was probably Cliff Richard or a sixties tribute act.

'The Chipboards.'

'Who?'

'The Chipboards - a bit like the Chippendales but cheaper, rougher and raunchier,' she said with a twinkle in her eye. 'We were both waiting to meet them at the stage door. Barry was the buffest by far, ooh and that Scottish accent. Kevin had a pot belly and Trevor was knock-kneed. But ohhh they were ever so good. Always remember the funny smell though…smelled like chip fat…probably couldn't afford baby oil. I thought they might have all dropped dead by now, but then it was on the news last month that they're doing a comeback tour soon! Who would have thought it after all these years,' and she momentarily drifted off into her memories.

'Anyway,' Brenda continued, 'Pippa had turned around in the queue at the stage door and asked me to hold her handbag while she took her jumper off so she could get Barry to sign her boob - and we've been friends ever since!'

It was at the mention of Pippa taking her jumper off for a Scottish stripper called Barry to sign her boob, that made Trip look at Brenda in total astonishment and drive his Jeep into the rear of a yellow Nissan Juke parked on the road.

On impact, he threw his head back against the headrest, knowing what was about to come next. He counted to ten and got as far as six, when there was a tap on his window and he buzzed it down.

'YOU HAVE GOT TO BE KIDDING!' Felicity fumed; all sense of client professionalism now evaporated. 'MY CAR – AGAIN! Have you been put on this earth just to make my life difficult?'

'It's actually starting to feel that bloody way, yes!'

Brenda quietly watched the exchange of heated words and smiled - *I must speak to Pippa about this later.*

CHAPTER 11

6am Friday morning, Trip woke up - again. *I really need to speak to Gav today about that bloody car alarm again*, he thought. After he'd showered and wiped the condensation off the bathroom mirror, he surveyed his black eye and was surprised he didn't have a matching pair after hitting Felicity's car again yesterday. He'd offered to give her the number of a garage again, but she'd made it abundantly clear that the last kind of help she would ever want - would be his. She really was the most stubborn woman he'd ever had the misfortune of meeting, but he'd given her his card with the garage's number written on the back anyway, just in case she changed her mind when she returned to earth from the orbit he'd propelled her into – yet again.

After checking for any overnight emails, he put on his running gear and headed out of his apartment for an early morning run. He'd learnt the hard way, that as a journalist, it was best to keep fit, as you never knew when you'd get chased down the road or find yourself in a tight spot. His friend Tooga had taught him how to fight when they were teenagers – and yet he still sometimes managed to not see a fist coming his way, much to Tooga's disapproval.

He exited the apartment building at 7am, jogged off down the road listening to his iPod and headed from the Buttermarket where his apartment was, up towards the fire station and without realising, detoured towards Felicity's coach house. Noticing her lights were on, he prayed she didn't come out as he went past - it was too early in the morning for another run-in, especially as he'd not even had his morning caffeine yet.

Throughout his run, his mind yet again, kept drifting back to Roni Porter and the tragic life she'd had. Trip himself had known dark times, but he would never have walked off a cliff, even on the darkest days after Gabby's death.

As he jogged towards the Bridport Road, his mobile rang and he eased to a stop to answer it.

'Trip,' he said breathlessly.

'Mr Hazard, Felicity Marche here.'

Well, that surprised him. 'Ms. Marche – how may I help you?' he said, still panting.

'Errm I've obviously caught you at a…errrr…bad time,' she said, painfully aware that he was in the middle of something that had caused him to be out of breath. 'Sorry, I wasn't expecting you to answer – I thought you'd still be in bed…asleep I mean…rather than…errr…'

As much as he was enjoying her obvious discomfort, he decided to end her embarrassment. 'Just out for a run – what can I do for you?'

'Oh right. Well, I've got a…*situation* I need to deal with this morning – so I wondered if I could move the appointment from 11am to a little later, say 1pm? I didn't want to phone Brenda on Pippa's house phone at this time in the morning, but I may not get an opportunity to call her before we were scheduled to meet.'

Trip noticed the uneasiness in her voice. 'Is everything OK?'

'Yes, fine.'

'OK well 1pm is alright for me - better actually - and I'm sure it will be fine for Brenda too. We'll see you at 1pm…and you're sure everything's OK Ms. Marche?'

'Yes. Thank you, Mr Hazard, I'll see you at 1pm,' and she hung up.

Trip strapped his mobile back onto his arm and slowly jogged off again. For some reason, he now had an uncomfortable feeling in his stomach. As much as the woman was stubborn and intolerable, she was still a woman and it didn't sit well with him that something may have happened to her.

He cut his run short and decided to go home – but would just detour back past Felicity's coach house again, for his own peace of mind.

***

It was 7am when Felicity had got the phone call from Detective Inspector Wicheloe from Dorset Police. He asked if he could come around to see her at 10am and when she'd asked why, he said two words which had made her blood freeze. *Connor Ryland.*

Connor Ryland was the only person to call her *Flic* and it had been many years since she'd last heard that name or seen him, although he was never far from her thoughts - and nightmares.

After she had ended the call, it was ten minutes later when she realised she was still holding the landline phone. It was a further twenty minutes after that, when she phoned Trip, to reschedule the hypnotherapy session. She'd been concerned that not only could the meeting with DI Wicheloe run past 11am, but that she wasn't going to be lucid enough to conduct a therapy session professionally – particularly with that infuriating man, *Mr. Hazard,* in attendance.

CHAPTER 12

Trip grabbed his car keys and mobile off the coffee table and headed out for his meeting at the Fire Station at 10am. He took the Jeep, even though it was only a five-minute walk from his apartment, so he could drive to Halfords for a new bulb for his indicator light, after hitting Felicity's car for the second time earlier in the week.

As he drove passed Felicity's coach house, he noticed a black Volvo had just parked outside. He immediately knew the car belonged to his best friend, Detective Inspector Jack Wicheloe.

Trip continued to the end of the road and wondered whether Jack's visit had anything to do with her rescheduling Brenda's hypnotherapy session. There was, of course, the tension he'd heard in her voice on the phone earlier and as he parked at the Fire Station, was still unable to shake the idea that it was somehow connected.

After the meeting with his friend, Leading Firefighter Dan Knight, regarding an article he was writing for the newsletter, he again drove past Felicity's house. Jack's car was still there and he was now convinced that something had happened.

He returned home for lunch and phoned Pippa's house to make sure Brenda hadn't changed her mind about the hypnotherapy session.

'No, no she's still up for it!' Pippa said, 'but anyway, tell me what's going on.'

'What?'

'The two of you. Brenda's been telling me all about it!'

'Who? What are you talking about Pippa?'

'You and the Hypnotherapist.'

'What about her? Has something happened?'

'I don't know – has it?'

'Pippa, what the bloody hell are we talking about here?'

'So, nothing to tell me then?'

'No – should there be?'

'Well, it appears not at the moment. But I have a feeling there could be soon.'

'Right, on the basis I have no idea what you're talking about, tell Brenda I'll pick her up in twenty minutes.'

'Will do, bye Trip', Pippa smiled and hung up.

***

At 12.50, Trip collected Brenda who was standing outside, looking surprisingly relaxed.

'Ready?' he asked.

'Oh yes! So glad I've already met her, I'm actually looking forward to a nice little doze. But you will still come in with me, won't you?'

'Yes, absolutely Brenda.' He knew it gave him an excuse to see if Felicity sounded less anxious than she had this morning – and also any clue as to why Jack was there earlier.

Minutes later, Brenda was ringing the doorbell and Felicity opened the door smiling and stepping aside, welcoming her into the office. Trip hesitated waiting for the door to slam in his face again, but it didn't. Surprised, he took a tentative step inside and the dogs began to bark at him. He quickly closed the front door and once inside the office and out of sight, they stopped barking.

'Brenda – lovely to see you again,' Felicity said. 'Mr. Hazard,' she nodded her head very slightly in his direction.

At least she's acknowledged my presence this time, he thought.

'Is there anything I can get you before we start, Brenda?' Felicity asked.

'No, no I'm fine dear, thank you.'

'OK, well you have a seat over there in the alcove and *you,*' she glanced at Trip, 'can have a seat over *there,*' and pointed to a chair in the corner of the office, at the furthest possible location from where she was going to be sitting.

Trip smiled. 'On the naughty step you mean?'

'Well, you said it,' and she turned her attention back to Brenda.

Trip sat down smiling, noticing the unruly brown curls straining for release from its ponytail again.

After ensuring Brenda was comfortable, Felicity took a seat at her desk.

'OK Brenda, when we're ready to begin, I'll dim the lights down a little bit and put on some quiet background music to help you relax. There is absolutely nothing to worry about - all you will need to do, is simply close your eyes. I'll then slowly help your mind to rewind further and further back in time, to the point you can last remember seeing your engagement ring. When do you think that was?'

'It was a couple of months ago now - towards the end of June, I think. This sounds ridiculous, but I've got an image of myself getting dressed one morning and catching it on my tights. I had to get a new pair out the drawer and carefully put them on. So, I think that's the last time I can remember seeing the ring.'

'OK that's perfect. We'll go back a couple of months to June and then slowly move forward from there. There's no rush to remember things, just allow yourself to drift into a nice deep relaxation, follow the sound of my voice and everything will develop from there.'

Trip was already feeling he could curl up and go to sleep.

'Mr. Hazard?' Felicity said, making him jump, 'can I please ask you to ensure your mobile is turned off. Not on vibration, but switched *off.*'

'Already did that before I came in,' Trip said smugly, feeling as if he'd earned a brownie point, 'and I've brought my Kindle with me to read if that's OK?'

'Yes, that's fine,' she said, her eyes sending a silent threat not to make any noise whatsoever for the next hour.

She stood up and walked towards where Trip was seated, not looking at him once. As she dimmed the light switch and returned to her seat, he noticed the faint scent of her perfume.

'OK Brenda, when you're ready, just relax, close your eyes….and we'll begin in a few moments,' and she turned the background music on quietly.

Felicity opened a folder and picked up a pen off her desk and as Trip glanced over the top of his Kindle, he noticed how she seemed to become momentarily distracted, as though she was suddenly somewhere else in her thoughts. Her face took on a subtle sadness, tension drawing across her forehead and her jaw tightened. Most people wouldn't have noticed this slight change in a person's face, but Trip could read people well.

Then, just as soon as she had drifted away, her focus was back in the room once more.

She glanced up at Trip who was pretending to be engrossed in his Kindle and satisfied he hadn't noticed her pause, began to speak to Brenda.

'OK Brenda, I want you to feel relaxed and safe here today. Just keep breathing those nice slow relaxed breaths…and very soon, you'll notice that with every deep relaxing breath you take, you'll be even more comfortable… even more relaxed. Sleepy and relaxed. And the more relaxed you become, the more your subconscious mind will open up, which will help you to remember exactly where your engagement ring is.'

Trip could feel his eyelids getting heavy, *do not fall asleep Trip*, he kept saying to himself. Trying to focus on his Kindle, he realised he was reading the same sentence over and over. Felicity's voice had taken on a soft warmth and it was now beginning to draw him in.

'...and in a moment, I'll count down from ten to zero... but for now, just keep listening to the sound of my voice... relaxing, letting go...drifting deeper and deeper now...and with each count...of each number...going deeper and deeper...and using each number to let go of any stress and tension...to go deeper now...and every time you hear the word DEEPER...you will become more relaxed... sleepier...dreamier and deeper relaxed...'

STAY AWAKE TRIP, his mind was shouting at him.

'...TEN...as you allow each muscle in your body to relax now...letting go...becoming calm...peaceful... comfortable...feeling very heavy and deeper relaxed... NINE...relax your mind...and if you lose track of the series of numbers...that's fine...just let go now...more and more...deeper and deeper relaxed...EIGHT...relax even more now...sleepier...dreamier and deeper relaxed...'

Trip's eyes closed.

'...SIX...and as you breathe in...and as you breathe out...just release any tension and any thoughts with each and every breath...deeper and more relaxed...'

He forced his eyes open – *focus on Felicity's fiery temper,* he thought...*Ms. Marche 'with a bloody E'*... but he felt as though he was being pulled by some invisible force into a tunnel.

'FOUR…and now with each breath…I want you to think of the word *DEEPER*…see the letters of the word DEEPER in your mind now…DEEPER…DEEPER…'

As a last-ditch attempt at staying awake, he stretched out his calf muscle, turning his foot left and right.

'…TWO…as you focus on the word DEEPER…you can see that the letters are starting to grow paler now…fading, fading away…'

Trip kept twisting his foot - then the burning started in his calf.

'…ZERO…the word deeper has now disappeared completely and your mind is now totally relaxed…your whole body now feeling heavy…and sleepy and deeply, deeply, relaxed…'

Trip's calf muscle went into cramp, his leg spasming like a hot blade had been stabbed into the muscle. He shot bolt upright, grimacing as he put both feet firmly on the ground hoping the cramp would unknot itself quickly.

Felicity paused for a moment and glared at him. She quickly put her index finger to her lips, and silently mouthed *shush*. He held her gaze, still acutely aware of the agonising pain in his calf.

She continued. 'Brenda, you have now drifted down into a very deep and comfortable relaxation, so just keep relaxing more and more now with each easy breath you take. Don't resist your body and mind wanting to relax more and more…drifting deeper and deeper. Just let yourself completely relax now...there is nothing to worry about. You are safe and all of the suggestions you will hear from me today, will help you to remember all the events leading up to where you have put your engagement ring.'

Trip sat back down, rubbing the back of his calf. *That had worked spectacularly well*, he thought, feeling a total idiot.

'Brenda, your subconscious mind is now in the ideal state for visualisation and suggestions…and you're feeling so relaxed and so comfortable, as your mind gently drifts and wanders. Remember, there is absolutely nothing at all for you to worry or feel anxious about.'

Felicity paused again, looking up at Trip - making sure he was behaving himself, he assumed. He smiled at her and winked and she made no reaction whatsoever.

'OK, in a moment I'm going to ask you to visualise certain things - and you'll find that by imagining the scenes I describe, you will become so absorbed that you will actually feel and experience yourself there. All of those muddled thoughts that have bothering you until now, will sort themselves out - just like a jigsaw puzzle, with all of the random pieces falling into place to make the complete picture of the events, just before you misplaced your ring.'

Now that the pain in his calf had subsided, Trip went back to reading his Kindle. This next bit was going to be very tedious, he thought.

'So, I want your mind to rewind a couple of months now…and keep rewinding back to that morning you were pulling your tights on and you snagged the ring on them. Simply say *YES* when your mind has rewound to that morning.'
Felicity paused.
'Yes,' Brenda said a few moments later.

'OK, that's good. Now you're getting dressed, what time was that?' she paused again, waiting for a reply.

'It was quite late in the morning. I hadn't slept well again - about 11am it was.'

'So, as you pulled your tights on, you snagged them on your engagement ring. You then had to get a new pair and carefully put them on so as not to catch them too. Can you tell me what happened next Brenda?'

'I finished getting dressed, went into the kitchen, filled the kettle and put the telly on. Then I made some toast and a cup of tea.'

'Good. Is your ring still on at the moment?'

'Yes.'

'OK, let's fast forward a little bit now to the afternoon – let's stop at around 5pm. What are you doing now Brenda?'

'I'm getting ready to go out'

'Is your ring still on?'

'Yes.'

'And where are you going to?'

'Weymouth College. My neighbour Maureen is picking me up in fifteen minutes.'

'Is your ring still on?'

'Yes.'

'OK, fast forward to Weymouth College – what happens next?' Felicity asked.

'I walked into the room and everyone was getting set up ready, so I went to the back of the room behind the screen and stripped off.'

Trip's head shot up and his eyes flitted between Brenda and Felicity. *What?* he mouthed to Felicity, only to be silently shushed again.

'And then what happened Brenda?' Felicity asked.

'I put the robe on and walked into the middle of the room and sat on the chair. When Mrs Mackenzie nodded, I slipped the robe off.'

Trip's eyebrows shot up in disbelief – *she was a life model! This is not so boring after all,* he thought.

'And is your ring still on Brenda?'

Who the bloody hell is interested in the ring! Trip thought.

'Yes.'

'OK. Let's fast forward again to later in the evening now…say 10pm. What's happening now?' Felicity asked.

'I've made a mug of Horlicks hoping it will make me sleep, but I know I'll be awake most of the night as usual. I'm sitting in bed watching a Cary Grant film on TV.'

'And is your ring still on?'

'Yes'

'OK go forward again to midnight – what are you doing now?'

'I must have fallen asleep, but something woke me up …a noise. It must be the TV that's still on…and then I thought I heard a car. It worried me because you don't expect a car on my road that late at night. I got out of bed and looked out the window and saw a car drive past and I could hear a dog barking frantically in the distance…'

Trip nearly dropped his Kindle on the floor, which most definitely would have seen him sent to detention – but he couldn't quite believe what he'd just heard. Brenda lived on the Old Coastal Road near Pulpit Rock – *has she just said she'd heard a dog frantically barking…and saw a car on or around the date of Roni Porters death?*

Brenda continued, '…well, I was so wide awake then, I decided to get my Des's medals out the box and clean them. I took my ring off and put it in the fruit bowl on the table so I didn't damage it.'

'That's great Brenda.' Felicity looked up at Trip, who

looked as if someone had just punched him in the stomach, something which she was pretty sure he was very familiar with, considering the black eye that still lingered. She wondered what Brenda had said to cause such a reaction in him.

'You've done so well today Brenda,' she said, '…so just relax now and keep breathing those nice calming breaths. In a moment, I'll count from one to five and snap my fingers…and on the count of five and the snap of my fingers, you will become fully awake, feeling relaxed and refreshed. ONE…beginning to drift up now…TWO… becoming more aware…THREE…feeling as though you are back in the room with me…FOUR…feeling more aware and ready to open your eyes…and FIVE eyes open wide awake,' and Felicity snapped her fingers.

'Oh my! I remember taking my ring off at the kitchen table and putting it in the fruit bowl! Oh, how wonderful! Thank you, Ms. Marche…Felicity…this means the absolute world to me!'

Brenda beamed with happiness; Felicity felt satisfied with the result and Trip's mind raced with a hundred questions.

CHAPTER 13

After Brenda had paid for the hypnotherapy session and repeatedly thanked her for helping, Felicity opened the door for them to go.

As Trip unlocked the Jeep, he hesitated, 'I'm just going to pop back in a second – I forgot to ask Ms. Marche something…' and as his hand was still on the front door handle, he simply walked back in - without thinking of the possible consequences.

As he entered and was about to speak, she came out of the office towards the hallway. She gasped loudly with fright, not expecting to see anyone and inhaled so much air into her lungs, she thought she'd pass out. Trying to steady her breathing, she quickly put her hand out to the wall to stop herself from collapsing.

Trip grabbed her arm to steady her. 'I'm so sorry, I didn't mean to frighten you. My god, you're as white as a sheet - here, hold onto me and let me get you to a chair in the office.'

He carefully steered her towards a chair and crouched down beside her.

'Are you OK? I can't tell you how sorry I am,' he said softly.

'Fine…I'm fine…,' she said shakily.

'Well, you don't look fine. Is this something to do with this morning?'

'This morning?'

'Your *situation* you had and Jack being here.'

'Jack?'

'DI Jack Wicheloe. I saw him at your house this morning.'

She looked up at him. 'Are you some kind of creepy stalker?' she asked bitterly.

'Feeling a bit more like your old self I see,' he said with a smile.

'I've said I'm fine,' and she looked away from him.

'Right. Of course, you are. Look you don't need to tell me…'

'Oh good, I wasn't planning to!' she interrupted.

'BUT,' he continued pointedly, 'was Jack here regarding Pulpit Rock?'

'Pulpit Rock? You mean where a woman committed suicide the other month?'

'Yes. He was the DI at the scene.'

'He wasn't here for anything to do with that,' she said, confused.

Trip searched her eyes for any clue, but none was forthcoming. Whatever Jack had been here for, it was nothing to do with Roni's death, of that he was now sure.

'What's going on Mr. Hazard?'

'Trip – *please* call me Trip. I'm not sure, but something isn't right…,' he trailed off.

She looked up into his eyes hoping he'd elaborate, but he didn't.

'Are you feeling OK now Ms. Marche?'

'Yes, I'm fine now thank you. You just made me jump,' she said quietly.

That reaction was far more than just being startled - that was absolute fear, he thought, but he didn't push her anymore.

'Right then, well if you're sure you're OK, I'll leave you

in peace. You have my number if you need me.' Felicity went to speak but he anticipated what she was going to say. 'Yes - I know, *you're fine*,' he smiled.

As he left her office, the dogs began barking again and he briefly hesitated outside until he heard her lock the door.

'Everything OK?', Brenda grinned when he got back into the Jeep.

'Yep, all good. Where to?'

'Would you be able to take me home? I'm desperate to look in my fruit bowl to get my ring.'

'Absolutely – do you need to pick anything up from Pippa's?'

'Yes please – my overnight bag.'

'Pippa's it is then,' he said and glanced back to the coach house once more before driving away.

***

After a brief stop to collect her bag, they set off towards Portland.

'Isn't Ms. Marche excellent,' Brenda said, 'I will be so glad to get my ring back on again. Felt lost without it. She's lovely isn't she Trip?'

'She seems very good at her job, yes.'

Brenda glanced towards him and smiled. 'So how do you know each other exactly?'

'Oh that's a long story, but we first had a run-in, literally, in the supermarket car park a while ago in June. We were pulling out of parking spaces and our cars collided. She blames me, but actually we were both at fault. But that's fine, I don't mind,' he shrugged.

Brenda couldn't help wondering if there was slightly more to it than that.

'So, tell me a bit more about these Chipboards then!' Trip laughed.

They drove the rest of the way to Portland, with Trip

hearing wild stories about Pippa and Brenda as groupies to three male strippers, who sounded like they definitely should not be getting their stage thongs back out of storage, any time soon.

CHAPTER 14

After dropping Brenda home, he briefly accompanied her inside to make sure everything was OK and also curious to see whether the ring was in fact in the fruit bowl - and it was.

Minutes later, he drove away from her house and headed back down the road to Pulpit Rock, parking near the lighthouse. As he walked over to where Roni had died, he thought *this must have been the last thing she saw in her life.*

A voice behind startled him – it was Mick.

'Hello again Mick, how are you doing?'

'Yeah, I'm OK. Will never feel the same being here though after…well, you know…,' Mick nodded towards the cliff edge.

'I know,' Trip said, placing his hand on the old man's shoulder.

'Nice piece you wrote about her in the Echo. Sad no one knew her really. And that dog of hers, hope he's got a nice home now.'

'Yeah, I'm sure he has,' Trip said.

Mick nodded and wandered off back towards the lighthouse garden, while Trip walked around the area, not really sure what he was hoping to find. He was concerned about Brenda's comments during her hypnotherapy session, regarding a car near the lighthouse late at night, so walked across the car park and headed back towards her house on foot. It had been a couple of months now and had rained many times since Roni's death, so even if there had been tyre tracks or something on the ground, rain would have long since washed it away.

Half an hour later, having found nothing, he returned to his Jeep in the car park and called Felicity. It went to answerphone. He wasn't actually sure why he'd phoned, so left no message.

As he drove out of Portland towards Weymouth, he thought about the dog. On impulse, he decided he'd stop off at the animal shelter on the way back to Poundbury, just to make sure he had found a good home.

***

Pulling into the shelter a short while later, he saw a small office next to the parking area and walking inside, smiled at a woman talking on the phone.

'Yes, yes, I appreciate that but we need those puppy pads ASAP – we've got Jack Russell puppies crapping all over the place at the moment!' The woman looked up at Trip and rolled her eyes. 'Well, I want them delivered first thing in the morning or I won't be ordering from you again - goodbye!' and with that, she hung up the phone.

'Sorry about that, bloody suppliers! Been driving me nuts lately,' she said.

'Sorry if this is a bad time…?'

'No, no, not at all – how can I help?'

'My name's Trip Hazard…,' he started to say when she interrupted.

'Trip Hazard? Seriously!' she laughed, pointing to a yellow A-board in the corner of the room.

'Yeah, my dad had a good sense of humour,' he smiled

and continued. 'I understand a dog was brought in here a couple of months ago. Bear? Big, black and looks like he could swallow you whole.'

'Ah yes Bear, the Belgian Malinois cross,' she said.

'The what?'

'Belgian Malinois - bit of German Shepherd in him too I'd guess. It's such a shame though…'

'Shame? Has something happened to him?' Trip interrupted.

'No, well not really - not in the way you're thinking anyway. I meant he'll be with us a long time, bless him. Big dogs are always harder to find homes for, even more so when they look quite scary. I'm afraid it's unlikely we'll find a home for him anytime soon, shame though, as he's a big softie really. He's out in the yard, come say hello,' she said, walking outside.

Trip went to speak, but she was already striding away in her muddy wellington boots, so he followed.

There were a few dogs running around playing and at first, he couldn't see Bear. Then, he spotted him. He was lying in the corner watching the other dogs play, head resting on his huge front paws.

'There he is,' she pointed, 'such a quiet gentle soul. That's all he does, just watches the world go on around him.'

Bear's head suddenly looked up, his eyes locking onto Trip.

'He recognises you!' she said, 'go and say hello, it'll cheer him up no end.'

'Oh, well errm…dogs don't really like me!' he said, thinking it had been a mistake coming here.

'Nonsense!' and she opened the gate for him to enter.

As he walked into the yard, the other dogs momentarily stopped to eye him up, then quickly resumed their boisterous play. He went over to Bear in the corner and crouched down at his side.

'Hello Bear – how's everything with you fella?' and he reached over and rubbed the top of the dog's head.

Bear sat up, nudging the hand resting on Trip's knee.

'Just wanted to check in on you buddy, make sure you were OK.'

Every time Trip stopped rubbing his head, Bear would nudge his hand again.

'Gotta go fella, but I'll come and see you again soon though, promise.'

He looked into his dark eyes and wondered if he could understand him.

As he walked back towards where the woman waited, he turned around to shut the gate and Bear was by his side, looking up at him.

***

'Listen,' Trip said, 'there are some ground rules if this is going to work.' He looked up in his rear-view mirror at his passenger sitting on the back seat.

'So, number one, you are *not* allowed on any furniture – including the bed. Number two, no chewing - of anything. Number three, no begging for food at the table – or anywhere. Number four, no barking at me whenever you see me, like Ms. Marche's bloody dogs!'

The dog stared back at him in the mirror, his tongue hanging out.

'Oh, and number five – you're having a bath when we get home!'

He looked in the mirror again and saw Bear, head tilted to one side, listening intently.

When he parked at his apartment building, he opened the back door of the Jeep and Bear jumped out, looking up at him.

'Come on then, let's get you in the bath.' The dog obediently followed, unaware of what was soon going to be happening.

He unlocked the door to his apartment and quickly

grabbed Bear's collar before he could disappear, herding him into the bathroom. 'How much do you actually weigh!' he said as he picked him up, his knees buckling under the weight of the dog.

After a fraught twenty minutes with a large wet dog thrashing about, Trip finally dried them both off – together with a soaking wet bathroom.

As he walked into the lounge feeling exhausted, he found Bear lying comfortably on the sofa.

'Rule number one – not allowed on the furniture, especially when you're wet!' and he scooted him off onto the floor.

'Right come on, we're going for a walk – you'll dry off much quicker in the evening sun than you will on my furniture.'

They headed out of the apartment and Trip decided to walk towards Felicity's house, although he wasn't quite sure why. She clearly disliked him – but that was understandable considering how badly all of their previous meetings had gone. He found her abrasive, stubborn and infuriating, but he was grateful for her helping Pippa's friend find her ring and also possibly unearthing something more sinister concerning Roni's death. Brenda's comments regarding the late-night car on the same night as a frantically barking dog, was still gnawing away at him.

Nearing her coach house, he noticed her still-dented car was parked on the road. He rang the doorbell and waited. The dogs inside began to bark, but she didn't come to the door. He gave it a moment and rang the bell again. Nothing. He looked at his watch – 6pm. He assumed she'd gone out and was just about to walk away, when one of the upstairs windows flew open and her head poked out. Her wild curly hair was springing out at all angles and her face was flushed.

'Mr. Hazard!'

'Ms. Marche – everything OK?'

'Oh god not really no,' she said and Trip felt a knot twist inside.

'What's wrong?' he asked urgently.

She hesitated, weighing up whether to say nothing at all and get rid of the man that wound her up so easily – or swallow her pride and ask for his help. She closed her eyes, silently cursing her bad luck, *of all the people who could have knocked on my door at that moment, it had to be him*, she thought.

'Are you any good with tools? Capable I mean - or are you as good with tools as you are at driving?' Even as the words left her mouth, she heard the bitter tone to them and regretted it.

He could have gone one of two ways at this point – option one was to tell her to sort her own problems out and walk away. Option two was to ignore her abrasiveness and do the decent thing and try to help. He went for option two.

'What's the problem?' he smiled up at her, biting his tongue - *hard*.

'I'm coming down to let you in,' and with that her head disappeared and the window slammed shut. A moment later she opened the front door, dressed in grey jogging bottoms and a baggy pink sweatshirt.

She looked down at Bear. 'You've got a dog?' she said, surprised. 'I didn't think you liked dogs?'

'Dogs don't like me, but for some reason this one followed me home, literally. About two hours ago actually,' he said. 'Only just got home and the first thing I did was chuck him in the bath and that turned out to be fun.'

She desperately tried to stifle the smile threatening to appear on her lips. 'I've got an issue with a towel radiator that's fallen off the wall – can you help?'

'How does a towel radiator fall off a wall?'

'Long story. Can you help or not?' she again winced at her harsh tone.

He looked at her. There were many words on the tip of his tongue at that moment, but he chose, 'I can help. Will your dogs be OK with Bear?'

'Oh…errr I'm not sure actually. They aren't very good with other dogs when we're out walking - but I've never had another dog in the house.' She was now unsure of what to do as she really did need his help. 'Come in - Bear could stay in the office while you're upstairs?'

'Sounds like a plan,' he smiled.

She moved to the side and opened the office door for the dog.

'Remember rule number one Bear!' Trip said, following Felicity upstairs.

'Rule one?'

'Not allowed on furniture. He's not so good with rules yet, it's a work in progress.'

She smiled, her back turned to him so he didn't notice and showed him into the bathroom.

He couldn't have made up the scene before him. The entire four foot tall towel radiator was hanging off the wall and held on simply by the two pipes going into it, at the bottom of the wall. They were completely bent out of shape from the weight of the radiator and chunks of plaster lay on the floor below where the pipes had shifted and dropped under the strain. Wedged between the radiator and the shower cubicle door were two pink fluffy slippers.

'How the hell…?' he asked, turning around to look at her.

'Like I said, long story…,' and she bit her bottom lip. 'I was trying to change the brackets holding the radiator to the wall, as one of the them had broken. But as I unscrewed the first bracket, it snapped in half and the radiator slipped. It then pulled the remaining two brackets out the wall and fell forward, pinning me up against the shower cubicle. The only thing I could reach to stop it hitting the glass shower door and ripping the pipes out the wall, were those,' and she pointed to the fluffy slippers.

'Jeez,' he said raking his hand through his hair, 'got a screwdriver by any chance?' still bewildered at the state of the bathroom.

She turned to the cupboard on the landing and opened the doors. Inside was quite possibly the neatest cupboard he'd ever seen. There were several shelves containing tool bags, boxes, a drill and cordless screwdriver. Small jars with nails, screws and picture hooks – all labelled and lined up. There was a rack of every size spanner hanging on the wall; two step ladders of different heights, as well as a small stepping stool, all stacked one in front of the other, in descending height order.

He was speechless and not for the first time in her company, he thought.

'What do you need? I'll have it,' she said surveying the cupboard contents, hands on her hips.

'I have no doubt you do,' he smiled looking inside. 'Pass me a Philips screwdriver and we'll see if we can't get these two brackets that aren't broken, back up in some way.'

'That's the flower-head isn't it?'

'The what?'

'The one that looks like a flower head,' and she passed him a screwdriver.

He looked at it, thinking it did indeed look like a flower. 'Thanks, that'll do.'

She picked up the two broken brackets from the floor, passing them to him and he miraculously managed to get the radiator back up on the wall, luckily with no permanent damage to the pipework.

While she tidied away the tools and mess, Trip leant against the door frame watching her.

'What?' she asked.

'Lot of tools in there,' he nodded towards the cupboard.

'Dad brings me something whenever he comes to do any jobs – it's like a duplicate garage for him in that cupboard. But I have absolutely no idea what to do with 95% of it. He perseveres with me though, in the hope that one day I may grasp what to do with it all.'

'And dad isn't nearby for radiator repairs?'

'Sadly not – they're at their house in France at the moment. I should have known better really and not tackled the job – I haven't got a good track record. But when I get it in my head to do something, I just have to do it. I'm quite stubborn.'

'No! Really?' he laughed.

For the first time *ever,* he actually saw Felicity smile - properly smile. *She should do that more often*, he thought.

'Thank you, Mr. Hazard, I really am very grateful for your help.'

'*Trip*. Please call me Trip.'

'Trip,' she said, looking away.

They walked across the landing into the open plan lounge and lying on Felicity's sofa, was Bear. Her smallest dog, Pickle, was lying by his side with her head on his paw, which was almost the same size as her head and her other dog, Dusty, was lying the other side, snoring.

'Shit, sorry - I told you he's not so good on the rule thing yet,' he sighed and went towards the sofa to scoot Bear off.

'No don't. Leave them,' she said. 'Coffee?'

He hesitated. 'That would be good, thanks.'

Due to the fact that the only sofa in the lounge was taken up by three dogs, Trip leaned against the worktop in the kitchen, at the back of the lounge. He looked around at all the quirky furniture. Rustic wood shutters, mock lintels above the windows, a wonky wooden fire surround with a fire in the hearth, where two cats were intertwined on a large cushion in prime fireside location.

She noticed him looking around, 'I've got a thing for unusual wood furniture,' she said, feeling she needed to explain her décor for some reason. 'Milk, sugar?'

'Just milk, thanks.'

She opened the fridge to get the milk and it was like looking into her tool cupboard again. Every jar and bottle were neatly lined up inside - Tupperware labelled, with all labels pointing to the front.

After placing the two mugs on the worktop, she moved them slightly so they were lined up at a perfect angle. As she opened a drawer, he glanced inside and wasn't quite sure what to make of the contents. She looked up at him and saw him intently watching, his eyebrows slightly raised.

'What?' she said defensively.

'No, nothing,' he paused, 'well, something. Is your cutlery colour-coded?'

She looked away, feeling embarrassed, 'I'm a bit OCD.'

Trip, at that point, had a twinge of something deep inside him. He unexpectedly felt...*sorry for her*? No, that wasn't it, he thought. *Protective of her*? Yes, kind of, but still not the right word. Unable to find a name for the response, he tried to sweep the thoughts away.

'I blame my dad,' she said.

He realised she'd spoken again, snapping him out of his own thoughts. 'Sorry, what?'

'I blame my dad - for the OCD. He's the same. Mum is the polar opposite and whenever she's here, she purposely moves everything about so it's not lined up. She does it to dad in his study too. Drives us both nuts.'

He crossed his arms casually and smiled, liking this vulnerable side to Felicity. It was a stark contrast to the snapping piranha he'd witnessed on too many occasions.

She noticed him grinning at her - *probably mocking my OCD,* she thought, feeling defensive again and passed him his coffee.

'Have you lived in Poundbury long?' he asked.

'Maybe eight or nine years now,' she said vaguely.

'I've only been down here just over a year,' he said. 'I inherited my parents holiday apartment at the Buttermarket, so I'm living there for now.'

'Oh, I'm sorry for your loss.'

'So where were you before Poundbury?' he asked.

She noticed the change of subject and simply said

'Australia.'

'Nice! What on earth made you come back to the UK's weather!' he joked.

Hesitating, she then quickly changed the subject, as she was not prepared to talk about Australia to him – or anyone. Only her parents and best friend Phoebe, were aware of her past.

'What do you do in Poundbury?'

He sensed her shift in mood and noticed her jaw tightening at the mention of Australia, so decided not to pursue it.

'I write the Poundbury Charitable Foundation newsletter, for my sins!'

'Really? I thought Roger did that?'

'Well, he used to - he still tries to. But it keeps me occupied and gives me the quieter life I wanted when I came down here.'

She wasn't sure whether to ask him what that meant by that, but decided not to. If he'd wanted her to know anymore, then he would have continued the sentence - but he didn't.

Her phone rang suddenly and he noticed her flinch. She walked over to where it was lying on the table and peered down at the screen, as though not wanting to physically touch it. Her shoulders then relaxed and she picked up her phone.

'Hi mum - how's things?...oh that sounds like a nice place…really?...yes, I'm fine…oh Hi dad…well no…but I had to try and fix it…no it didn't go well…yes, I know…but it ended well and it's all fixed now!' she looked over at Trip, who was watching her. 'Don't sound so surprised!...yes they're all fine – Pickle's got a new friend…no I haven't bought another dog!...yeah, well animals are nicer than people generally…'

He wondered what she meant by that and had a feeling, like him, that there was an awful lot more to Felicity Marche, *with an E,* than met the eye.

As he watched her end the chat to her parents, his mobile buzzed in his pocket - a text from Coop saying he had more information on Roni Porter.

'I've got to go, sorry. But thank you for the coffee.' He looked over at the pile of dogs on the sofa, 'Bear come on, time to go.' The dog opened one eye, looked at him and closed it again, clearly far too comfortable.

'Before you go, have you been shopping to get him some food?'

'Damn it, no!' he said running his hand through his hair. He'd never owned a dog before and hadn't expected to be owning this one, so wasn't prepared in the slightest.

'Right, let me just…,' and she began looking in one of the kitchen cupboards. 'OK, you'll need one of these…and this…some of this…oh and this may help too.'

She put on the worktop in front of him two bowls, half a bag of dried dog food and a big squeaky stuffed duck.

'The food's not ideal for a big dog like Bear, it's meant for small dogs, but it'll do for him for tonight. And a client gave me the squeaky duck for my dogs, but it's bigger than them! Make sure you go to the pet shop near Halfords tomorrow and get him some proper food. Talk to the staff, they'll tell you what you need.'

'Ms. Marche, thank you. I'm not sure what to say. How much do I owe…'

'Felicity,' she interrupted.

'Felicity' he repeated, surprised.

'You owe me nothing, they're all spare - I have spare of everything, OCD remember. It's the least I can do as a thank you for your help tonight,' and she began putting the food, bowls and duck into a bag for him.

'Thank you, Felicity – that's really kind of you,' he smiled. 'Bear, come on I've got to go.'

She could sense his urgency and assumed the text was from his girlfriend, wife or significant other.

'Come on, time for a walk!' she called across to her dogs,

who both leapt off the sofa and ran to the top of the stairs, Bear quickly following. Impressed, he looked at her and for the very briefest of moments, their eyes locked, until they both looked away.

She opened the stairgate, which Bear had clearly originally jumped over and let all three of the dog's downstairs, herding her two into the office.

He clipped on Bear's lead. 'Thanks for the coffee, Felicity. Hope the radiator doesn't pull the wall down in the middle of the night. If it does. I'll deny all knowledge of ever having been here!'

She laughed, completely taking him by surprise. 'Thanks for helping me out, I really appreciate it. I'm not sure what I would have done to be honest,' and she looked down at the floor, unwilling to look into his eyes again. 'Bye Bear – nice to meet you', and she stroked his back as the dog wagged his tail happily.

'Good night Felicity,' he smiled with a single nod of his head and walked out into the warm evening air.

After a few steps, he turned back as she closed the door and waited until he heard it lock. Satisfied, he walked away, Bear trotting along beside him. He was sure this would come back and bite him at some time, but he had to admit, she wasn't as bad as he first thought.

Felicity locked the front door and heard Trip walk away on the gravel outside. She had been so angry that he of all people should knock at the very moment she desperately needed some help. But actually, she begrudgingly admitted, he wasn't as bad as she'd first thought.

CHAPTER 15

He awoke the next morning at the usual time, thanks to Gav and his car alarm. He stretched his arms up and yawned. To his left, he became aware of the warm body lying next to him, snoring lightly.

'Bear! RULE ONE!'

The dog opened his eyes, yawned, stretched out his dark hairy body and closed his eyes again.

'Oh no you don't!' Trip said, rolling onto his side to shove the dog out of bed, but as he did, felt a pain in his side and reached down.

'RULE TWO!' and he pulled out a shoe from beneath him – very well chewed. He had a feeling that this rule learning was going to take some time for the dog to master.

Trip got up out of bed, treading on the other shoe, so far, unchewed.

After showering, he went into the kitchen for his morning coffee.

'OK time for breakfast – then we'll go and get you some proper food from the pet shop.'

Just as he sat down to read his emails, his mobile rang.

'Trip.'

'Morning – let you have a lie in so I didn't interrupt your beauty sleep this time.'

'Very decent of you Coop, cheers. Tried calling you last night after your text, everything OK?'

'Yeah, sorry about that, had an urgent Tooga thing crop up in Plymouth.'

Trip had learnt over the years that the less he knew about things that involved the words *urgent* and *Tooga*, the better.

'What you got for me?'

'Had a bit of a poke around in the Co-op's computer files and there was a letter saved, addressed to Roni, confirming her promotion to Assistant Manager – dated two days before she died. Quite a jump in salary she'd be getting too. Just thought you might find that interesting.'

'Yeah, that is interesting. Things were finally going right for her, probably for the first time in her life and she kills herself two days later? Sounds a bit odd to me.'

'Yeah, I thought the same when I saw it. Anyway, if I stumble across anything else, I'll let you know. Laters,' and Coop was gone.

The nagging feeling Trip had about Roni's suspicious suicide, began to itch and intensify.

CHAPTER 16

The man sat alone in the dark, eyes closed and head bowed forward. His body began rocking slowly backwards and forwards. The voices were always loudest at night, saying the same things over and over again in his head…taunting him, daring him.

'For they cannot rest until they do evil, they are robbed of sleep 'til they make someone stumble.'

The voices were visiting him more frequently now. For years they had only occasionally called upon him, but now, they wanted his services more often. And for three days now, the voices had been relentless and the repetitions constantly echoing around his mind.

His right fist pounded on his forehead trying to stop the invocations, but their silence would elude him. He knew what was expected in order to award him some peace, even if it only lasted a short while.

He grabbed the screwdriver lying next to his foot and faintly drew an imaginary circle on the floor, repeating it again and again, the movement gaining momentum. After a few moments, he stabbed the point into the floor in the centre of the circle and stood up, walking to the back of the room. With effort, he pushed a heavy unit to the right, then crouching down, loosened the screws holding the front of the small rectangular panel to the wall. He placed the panel and screwdriver on the floor and carefully pulled out a shallow metal box. He sat on the floor, his back resting against the wall and opened the lid. Inside, the contents were faded and damaged and he touched a photograph, tenderly tracing the outline of the image in the picture with his finger. A flame immediately ignited inside him and he placed the picture on the floor. Next, he picked up an old worn Bible and held it in his left hand, placing his right hand on top, then he closed his eyes and quietly repeated;

'The sea gave up the dead that were in it and death and Hades gave up the dead that were in them and each person was judged according to what they had done.'

The flame spread through his body like a wild fire and he opened his eyes. From the back of the Bible, he removed an old, folded envelope and carefully opened it. Inside was a small dark lock of hair, tied at one end with a piece of red thread. He held it to his nose, inhaling the scent still embedded in its fibres, then gently placed the hair against his face, stroking it across his cheek.

It was almost time again.

PART TWO

KILLER IN THE SHADOWS

CHAPTER 17

A warm September was beginning to disappear into the cooler months ahead, October now only a week away. The evenings were slowly becoming darker earlier, in readiness for the end of British Summer Time and fate had been unusually quiet in endeavouring to interfere in the lives of two people, who reluctantly kept being thrown together.

'Hello, Felicity Marche.'

'It's Trip. Radiator still on the wall?'

'Mr. Haz…Trip, good morning. Yes, it is thankfully! Are you phoning because you doubted your workmanship and thought the wall may have fallen down by now?'

He thought he sensed she was smiling, but with Felicity he'd learnt you could never really be sure.

'Never doubted my ability once,' he laughed.

'So how can I help you?'

'Can I ask you something regarding hypnotherapy?'

'Yes of course.'

'I know it's been a while since the first session, but do you think if you hypnotised Brenda again, you'd get any more information about the car she heard that night?'

'Well in theory yes, but it depends on whether she

actually saw or heard anything other than what she already said.'

'Right,' Trip said and was quiet for a moment, thinking. 'Why do you ask?'

'I still can't shake the feeling that something isn't right about Roni Porter's death.'

'Is that the girl who killed herself at Pulpit Rock in June?'

'Yes. This girl had a crappy life Felicity – from childhood all the way through to present day. Then finally things turn around for her and she gets offered a good promotion at work. Probably the first good thing that's ever happened to her - but two days later, she walks to Pulpit Rock and jumps off in front of her dog, leaving him to run around alone, barking all night. Does that sound odd to you?'

'It does sound a bit strange. Maybe she just couldn't deal with the fact that something good had happened to her. Often when people are so used to having bad things happen all the time, they don't know how to deal with good things.'

'But step off a cliff? And wouldn't she have left her dog with someone if she was planning on killing herself? Wouldn't you make sure that you're only friend, a loyal friend, was going to be looked after by someone you trusted – or at least knew? Other than the dog, her neighbour was the closest thing she had to a friend – and he says she loved Bear more than anything.'

'Wait, Bear? *Your* Bear? Is that how you've ended up adopting him?' she asked, a knot of emotion tightening in her chest.

'Yeah. I was at Pulpit Rock the day after she died to write an article on it for the Echo and poor Bear was there with a Policewoman waiting for the dog van to take him to Weymouth shelter. He looked so sad. Then a month or so later, I called into the shelter to make sure he was doing OK and that he'd got a nice new home. But big scary looking dogs are hard to rehome, apparently. I'd gone over to him to say goodbye and he followed me back to the shelter's office. Next thing I knew I had this smelly moody dog on my back seat.'

Felicity was momentarily stunned. She would never have thought the man who had wound her up so quickly on numerous occasions, would have done something so caring and thoughtful.

She snapped herself out of the moment. 'That was a good thing to do Trip,' she said, aware of the fact that if she'd said much more on the subject, her voice would have faltered.

'He's a big softie, I could see that. Didn't seem right leaving him to probably live his days out in a shelter.'

On the other end of the phone, Felicity smiled.

'Anyway,' Trip continued, 'if you're willing, I'm going to ask Brenda if she'd be happy for you to hypnotise her again, to see if she remembers anything else about that night. I'm interested to know more about the car she heard, if possible. Was it involved in her death? Or perhaps the person saw something? Anyway, would you be OK with that before I speak with her?'

'It's really playing on your mind, isn't it? Yes, of course I'd be happy to help,' she said, beginning to feel intrigued as to what Brenda may remember.

'That's great – thanks Felicity. I'll give her a call now. Have you got any appointments available soon?'

'Don't worry about that, speak to Brenda and see when she would be free and I'll work around it – whatever time of day it is.'

'OK, that's great - I'll call you back shortly.' He ended the call and phoned Brenda straight away.

'Brenda, it's Trip.'

'Hello Trip. How are you? - and that lovely Ms. Marche?'

'It's her I'm phoning you about – well kind of. How would you feel about being hypnotised again, regarding the noises and the car you heard when you lost your ring in June?'

'I'm not sure I understand?'

'The night you heard those noises, a woman killed herself at Pulpit Rock. I'm just interested if you heard or saw anything else. Just my journalistic nose twitching really!' he said, so it didn't worry Brenda unnecessarily.

'OK, well if it will help you, then of course I will. And I get to have a nice snooze in that comfy armchair of hers again!' she said cheerfully.

'Thank you, it means a lot to me that you're willing to do this. When would be convenient?'

'Is today any good? - I've got nothing on at all.'

He hoped she meant that she was free all day – as opposed to having no clothes on again, modelling in an art class.

'Perfect – pick you up at 4pm?'

'4pm it is, I shall be ready and waiting.'

'You're a star Brenda – see you later,' and he ended the call.

***

'Felicity Marche,' she said answering her phone.

'Trip again. I've just spoken to Brenda and she's happy to help my journalistic twitch. Would 4pm today be OK for you?'

'4pm is fine – I'll see you both later,' and she hung up.

He looked at his phone. The call had ended very abruptly. He had that heavy feeling in his stomach again and wondered if something had happened in the space of the few minutes he'd been on the phone to Brenda.

CHAPTER 18

Trip arrived at Felicity's coach house just before 4pm. Brenda was sitting in the back with Bear and Pippa sat in the front.

'Pippa, I'm not sure this is a good idea you know, just turning up like a bus full of tourists to see Felicity. You should have let me call to give her advance warning that you wanted to meet and no doubt interrogate her. She can be very volatile you know and I'm pretty certain that springing you on her like a jack-in-the-box isn't very wise.' A feeling of impending doom began to loom, the closer he got to Felicity's coach house.

'Nonsense!' Pippa said, 'I'm desperate to meet her after Brenda has been eulogising her for so long. I'm only going to say a quick hello, so don't get your knickers in a knot.'

Trip sighed, knowing there was no point in trying to change Pippa's mind once it was set on something. He looked in the rear-view mirror at Brenda, who simply shrugged and rolled her eyes.

Before Trip had even got out of the Jeep, Felicity opened the front door, dressed in denim dungarees, a t-shirt and a red spotty headscarf keeping the rebellious curls off her face. There was a paint brush in her hand and flecks of white paint on her face.

'I'm so sorry I completely lost track of the time,' she flustered. 'Give me five minutes to get changed and cleaned up!'

'I'm hoping you're better with a paint brush than you are a screwdriver? Although judging by the paint splashed all over you, I guess not!' Trip smiled.

She rubbed the back of her hand across her face, which only made it worse. 'Brenda, hello again!'

'Felicity, this is Pippa, Brenda's friend…and mine too. She insisted on coming to meet you, *quickly*,' and he glared at Pippa. 'Sorry I didn't pre-warn you, but she ambushed me while Brenda was getting into the car.'

Trip held his breath waiting for the fall-out.

None came.

'Pippa! Hello! I've heard so much about you from Brenda – and the Chipboards of all people! I went to see them years ago in Bognor Regis! They're touring again soon you know.'

Pippa beamed with approval and Trip let out his breath before he passed out. Firstly, he wondered when Brenda had spoken with Felicity, as he'd been there during both visits. And secondly, he found it hard to believe that a night out watching Barry and his pot-bellied stripper mates, would have been Felicity's idea of a good night out.

'Please come on in while I get changed – Trip will you make them a drink while I get cleaned up?'

'Not for me thanks!' Pippa said, 'it was so lovely to meet you Felicity – we'll go for lunch next week so we can have a proper chat then. Got to dash, off to keep an eye on Roger at the printers – poor girl in there is bloody terrified of him!' And with that, Pippa scurried off down the road.

'Cup of tea would be lovely, thank you,' Brenda said getting out of the car.

'Let Bear upstairs Trip – he'll be fine up there,' and she

disappeared up the stairs.

Brenda went into the office and made herself comfortable in the armchair, while Trip followed Bear upstairs.

His dog trotted into the lounge as though he owned the place, only to be immediately pounced on by Pickle, who'd appeared from nowhere. For once, Trip noticed, Felicity's dogs hadn't barked at him and he felt a huge sense of triumph. Even before he'd finished filling the kettle with water, all three dogs were lying on the sofa, Pickle licking the side of Bear's face. He looked around the room for her two cats, concerned they may be startled by the large dog's sudden appearance – but they were both fast asleep on the window seat, basking in a ray of sunshine streaming in through the shutters, totally oblivious to the visitors.

'Use the cups with the cats on the front for you and Brenda, the teaspoons for making drinks are in the top drawer – the red handled spoons,' she shouted from the other room.

He opened the cupboards trying to find where the mugs were. Every single item in each cupboard was neat, tidy and lined up like soldiers standing to attention. Finally, he found the mugs and pulled open the top drawer which revealed the colour-coded cutlery and a large grin spread across his face.

A few minutes later, Felicity appeared in black jeans and a Nik Kershaw t-shirt, paint splatters still peppering her face. He opened his mouth to tell her, but then changed his mind and simply smiled.

'Nik Kershaw?' he said.

'I love the 80's,' she said happily, walking in front of him to pick Brenda's mug of tea up. 'Come on, let's get started,' and she opened the stair gate to go downstairs.

As they entered the office, a light snoring was coming from Brenda in the armchair. He looked at Felicity, raised his eyebrows and shrugged. She nodded towards the chair he'd previously sat on, when he'd been banished across the room. However, the chair was now at the other side of her desk instead and reading his thoughts, she quickly justified her reason.

'If you sit across the desk from me, it means you can write any questions down you'd like me to ask during the session.'

He looked down, noticing the notepad and pen, neatly placed on the desk in front of his chair. 'Good thinking,' he said and took his seat.

Felicity went over to Brenda and quietly spoke. 'When you're ready, you're mug of tea is on the table to the side of you.'

Brenda flinched, 'What?...oh…yes, sorry, I nodded off!' She sat upright and picked up her tea. 'So, what are we hoping to find out today?'

'We're just going to go back again to the evening where you put your ring in the fruit bowl. I want Felicity to see if you remember anything else about the noises outside when you woke up. That kind of thing,' he said.

'Your ring is beautiful Brenda,' Felicity said, looking down at her hand.

'Thanks to you, I can feel my Des back with me again now,' she said, her finger gently touching the dark blue sapphire.

Felicity's mind momentarily drifted back in time…back to when she'd had a diamond on her own finger…

The total surprise of waking up to see the box on the pillow next to her head. The diamond sparkled so brightly in the sunlight. His head appeared around the doorframe grinning. Being lost for words looking from the ring, to him. The warmth of his arms as they wrapped around her, kissing her lightly on the top of her then blonde head. She remembered looking up into his eyes as he'd said, will you marry me? She had of course said Yes.

But then he'd died.

Trip glanced up at Felicity and noticed she was sitting with her head slightly forward, looking down at her hands. Assuming she was preparing the questions to ask Brenda, he went to say something, but then noticed a tear roll down her cheek. He watched her for a few moments puzzled, then discreetly looked back down at his notes, pretending to write.

She wiped the tear away and looked over at Brenda who had already finished her tea and was reclining back in the chair once again, eyes closed. She glanced over at Trip, who was busy writing notes.

'OK Brenda, if you're ready then shall we begin?' she asked.

'Hmmm yes, ready when you are,' Brenda muttered sleepily and Felicity began her hypnotic induction once more.

Having learnt from the last time, Trip tuned his ears out to Felicity's soothing voice to avoid any repeat of his previous behaviour and continued to make notes until he felt sure he wouldn't be pulled down into a deep sleep. When he felt it safe to look up and pay more attention to her words, she was nearing the end of the induction and Brenda's head had lolled to one side, lightly snoring once more.

'…TWO…the letters of the word deeper starting to slowly fade away…ONE…the word deeper harder and harder to see now…ZERO…the word deeper has now disappeared completely and your mind is now totally relaxed…deeper relaxed than you have ever been before…your whole body is now feeling heavy…and sleepy and deeply, deeply relaxed.

You have now drifted down into a very deep and comfortable relaxation, so just continue to allow each easy breath to relax you more and more, drifting deeper and deeper…'

Felicity looked up at Trip, pleased to see he wasn't asleep or creating a spectacle with a cramped leg again. He sensed what she was thinking and winked back at her, pleased with himself that he'd successfully got through it this time, without incident.

'OK Brenda. We're going to slowly drift back again to 23rd June this year – the night we have previously taken you back to. And I want you to rewind your mind to that evening when you'd made a mug of Horlicks to take to bed…,' Felicity paused.

After a few moments Brenda said, 'yes.'

'OK that's good. Now what is the next thing you remember?'

'I'm carrying my mug of Horlicks into the bedroom and getting myself comfy in bed. A Cary Grant film is just starting on TV.'

Satisfied Brenda's mind was at the time they wanted, Felicity continued. 'OK, fast forward again a little to midnight – and slowly tell me what's happening now…'

Trip slid his questions forward across the desk to Felicity.

'I'd dozed off. But something has woken me up.'

She looked down at Trip's questions. 'What do you think has woken you?'

'A noise.'

'Can you describe the noise?'

'I'm not sure…the TV is still on, but…,' Brenda paused.

'Describe the noise Brenda, it's there in your mind, stored away.'

'I heard a scream.'

Felicity and Trip both looked at each other and he nodded his head and mouthed, *go on.*

'Can you describe the scream for me?'

'It's in the distance but it's a woman, definitely a woman screaming, but not for long. Then it's silent.'

Felicity looked briefly at Trip again and continued, 'and what's the next noise you hear?'

'A car – I can hear a car slowly approaching.'

Trip pointed at a question on the notepad. She nodded and said, 'how long after the scream, did you hear the car?'

There was a pause. 'A minute or two at the most.'

'What happened next?' she asked, feeling increasingly intrigued by her answers.

Trip scribbled a quick note on the notepad and slid it over.

She glanced at the paper. 'Could you hear the dog barking *before* the car drove past?'

A pause. 'Yes.'

'What happened next?'

'I got out of bed and walked over to the bedroom window and looked outside.'

Trip got up, his anticipation building and walked around the other side of the desk to stand beside Felicity.

'And what did you see when you looked out of the window Brenda?'

A pause again.

'I saw a car drive past…'

Trip leant down at Felicity's side and pointed to a question on his notepad.

'Can you see the colour of the car?' Felicity asked and held her breath.

'Yes…'

They looked at each other, their faces only inches apart. Still aware she was holding her breath, she let the air slowly out of her lungs.

'Well, no…' They both turned their heads around to look at Brenda. 'I'm not sure exactly, but it's a dark car. I can only see the back of it as it goes past the street light, but it's definitely dark…blue maybe…'

Trip pointed at the notepad again.

'Can you tell what sort of car it is?'

'No.'

They both felt a sense of disappointment.

'Can you see or hear anything else Brenda?' Felicity asked.

'The dog's still barking.'

That was Bear Trip thought sadly, *running around frantically trying to find his owner in the dark.*

Felicity looked up at him and could sense his sudden sadness. He glanced down at her and smiled, but it did little to hide the sorrow in his eyes as he went back around the desk and took his seat again.

'That's great Brenda, you've done so well today. Now in a few moments, I'm going to count from one to five and snap my fingers…and at the count of five and the snap of my fingers, you'll be wide awake, feeling calm, relaxed and refreshed.'

Felicity paused.

'ONE…just slowly and gradually beginning to drift up now. TWO…becoming more aware. THREE…feeling as though you're back in the room with me now. FOUR…more and more aware…and ready to open your eyes now on FIVE…*snap*…eyes open, wide awake.'

Brenda's eyes fluttered open and after a few seconds she looked at Felicity and then Trip. 'Did it help?' she asked.

'I think it did,' Trip smiled.

A few minutes later, Brenda disappeared upstairs to use the bathroom and Trip pushed the office door closed.

'Thank you so much Felicity - how much do I owe you for today?' he asked reaching for his wallet.

'Absolutely nothing.'

He looked up at her surprised. 'No, really…'

'Nothing,' she smiled. 'So did she say everything you hoped to hear?'

'Yeah, pretty much. My suspicions have been confirmed, sadly.'

'What are you going to do with the information?'

'I'm going to speak to Jack Wicheloe, although I have a feeling I know what he's probably going to say.'

'Which is what?'

'That there's nothing to suggest it was anything other than a depressed woman jumping off a cliff.'

'But you don't think that, do you.'

'Do you after hearing what Brenda's just said?'

'No.'

He ran a hand through his hair and looked up at the ceiling, then glanced down at Felicity when he heard the stairgate open.

'Can I call you after I've dropped Brenda off at Pippa's – she's staying there tonight.'

'Yes, of course. Or you could just leave Bear here then pop Brenda home and come back for coffee and a chat. You look like you need to talk this through with someone,' she said, hoping he'd say yes as she'd become completely intrigued by what had unfolded in the session.

'That sounds good – are you sure?' he asked, fully aware that this woman, who was now offering to listen to his muddled thoughts and theories, was the same person who had previously flown off the handle, making no secret of her hostility towards him.

'Of course I am. Plus, the fact that Bear is probably being used as a pillow by Pickle right now and it seems mean to disturb them,' she smiled again.

Brenda walked back into the office, noticing the exchange of smiles.

'OK then Brenda, let's get you dropped off at Pippa's.'

***

The dark coloured car was parked on the road opposite Felicity's coach house. It was there most nights. Watching. Waiting. The figure slumped well down in the seat, so as not to be easily spotted by any passing traffic or pedestrians.

I've noticed the journalist visiting your house on several occasions now. What are you to him Felicity? Why was he in your house so long the last time? Is this more serious than I first thought?

CHAPTER 19

After dropping Brenda off and escaping relatively unscathed from Pippa's interrogation about Felicity, which even now was still baffling him, Trip called in at his apartment to pick up some of Bear's new dog food and collect his laptop and notes on Roni Porter. He was about to pick up a bottle of wine from the kitchen, then thought better of it - this wasn't a date after all. He laughed to himself…*can you imagine us on a date! Never in a million years! She's most definitely not my type, way too stubborn and stroppy! And all the OCD stuff! - she'd spend the whole time trying to organise me!*

Before he left, he called Jack Wicheloe.

'Hey Trip, how's things?'

'Yeah, good thanks mate. Listen, the woman who died at Pulpit Rock in June, Roni Porter.'

'The suicide?'

'Yes, well…maybe, I'm not so sure Jack.'

'What do you mean?'

'This may sound a bit farfetched, but hear me out. There's a lady, Brenda Talbot, who lives in one of the Old Coastal Cottages near the lighthouse. On the night of Roni's death, she heard a noise that woke her up – a

127

woman's scream, then moments later, a dog frantically barking. She then heard a car coming down the road, looked out her bedroom window and saw it was dark-coloured, possibly blue.'

Trip hesitated, hoping Jack was still on the other end of the phone.

'OK. And how do you know all of this exactly?'

'Well, this is the really farfetched bit.' He cleared his throat. 'Hypnotherapy.'

'You're kidding me, right?' Jack laughed.

'Nope.'

'Oh, come on Trip! This is ridiculous! Who is this Brenda exactly and how did the hypnotherapy come about?'

Trip sighed, knowing this would be the point Jack would probably hang up, roaring with laughter.

'She's a seventy-year-old woman who'd lost her engagement ring and I accompanied her to a hypnotherapist in Poundbury, to help her remember where she'd put it.'

Jack interrupted. 'Hypnotherapist in Poundbury?'

'Yeah, that's right.'

'Near the Fire Station by any chance?'

'Yes, why – something up?'

'No, go on.'

'OK, so the hypnotherapist succeeded in getting her to remember exactly where she'd put her ring – so I really do believe that the screaming, the dog barking and the car all happened too.'

'Seriously Trip, we can't open a murder case based on a seventy-year-old woman's hypnotherapy session! Roni Porter was a depressed woman, with a troubled past. There is absolutely nothing to suggest foul play. Honestly mate, it was just a very tragic end to a woman with a very tragic past.'

'But she had a promotion at work, two days before she died. That alone was something worth living for surely?'

'And how do you know about that exactly?'

Trip cleared his throat again. 'Errr, I may have stumbled across some information online.'

'You mean your hacker-friend stumbled across it.'

Trip purposely ignored the last comment. 'There's Bear too.'

'Bear?'

'Her dog…and now my dog.'

'Wait, you've got her dog?'

'Yeah, I went to see it at the shelter.'

'To interview it?' Jack laughed.

'No, to make sure he'd found a new home.'

'And it did – yours! You don't even like dogs mate! Do I have to remind you of that Rottweiler who kept humping your leg when you were trying to interview the ex-Mayor of Birmingham, who was fiddling his expenses. What was the dog's name again?'

'Princess Twinkle Toes.'

Jack began laughing. 'How could I forget that!'

'Yeah, trust me that's a name I'll never forget. Actually, I do like dogs,' Trip continued, 'they just don't like me. And Bear…well, he just kind of followed me home. Anyway, Roni loved him and don't you think it's strange that if she was going to jump off a cliff and kill herself, she'd take her dog along for the show? Wouldn't she have left it with someone so it would be looked after, rather than getting dragged off to a shelter?'

'Mate, she was depressed and I don't think she would have been thinking that clearly to be honest. Plus, she didn't have any friends at all by the sounds of it. So, who would she have been able to leave the dog with?'

'Finn.'

'Who the hell's Finn?' Jack said, frustratedly.

'He's her neighbour and pretty much her only friend. He owns the Fryer Tuck chip shop in Portland. He liked Bear – used to bring him a saveloy home sometimes and…' Trip was interrupted again.

'Whoa a minute! Let's just recap here. A seventy-year-old woman loses her ring and has a hypnotherapy session to remember where it is. Then there's a depressed woman with a terrible past, rattling with antidepressants, with no friends or family – other than a bloke who owns a chippy that gives her dog the occasional sausage! Come on Trip, you've got to realise how crazy this sounds!'

'Yeah, I thought you'd say that,' he sighed.

'And where was it?'

'Where was what?'

'The ring?'

'In the fruit bowl.'

Trip had to move his phone away from his ear as the laughter from the other end of the phone was deafening.

'That's the best punchline ever mate! Listen, I've got to go, but I'll have another read over the case files for you. If I think anything looks like it needs revisiting, then I promise I'll follow it up. OK?'

'Thanks Jack, that's more than I thought you'd do to be honest. Anything you come across, give me a call.'

'Yep, no worries, will do,' and Jack ended the call.

As Trip grabbed his car keys and left the apartment, he thought that went slightly better than he imagined it would. While he walked across the car park, his mind drifted back to when he first met Jack. They were both living in Birmingham then and Trip was studying Journalism at Birmingham City University - Jack studying Criminology, Policing and Investigation. They played Rugby together in between lectures and soon became friends and drinking partners. It turned out that their fathers had gone to school together, but had lost touch years before. Through the two sons, the fathers became good friends again and both sets of parents often holidayed together.

One night, Jack's parents had been at the Birmingham Hippodrome to see a musical. After the show, they were driving home on the A38 towards Edgbaston, when a white van had driven through a red light. The driver had only closed his tired eyes briefly at the wheel, but it was long enough for him to collide at high speed into the side of the black Peugeot carrying Jack's parents. The car had spun across the road, hit a concrete bollard on the crossing between the two lanes and catapulted into a tree, bursting into flames.

Standing at the side of the freshly dug hole in the ground, staring down at the coffin, Trip's father had made a silent pledge to his deceased friend, that he would look after Jack as if he was his own son.

From that moment on, they became like brothers. Trip's father had funded Jack through University and sat with pride when he graduated to join the police force.

When years later Trip's own parents were killed in a house fire, they relied on their brotherly bond more than ever.

***

As Trip drove towards Felicity's coach house, he noticed the dark coloured car was still parked on the road opposite. He had seen the car there a few times now and slowed his speed approaching the courtyard, but couldn't see anyone inside the vehicle. Call it that journalistic itch again, but an uneasy feeling now started to take root.

He parked his Jeep, grabbed his laptop and files and got out of the car. Still focussed on the dark car across the road, he knocked on her front door, deciding if she didn't answer within ten seconds, then he'd kick it down. He began to count in his head and when he got to five, knocked again. At eight, he was rattling the handle and banging loudly on the door. When he reached ten, he pulled his mobile out of his pocket, at the same time as peering through the letterbox. He could see no movement and the office door was shut. There was also no barking, but he could hear music.

Her mobile went straight to voicemail.

'Felicity!' he shouted through the letterbox.

No reply.

'Felicity!' more frantically this time.

He rang her mobile again. Voicemail.

'Felicity it's Trip,' he shouted through the letterbox, '– DI Wicheloe is with me too. We're just off to the pub for a drink and I realised I left my…errrr…*melons*…in the office earlier. I'm going to need them tonight so, just passing to collect them please!' he lied, desperate to gain entry now, not knowing what to say without having to kick her front door down.

The door suddenly flew open.

'*Melons*?' Felicity shouted, her hair springing all over the place and her face flushed pink. 'What the hell are you going on about?'

Trip nearly collapsed on the floor with relief.

'For the love of god Felicity!'

'Have you completely lost your bloody mind?' she said, her voice three octaves higher than normal, 'why on earth were you shouting about melons through my letterbox!'

'It was the first thing that came into my head,' he sighed, starting to feel annoyed at her ingratitude.

'Why would melons be the first thing to enter your head!' and she instinctively looked down at her chest.

Trip unconsciously followed her eyes and she looked up at him at that exact moment; quickly zipping her fleece jacket up.

'The entire neighbourhood must have heard you yelling!' she said, feeling awkwardly embarrassed suddenly.

'Well, all except you apparently! Why the hell didn't you answer the door, or your phone, anything!' His own voice was now beginning to rise too.

'Because I was washing the dogs' feet!'

'The…hang on, what?' he said bewildered.

'I've just got back from walking the dogs and it's been raining, so their feet needed washing,' she explained, as though it was the most normal thing in the world to have been doing.

'Huh?' he said, still none the wiser. 'Bear too?'

'Yes, Bear has feet too you know – one at each corner! You frightened the life out of me shouting through the letterbox and banging on the door. Can't you do anything…*normal!*' She was still shouting, but was beginning to question why.

'Normal! You have got to be kidding me!'

'And what's that supposed to mean?' she snapped.

'You are the most *un*-normal person I have ever met!' He was unable to bite his tongue any longer.

'Oh really!'

'Yes really! – you're like no woman I've ever met before in my life, thankfully! You're stubborn, stroppy and opinionated. You wash dogs' feet after a walk on tarmacked pavements after a bit of drizzle – who does that! And you've got colour-coded bloody teaspoons for god's sake!' Trip finally purged himself of months of repressed annoyance towards her.

'Well fine!' she raged, feeling stung by his words.

And Felicity, repeating history, slammed the door in his face.

He could hear her footsteps pounding up the wooden staircase. *That woman is absolutely unbelievable! I was concerned someone was watching her house and panicked something bad had happened to her! Well, bloody good luck to any psycho stalker who takes that infuriating woman on!*

Trip unlocked his Jeep, threw his files and laptop on the passenger seat, then walked around to the driver's side and got in. He started the engine and glanced in the rear-view mirror, then dropped his head back against the seat and closed his eyes. Throwing the car door open, he got out, marched back to her front door and knocked.

Footsteps pounded back down the stairs and the door flew open again.

'Bear, please,' is all he said.

'The cats are asleep on him,' she said, 'I'll return him in the morning,' and she went to slam the door.

'You don't even know where I live!'

'Oh, I'm sure if I ask any woman in Poundbury they'll know where you live! I don't think I'll have any problems finding you.' Her hands were now on her hips and her tongue was still as sharp.

'What's that supposed to mean!' he said indignantly.

'You think every woman just melts in your company! Everywhere you go, you're winking and smiling at women. Even when YOU crashed into my car – THE FIRST TIME, you charmed the bloody witness! Well, this woman here can see right through you and I will never EVER feel charmed OR melt in your company. That's a promise!'

She immediately felt angry at herself for getting so personal and insulting.

He looked over her shoulder, to the top of the stairs. Two cats and three dogs were watching the entertainment below.

'It appears my dog is now awake, so if you would be so kind…,' he said nodding towards Bear.

She spun around, stomped upstairs and opened the stairgate for Bear to go down, but he didn't budge.

'Come on Bear,' Trip called calmly to his dog.

'Ha!' she laughed, 'see Bear isn't charmed by you either!'

'Well, as Bear is a male then I'm not offended by the snub,' he smiled through gritted teeth and then to really wind her up, he winked.

That most definitely tipped her over the edge. She needed him gone before she threw something.

'Go on Bear, time to go home,' she said far more calmly than she felt.

The dog looked up at her with his big dark eyes. His tail started wagging, but he still had the look of a trained killer, which was just the way his face had been created.

'Bear - home *now*,' Trip said a little more firmly, desperately wanting to distance himself from her.

Finally, the dog trotted down stairs, followed by a stomping Felicity and he opened the rear door of the Jeep for Bear to jump in.

She slammed her front door.

He slammed the car door.

And they both couldn't remember what they were originally arguing about.

***

The figure in the dark car watched with enjoyment as Felicity yelled at the journalist and angrily slammed the door in his face.

Well, isn't that interesting. I don't think I have anything to worry about regarding the two of them afterall.

And the car, once again, drove off unnoticed into the darkness.

CHAPTER 20

Abigail Hart sat down in front of her dressing table mirror and stared at her reflection. Her long dark hair was wet and hung limply onto her shoulders. It was the first time she'd showered and washed her hair in a week. Laura, her best friend, had let herself into Abi's house earlier that morning, having been fed up with her friend telling her *everything's fine*, when quite clearly, it wasn't.

'You stink!' Laura said, 'this isn't doing you any good whatsoever. What's it achieving? You're locked away in this huge house, not getting out of bed, not eating and getting smellier and more depressed by the hour! Meanwhile, dickhead is out shagging his newly knocked-up girlfriend and travelling around Europe First Class!'

If Abi hadn't known Laura since they were five years old and been inseparable ever since, then she could quite easily have been hurt by her harsh words.

'Laura, don't. I'm fine, I just need time.'

'You're evidently NOT *fine*. And you need time? - it's been three months since he left!'

Three months felt like a lifetime to Abi. She hadn't been prepared for what had happened at the end of April and had no idea anything was wrong, well apart from the obvious.

Five years ago, she'd gone to work for Richard Hart as a temp covering for his secretary, who'd gone on holiday for three weeks to Canada for her daughter's wedding. Richard was the founder and Chief Executive of PR and Marketing company, Hart Media & Communications, based in Poole.

From the first time she was introduced to Richard by the Head of Human Resources, she'd liked him. He was ambitious, confident, intelligent, creative and handsome, with a sharp sense of humour. His dark hair was peppered with grey at his temples and his tall, athletic body wore only the best tailored suits. He was the full package as far as Abi was concerned.

For hours she would sit in meetings, taking minutes and watching how staff and clients listened to him intently whenever he spoke. All of his staff were encouraged to aim for their greatest potential – and they were rewarded with good bonuses and incentive schemes. There was even a creche available in the building.

Two weeks after she'd started working for him, his secretary had broken her leg following a nasty fall in Canada and needed surgery. As she was nearing retirement age, she decided not to go back to work. Richard had then offered to make Abi's position permanent.

Two weeks after that, he'd asked her if she'd like to accompany him to an exhibition at the NEC in Birmingham, where they were running the Press Office for the events company.

They'd flown from Bournemouth to Birmingham and she'd booked him a suite at The Hyatt Regency and a bedroom with a canal view for herself. She had loved the buzz and excitement of the press office and had walked miles around the exhibition, talking to exhibitors and journalists. That evening, after dinner, they sat drinking cocktails in the Aria Bar. It had been the best day of her life so far. At midnight they had gone to the lifts, laughing and joking, flushed from the alcohol. As the doors of the lift opened at her floor, she'd thanked him for a lovely evening and stepped forward to leave, but he'd grabbed her arm, spun her around and kissed her. She'd melted into his arms as the lift doors closed.

No one had got out at that floor.

The next morning, she woke up in his bed in the executive suite. He'd rolled over, pulled her gently towards him and softly kissed her forehead. She was totally and utterly in love. He was the kindest, most caring man she'd ever met in her life and six months later, they'd married on a private yacht in the South of France.

Over the next two years they often spoke about having children. Richard was then forty-two, Abi thirty-four and they had both felt ready to start a family. But it never happened. They had numerous tests and all of them came back saying the same - there was no medical reason why Abi wasn't able to conceive. For four years they tried and the more time that passed, the more desperate and despondent Abi became. Richard began working later into the evening, often not coming home at all. Then three months ago, he was home early for once, saying he was leaving her. Apparently, she was no longer the woman he'd married. He went upstairs and packed a suitcase - she went upstairs begging him to stay. She hadn't seen him since.

One afternoon on social media, she'd seen photos of him with a young blonde-haired woman, embracing her from behind, hands resting on her rounded stomach. Abi hadn't got out of bed since. All she'd eaten for three months, were antidepressants washed down with tap water and any food Laura had managed to force into her.

From the day he'd left, Richard had changed beyond all recognition. No longer the kind and caring man she once knew. Any calls she made to him were ignored and all communication had to go through his solicitor. One day he'd even sent someone from the office around to collect his belongings. She'd lost her job, her husband and very soon, her home.

Then this morning, Laura had turned up to give her a stern talking to saying she'd booked a table at the Blue Vinny pub in Puddletown that evening. It wasn't open to discussion – she *would* be going.

Abi's phone rang, it was Laura. 'Just making sure you're up, showered and getting ready. I'll be there in half an hour and we're meeting Becky and the rest of them in the pub at 8pm.'

Abi said nothing, just listened to the instructions.

'Come on Abi,' Laura pleaded, 'we're all so worried about you. It'll do you good tonight, honestly it will and you'll end up feeling a bit better by the end of the night, I promise. He's not coming back and you're wasting your life away hoping he will. It'll just keep eating away and eventually kill you. And I will NOT LET THAT BLOODY HAPPEN!'

'I know Laura - I'm trying, really I am. I just…feel… so…unhappy and lost,' she said sniffing back a sob.

'You can do this. I'll be there in…,' she paused to check her watch, '…twenty minutes. And wear something nice!'

Abi smiled weakly as the call ended. She loved her friend so much for what she was trying to do and was determined to make an effort this evening for Laura's sake.

***

At 7pm Laura arrived and let herself in. Abi was still staring into the mirror in her bedroom.

'Abi, come on, let's get that hair sorted – it looks like something has died on your head!'

Laura then set about styling her hair and applying some make-up. She sorted through her wardrobe and chose a white Victoria Beckham t-shirt and pair of jeans, which Abi hadn't been able to fit into for three years.

'Look at you all clean and non-smelly! You look amazing Abi. One good thing to come out of all of this, you can get your arse back in those skinny jeans again!'

She looked at her reflection in the mirror, but all she could see was a lonely woman unable to have children.

They decided to walk down to the pub as it was only fifteen minutes away from where Abi lived and Laura chatted non-stop about her latest boyfriend.

Just before 8pm, they arrived at the pub and Laura went to the bar, returning with two large gin and tonics.

'I'm not sure I'm supposed to drink while I'm taking these tablets,' Abi said.

'It's just one glass, it won't do any harm', Laura said, clinking their glasses together. 'Cheers! To new and happy beginnings.'

By the time Becky and their other two friends had arrived, Abi was surprised to realise she was feeling quite hungry, so they ordered their food and two bottles of Chardonnay.

At the end of the meal, Abi was not only feeling bloated and full from the first proper meal she'd eaten in months, but was also feeling very sleepy from the alcohol.

She looked at her friends around the table and smiled. 'Thank you everyone, I've really enjoyed this evening,' then grabbed Laura's hand and squeezed it. 'Thank you for arranging this and dragging me out, *literally!* It's made me feel a little bit more human again,' and she kissed her friend on the cheek.

Laura hugged her. 'It's so lovely to have my friend emerging from her pit at last! Seriously though Abi, I'm so glad you came tonight. Things will get better I promise and once the divorce is all sorted with dickhead, you can start a new chapter in your life.'

'Well funnily enough I've been thinking during the meal tonight that I might go back to college and study for a PR degree – I loved my job and I miss it so much.'

'Really? Oh, Abi's that's a great idea! And I was serious when I said that when your house is sold, you can move in with me. Mr. Mistoffelees will love you being there for him to curl up on your lap too.'

'That sounds perfect, thank you. Would you all mind if I head home now, I'm feeling woozy from the alcohol and really stuffed after that huge steak. I'm going to walk to clear my head and help my food digest.'

'I'll come with you,' Laura said and went to get up.

'No don't be daft, your dessert hasn't come yet. Honestly, I'll be fine, it feels good wanting to actually be outside rather than hiding under my duvet!'

'Sure?'

'I'm sure,' Abi said and hugged her friend's goodbye.

It had rained lightly while they'd been inside the pub and as soon as she felt the cool damp evening air on her face, she suddenly felt quite light-headed. As she perched against one of the wooden bench tables in front of the pub, she closed her eyes for a moment and enjoyed the light breeze on her face, but quickly felt as though everything was starting to spin. She opened her eyes, waited for the spinning sensation to ease, then stood up and crossed the road, slowly and unsteadily walking towards home.

After walking a few yards, she heard a vehicle approaching behind her. The car slowed down and Abi looked to her right.

'Hi Abi, you OK?' the voice asked.

'Oh, hello. Yes, I'm fine thanks, just had a meal and a few drinks in The Blue Vinny and feeling a bit woozy now!' she smiled.

'Let me give you a lift, I'm on my way home so I'll be driving past your house,' he said.

'No really, I'm fine, honestly.' She wobbled and her ankle twisted, forcing her to put a hand on the car's roof to steady herself.

'I really think it'll be safer for me to give you a lift and it looks like it's about to rain again,' he said looking up at the sky.

'Yes, maybe you're right, thank you that's very kind of you,' and she reached down to open the passenger door to get in.

'Haven't seen you around in a while Abi, everything OK?'

'Richard and I have separated, so I haven't felt like going out…,' her voice trailed off as she looked out of the side window.

'I'm sorry to hear that.'

She didn't reply.

For the next few minutes there was silence in the car. She was desperately trying to keep her sleepy eyes open and every time her eyelids blinked closed, they stayed shut for a few seconds longer. Eventually, in an attempt to stay awake, she tried to buzz the window down for some fresh air, but suddenly realised he'd driven past the turning for her road.

'That's my road back there…,' she said, at the same time as her head was viciously slammed against the side window.

Darkness immediately enveloped her and Abi's body slumped forward, restrained by the seat belt.

The car drove past Puddletown Middle School and the road swung around to the right. The lane was dark and narrow with a canopy of leafy branches, their fingers entwining to form a dark and menacing tunnel. Old, crooked and twisted trees stood at the sides of the lane, resembling shadowy figures with gnarled walking sticks, stooping down to look inside the cars at the strangers driving past. The road then curved around to the left into Rhododendron Mile, snaking its way through Puddletown Forest, eventually leading onto the A35 bypass. The nights were beginning to draw in now and the sun had already disappeared behind the trees, ready for it's slumber.

He'd been driving for ten minutes, heading towards Bridport, when Abi's head started to move and a mumbled noise left her lips. As she lifted her head, conscious awareness slowly began to return to her fogged brain. Aware of her movement, he swiftly unfastened her seat belt, grabbed the back of her hair and rammed her head forward violently onto the dashboard. There was a sickening crack as her forehead hit the solid plastic panel and her body once again became motionless.

The road now curved to the right and her body slid towards him. He forcefully shoved her over to the left, as though she were diseased roadkill which he needed to distance himself from.

As he reached a roundabout, he turned onto Burton Road, then headed towards Abbotsbury. After a few miles, he bore right onto Cliff Road near Hive Beach on the Jurassic Coast and pulled into a rough patch of ground at the cliffs edge. It was now raining hard, the area deserted.

He turned the engine off and sat quietly for a few moments, staring out at the dark horizon. His eyes closed and his thoughts retreated into the murky shadowy corners of his mind. Silent ghostly figures summoned him, their faceless voices beginning their sermonising once more - quietly at first, then increasing in volume. Their repetitive whispers swirling around like a thick heavy mist in his head.

The sea gave up the dead that were in it and death and Hades gave up the dead that were in them and each person was judged according to what they had done.

His eyes flickered open and he looked out across the dark water, knowing the gateway to Hell lay beneath the sea's surface; the endless souls swimming aimlessly, trapped in their watery gloom forever. He glanced towards Abi, still slumped against the car door. *Worthless bitch*, he thought. *They all were. God's so-called divine creatures were filthy pustules of poison, their softly curved bodies only acting as a vessel to carry around the evil decaying inside them.*

He opened the glove box and removed some scraps of material, then reached over to Abi and grabbed her hands, loosely binding her wrists, being careful not to leave any marks on her skin. Next, he took the black hood he'd crudely made from his father's old cassock, an appropriate upgrade to the previous hessian hood that had blown over the cliffs at Portland. Finally, he picked up a piece of string and shoved it in his pocket, along with the hood.

Checking the rear-view mirror and satisfied they were alone, he got out of the car, walked around to the passenger door and pulled it open. Abi immediately fell to the ground like a leaden weight and he kicked her hard in the stomach. A pained and defeated noise escaped from her lips.

He grabbed her long dark hair, wrapping it tightly around his fist, then wrenched her head up.

'Stand up,' he snarled angrily, staring down at her.

She whimpered again, but didn't move.

'I SAID, STAND UP!' and he pulled her hair sharply upwards towards him.

She tried to stand up but pain seared through her scalp and her vision blurred. He grabbed the back of her neck with his hand and hoisted her to a standing position. Her legs kept buckling beneath her but he pulled her backwards, closer to him, keeping his hand firmly on her neck to stop her from collapsing to the ground. The breeze whipped her long dark hair across his face, its soft silky fingers caressing his skin and he closed his eyes briefly, inhaling the smell into his lungs. Seconds later, he pulled the hood from his pocket and slid it over her head, tying the string around her neck to secure it, but tighter this time so as not to lose another hood in the wind.

The air was cool and he could smell rain coming in from the sea. Abi stood unmoving, not lucid enough to understand what was happening. Slowly, he walked her towards the cliffs edge, stopping when she was merely inches from it. After untying the string from the hood, he released the loose cloth bindings from her wrists and her arms fell limply to her sides.

'And I looked…' he paused and removed the hood, *'…and behold a pale horse…and his name that sat on him was Death…'* and with one sharp heavy push, Abi plummeted over the cliff edge, *'…and Hell followed with him.'*

After the last word was spoken, the man looked over the cliff edge and smiled. Her body lay broken and crumpled on the rocks below and as he briefly closed his eyes, it was as though he could hear her being pulled towards Hell, to join the other meaningless souls.

CHAPTER 21

Trip didn't need Gav's car alarm to wake him up this morning - he'd lain awake most of the night. After he'd driven away from Felicity's house the previous evening, he noticed the dark car had disappeared. Not that it should concern him, he thought. From the first time he'd met her, when their cars had collided in the car park, she'd done nothing other than irritate the hell out of him. She was volatile, obstinate and apparently, could never possibly be in the wrong. But despite this, her hypnotherapy sessions with Brenda had helped confirm his suspicions regarding Roni's alleged suicide and for this, he was very grateful.

What had kept him awake for the majority of the night and hurt him the most though, was her implication that he was some kind of lothario. The thought he would want to be with anyone after what happened to Gabby, incensed him. There had been no dates, no girlfriend, no woman in his bed since she had died a few years ago. It would feel like he was cheating on her, even after all of this time.

His anger and frustration had eased slightly by going for a run at 2am, but was then replaced by a gut-wrenching sadness over his loss.

In 2011, he was working as an investigative reporter for the Birmingham Evening Mail. Whilst researching a story on rioters attacking Birmingham Children's Hospital, he'd gone to interview the Chief Executive, Barbara Stewart. On his arrival, her secretary explained that Mrs Stewart had been delayed at a previous appointment, so Trip had gone for a walk around the building. As he'd been about to kick a vending machine that had taken his money but not dispensed his Mars Bar, a voice behind him spoke.

'If you press the button…,' a hand reached forward, '…and thump just here…,' and the Mars Bar dropped into the slot below.

He'd looked around to say thank you and before him stood a woman in scrubs, with hair the colour of chestnuts. Her deep brown eyes smiled at him and she introduced herself as Gabby Williams - a children's nurse at the hospital. They'd gone for a coffee in the canteen and shared his Mars Bar.

Eight months later, they moved in together.

On their one-year anniversary, Trip proposed while they were ice skating one evening. He fell over for the hundredth time, but on this occasion, instead of struggling up to his feet, he stayed down. Gabby laughed trying to pull him up and he produced the ring from his pocket. She'd flung her arms around his neck and burst into tears. He'd taken that to mean _yes_.

Two years later, she was driving home from a long night shift, where one of the children on her ward that she'd grown particularly fond of, had died. It was 5am on a Sunday morning, when her car left the road and collided with a tree. She died instantly. The police report said, '_it was a tragic accident, most likely caused by tiredness at the wheel after a long shift. She would also have been particularly emotional, following the death of one of her patients._'

For six months following Gabby's death, Trip had been in freefall. On several occasions, his friend Tooga had to keep him from sinking so deep that he would have never resurfaced.

Then, nearing seven months after her death, Trip received a phone call from Tooga, asking him to meet him at his club that evening. Reluctantly, he'd agreed, knowing it was his friend's way of forcing him back out into the real world. At 8pm, he arrived at The Broadsword Club, located in Birmingham's Jewellery Quarter. Moments later, Tooga was pouring him a double Aberfeldy Whisky, telling him that his contact at the Forensics Unit had been in touch. Flecks of red paint had been found scraped deep into the side of Gabby's crashed white car. No marks were on her car before the accident, according to the CCTV pictures of her pulling out of the hospital car park that morning. But a red car could be seen on the camera footage, pulling out immediately behind her. Tooga explained that he'd put the word out on the street to all garages and scrap yards in the Midlands, to look out for any red cars coming in for repairs, respraying, crushing or any that had been abandoned and torched.

Trip's mobile rang, jolting him back from his memories.

'Hey Jack,' he said quietly, struggling to pull himself out of the past.

'Trip, there's been another suicide - off the cliffs near Hive Beach. I think we should meet.'

CHAPTER 22

The following evening, Trip waited for Jack in The Duchess of Cornwall pub in Poundbury, still thinking about the explosive row with Felicity a few days earlier. He wasn't sure what annoyed him most; the immeasurably irritating woman that she was – or the fact that he was still thinking about it. He was starting to think that Poundbury wasn't big enough for both of them.

At 8.30pm, Jack finally arrived.

'Sorry mate, got held up at work. Pint?'

'Yes please,' Trip said and finished his drink.

A few minutes later Jack returned.

'Cheers,' Trip said, tapping glasses, 'so what's going on then?'

'Yesterday morning, we were called to Hive Beach, near Bridport. A man and his son arrived that morning to set up for some early morning fishing and discovered the body at the bottom of the rocks. Looks like she jumped off near Cliff Road.'

'And you think this is suspicious because?'

'Well, that's the thing. It's not suspicious at all. The woman's name was Abi Hart and she lived in Puddletown.

Apparently, Abi and her husband had been trying for kids for a few years, but it wasn't happening and she was becoming desperate. So, when her husband came home one night a few months ago, packed a bag and left with his pregnant mistress, it understandably destroyed her. Laura, her best friend, said Abi had been in a right state ever since.' Jack paused for a drink. 'I would have just closed this case as another tragic end to a desperately sad woman's life, but then you phoned the other night, going on about your seventy-year-old with her hypnotherapy and Roni Porter committing suicide in Portland - saying something good had recently happened in her life, so why kill yourself. Then we get another apparent suicide, by another depressed woman, who again had just made some positive decisions in her life.'

'What decisions?' Trip asked, his journalistic itch reigniting.

'Laura had persuaded her to go out for a meal at the Blue Vinny in Puddletown that night, with three other friends. Abi had been very reluctant to go, but Laura pretty much dragged her there. In the pub and a few drinks later, on top of anti-depressants, she actually started enjoying herself and relaxing – to the point where she told her friends she'd decided to go back to college to get a PR degree and was going to move in with Laura while she was studying.'

'This is sounding a bit too much of a coincidence mate.'

'I agree. The problem is though, if something more sinister is going on here, then we can't find any connection whatsoever between these two women. They had very different lives and backgrounds – Roni with the death of her parents, bouncing around foster homes, drug addiction etc. Then there's Abi with her normal childhood, loving parents, large circle of caring friends who would have done anything to help her and currently living very comfortably in a big house, with a sizeable divorce settlement coming her way,' Jack paused, and finished his pint. 'Same again?' he nodded towards Trip's almost empty glass.

'I'll get them,' and Trip disappeared to the bar.

When he returned, Jack continued.

'Since you phoned the other night, I have cross-checked these two women's lives completely to find something in common about them or people they've met – anything, that may mean someone wanted to kill them. The only person with anything to gain was Abi's soon-to-be-ex-husband, because with her dead, he'd have no divorce issues and no settlement to pay. But he's got zero connection with Roni Porter.'

'And what do you know about Abi's husband?'

'Richard Hart owns Hart Media & Communications, in Poole. All his staff love him - I think he's a bit of a dickhead personally, which ironically is how her best friend described him. But do I think he's capable of murder...,' Jack paused momentarily, 'no, I don't think he's got it in him at all.'

'You know that people do strange things when money is involved though.'

'Yeah, but if you met him, you'd know what I mean. He's got it all – good looks, charming, successful, but would never get his hands dirty doing something like this.'

'Well, if he's that successful he could have paid someone.'

'Yeah possibly, but it still doesn't make any connection with Roni though.'

'Maybe they aren't connected. Roni could genuinely just be a tragic suicide - and Abi's too, I suppose.'

'Hang on a minute, you're the one who came to me remember, saying you thought something was a bit off with Roni's death!'

'Yeah, I still do think something isn't right about that. But from everything you've just said, I can't see any connection between Roni and Abi.' Trip was feeling more disheartened by the minute.

'And that's why I asked you to meet me tonight,' Jack smiled.

'Go on,' Trip said, confused.

'As I say, we can't find anything at all to connect these

two women. Your seventy-year-old lady who heard and saw a dark coloured car the night Roni allegedly committed suicide, does now seem a bit of a coincidence. But we have absolutely nothing to indicate that her death was murder. Cliff suicides happen – but two, only months apart for no solid reason when both of them finally had something positive to look forward to, is starting to gnaw at me and I'm beginning to think perhaps something disturbing is going on in Dorset. Anyway, I think it's worth digging a bit deeper. Now I can't ask you to do this in an official capacity and I'll certainly deny ever having this conversation – but you have contacts mate, ways and means of finding things out that I can't officially. So can you poke about and ask some of your shadowy friends if they can find anything we've missed?'

'Well, I'll try not to take offence at the implication that I hang around with anyone other than respectable members of society, but yes, I'll make a few phone calls and see what I come up with.'

'Right answer, thanks mate. So, changing the subject, how's things with you? I don't suppose there's any new woman in your life?' he smiled, knowing Trip hadn't had a girlfriend since Gabby's death.

'Well, strangely enough, there is a new woman in my life – but not in the way you mean. She's a bloody pain in the arse and I could most definitely do without her.' Trip's jaw tightened as Storm Felicity raged through his mind. However, a few moments later, as he took another swig from his pint, her softly smiling face swam into his thoughts.

Across the table, Jack watched his best friend. 'Who is this pain in the arse then?'

'Felicity bloody Marche – with an E!'

'The hypnotherapist?'

'The very same.'

'Interesting.'

'Trust me, it's not.'

Jack sat back, thinking. *Two damaged people…complete polar opposites…yeah that could work…*he smiled to himself.

CHAPTER 23

Later, when Trip returned from the pub, he phoned one of the shadowy contacts Jack referred to.

'Yo.'

'Hey Coop, how's things with you?'

'Armed and ready.'

Trip wasn't quite sure whether that meant he was OK or not, considering he knew so little about him.

'That's good then,' he said, going with a safe reply. 'Listen, can you do a bit of digging for me on a woman called Abigail Hart - Abi. Married to Richard Hart. Lived in Puddletown, Dorset.'

'Puddletown? – that a real place?' Coop laughed.

'Yep, sure is. Anyway, this woman allegedly jumped off a cliff yesterday at Hive Beach, near Bridport.'

'Shit, you get a lot of women jumping off cliffs down there don't you mate!'

'Yeah exactly. I'm starting to feel something more is going on here, as it's a bit odd that two similar deaths happen within a few months of each other. Even the Police are starting to agree with me now. Can you also see if you can find any connection whatsoever between Roni Porter, the woman who killed herself at Portland - and Abi Hart.

Any link at all, no matter how tenuous - mutual people they knew, places they went, their childhoods, anything.' Trip paused looking down at his notes after his meeting with Jack earlier, 'and can you find me a phone number for a Laura Taylor – she was Abi Hart's best friend.'

'On it. Laters,' and Coop was gone.

Trip slumped down on his sofa and switched the television on, as his mind was too alert to go to bed. A decent night's sleep had alluded him for several days now, in fact, if he was honest with himself, since he'd had that colossal argument with Felicity. He'd had no contact with her since that night and frankly, it was no loss in his life. He didn't need someone so bloody difficult to battle with constantly, that's for sure. So why did he keep going over it in his mind all the time? He made a pact with himself that he'd analyse it now for the final time, then no more dwelling on it and forget all about the words they'd both slung at each other.

OK, Trip thought - *she's 100% not my type. She is unrelentingly stubborn – beyond mule-like, more like a camel as she's just as likely to spit in your face. She's single-minded, inflexible and intransigent - and she can never be wrong about anything! She insulted me – on more than one occasion, implied I'd been ogling her chest – the very last chest I would ever want to ogle and most unforgivable of all, she made me dredge up locked away memories of Gabby.*

And yet, even after analysing it in depth, he still couldn't completely put Felicity Marche *with a bloody E* out of his mind when he tried to go to sleep that night.

***

The man lay in the dark, on the hard metal framed bed in the corner of the room. He thought back to the moment he saw the woman's dark hair fan out like ethereal wings, desperately trying to stop the weight of the falling body and fly her away to safety. But those wings had failed and the body had dropped heavily down onto the rocks, settling onto its final resting place, bloodied, bruised and broken.

For now, the voices were quiet, but he knew the respite would not last long and they would soon be calling on him again.

CHAPTER 24

Felicity sighed and looked at her reflection in the full-length mirror. To the side of her were six different dresses ordered online, hoping that one of them was adequate for the annual Pumpkin Fundraiser Ball, in a few weeks' time.

The Ball this year was being held in a vacant commercial office building, overlooking Queen Mother Square in Poundbury. Every year the Ball raised money for three different charities – and this year, one of the charities was the animal rescue shelter in Weymouth, where Bear had been temporarily placed, before Trip adopted him. This alone was the only reason Felicity was prepared to attend the Ball for the first time.

However, she was now faced with two problems. One, what the hell was she going to wear, as there was a strict dress code which filled her with dread. And two, it was organised by Roger, who'd said he would seat her on his table.

Even though Roger had never done or said anything that most people would have considered amiss - other than being a pompous prat - to Felicity, any sort of male attention made her freeze in fear. That was the reason she never wore make-up, why her hair was always pulled back into a ponytail and why she wore plain loose clothes, that drew no attention to her body in any way.

She glanced at the pile of discarded dresses on the bed and then back at the image reflected in the mirror. She hated what she saw. It wasn't the dresses that were the problem, it was her. The outfits she'd ordered were beautiful – long, black and elegant, which all complied with the dress code. However, in her reflection now, all she could see was a female form, that in her mind, was too damaged to be seen and one which should certainly not be dressed up in elegant feminine clothes.

Sighing, she took off the sixth dress and repackaged it to be returned in the post tomorrow, together with the other five outfits. Then miserably, she flopped down on the bed feeling utterly fed up. Her two dogs yawned and stretched from their sleep, where they were curled up on the bed. The littlest dog, Pickle, pounced on her chest and licked her nose, while her other dog Dusty, rolled over onto his back, thinking surely a tummy tickle would cheer his owner up.

She had only one option available to her now and reluctantly picked up the phone.

'Hello, it's me,' she said glumly.

'Felicity, how lovely to hear from you. Everything alright?'

'Not really Pippa. How about you?'

'Yes, yes all good – everything is starting to come together marvellously for the Ball. The empty offices will be transformed and should look fabulous! But that's not why you've phoned is it. So, tell me why do you sound so miserable, what's happened? Don't tell me Trip has been a bloody idiot again!'

'No, I haven't spoken to him for a while now, ever since…well, you know the whole melons event.'

'So what's happened then?'

'It's the damn Ball. I really don't want to go…but I also do want to support the charities involved this year, particularly the animal shelter. But, oh Pippa, I don't know what to wear! It's been so long since I've had to wear an evening dress or even do my hair and make up for god's sake! I've ordered a load of dresses and they all look ridiculous on me and…' Felicity was interrupted midway through her depressing monologue.

'Right, stop a moment and let me think…,' Pippa said firmly.

She shut up, as instructed.

After what seemed like several minutes, Felicity spoke. 'Errrr, Pippa…are you still there?'

'Yes, yes just looking through…ah, yes here we are!'

'Here we are what?' she asked nervously.

'Give me a moment and I'll call you back,' and Pippa hung up.

She closed her eyes, suddenly feeling that calling Pippa had been a huge mistake.

Ten minutes later, Pippa phoned back.

'Right then, as you know the Ball is a few weeks away. I've arranged for you to go and see my goddaughter, Isabella, on the Friday of the Ball at 9am. We decided you were going to need all day.'

'All day for what?' Felicity asked, filled with dread.

'All day to look like an actual woman!'

She wasn't sure whether to be insulted or not. 'Oh Pippa, what have you done!'

'Calm down, it's nothing to worry about for heaven's sake. Isabella has a boutique in London, but she's coming up to see her mum at the end of October, so she's going to bring a tonne of dresses with her - and before you start having a meltdown, I've told her about the Ball so she knows what sort of dresses and I've also told her a little about you too and what you wouldn't be prepared to wear. Now the *pièce de résistance* is that her mother was a hair and make-up artist on magazine shoots for Vogue, in her day. So, my dear, you will be getting the entire works! And no disrespect, but you really do need it. Such a natural beauty and you don't even know it!' Pippa said managing to swerve a downright insult with a compliment.

'Oh god, no way, I can't! It's just not me. I want to just disappear into the background, you know that,' she said, filled with panic.

'Nonsense! It's all arranged now – and they both love a challenge!' Pippa laughed not even bothering to end this insult with a compliment.

'But…'

'No buts! Enjoy yourself – you deserve a day of *you* time. You spend all your days helping and fixing everyone else, so let someone help and fix you for once. I'll text you the address – her mum lives in Poundbury, so it's not far at all.'

Felicity slumped back on the bed and closed her eyes with absolute dread for what was in store. 'Oh Pippa,' is all she could find to say.

'You're going to have a fabulous time, I promise. And her mum has got a million and one scandalous stories to tell about her Vogue days – makes my stories sound tame!' Pippa snorted down the phone. 'Oh and shave your legs before you go!' and with that, she was gone.

She opened her eyes and stared at the ceiling, wishing now that she'd opted for that sixth dress instead.

CHAPTER 25

A few days after meeting Jack in the pub, Trip's mobile began to buzz at the side of the bed.

'Trip,' he muttered.

'Do you do anything other than sleep mate?' Coop laughed.

He looked at the time on the phone through bleary eyes. 'It's 4am mate.'

'Oh, yeah, right – keep forgetting it's night there. Sorry 'bout that.'

'You really need to work on making your voice sound at least a bit remorseful,' Trip yawned.

'I've got that number you wanted for Laura Taylor and also Richard Hart's mobile too. I held back phoning you straight away with the information, as I've been following a few leads.'

'You could have just texted this to me, considering it's the middle of the night and all that.'

'But then I wouldn't get to hear the satisfaction of you saying how brilliant I am.'

Trip sat up. 'Why, what you got?'

'Right – I found all the obvious stuff out on Abigail Hart. Normal childhood, good parents, lots of friends, blah blah

blah. She met her husband, Richard, when she went to work for him at his PR company in Poole – Hart Media & Communications. Married after six months together. All good so far, but then they want kids and can't have them. I found loads of medical stuff to do with tests, but no obvious reason why she wasn't getting knocked up though. She gets more depressed and he gets a wandering eye. He starts an affair with one of the PR girls at his company, gets her up the duff and runs off around Europe with her, First Class. Lots of antidepressants later and we're up to date with Abi being out with her friends at the pub in Puddletown on the night she dies.'

'And…?' Trip said, knowing there'd be something more than that to justify Coop phoning rather than emailing all that information.

'And her husband's a crook.'

'What sort of crook?'

'The sort that wouldn't want divorce lawyers and Court Judges poking around in his finances. And it gets better,' Coop continued, 'I stumbled across a known contact of his – Slasher Stevens. You remember Slasher I assume…?'

'I remember him alright. Big bloke, spider tattoo on his hand – enforcer to the lowlifes of this world.'

'That's the one.'

'Interesting, because one of my neighbours, who mixes in the company of some of Dorset's dodgiest residents, recently described him perfectly to me. He's clearly been in the area for a few months.'

'Why would your neighbour know him?'

'With Gav, who knows. He'll have trodden on someone's toes he should have kept away from. But that's his problem, not mine - well, apart from the fact I'm hiding a USB for Gav that Slasher may be looking for.'

'Why are you doing that for a dodgy neighbour?'

'Because even though he drives me bloody insane with his damn car alarm, I don't want to see him getting beaten up, or worse.'

'Mate, you're too nice.'

'Yeah, I know. Anyway, I'm guessing you've spoken to Tooga about the Slasher connection?'

'Indeed – you know Tooga likes to know everything he can about that piece of shit. He's still very keen, even after all these years, to speak to him about the money he stole when he used to work behind the bar at his club. Anyway, Tooga asked around and the last time anyone knew of his whereabouts, was at a motorway service station near Exeter about a week ago. He got pissed off at a BMW driver who nipped in the parking space he was about to reverse into. Mr. BMW opened his window to laugh at beating Slasher to it and Slasher dragged him through the window and beat the living shit out of him. I'm thinking Exeter isn't a million miles from sunny Dorset, is it?'

'No, it's not. Sounds like Slasher's back in town. Coop, as ever, you're a prince amongst thieves. Thanks mate.'

'Yeah. Laters,' and he disappeared into the ether once more.

Trip's mind was now running at a hundred miles an hour. This last piece of information seemed pretty crucial and he wasn't surprised that during Jack's official police investigations, he hadn't discovered this dubious side to the seemingly perfect Richard Hart.

CHAPTER 26

Trip had slept fitfully after Coop's phone call a few hours earlier, which meant he'd slept through the usual 6am wake-up call, courtesy of Gav's car alarm. Occasionally there were some silver linings, he thought as he stretched. With a heavy head, he got out of bed hoping that a run would help clear his mind and energise his body.

As he exited the apartment building fifteen minutes later with Bear, he noticed Gav's car wasn't in the car park. No sane person would steal that heap of junk, however, he also found it hard to believe that Gav ever woke up before midday. Perhaps today was the day that Slasher Stevens had come looking for Gav and his mysterious USB stick, still hidden away in Trip's apartment.

After Bear had sniffed an appealing lamppost for a frustrating amount of time, he finally jogged out of the car park and headed away from the Buttermarket, hoping a run would help to organise his thoughts. Today his head was crammed full of so many different pieces of an impossible jigsaw, which he didn't know how to solve and he needed to find some clarity to help unscramble the mess in his muddled mind.

When he finally returned from his run, he noticed Gav's car was still missing and wondered if it was too early to hope it had finally been laid to rest in a scrapyard somewhere.

After showering, he sat down at his desk, Bear snoring on the sofa - all rules long since forgotten. Looking at the scattered files in front of him, he was beginning to get a sense of déjà vu. His initial gut feeling that something was strange about the circumstances of Roni Porters death, was now including similar suspicions regarding Abi Hart's supposed suicide. As both women had finally found something positive to focus on, he was becoming increasingly concerned that the deaths were now turning into something worryingly more sinister. There may, of course, be no connection whatsoever between the two dead women – random suicides or random murders. But his instinct was telling him otherwise.

He picked up his phone and called one of the numbers Coop had given him earlier.

'Hello?' a woman's voice said.

'Laura Taylor?'

'Yes,' she said simply, sadness still evident in her voice.

'Hello, my name is Trip Hazard. I'm a freelance journalist in Poundbury and also a friend of DI Wicheloe's.'

'OK. What's this about?' she asked, her voice starting to falter.

'I want to try and find out as much as possible about Abigail Hart and I understand you were her best friend. I wonder if now is a good time to ask you a few questions Laura?'

'Yes of course. Did DI Wicheloe tell you I don't think Abi jumped? Not willingly anyway.'

'He did, yes. Could you tell me a bit more about why you think that?'

'We'd been out for a lovely meal at the Blue Vinny that night. Poor Abi had been feeling so sad for months, but I'd finally managed to get her out of the house. She really didn't want to go out that night, but I forced her…' her voice caught in her throat. Sniffing backs tears, she continued, 'I convinced her to come out and told her it would do her the world of good, but look how it ended.'

'I'm so sorry for the loss of your best friend Laura, but you need to know that what happened to her was not your fault, so don't punish yourself. I have contacts that the police simply don't have access to and that's why DI Wicheloe asked me to quietly look into this for him. We both agree that something doesn't feel right about it, largely based on what you told the police. This conversation and my investigations are completely off the record and not for publication. I will only pass information onto the police which I believe may be relevant or important, so please feel you can speak freely to me.'

'Thank you for trying to help Mr. Hazard. I was convinced the police thought I was just being crazy and emotional when I kept insisting it wasn't suicide. But I'm telling you, a different Abi left the Blue Vinny that night, to the one that had walked in there earlier in the evening.'

'In what way?'

'She'd locked herself away in that big house for months. She wouldn't see anyone other than me – and that's only because I had a key. Richard was being a dickhead and would only speak to her through his solicitor, which was just making everything worse. Then when she saw the pictures on social media of him hugging the pregnant blonde woman, well that nearly finished her off. If Abi had died then, it wouldn't have surprised me at all and I would have said that it would definitely have been suicide. But these last few days, she was starting to at least try a bit – and the fact I'd managed to get her to come out that night was amazing. There would have been no chance a few weeks earlier and trust me I'd tried. Then in the pub that night, traces of the old Abi started to re-emerge. I know the alcohol mixed with the antidepressants was probably unwise, but actually it really relaxed her so much that she was laughing and smiling – both things that she hadn't done for months…' Her voice faded away, remembering those last precious minutes that she would ever see of her friend. 'Then at the end of the meal, she was saying that she needed to kick herself into action and sort out her future, without Richard. She was talking about going back to college to get her PR degree. Dickhead was insisting the house would be sold in the divorce, so we even talked about her moving in with me while she was studying.'

'Do you think she could have just been saying that for your benefit?'

'No, absolutely not. I've known Abi since we were five years old – we always told each other everything. I could tell when she was lying from a mile off.'

'And what can you tell me about her husband Richard?'

'He's a Class A dickhead. I never liked him from the first time Abi introduced me to him. He's good looking and says all the right charming things, but there was always something a bit, well, sort of oily about him, you know? Like it was all a bit of a false façade and this whole package thing of good looks, successful business, nice guy, was just a bit too good to be true.'

'Did Abi know what you thought about him?'

'Oh yes. Like I said, we'd known each other almost all our lives and there would have been no point pretending I liked him when I didn't, because Abi would have seen straight through it.'

'And did you ever see or hear anything to do with Richard that confirmed your thoughts about him?'

'No, I just thought he was a fake. Why? Do you think he had something to do with Abi's death?'

'At the moment, no. Just trying to get an understanding of who he is. I believe he's still travelling around Europe and I'm having trouble contacting him as his mobile always seems to be switched off.'

'Well, I hope he stays away – she was far too good for

him and I'll always hold him responsible for Abi's death, whether he was or not.' She sniffed back her tears once more.

'Thank you, Laura, you've been really helpful. If there is anything at all you remember that you think might be useful, please don't hesitate to give me a call, whatever time of day it is.'

'I will Mr. Hazard…and thank you for doing this for Abi…,' and her voice broke into quiet sobs.

'Please call me Trip. Look after yourself Laura and I'll be in touch.'

'OK, Trip…thank you again,' and she ended the call.

He sat back in his chair digesting everything that had just been said. He really would have liked to speak to Richard Hart face to face, or at least on the phone, to see if he had the same gut feeling about the man as Laura and Jack did. Somehow, he thought he probably would. Grabbing his car keys, he decided to drive out to Puddletown with Bear.

Firstly, he retraced the route Abi Hart would have walked with Laura, from her home to The Blue Vinny pub. Next, he drove through the winding country lanes to get to where she died at Hive Beach, near Bridport. He couldn't shake the feeling that it seemed a long way to go to kill yourself. There were several houses Abi would have driven past, or been driven past by someone else, to get to where she went over the cliff edge. However, as it was out of the main holiday season when she'd died, there wouldn't have been the usual throng of tourists about that may have seen her. It had also been raining heavily that night, which meant that even local people probably wouldn't have ventured outside unnecessarily.

Looking out across the sea, most likely the last view Abi had seen, Trip picked up his mobile from the passenger seat.

'Hey Jack.'

'Trip, what can I do for you?'

'Just a quick question – were there any vehicles acting suspiciously either in Puddletown or near Hive Beach, on the night of Abi's death?'

'None that we're aware of, no.'

'What about her own car?'

'In the garage at her home.'

'Any local taxi firm taken any bookings or passengers to where she killed herself?'

'None.'

'Well, unless Abi had miraculously teleported herself here, I'm beginning to believe she must have been driven by someone else, for the sole purpose of killing her.'

'Yep, I know exactly what you mean, which is why I asked you to dig around a bit. Unfortunately, my soon-to-be-retiring boss wants this filed away as a tragic suicide.'

'But how else do you explain Abi getting from Puddletown to Hive Beach? And don't you think it's a bloody long way to go to kill yourself? Plus, she'd been drinking wine on top of anti-depressants – not the best mix under any circumstances.'

'Yeah, like I say, I completely agree with you. We did have a witness saying that she swayed a bit as she walked out the pub.'

'So, the fact that her own car was still in the garage at home, means she would have randomly driven another car all the way to Bridport? Even if that had happened, surely she would have had a prang during the journey if she was that woozy? Have you spoken to Richard Hart yet?'

'No haven't managed to get through on his mobile. You?'

'No, me neither. There is a name that has popped up connected to Richard Hart though.'

'Go on.'

'Slasher Stevens.'

'You're kidding me.'

'Sadly not.'

'How is the perfect and popular Richard Hart connected to that lowlife?'

'That's something I'm still trying to find out – but he was recently seen in Exeter and strangely enough, by my annoying neighbour, Gav. Jack, I can't shake the feeling that something is very amiss here.'

'I agree – and the Slasher Stevens connection is particularly worrying, especially as he's been seen in the area recently. Listen, I've got pressure from above to file this away quickly, so we need to find any evidence as soon as possible.'

'I'll let you know the minute I hear anymore.'

'Cheers mate', and Jack hung up.

CHAPTER 27

It was 8am on the day of the Fundraising Ball and Felicity already wished that the day was over before it had begun. October was her favourite month of the year and there were many reasons why she loved it. The autumnal leaves changing colour on the trees, colder weather, clocks changing ending British Summer Time, frosty misty mornings and evenings getting darker much earlier. But the main reason she loved October, was because it was the month she had flown back from Australia, to live in the UK once again and start to rebuild her life.

But right now, not only did she have to go through the pain and discomfort of attending the Ball tonight, she had to endure the pain and discomfort from a day of primping and preening at the hands of Pippa's friend and goddaughter. Reluctantly, she dragged herself out of bed, grabbed a razor and disappeared into the shower.

She was just wrapping the towel around her hair, when her mobile rang.

'Just making sure you haven't chickened out of your pampering day!' Pippa laughed down the phone.

'No, no I'll be there,' she sighed.

'Now listen, I don't want you worrying about your dog's bladders while you're being fussed over all day. So, on your way to Isabella, pop in to mine and leave them with me - Brenda's coming up this morning and staying the night, so she'll be with them while we're at the Ball too. OK?'

'I hadn't thought of that. Hang on a minute - how long do you think they're going to take with me today?' she said alarmed.

'I told you, it's a whole day jobbie!'

'Oh,' Felicity's heart sank, 'that's really good of you – and Brenda. The dogs will love being with her all day.'

'Think nothing of it. Right, you need to get a move on. I'll see you shortly.'

'Pippa?'

'Yes?'

'You'll be pleased to hear I've shaved my legs.'

'Thank bloody goodness for that!' and Pippa was gone.

Felicity had never met a woman like Pippa before in her life - *ever*. For someone who had many enemies and opponents, she could honestly say that Pippa was one of a kind, with the biggest heart of anyone she knew. And it was for that reason alone, she was willing to put herself in a situation which would reveal the very worst of her insecurities and inner demons.

Thirty minutes later, Felicity had dropped the dogs off at Pippa's and driven the short distance to meet Isabella. She parked on the road outside the townhouse and rang the doorbell and within seconds, the door was opened by a stunning woman with long blonde hair.

'Felicity I presume! I'm Isabella, come on in.'

Felicity didn't move, momentarily frozen on the doorstep. 'Errrr aren't you…Isabella Brock?'

'That's me! Come on in, it's freezing out there and mum can't wait to meet you. Pippa's said so many wonderful things about you,' and she moved aside to let Felicity enter.

The house was as stunning inside as the woman who'd answered the door. The hallway and rooms were painted white, with dark wooden floors and furnishings in soft creams and toffee colours.

'Felicity!' a voice called from a room in front of her. The door opened and a beautiful platinum haired woman, clearly Isabella's mother and from whom she'd inherited her looks, appeared in the doorway, hands outstretched in greeting.

'I'm Georgina, Isabella's mother. It's wonderful to meet the woman Pippa's been talking so fondly about. She's a very difficult woman at times and it takes a special person to impress her, trust me!'

'It's so lovely to meet you both – but Pippa failed to mention the *Isabella* I was meeting was in fact *Isabella Brock* the fashion designer!'

'Good old Pip! Always likes to shock and surprise. The stories I could tell you about her!' Georgina laughed. 'Right then, let's go upstairs and see what we can do to transform you.'

'I, errrr, look I…,' Felicity stuttered, unsure how to say what she needed to, without sounding ungrateful to them.

Georgina interrupted. 'Listen Felicity, Pip has said a few bits and pieces – not much and certainly not enough for you to worry that she's been talking about you behind your back. She admits she completely railroaded you into coming here today and none of this will be easy for you. But she just wants you going out tonight, feeling pampered and happy - and well, being looked after for once, instead of being the one that always helps everyone else.'

Felicity really didn't know what to say, which was quite unusual for her. She could have hugged the two women for being so nice and prepared to tussle with the insecurities which were about to be unleashed.

'Thank you', she said to them both.

'Come on then, let's get started,' Isabella smiled.

She followed them upstairs to the third floor of their house and stopped in her tracks. In one room, there were rails and rails of clothes, steam presses and sewing machines. Three full length mirrors were angled around a small round podium in the centre of the room and to the side were half a dozen or more clothes dummies, lined up like soldiers dressed in various half-finished garments. There were rolls of satin material in every colour of the rainbow lying on a large table and a mountain of shoe boxes stacked up high in one corner.

Across the landing, was clearly Georgina's domain. Dressing tables filled one entire wall, with lights all around the table top mirrors. Every electrical hair appliance available, appeared to be plugged in ready for use at one table. Numerous bottles, tubes and sprays were arranged on another, together with palettes of every conceivable colour of eye shadow and face make up. A vast array of lipsticks, pencils, mascaras, brushes and sponges were all arranged in various pots, boxes and display racks. There were perfumes in bottles of every shape and colour and huge books containing hair colour swatches. Although Felicity had been speechless when the famous dress designer opened the front door to her ten minutes ago, this was something else.

'Oh my…'

'Spectacular isn't it!' Georgina beamed.

'I've never seen anything like it.'

'Right then, Isabella needs you first to get the dress sorted because she may need to make alterations – plus the fact we don't want your hair and make-up ruined while trying clothes on, so we'll do that after.' She grabbed Felicity's hand. 'Come on, this is going to be so much fun!'

That's not the word Felicity would have used and she reluctantly followed her back into the other room.

'OK, now why don't you tell me what you *aren't* happy to wear,' Isabella said.

'Well…it's been a long time since I've worn a dress…'

174

She looked down at the floor, momentarily lost in her thoughts. '…and there are…well…I can't errr…,' she didn't know how to explain her restrictions.

Isabella, who was still holding Felicity's hand, squeezed it. 'You don't have to explain or say anything you don't want to. Why don't you just have a wander around, look at the rails of dresses, point out the things you aren't comfortable with – and show me the one's you do like. Remember, nothing is going to be exactly right – I can alter anything, in any way, to make it perfect for you.'

'Thank you,' she said quietly, tears stinging her eyes.

'Take your time,' Isabella smiled and let go of her hand, gently ushering her forward towards the clothes.

For the next hour, Felicity looked through the dresses which were all exquisite. But, as she moved amongst them, she felt utterly overwhelmed. It had been many years since she'd worn anything other than trousers and long shapeless sundresses.

As she began to feel more comfortable in Isabella's company, she tried to explain her insecurities. 'I can't wear anything that's too low cut at the front, or has side splits too high. And definitely no front split to the dress.'

Isabella nodded and swept around the room, hanging dozens of dresses onto an empty rail.

'OK, what do you think of this lot?'

She nervously walked towards the rail. 'They are all so lovely – stunning, but too stunning for me and I think…well, I'd feel…exposed.' She suddenly felt quite sorry for herself. 'Oh Isabella, I think I'm a lost cause!'

'No such thing,' she smiled. 'Hmmm let me think…,' and she disappeared behind a rail full of black zipped bags. 'So, how do you feel about backless?'

'Err…OK, I suppose. Although I would much prefer trousers and a shirt!' she laughed.

'Hmmm…well, I could take this piece…join that…and remove this bit…then take that panel from this one…put it all together…yes perfect, I think this is going to work!' she mumbled triumphantly from behind a sea of unzipped dress carriers.

All Felicity could see however, were a pile of different dresses heaped on the floor.

'Right, let me draw you a rough sketch to give you an idea of what I can see in my head,' Isabella said.

Felicity soon realised that her idea of a *rough sketch* was in fact an incredible piece of artwork. The sweeping lines, folds and shading she gave to the drawing, brought the image to life.

'Oh, it's…perfect,' she said, having an overwhelming urge to cry.

'Ha! Knew it! OK, slip this one on first, but ignore the top half because I'll be removing that…and wait while I just…,' and she disappeared out of the room.

Moments later, she reappeared with a trifold screen for Felicity to undress behind.

Relieved by her thoughtfulness, she went behind it and slipped on the first outfit.

'When you're ready, jump on the podium so I can pin it,' Isabella called over the top of screen.

When Felicity emerged, she looked awkward and uncomfortable.

'Don't worry, by the time I have finished you'll feel like Cinderella,' Isabella reassured her.

'I don't want to find a Prince Charming tonight – and I certainly don't want to stand out. I just want to survive the evening!' she said, wondering what excuse she could come up with to flee the country.

'When we've worked our magic on you, you'll feel completely comfortable, confident and ready to face anything, I promise. OK, you can slip that off now, but be careful of the pins.'

She disappeared behind the screen again and Isabella draped the next dress over for her to try on. This continued for what felt like forever, but eventually Isabella seemed satisfied.

'OK all done – you can go see mum now to sort those curls out! I'll shout when I need you to try anything on again,' and Isabella set about flinging open boxes of threads and lining up an array of cutting implements, clearly in her element.

As if by magic, Georgina appeared in the doorway and putting her arm around Felicity's shoulders, led her into what resembled a complete hair and beauty salon, tucked away in a large three-storey townhouse in Dorset.

'Right then, what are we going to do with these curls tonight?'

'I don't know – it's been years since I've done anything with this,' and she pulled a long curl straight before letting it go to bounce back. 'I just drown it in anti-frizz serum each day and then tie it back,' she sighed.

Georgina studied her and unleashed the ponytail, wayward curls springing out in every direction. 'What about colour?'

'Colour! I thought we could maybe just, I don't know, pin it up?'

'Oh no, no, no! Something far more special can be done with this!' and she tilted her head from left to right, clearly planning her strategy.

'I see you have a natural blonde streak tucked away amongst this mass of curls.'

'Yes, I was always teased about it when I was younger and for years had my hair blonde to hide it, but…well, since I've been back in the UK, I've just let my hair do its own thing. So, this boring brown is all me!' She suddenly felt very self-conscious about the unruly mop of bramble twigs on her head.

'I think you need to embrace that beautiful blonde streak and make a feature of it - it's very unusual you know. So, how about we put a lovely rich chocolate brown through your hair to give us a nice depth of base colour all over. Then I'm thinking, blend some warm caramel and toffee low-lights through. Then finally, tone the blonde streak with a subtle creamy honey, to blend in with the rich shades of chocolate pudding, sweet toffee and gooey caramel. Sound good?'

'Good enough to eat!' she said, feeling very hungry.

'Excellent!' and she led Felicity over to a basin in the corner.

CHAPTER 28

Grace Jefferies walked into her kitchen and made a flask of coffee for her journey into work, as she did every morning. Fridays were always her busiest day of the week with the mad rush of exchanges and completions happening, but throw into the mix the Bailey-Thompsons client-from-hell and it was going to be like wading through treacle today.

Her husband, Peter, was a food critic and he'd booked a short weekend away to Plymouth to do some restaurant reviews. The original plan was that they were supposed to be going to the hotel this morning and return on Monday. Grace, however, had the Bailey-Thompsons completion scheduled for today and as there had been numerous problems throughout their house sale, she needed to get it finished. As it was her own business, she felt it unfair to leave those particularly difficult and obnoxious clients to any of her staff to deal with as none of them deserved that punishment.

After several arguments, Grace and her husband had agreed that he would still go on ahead to Plymouth alone, so he'd left earlier that morning and she would drive there as soon as she could get away from the office later.

Over the years he'd grown tired of her always putting her work first. They had no children, which was her choice not his and he'd added that to his list of resentments towards his wife. However, they had a large house, nice cars, went on luxury holidays and as Peter's income was far less than Grace's, he bit his tongue the majority of the time.

Grace's law firm, Bartlett-Jefferies Solicitors, was based in Dorchester. She'd started the company ten years ago using her maiden name combined with her married name. She had successfully established her business and now had a good reputation, with a very healthy client base.

As she was leaving her home in Broadmayne, she phoned her secretary.

'Morning Caroline, just leaving home now – any calls yet from the Bailey-Thompsons?'

'Hi Grace, no calls yet thankfully, but I'm guessing it won't be long!'

'OK, good - on my way,' and she hung up.

Twenty minutes later, she parked at her offices in Brewery Square in Dorchester and walked into the building, where she could immediately hear Caroline on the phone.

'Yes Mr Bailey-Thompson I will pass that onto Mrs Jefferies when she's finished on her conference call. No, I don't imagine she'll be much longer. Yes, your completion is still scheduled for today. No, we don't envisage any more hitches.' Caroline looked at Grace and rolled her eyes. 'No, I won't forget to pass your message on, just as soon as I am off the phone from you,' she said politely, through gritted teeth. 'Yes OK. Goodbye Mr. Bailey-Thompson,' and Caroline finally escaped off the phone.

She flung her head down dramatically on her desk and groaned. 'It's only 9am and I need chocolate already!'

Grace passed her a Twix from her handbag. 'Another few hours and it'll all be over and no more Bailey-Thompsons!' she smiled and walked into her office.

The rest of the day passed in a blur of phone calls and emails. The Bailey-Thompsons completion eventually took place, much to the huge relief of all of her staff and after finishing some other client letters, she finally left the office at 3pm.

She phoned Peter as she pulled out the car park and was diverted to his voicemail.

'It's me - I'm on my way home to collect my bag and get changed. I reckon, traffic permitting, I should be there between 5.30-6pm.'

Ten minutes later, she was driving down the A35 towards Puddletown, when suddenly there was a loud pop as a tyre blew. She panicked, feeling out of control and quickly pulled over onto the side of the bypass. By the time she'd switched off the ignition and got out of the car, her heart was pounding and it took several minutes before she got her breathe back.

Eventually feeling calmer, she called the telephone number on the AA sticker on the windscreen, only to discover that Peter had forgotten to renew their policy six weeks ago. Frustrated, she threw her mobile onto the passenger seat and leant against the car, closing her eyes as she rubbed at the tension forming across her forehead.

The noise of a car engine close by interrupted her fractious thoughts towards her husband and she opened her eyes to see a man walking towards her.

'Everything OK? Do you need any help?' he asked.

'My tyre has just blown – frightened the life out of me.'

'I'm sure it did. Have you called anyone?'

'Yes, the AA - but my policy has expired, so I was just about to Google local garages to see if anyone can help. I'm supposed to be going on holiday right now – typical isn't it!'

'There's a garage not far from here, they had to tow me a few months ago when I had smoke billowing from my engine. I've got the number on my mobile, let me get it for you,' and he walked back towards his car.

When he returned with his phone, he scrolled through his contacts, giving her the details of the garage and she rang the number.

'Harris Recovery,' a man's voice said.

'Oh hello, my name is Grace Jefferies and I'm stuck on the A35 bypass, just near the turning for Wareham. One of my tyres has blown and I haven't got a spare, although I have got one of those foam kit things. But to be honest, I wouldn't know what to do with it anyway! A kind man has just stopped to make sure I was OK and he recommended you. Are you able to help me at all?'

'Certainly can, Mrs Jefferies. Actually, I'm just on my way back to the garage from Dorchester now, so I should be with you in about five minutes. OK?'

'Oh, thank you, yes! White Range Rover - three tyres!' she laughed with relief.

'No problem, be with you soon,' and he hung up.

Grace turned towards the man at the side of the road.

'Thank you so much, he's going to be here in a few minutes. I can't thank you enough for stopping to help me.'

'My pleasure. Now make sure you stay out of the vehicle and keep on the grass verge away from the road until the mechanic arrives. This is such a fast road, so you need to be careful.'

'Thank you, I will.'

'The garage was great with my car and it was fixed the next day, so I'm sure a tyre can be sorted in no time.'

'What's frustrating is that I only live in Broadmayne, I can't believe it's happened so close to home.'

'My sister lives in Broadmayne, just near the Black Dog pub.'

'I live literally just around the corner from there,' Grace said. 'The thatched cottage with the old wishing well in the front garden.'

'Yes, I know the one — beautiful house. My

granddaughter always insists on making a wish and throwing a penny in the well whenever we take her to see my sister.'

'Oh, that's nice. Listen, thanks again for stopping to help me out, you're very kind.'

'No problem at all – do you still think you will be able to go on holiday today?'

'I'm not sure – it's not looking likely at the moment though. My husband won't be impressed as he's already gone on ahead, so I'll be cooking for one tonight instead of eating in a lovely restaurant on The Hoe,' she sighed.

'That's a shame. Right, stay safe while you're waiting for the recovery truck and hopefully, you'll be on your way soon.'

'Thanks again', Grace said and watched him walk back to his vehicle.

As he got back into his car, he looked at her in the rear-view mirror for a few moments. The breeze caught loose tendrils of her dark hair, whipping them forward, bringing back memories from his childhood.

Finally pulling his attention away from her, he slowly drove off into the traffic and disappeared from sight.

A few minutes later, the recovery truck pulled onto the verge at the side of the bypass in front of her car. A tall man in overalls got out and walked towards Grace.

'Mrs Jefferies?' he said.

'Yes – thank you for getting here so quickly.'

'No problem at all, let's see what we can do about the tyre.' He crouched down at the side of her car and looked at the damage. 'OK this isn't repairable I'm afraid – the walls of the tyre are ripped and you'll need a new one.'

'I was worried you'd say that.'

'I might have one in stock though, so let's get you towed away from this busy road, back to my garage – it's only down the road at Troy Town. If I've got one of these tyres, then I'll fit it straight away and you'll be on your way in no time.'

'Thank you so much. I'm supposed to be going on holiday now, so that would be great. I'm not far from home here either,' she said relieved.

'OK, jump in the passenger seat and I'll get your car loaded onto the truck - but ignore all the sweet wrappers on the floor!' he laughed.

She walked around to the front of the truck and got in, kicking the sweet wrappers to one side to make room for her feet. Minutes later, he got in beside her.

'OK, all set,' he said.

'You weren't kidding about the sweet wrappers were you!' she laughed.

'Yeah, it's a bad habit – gave up smoking, took up sweets instead!'

'I can't believe this has happened on today of all days. My husband went on ahead to the hotel this morning and we were supposed to be having a weekend away.'

'Well hopefully we can still get you on your way tonight.'

'That would be great if I can.'

'So, who recommended me?'

'I didn't get his name, tall man with a white beard wearing a baseball cap and sunglasses. Sorry, that's not very helpful description is it.'

'Wasn't Santa Claus in disguise, was it?' he laughed.

'Only if he's traded in his sleigh for a blue car!'

He drove the truck three miles along the bypass, turning off at the exit for Troy Town, then minutes later, they were pulling into his garage.

'Right, let me have a look and see if I've got one of these tyres,' and he disappeared around the corner while Grace called her husband.

'Peter, I may be a bit delayed', she heard him sigh and mutter under his breath. 'Before you start, one of the damn tyres blew on my way home, on the bypass. A man stopped and gave me the number of the local garage, which is where I am now. Hopefully he has a tyre in stock and can change it straight away, which means I won't be too much later getting to you.'

'Why didn't you phone the AA? That's what we pay them for.'

'Because *you* forgot to renew the policy.'

There was silence at the other end of the phone.

'Fine, let me know what's happening.' The unimpressed tone was clearly evident in his voice.

'I'm OK though, *thanks for asking*. Look, I don't want to argue about this now - I'll call you when I know more.'

'Yep, sure,' and he hung up.

Grace dropped her mobile back in her bag and counted to ten, in the hope her anger towards her unsympathetic husband would pass.

'Well, there's good news and bad news,' the mechanic said as he reappeared.

'Go on…,' Grace sighed.

'Well, the bad news is that I don't have one of these tyres in stock. But the good news is, I've tracked one down and I can get it delivered first thing in the morning and it should be ready for you by 9am at the latest.'

'Really? Thank you so much. I appreciate all your help and at least I can be in Plymouth by mid-morning tomorrow. If you let me know when it's ready in the morning, I can get a taxi and collect it.'

'I'm just sorry I can't sort it for you now.'

'Honestly you've been great – and I'll have a peaceful night alone tonight, which is a rarity these days.' Her mind flitted back to Peter's lack of concern over the tyre blow out. 'I'll give my secretary a call now so I can catch her before she leaves the office and she can collect me on her way home,' and she walked outside to make the call.

'Caroline, it's Grace. My tyre burst on the way home on the bypass and I've been towed to a garage in Troy Town. Could you swing by and pick me up on your way home and drop me at my house please?...you're an angel, thank you!...yes, it's called Harris' Garage in Troy Town...errrm not sure there's a road name...OK, great – good old Google! Thanks Caroline, see you soon,' and she ended the call.

'Right, my secretary is going to leave work now, so she'll be here in about ten or fifteen minutes. Is there anything you need from me before I go?' she asked.

'I'll fill in the invoice now if you like, it'll save you time in the morning. I just need your name, address and contact number,' and he grabbed his pad and a pen.

After giving him her details, she walked outside and phoned her husband again to update him while she waited.

'It's not good news I'm afraid. The garage can't get a tyre until the morning, but it should be first thing, so hopefully I'll be with you by 11am,' she said.

'Right OK – well at least the whole weekend won't be ruined.'

'Peter, I haven't done this on purpose you know. I was actually looking forward to a break.'

'Yeah, I know. It's just so damn bloody annoying that something always gets in the way.'

She knew he was complaining about her work as usual, but let the insinuation pass.

'I'll phone you when I'm leaving home tomorrow morning.'

'Yep OK. Goodnight,' and he ended the call.

Fifteen minutes later, Caroline arrived and took Grace home. 'Thanks for the lift,' she said, getting out of the car.

'Have a lovely weekend away – and relax and enjoy yourself tonight!' her secretary shouted as Grace walked towards her house.

Caroline, along with everyone else, knew nothing of the problems in her marriage.

CHAPTER 29

Over the next five hours, Felicity was herded between standing on a podium getting pinned and twirled around, to sitting having her hair colour transformed. Georgina regaled some spectacularly salacious stories about the wild times she and Pippa had enjoyed as teenagers in London and the celebrity parties they'd gate crashed.

'…and then we legged it down the road with his guitar! Pippa still has it now, I think,' Georgina laughed at the memory.

'Oh and the funniest was when Pippa and I were both at a party, well before she changed her name to Pippa – and that's a story in itself! The whole National Security thing was a nightmare…still not sure she's allowed to travel overseas,' and she briefly paused to mix a different colour hair dye.

'Anyway, we often managed to sneak into the wrap parties at Pinewood Studios and this one particular party we were desperate to gatecrash. We were talking to a couple of gorgeous stuntmen, when Pippa nipped off to the toilet. Twenty minutes later I'm panicking because I can't find her and then I overhear someone asking if they've seen that greasy little shadow cabinet MP…oh, what's his name?…

can't remember at the moment, but ask Pippa when you next see her, she never forgets anything. Anyway, the MP's wife started to pound on one of the office doors, yelling and shouting for him to come out, wanting to know who he was in there with. Next thing I heard was that the police had caught him climbing out of the back window practically starkers, apart from his socks, underpants and a bra dangling out of his left sock, which he hadn't noticed in his rush to get away! One of the police officers eventually gave him an old rugby shirt to cover himself up – the press got hold of that bit the next day, poor sod! Pip was vague with the details afterwards, other than to say she'd been asked to tail him for a while and at the party she'd caught him in a compromising position with a fellow MP's wife. Ah well, those were the days…,' she laughed.

Finally, the colouring process was complete and Georgina combed through her damp hair, studying the wet springy mass of curls. 'Do you trust me?'

'Completely,' Felicity smiled.

'Right answer!'

'Do you think Isabella is getting on OK out there?'

'Oh, she'll be in her element! She was destined to be a designer since she was a girl you know. Always cutting clothes up and stitching them back together. I have no idea where she gets her talent from - I can't even thread a needle!'

'I still can't quite believe I'm in the same house as her to be honest. I've seen her dresses so many times in magazine articles and drooled over them!'

'She's just started working on the gowns to be used in the new Cinderella film – seems quite apt with what we're doing today, don't you think?'

She was indeed beginning to feel like Cinderella now.

At that moment, Isabella shouted from the other room. 'Is now a good time to steal Felicity for a few minutes for a preliminary fitting?'

'Yes, perfect timing, she's on her way!' and Georgina

herded her across the hallway.

As she walked into the room, patterns were strewn across the floor and rolls of material draped across a large wooden table. It looked like a whirlwind had sped through the room.

'Don't be put off by the mess – think of it as organised chaos!' Isabella grinned. 'Here - go and carefully step into this.'

Felicity disappeared behind the screen once more and stepped into the garment as best as she could, trying to minimise the number of pins jabbing into her skin. Once on, the dress felt snug but not tight, feeling as if she had stepped into a new skin.

She stood on the podium, her back to the mirrors as instructed by Isabella, who needed to focus on the rear of the dress.

'I don't want you seeing it properly until it's finished!' she laughed. 'Right, almost there now…that bit just needs to come a little higher now… and hmmm…there's something missing…' Isabella studied her creation, tilting her head from side to side.

'I can't believe this is really happening – being fitted and dressed in an Isabella Brock creation. All feels a bit surreal and you must let me pay for everything today.'

'Absolutely NOT! All of the dresses I've used to create yours are one's that have been used in films – so they've already been paid for, technically!'

'Really?'

'Yes, I do a lot of design work for films – anything that requires a bit of special glam. You have parts of dresses here that were used in several Hollywood blockbusters! When they've finished filming, I have the dresses back and alter them in some way, then sell them in my shop in London - Brock's Frocks. I have a lot of clients that love to think they are swishing around in a dress worn by a famous actress.'

Isabella was still eyeing her intently when she suddenly said, 'got it!'

'Got what?'

'The perfect finishing touch I was looking for! OK, you can carefully slip out of the dress now. Mum?' she shouted across the hallway, '– she'll be back in a minute for you to finish the hair and do her make up.'

After taking the dress off, she wandered back into see Georgina, leaving Isabella to finish off her bespoke creation. It was now 5pm and the light was beginning to fade outside and she couldn't quite believe she'd been here since 9am that morning.

'Right then,' Georgina said, seating Felicity with her back to the mirror, 'let's get this hair looking incredible.'

Forty minutes later, she spun her around in the chair. With utter amazement she saw that her hair had been transformed from a frizzy bundle of ponytailed curls, to a wavy, shiny image of perfection. Georgina had taken some length off and cut in layers, straightening her hair so it fell in soft, delicate waves down her back. It was parted slightly off centre, the sides softly sweeping away from her face and draping over her shoulders. The different shades and colours reflected and danced through her hair and down one side, the blonde streak that she'd spent a life time disguising, now shimmered with a honey blonde warmth.

'Oh. My. God.'

'I told you we'd transform it!' Georgina said, grinning behind her.

'How is this even my hair? It's absolutely incredible! I can't believe you have achieved this from what you were faced with this morning,' and her eyes began brimming with tears.

'Don't cry, we need to do your make up yet! I'm thinking something subtle?'

'Yes definitely, I don't want to stand out.'

'Oh, I'm sorry my dear, you'll be standing out whether we put any make-up on you or not!'

She turned her around and started applying creams and powders - sponges and brushes flashing before her eyes. In the other room, the sound of a sewing machine hummed in the background.

Eventually, Georgina stepped back to admire her work. 'Done!' she said and turned her around to face the mirror.

Felicity couldn't believe the reflection looking back at her. She still looked like herself and wasn't painted like a doll or unrecognisable, but she looked flawless as though she was an airbrushed photograph in a magazine.

'But how…'

'Felicity, you are a beautiful blank canvas - I haven't done that much to be honest! Just some subtle smoky eye make-up, a dash of blusher and a tinted lip gloss called *Spiced Pumpkin*, which I thought very apt!'

'It's incredible,' she said, completely stunned at the person looking back at her.

'Tell me, is there a lucky gentleman picking you up tonight to go to the Ball?'

'No! Definitely no,' and she suddenly, inexplicably, felt a little sad.

'So, you really will be like Cinderella going to the Ball alone! And you never know, you may just meet your Prince Charming there too.'

'That is *never* going to happen, trust me. Everyone who's going will be married, ancient or like Roger!' she laughed, still with that slight feeling of emptiness inside, which was being irritatingly stubborn to leave.

Isabella appeared in the doorway. 'Ready!'

'Oh, one last thing…,' and Georgina walked over to the bottles of perfume, 'which one do you usually wear?'

'Dolce & Gabbana, Light Blue Intense.'

'Good choice - fresh and vibrant, mellowing into enigmatic and sensual undertones - perfect!' Georgina grinned, passing her the bottle.

Isabella grabbed her hand. 'Now pop into the bathroom across the hallway first – get yourself freshened up and there is some underwear laid out for you – all new, not previously worn by an actress or anyone else you'll be pleased to know! I designed the underwear too by the way and this will fit perfectly under the outfit.'

She was ushered into the bathroom and as the door closed, she caught a glimpse of herself in the mirror. There was a huge smile on her face and she realised quite suddenly, that she couldn't remember the last time she had smiled in this way. That's when she looked down and noticed the tiny sheer black thong with the distinctive *IB* logo discreetly embroidered on the back. The smile immediately disappeared. She was pretty sure something this small couldn't be classed as underwear.

After pulling on the scrap of material, she wrapped the long robe around her which had been draped on a chair beneath and emerged from the bathroom.

'Isabella, that's not underwear!'

The two women laughed. 'Well, no type of bra is possible with this dress, but the front is safe and secure, so don't worry about doing a Pippa!'

She was too afraid to ask what *a Pippa* was.

After disappearing behind the screen for the final time, she slipped off the robe and stepped into the dress.

'Let me know when you're in it and I'll do you up,' Isabella called over the screen.

She appeared and walked over to the podium.

'No taking a sneaky look!' Isabella said, who then proceeded to zip and button various parts of the dress.

The two women stood in front of her.

'Oh Isabella, you've excelled yourself', Georgina said hugging her daughter.

'It's pretty spectacular isn't it. OK, turnaround Felicity – time for a look.'

She slowly turned around towards the mirror, holding her breath. The image that reflected back, left her utterly speechless. A black, velvet, Bardot-style off the shoulder bodice, clung to her figure perfectly and the full-length velvet sleeves, felt soft and luxurious against her skin. Draped from the waist and skimming her hips, was a floor-length black satin skirt, split entirely up the front. The skirt only came three quarters of the way around her waist, leaving her stomach and legs exposed. However, underneath the skirt were slim fitting black satin trousers, which silhouetted her slender legs, accentuating her feminine shape. Finally, the inside lining of the skirt was a rich, deep burnt orange satin.

As she turned slightly to the side – she could see that the back of the velvet bodice was cut entirely away, exposing her back all the way down to the very base of her spine and the reason for the miniscule thong now became apparent.

At this point, she'd still not uttered a word, feeling completely overwhelmed.

'And the finishing touch!' Isabella said, breaking the silence. She placed two black shoes on the podium in front of her.

Felicity looked down and saw a pair of Christian Louboutin black high heels, their signature red soles peeking out from underneath.

'Oh…but…', she began to say.

'Gorgeous aren't they! Go on, put them on - I can't wait to see the finished look!' Isabella said.

She slipped the shoes on and grew several inches in height. It was as though they had breathed life into the dress. All of the layers and drapes of material now hung perfectly with the elevated height.

'They fit!' Felicity said with amazement.

'You have Pippa to thank for that – she had a sneaky look at you shoe size when you saw her yesterday,' Georgina laughed.

'Oh! She popped around yesterday to give me your

address, I thought it was odd she didn't just text it. Then I thought, well it is Pippa! She went upstairs to use the loo and must have looked then.'

'Pip's very sneaky and resourceful when needs must,' Georgina grinned.

For one final time, she looked at her reflection in the mirror, unable to believe who she now was, compared to who she had been at the start of the day.

'I can't thank you both enough – and Pippa, for doing all of this for me. I don't know how I can possibly repay you for making me feel…so special,' and her voice broke with emotion.

'For god's sake don't cry!' Georgina laughed, 'your make-up!'

'I nearly forgot!' Isabella said, 'here…,' and she handed her a small black purse.

'And I've put the Pumpkin Spice lip gloss inside, just in case Prince charming arrives!' Georgina winked.

The two women looked at their masterpiece standing on the podium, 'Well Cinderella, it's very nearly time for your Ball.'

CHAPTER 30

Trip looked at his watch. 'Shit!'

It was 6.15pm and he was supposed to be attending the Pumpkin Ball, which started at 7pm.

A few hours ago, in abject frustration at achieving nothing else in his investigations regarding Abi and Roni's deaths, he'd driven over to Hart Media & Communications in Poole and spoken to some of Richard Hart's staff. It was a complete dead end as all of his employees seemed to idolise him and think he was the most faultless person on the planet.

He jumped into his Jeep with Bear and drove back home as quickly, but safely as he could from Poole.

Twenty minutes later, he pulled into the car park and noticed Gav's car had returned and felt strangely comforted by this fact - although at 6am tomorrow morning, he probably wouldn't be. As he let Bear out of the back of the Jeep, the dog immediately started sniffing around suspiciously.

'Bear, come on - I'm running late so if you need to go - go!'

The dog seemed oblivious and started slowly wandering

around the car park, heading for the grassed area in the corner. Trip waited patiently for five minutes, but on the sixth minute his patience had run out.

'Bear, come on, we need to go!'

The dog didn't budge, still following the scent of something that was clearly bothering him.

He was just about to retrieve Bear, when his mobile rang. It was Tooga.

'Alright Trip, how's life with you?' he said in his broad Birmingham accent.

'Good thanks Tooga – how's the mother-in-law…still with us I'm hoping?'

'Yeah, going to see the Hypnotherapist again tomorrow, need a top-up session – that hot tub is starting to look very appealing again,' Tooga said, sadly not joking.

'Funny you should say that – I went to see a Hypnotherapist not that long ago.'

'Really? That's something I didn't think you'd ever say!' Tooga laughed. He remembered all too well how mercilessly Trip had mocked him for going to see one himself.

'Well not for me – I was railroaded into taking one of Pippa's friends, who then persuaded me to go into the session because she was so nervous.'

'How is Pippa? - dragged you into any more of her covert night time ops lately!'

'Thankfully not. So, what can I do for you?'

'I was thinking of coming down for a visit to sunny Dorset soon – thought you could take me out for a pint.'

'Are you that close to drowning the mother-in-law then?' Trip laughed.

'I'm always that close,' Tooga sighed. 'I've also got some business down in Plymouth to take care of, so figured I'd visit my oldest friend on the way.'

'It'll be good to see you mate,' Trip said, not wanting to know what the *business* actually was. 'When were you thinking?'

'Next week some time, not exactly sure when, depends how long it takes to sort the problem out. I'll give you a call when I know.'

He noticed *business* had now changed to *problem* and decided he definitely didn't want to know what would be happening in Plymouth.

'OK great, look forward to it. You can meet Bear too.'

'Bear? Who the hell is Bear?'

'My dog.'

'You've got a dog? You've got to be kidding me! Don't you remember that huge Rottweiler called Princess Twinkle Toes who, like every other female on the planet, was desperate to hump you!'

'Yeah, funny mate. Bear was Roni Porter's dog and he just sort of followed me home one day.'

'Sounds like something that would only happen to you mate. I'll see you and Bear next week then. Oh and tell Pippa she can try and win her money back in a Blackjack game while I'm there!' and Tooga hung up laughing.

Trip knew him very well - after all, they had been friends since they were ten years old. But because he knew him so well, he had a hunch there was a second reason behind his visit to Dorset.

He glanced at his watch, seeing twenty minutes had passed and looked around the car park for Bear, but couldn't see the dog anywhere.

'Bear.'

'Bear!' he said, louder.

Frustrated, he grabbed a torch out of the Jeep and started to search around the car park, suddenly becoming aware of a noise in the corner. As he got closer, the torch illuminated a dark unmoving figure.

'Bear?'

He could hear a pathetic whimpering and snivelling noise.

'What are you doing?' he asked the dog, clearly not

expecting an answer.

Standing in the corner was Gav's greasy mate. Bear was on his hind legs, front paws resting on his shoulders, pinning him against a wall.

Trip shone the torch in the man's face.

'Everything alright there, Scooter?' he asked, unable to hide his smile.

'Do...g,' he stuttered.

'What you up to then?'

'I...was...just...'avin...a...fag...and he...'

Bear started growling in his face.

'...and he just...ran...at me...and...I...been...here...ever...since...'

'How long you been like this?'

'Twenty...minutes...been counting...every bleeding second...hoping...it weren't me last,' he sniffed.

The dog started baring his teeth and growling deeper.

'W...why...is ...he...doing that?'

'He's hungry,' Trip smiled.

'Aww man...I'm too young to die...I got so... much...I wanna do yet.'

'Really? Like what?' Trip asked amused.

'Huh?'

'What's the *so much* you've got to do?'

'Well, I can't think under pressure can I.'

'Come on Bear, leave this...,' Trip paused thinking of the right word, 'idiot alone. Let's get you something more nutritious to eat.'

'You...g...getting pizza?'

'Not for you moron - for the dog!' He patted the side of his leg and Bear immediately released Scooter from his clutches and stood beside Trip.

'Th...thanks man. Thought I was a gonna,' and he shakily tried to light the end of his cigarette.

Trip shook his head, walking away towards the entrance of the apartments.

After a quick shower and with no time for a shave, he got dressed in his dinner suit and white shirt, ready for the Ball. He grappled with the bow tie for a few minutes, wondering why the hell he hadn't bought a ready-tied one. On the seventh attempt at tying, he finally gave up, leaving it resembling a bow, tied by a child for the very first time. He looked in the bathroom mirror, ran his hand through his wet hair and scratched his stubbled chin.

'You're no Prince Charming tonight, but you'll just have to do,' he said to his reflection.

He turned to his dog. 'Any chance of remembering those rules while I'm out tonight?' Bear was already snoring on the sofa, head on a chewed shoe.

He needed to make a quick phone call to Coop to see if he'd turned up any new information, then finally he'd be ready to leave for the Ball.

CHAPTER 31

As Felicity pulled her car keys from her handbag, Isabella gasped, almost making her drop them.

'Wait - Cinderella can't drive herself to the Ball, she needs a carriage!'

'Definitely', Georgina agreed. 'I'll nip you down there and you can leave your car here and collect it in the morning.'

'No honestly, you've both been so kind – it's only down the road and…'

'I really don't think driving in those Louboutin's is probably a wise idea with the height of that heel! It'll only take me two minutes, come on,' Georgina said and opened the front door.

Felicity realised there was no point in protesting, so she followed her outside into the cold October air.

'Wait in the car mum, I'll just be a sec,' and Isabella disappeared inside the house.

A moment later, she reappeared with a beautiful black cloak.

'Here,' she said, holding it for Felicity to drape around her shoulders.

'Don't tell me you've just whizzed that up on your

sewing machine too!'

'No, it's one I made earlier - it's going to be couriered to Pinewood Studios on Monday for a film, so look after it!' She hugged Felicity and kissed her cheek. 'You look absolutely stunning and I hope you feel like a million dollars tonight, because you sure as hell look it.'

'Thanks for everything,' Felicity whispered as she hugged her.

'Come on Cinders,' Georgina shouted from the car, 'you're already late!'

When Georgina pulled into the car park, there was a steady stream of people going into the Ball, with a few small groups chatting on the steps outside. Felicity thanked her for the hundredth time and got out of the car, suddenly feeling quite nervous.

As she started to drive away, Georgina shouted, '…and make sure you don't lose a shoe!'

A voice behind her made her jump, 'Felicity?'

She turned around. 'Pippa! I have had the most amazing day, thank you!'

'Bloody hell you look absolutely stunning! Who knew this…,' and she swept her hands up and down, '…lurked underneath all those curls and baggy clothes!' She was clearly astounded and *almost* lost for words.

'I'm feeling pretty nervous suddenly to be honest and very apprehensive about walking in there on my own.'

'Well, you aren't alone now, you have me to walk in with,' and Pippa looped her arm and headed towards the building.

'This reminds me of when I was summoned to the Russian Embassy in London all those years ago…such a ridiculous misunderstanding.'

Felicity turned her head to face the woman beside her, who continually kept surprising her.

They entered the building and walked over to a

cloakroom, which had been set up just inside the entrance. Pippa passed her coat over to the attendant.

'The room looks amazing!' Felicity said.

Everywhere had been decorated with stunning autumnal flower displays of orange gerberas and roses with twisted hazel and willow twigs. Pumpkins were scattered around on circular tables with candles lit inside them, illuminating their carved faces. Drapes of material hung from the ceiling and a dance floor had been positioned towards the side of the room.

Felicity unbuttoned her cloak and carefully passed it over, 'please be careful with that, I've borrowed it!'

'BLOODY HELL!' gasped Pippa, 'Felicity that dress is absolutely incredible! I need to keep Roger away from you tonight, his eyes will be out on bloody stalks!'

'Is it too much do you think?' she asked, suddenly feeling very self-conscious.

'Good grief woman, you look sensational, bloody own it and enjoy it! Just steer clear of Roger! Come on, let's mingle. I'm dying to see what that old trout Marjorie's wearing, she's desperate to muscle in on the newsletter and squeeze me out. She may have wrapped Roger around her little finger, but she's picked the wrong woman to mess with in me. Plus the fact...I *know* people...,' she winked and tapped the side of her nose before disappearing into the sea of black jackets and gowns.

Felicity stood for a moment unsure of where to go, looking for somewhere to hide in the background. A waitress walked past with a tray of champagne flutes and she grabbed one - if there was ever a night she needed Dutch courage, she suddenly decided it was tonight. She glanced around the room becoming very aware of several eyes looking her way, then with relief noticed one of her clients with her husband and squeezed through the chatting groups until she reached the familiar faces.

'Hello Liz, how are you?'

Liz paused talking to her husband and looked at Felicity. As soon as the penny had dropped, she said, 'my god Felicity - wow! I would never have recognised you if you hadn't spoken to me! Neil, you remember Felicity – the hypnotherapist who sorted out my fear of flying a couple of years ago.'

'Yes, hello. You look very different to how I remember you!' he said shaking her hand.

'It's amazing what a bit of lip gloss can do!' Felicity smiled self-consciously, hoping to change the subject quickly. 'So, been on any lovely holidays lately?'

'Yes, we were in Australia in April for a month and we fly out to Toronto on the 10th December to spend Christmas with our son, daughter-in-law and our new granddaughter - it'll be the first time we've met her!' Liz said.

'That's fantastic!'

'It's all thanks to you Felicity.'

As the waitress reappeared with more champagne, Neil and Liz picked up two new glasses.

'Another one?' Neil asked.

She looked down at her glass, surprised to see it was empty having obviously finished it without even realising. Before she could answer, Neil passed her a full glass.

'Thank you,' she said, placing her empty glass on the tray. *I need to make this my last,* she thought.

Trip had decided to walk to the Ball, feeling the need for a few drinks tonight as his mind was still spinning with theories on the two women's deaths. He needed a solid connection between them, or find someone they both knew, that had reason and motive to kill them.

As he walked up the steps and into the building, he was immediately impressed at how an empty office building had been transformed into a ballroom, complete with softly lit dance floor and more importantly for Trip - a bar. He gently pushed and squeezed his way through, then leant up against the bar, waiting to be served.

As he waited, his phone buzzed in his pocket with an email from an ex-colleague in Birmingham and just as he began to read it, someone nudged into him to get past.

'Trip! Sorry about that, nice to see you here tonight. Looks spectacular doesn't it!'

'Roger,' Trip inwardly groaned, 'yes, you've done a great job putting this all together,' he replied hoping that Roger wasn't going to stay chatting for too long. 'Hillary with you tonight?'

'Yes, she's somewhere around…,' Roger said half-heartedly looking for his wife.

Trip also looked around for Hillary, hoping to catch her eye so she could save him from Roger as she was fully aware of how obnoxious her husband could be.

As he glanced around the room, his eyes hesitated on the back of a woman. She was wearing a black dress, exposing her back, all the way to the base of her spine. Dark, soft waves of hair tumbled between her slender shoulders and his eyes lingered on her for longer than they should.

Across the room, Pippa was talking to Roger's wife, Hillary, while surreptitiously trying to spot Roger, to see if Marjorie was stuck to him like a limpet. That's when she noticed Trip. She began to wave at him, then realised his eyes were locked onto something else. When she followed his gaze, she could see the *something*, was in fact a *someone*.

Interesting, she thought and could feel the stirrings of a plan inside her. A smile twitched at the corners of her mouth.

Trip gradually became aware that Roger was still talking.

'Sorry Roger, just spotted someone I want to say hello to over there. I'll catch up with you later,' and he walked away, drink-less from the bar, before Roger had chance to say anything.

He was moving between people and tables, curious to see who the woman in the black dress was, when a waitress suddenly walked across in front of him, breaking his concentration. Apologising, he smiled at the waitress for nearly colliding with her and continued on his journey towards the woman. However, he immediately noticed with some disappointment, that she had since disappeared.

Felicity found a quiet table nicely tucked away behind the dance floor and cautiously looked around the room to make sure Roger was nowhere nearby. That's when she saw Trip. She was surprised to see him looking so smart, *in a Trip sort of way*, thinking that he was a man you would notice in any crowded room. He was talking and smiling to a waitress. *Typical - flirting*, she thought. His hair was ruffled, chin stubbled and his bowtie messy. *What is it that all these women see in him*, she wondered? He always looked to her like he'd just fallen out of bed – *probably some woman's bed*, she wagered. Every time she had been in his company, he'd either caused her some damage in some way, or completely insulted her – then assumed a wink and a smile would make everything OK.

Pippa came and sat next to Felicity, disrupting her thoughts. Moments before sitting down, she had seen exactly where's Felicity's gaze had been sited. *And it gets more interesting...Brenda was right*, she thought to herself.
'Enjoying yourself?' Pippa asked.
'Actually, more than I thought,' her eyes drifting back to the middle of the room, noticing Trip had now vanished.
Pippa smiled, *oh, this was going to be very interesting indeed*, she thought.

***

The room was dark and dirty, the only noise coming from the small fan heater in the corner. The man was sitting quietly on the floor, his skin damp and clammy. The voices were beginning to get louder again,

Inhaling deeply, he closed his eyes once more as the indoctrinated verses organised themselves in his mind. He now knew what he needed to do.

'…among them are those who enter into households and captivate weak women weighed down with sins…'

As he opened his eyes, he stood up, kicked a discarded screwdriver across the floor and walked towards the door.

CHAPTER 32

Grace Jefferies wrapped her wet hair in a towel, fastened the white robe around her warm damp body, then picked up her empty wine glass and carried it downstairs into the kitchen. After checking the front and back doors were both locked, she turned off the light and headed upstairs to bed, glad of an early night. She was completely unaware of the car driving slowly through the village, looking for her house.

As the driver rounded the next bend in the road, he knew his destination was approaching. The houses were becoming more infrequent and as he neared the edge of the village, he saw it - the cottage with the wishing well in its front garden. He slowed down, glanced in his mirror for any other vehicles, then driving slowly past the house, checked for any activity or lights. There were none. Immediately after the house, he turned into a narrow tree lined lane and pulled into a field gate entrance a short distance away. He switched off the car headlights and looked over his shoulder towards the back of the house. It was heavily shielded from the road by a high wall and tall leylandii trees, so he manoeuvred his car around and pulled back out onto the lane.

Slowly approaching the house once more, he turned into the driveway and parked alongside the garage, completely out of view of the road.

He closed his eyes.

The voices began.

'For they cannot rest until they do evil, they are robbed of sleep 'til they make someone stumble.'

His heart began to beat faster, the volume of the voices increasing in his head.

'It's time,' he said to the voices and pulled a black ski mask down over his face. He reached into the glove compartment and removed the dark leather gloves, sliding his hands inside. Next, he picked up the small torch and black pouch from the passenger seat, got out of the car and pushed the driver's door *almost* closed. It was a cold, damp evening and as he walked to the rear of the car, his foot slipped on some wet leaves, his hip slamming against the side of the vehicle. Cursing under his breath, he quietly clicked open the boot in readiness for the guest that would soon be joining him.

Once satisfied that there was no movement either inside the house or nearby, he walked towards the front door, hoping she may have forgotten to lock it. She hadn't, so he continued around to the side of the house. There was a tall back gate and this time fate was on his side; it was unlocked. Edging down the side of the house, he slowly approached the back door. Again, it was locked, but that would prove no obstacle. He removed the black pouch from his pocket and silently picked the lock, entering the kitchen.

He walked through the kitchen, down the hallway towards a low bookcase with a table lamp and small marble bowl sitting on top. Inside were a set of keys, *why were people so stupid and predictable,* he thought. At the front door, he silently unlatched the security chain and studied the keys in his hand, before choosing the most suitable one. Turning the key, the door unlocked and he retraced his steps, replacing the keys quietly back into the bowl.

As he reached the bottom of the stairs, he listened. In the distance, he could hear faint snoring and began to slowly walk up the stairs. At the top of the landing, he paused again to listen. The snoring was ahead of him and he proceeded in that direction. After passing several open doors which led into a bathroom, spare bedroom and a study, he stopped. The voices were now relentless in his head, the rage inside him burning. He continued down to the last door, which was slightly ajar. Through the small gap, he could see the woman asleep on her side, one foot sticking out from the bottom of the crumpled sheets.

Carefully he pushed the bedroom door open and crept towards the side of the bed. For a moment he watched the rise and fall of her chest, her long dark hair splayed across the pillow. He bent forward towards her and closing his eyes, inhaled the scent of sweet flowers from her hair. She stirred slightly and he quickly reached forward, clamping his gloved hand down hard on her mouth.

Grace's eyes flew open as she gasped, her airways restricted. He pulled her body back towards the edge of the bed. Her eyes searched the darkness for an answer, but could see nothing. Panic raced through her body, her mind scrambling to understand what was happening. In those few split seconds, she suddenly realised a hand was over her mouth and a body close behind her. She began to struggle and grabbed at the hand forcing down on her mouth, her fingers desperately trying to prise it away. As she thrashed onto her back, she stared up into the cold dark eyes looking down at her through small holes in the ski mask. Her legs kicked around frantically, sheets and pillows scattering onto the floor.

'Stop!' the man said.

But her instinct for survival continued and she fought, frantically trying to escape his hold.

He continued to clamp his left hand over her mouth, his right hand now formed into a fist and he smashed it down hard into the centre of her face. Blood splattered from her nose across the bed and her body instantly stopped moving. Removing his left hand, he pulled a cloth from his back pocket and wedged it roughly into her mouth, then removed some scraps of material from his jacket and bound them around her wrists in front of her body.

As he stood up straight, he looked down at her motionless body for a few seconds. Blood was smeared and drying across her face, her legs bent at angles. The slip she'd worn to bed, was now twisted tight around her body and her long dark hair spread like shadowy veins across the mattress.

Kneeling on the bed, he dragged her upright into a sitting position and her unconscious form slumped forwards like a ragdoll. He stood up and lifted her over his shoulder and began to retrace his steps to the front door.

Cautiously, he peered out of the small window, looking outside for any signs of movement. There was none. He opened the front door and walked out into the cold October air, pulling the door shut behind him. Adjusting her weight on his shoulder, he headed towards the car, carefully avoiding the wet leaves this time.

As he reached the open boot, he threw her body inside, pushing her floppy, lifeless limbs roughly in beside her, then slammed it shut - entombing her.

CHAPTER 33

Trip sighed, beginning to wish he'd never come to the Pumpkin Ball. At the bar, Roger had been waffling on for what seemed liked hours, concerning the pros and cons of bee keeping. Stifling a yawn, Trip glanced around at the circular tables, noticing a letter had been carved into the back of each the pumpkin centre pieces. The letters correlated to a seating plan pinned to a board near the entrance - and that's when he noticed the woman in the backless dress once again.

Felicity was anxiously scanning the seating plan, praying she wasn't on Roger's table. But as her eyes settled on her name, her heart sank. Roger had indeed kept to his word and seated her beside him.

Pippa suddenly appeared. 'How about we wind Roger up?' and with a twinkle in her eye, looked for a name to swap with Felicity's. 'Ah, perfect!'

She moved Jeremy Penworthy onto Roger's table, an obsequious little man with ruddy cheeks and halitosis - and Roger's arch-nemesis.

'Come on, let's bugger off quickly before we're spotted!' and she grabbed Felicity's hand and dragged her away.

Pippa's mischief, meant that Felicity was now seated on table E, the same table she'd been sitting at earlier, tucked away behind the dance floor. She took her seat, with her back to the room and after a short while, most of the guests were seated. There was a clinking of a glass and Roger's voice boomed from across the room.

'The buffet is now open, so please help yourselves and enjoy. No shoving or barging – and no throwing bread rolls…,' and he deliberately glanced down at Jeremy, scowling.

Around Felicity's table, were an eclectic mix of characters that Roger had clearly wanted seated as far away from him as possible. It turned out that while Roger saw these people as outcasts, to be shoved away in a corner, Felicity found them utterly fascinating to talk to.

There was Mary, a retired sex therapist, who shocked everyone with her stories. Phillip and his wife Tilly, who had retired to Poundbury from London, where he'd made his fortune psychoanalysing the rich and famous. Norman and his wife Kim, owners of a used car business, who shared amusing tales of questionable items they'd found stashed away in second-hand cars they'd bought. Cordelia, who used to teach belly dancing classes in Brighton and in 1984 was the Guinness World Record holder for hula hooping. And finally, Frank, a quiet Travel Writer, whom Felicity had first met many years ago.

A queue of people quickly formed at the buffet and waiters and waitresses wandered around the tables with bottles of wine and sparkling water. Felicity was deep in conversation with Mary, having bonded the moment they'd started to chat.

'I'm ravenous, my dear, let's go and queue before the scavengers strip the buffet bare,' and Mary linked arms with her, joining the back of the queue where they continued their conversation.

Across the room, Trip was talking to the owner of the company that printed the Foundation's newsletter, Tony. A waiter arrived at their table and as Trip asked him for red wine, he noticed standing in the queue at the buffet, the woman in the backless dress again. Once more, his eyes lingered on her, still curious as to who she was. He thought he knew all of the people who would be here tonight, but perhaps she was someone's guest. As she turned slightly to the side, she whispered into the ear of the woman with her. That was when he noticed a streak of blonde hair, snaking its way down her back, shimmering in the glow from the lights illuminating the buffet. He most definitely didn't know who this woman was.

'…don't you think so, Trip?' Tony said.

Trip snapped out of his trance. 'Sorry Tony, I missed that, it's been a long day. What did you say?'

'I was just saying, it's nice to see Mary here tonight. She's been really ill you know with pneumonia, but she's now looking like her old self again,' and he nodded towards where she stood in the queue.

'Yes, absolutely. Do you know who she's talking to? I'm assuming she's someone's guest?'

Tony craned his neck, trying to get a good look at the person. 'I've no idea – never seen her before. And I would definitely remember meeting her!' he laughed.

'Indeed,' Trip said as his eyes locked on the woman once more.

Mary and Felicity returned to the table with their plates and in their absence, two bottles of wine had appeared.

'Red or white?' Mary asked.

'Oh, I'd better stick to water. I've had two glasses of champagne already.'

'Nonsense! How often do you get all dressed up and let your hair down! Come on, I can't drink alone,' and Felicity reluctantly nodded towards the red.

'So, tell me, any man in your life? If you need any advice, you know, in *that* department…,' Mary winked.

'Absolutely not!' Felicity quickly interrupted, before she had chance to finish the sentence.

'Such a waste my dear,' and grabbing Felicity's hand, she lightly squeezed it.

'I'm happy being on my own and I don't need a man to fill a gap I don't have.'

'Noted my dear, but I still think it's a waste.'

As the guests finished eating, waitresses appeared removing plates and empty glasses.

Roger stood up once more. 'The DJ will be starting the music shortly and the bar is open for drinks, so…'

'Bloody hoorah!' shouted Jeremy, earning himself another glare for interrupting.

'…SO,' Roger emphasised, scowling, 'please feel free to dance.'

The lights were dimmed and a DJ appeared at the rear of the dance floor and sixties pop music quickly began to resonate around the room. Philip and his wife Tilly got up to dance to The Beach Boys, while Kim dragged a very reluctant Norman up towards the dance floor. A few songs later and Chubby Checker's, Let's Twist Again, started to play.

Frank, the quiet travel writer, leaned over to Felicity.

'Care to?' he asked.

By this time, Felicity's glass of red wine was sloshing around on top of the champagne, so she threw caution to the wind.

'Why not,' she smiled.

'That's my girl!' laughed Mary.

They both moved onto the dance floor and Frank immediately morphed into some kind of born-again teddy boy and was lost in the music. The champagne and wine inside Felicity, quickly began to lubricate her hips and within seconds she felt alive again for the first time in years.

Trip watched the woman on the dance floor as her hips twisted to the rhythm of the music, the incredible dress hugging her slender figure. Her dark hair swayed and bounced, brushing against the bare skin of her back. There were feelings stirring deep inside him that he hadn't felt in a long time and never thought he would ever experience again. He was now having to use a great deal of strength to suppress those feelings, so he forced himself to look away. But within moments, his eyes had drifted back, being pulled towards her like a magnet.

Pippa appeared at his side.

'Trip, haven't had chance to chat to you all night, how's things?'

She noticed he still hadn't taken his eyes of Felicity.

'Err yep good, all good,' he said finally pulling his eyes away. 'Tooga phoned me earlier – said he's coming down soon and you can try and win your money back.'

'Don't tell him this, but I've been practising! I rallied up a few of the WI ladies and we've been playing Blackjack on the evenings the husbands are at their Rotary meetings. Even managed to recruit Roger's wife, Hillary! My god he'd be mortified if he knew she was with me every Wednesday evening - corrupting her! Never did manage to master the art of card games – even holed up on a submarine with all those sailors.'

'Submarine?' he said distracted, his eyes finding the woman once more.

'Yes – a tale for another time. Listen Trip, could you do me a favour and go and grab Frank off the dance floor. Roger's having apoplexy in the corner, about not getting the photos of his Borneo travels emailed in time to be printed. I told him he's panicking over nothing, but he won't listen to me. Can you get Frank to calm him down before we have to call an ambulance?'

He looked down at Pippa, 'oh yeah sure, will do.'

'Thank you!' and she gently pushed him forward towards the dance floor.

He walked away, trying to spot Frank, which wasn't easy as his eyes were continually drawn back to the woman. As he was sidestepping around Kim and Norman energetically jiving, he spotted Frank, dancing on his own - eyes closed, sweat beading on his forehead.

'Frank,' he said touching his shoulder, 'sorry to interrupt your sixties flashback, but Roger's having a coronary in the corner about the printing deadline or something. Can you go and calm him down before he keels over?'

Frank opened his eyes, 'I've already told him twice tonight! Yeah, no problem I'll go and sort him out,' he sighed, walking off the dance floor.

Trip turned around to head back to the bar but walked straight into the woman still twisting the night away.

Felicity looked up to apologise.

She stopped dancing.

Their eyes locked onto each other.

The music seemed to fade away.

And neither one of them spoke.

CHAPTER 34

Her eyes slowly flickered open, but darkness surrounded her. She was confined, unable to move - a sudden terrifying realisation that her hands were tied in front of her. To her horror, she then realised she was moving in a vehicle and her whole body was constantly being jerked and thrown around. In desperation, she tried to kick out her legs, but space was too restricted. Was she in a boot of a car? The last thing she remembered, was being asleep in her bed. This was surely some kind of terrible nightmare…but that hope was quickly squashed as her body slammed to the right and her head smashed into something hard.

She gasped, suddenly remembering the feel of the hand over her mouth and the cold dark eyes looking at her through the holes in the ski mask. Screaming for help proved hopeless, as there was something stuffed in her mouth which tasted bitter and dirty. Her head jerked to the left, then was tossed from side to side and fear began growing inside her with every passing moment. Hot tears cascaded down her cheeks and merged with the mucous dripping from her nose.

She tried to manoeuvre her body around, but the limited space available meant she could only move very gradually.

Every time the car jerked, it would roll her back in the opposite direction. Eventually, with considerable effort, she managed to turn so that her feet were towards the end of the car, however, her head was now bent at an awkward angle. She tried kicking her feet against the inside of the boot, but nothing happened except pain shooting up her legs from the impact. The bindings around her hands were tight and unable to loosen or free them, she slammed them up into the space above her, hitting the ceiling of the boot. After several futile attempts, she only caused more damage to herself and as the pain in her hands became too much to bear, she had no option but to rest.

Suddenly, the vehicle stopped and everything went eerily silent, except for her own stifled, gasping breaths. As she listened, her senses became heightened. Behind her head she was aware of a muffled voice and she strained to hear the words, but the pounding in her ears made it impossible.

The car rolled as weight shifted, presumably from someone getting out. A door slammed and her eyes grew wide with fear, focussing on the closed boot. If she was lucky, she would get one opportunity.

She heard footsteps, scuffing on stones or gravel and she held her breath.

Movement at the rear of the car.

A click and the boot suddenly opened.

She'd expected to be blinded by daylight, but wasn't. A blanket of night time darkness cloaked everywhere instead. Tensing her whole body, she kicked her two legs out with all the force and power she could muster, adrenaline coursing through her veins. Her one foot struck his chest, as the other heel slammed into his throat, the impact snapping his head backwards.

The man choked and crumpled to the floor and she frantically scrambled out of the boot, stumbling and almost falling. The huddled figure by her feet, clutched his throat trying to draw air into his oxygen-starved lungs. He rolled from side-to-side gasping, moaning in pain like an injured

218

animal.

Grace began to run but tripped, landing heavily on the ground. Unable to move her one foot, she realised the man had lashed out and grabbed her ankle. She struggled and fought against his tight grip, as her skin scraped against the ground below her semi naked body, small pieces of gravel jabbing and tearing into her skin.

Again, she lashed out with force, trying to make contact with the man using her unrestrained leg, but missing her target and striking fresh air. She rolled onto her back to get a clearer view. Taking careful aim, she kicked down hard with her foot and it sank in between his legs, crushing his testicles.

The man fell backwards, searing hot pain scorching through his body, feeling as though he'd been torn in two. He released her ankle, his body screaming, as both hands instinctively grabbed between his legs, trying to protect an already desecrated fortress.

She rolled onto her side, scrambled to her feet and ran for her life.

Adrenaline continued to fuel her, propelling her body forward. She had no idea where she was, but could hear waves crashing in the darkness. Her feet were burning, as though she was running across hot coals, but still she kept running. *Don't look back* she thought, *keep looking forward*, even though every instinct was telling her to glance back.

Ahead, she saw a muddy track and ran as fast as she could onto it, stumbling clumsily on loose stones. Something dug into her foot and she cried out in agony as her leg buckled beneath her. But still she kept running.

A man's voice began shouting behind her, but she refused to look back. She saw a house ahead and a wave of relief crashed over her, but she tripped again, this time falling hard onto her front, smashing her face into the ground. She was too close now to give in and a final burst of adrenaline forced her to struggle to her feet once more. Warm, wet liquid trickled down her face and body, her feet suddenly leaving the uneven coarse path as it merged onto tarmac.

There was a door in sight and she sped towards it. Her body crashing against it and she pounded her bound fists onto the wood, over and over again. She tried to shout, but the material was still wedged tightly inside her mouth. There was no longer any feeling in her hands or wrists, they were too numb with pain, her feet burning in agony. Relentlessly she kept beating her fists against the door, hoping it would lead to her salvation.

Finally, a light appeared through the small window in the door.

The bolts slid back and a key turned.

Grace's body fell to the floor as the door finally opened.

CHAPTER 35

It was as though everyone in the room held their breath and waited. But in reality, time had frozen for only two people on the dance floor, their eyes still fixed on each other.

The DJ spoke, 'OK folks, time to slow things down a bit,' and Andy Williams began singing from the speakers… *Can't take My Eyes Off You.*

Finally, Trip broke the silence. 'Felicity.'

Not a question, just a name.

'Mr. Hazard,' she said quietly.

Realising they were both motionless, people slowly dancing around them, he reached towards her and gently picked up her hand.

'We may as well, while we're standing here,' he winked.

She looked down at his hand, aware of the warmth of his skin on hers. Before she had spoken a single word, he picked her other hand up and placed it on his shoulder. His hand then rested lightly against her exposed back and she flinched. Panicked eyes looked into his.

He quietly sighed at the feel of her bare skin beneath his hand, then noticed the look in her eyes.

'It's either the back…or lower…,' and he smiled, tilted his head and looked around towards her hips.

'The back is fine,' she said, finally finding her voice again.

Her body was tense and rigid, unlike when he'd been watching her dancing moments before.

'I'm sorry about the other week, I didn't mean to upset you so much,' he said quietly.

She searched his eyes and sensed sincerity in his words.

'I'm sorry too. I know I'm stubborn.'

He looked down at her and noticed the faintest of smiles on her lips.

'At the risk of getting a slap across my face, I need to tell you that you look absolutely stunning.'

Again, he felt her body tense and she didn't speak for a few moments.

'I see you haven't shaved,' and she glanced down at his bow tie, 'and who the hell tied that for you!' her smile briefly reappearing.

'I've showered at least, be grateful for that,' he grinned.

She looked into his eyes for a few quiet seconds and then glanced away. *It's just the alcohol in me,* she thought, *remember who this man is and how much he winds you up.*

'So, is this a permanent new look?'

'It's just a bit of lip gloss,' she shrugged.

'This…,' his eyes roamed down to her feet and back up again, '…is more than a bit of lip gloss Felicity. Haven't you noticed that every single pair of eyes are on you tonight? The women wondering where that incredible dress is from - the men wondering where the incredible woman inside the dress is from.' He paused as a thought filled his mind, 'and I hope to god Roger has kept his paws off you?' suddenly feeling alarmed at the prospect.

'Pippa has done stellar work tonight, keeping him otherwise occupied,' she said, blocking her ears to the compliment.

He caught sight of Pippa at that point, standing next to the DJ smiling, her eyes fixed on Trip and Felicity. She waved at him and winked.

'So,' he said looking down at Felicity's dress, 'where on

earth in Dorset did you find that outfit?'

'Ah, long story, but Pippa's goddaughter is Isabella Brock…'

Trip interrupted, 'the fashion designer?'

'I'm impressed you know! Yes, the very one. Pippa arranged for a bit of pampering for me today and when I turned up at the house, Isabella opened the door. Oh and her mum was a hair and make-up artist for Vogue!'

'Yes. The hair,' he said simply.

'It's been a long time since my mass of curls have been tamed…or coloured.'

'I like the streak.' He was suddenly aware that she probably didn't care whether he liked it or not. 'I hadn't noticed that before.'

'I've spent a lifetime trying to hide it.'

'You shouldn't, it's very unusual…,' and he briefly hesitated. 'My mum had one.'

She sensed a sadness in his voice and they fell quiet. He was conscious of the fact that her body was still tense, but without realising, his hand now rested lower on her back, slightly firmer against her soft, warm skin. The familiar scent of her perfume floated around him – and he wondered when it had become familiar to him. Before he could stop himself, he inhaled a little deeper.

'Trousers,' he uttered.

'What?' she asked looking up at him.

Realising he'd said it out loud, he quickly tried to explain. 'Trousers, I mean, under the dress – very unique…and very *you*,' he smiled.

'Meaning?'

He felt her body tense more.

'Meaning no insult whatsoever!' and he tried to think quickly, but was finding it more and more difficult holding her so close.

'I'm happier in trousers,' is all she said and he noticed her eyes glance down at her legs.

He was seeing a very different side to Felicity tonight.

Yes, she looked stunning in her dress. Yes, she had make-up on for the first time he'd ever seen - and yes, her hair looked lovely. But that all came second to the person he was seeing underneath. However, the prickly barbed wire fence still seemed to surround her whenever he was near.

'I'm surprised you're here tonight,' he said quietly.

'So am I! If it wasn't for the animal shelter being one of the charities benefitting from this evening, then I would be tucked up in bed with a book right now, trust me!'

'Well, I'm very grateful for the animal shelter then,' and he desperately fought the urge to pull her closer towards him and move his hand even lower on her back.

As he turned his head slightly, he noticed the sweet coconut scent of her shampoo and he closed his eyes. Instinct took over and his hand moved lower down her back, unable to resist any longer.

Her body completely froze, but her mind was confused - was this a different sensation to the terror she normally experienced?

They remained quiet for a few moments, but then both suddenly became aware the music had ended and a more upbeat song was now playing. He begrudgingly removed his hand from her warm back.

'Drink?' he nodded towards the bar.

She hesitated. 'I think I've had enough tonight, but a glass of water would be nice.'

'Water it is then.'

'I'm just going to nip to the toilet, I've danced all that alcohol down!'

His eyes were fixed on her as she walked away and he noticed the top of a small tattoo at the very base of her spine. *Felicity*, he thought. He still couldn't quite believe that the woman who had intrigued him earlier in the night, was the same woman who looked like she could have throttled him on several occasions. In fairness though, when she went off on one of her explosive rages, he could quite easily throw a bucket of ice over her.

As if by magic, Pippa appeared quietly by his side. She stood next to Trip watching Felicity disappear out of sight.

'She looks amazing doesn't she,' Pippa said.

'Stunning.'

She smiled and walked away. Her work here was done.

Trip sat on a stool at the bar waiting for Felicity to return, but after several minutes when she didn't, he began to feel uneasy. He got up and walked towards the toilets, just as she walked around the corner and straight into him.

'You really need to stop crashing into me Ms. Marche, *with an E*,' he smiled.

'Are you following me?' she grinned.

He wasn't sure he'd seen her grin before and he liked it.

'I was worried Roger had!' he laughed.

Her eyes looked down at his bow tie again.

'Here,' she said, 'I can't bear looking at this mess any longer. I have OCD you know!'

'That, Felicity, is something I will never forget,' he smiled.

She undid his bow tie and gently retied it, becoming aware of how close her fingers were to his face and skin, making her anxiety increase once more.

He glanced down at her hair and bare shoulders, the perfume swimming around him again. She was biting her bottom lip in concentration as she tied the bow and his eyes lingered on her lips. At that moment she glanced up at his eyes and her fingers momentarily froze in their task.

This was a path she was not ready to walk down.

'There, all done,' she said quietly, 'much better,' and stepped back to a safer distance.

'Thank you.'

His eyes were not willing to leave her just yet.

As they walked back towards the bar, a voice said, 'Trip! Looking smart mate, not used to seeing you without a black eye!'

He turned around.

'Dan, good to see you.' The two men shook hands, 'didn't realise you would be here tonight', Trip said.

Felicity hesitated, completely aware that he was the fireman who had rescued her when she'd been stuck up that damn tree.

'Dan, this is Felicity Marche. Felicity, this is Dan Knight, Dorset Fire and Rescue. She's a Hypnotherapist here in Poundbury…,' he suddenly paused. 'Actually, didn't you rescue her from a tree a few months ago?'

She withered inside, hoping the ground would consume her.

'I did indeed! Almost didn't recognise you with your clothes on Flippity! The tattoo gave you away though! Very nice to see you again,' Dan grinned and took her hand and kissed it. 'You look stunning.'

She subtly pulled her hand away.

'Nice to see you again Dan.' She felt embarrassed, vulnerable and awkward.

Trip watched the exchange, feeling puzzled which was quickly replaced with jealousy - an emotion he realised he had no right to feel. *Flippity?*

'So, you know each other beyond the tree rescue then?' he said sounding slightly more fractious than he intended.

Before Dan had answered, a voice called out.

'Ms. Marche? My god I would never have recognised you!' and Roger walked towards them.

Have these two men never heard of the saying, two's company, three's a crowd. What the hell did four make then? Trip thought irritably.

'I can't believe it's you!' Roger continued. 'I kept seeing fleeting images of this beautiful creature in the room…'

Creature, thought Felicity, one of the many reasons I dislike you Roger.

'…and I thought, I need to speak to this woman! But then bloody Pippa kept ambushing me all night. Wretched woman, I swear she's been on the sherry before she even arrived this evening. Dan, good to see you,' Roger added turning towards the fireman.

Trip sensed Felicity's obvious discomfort and interrupted Roger's waffling monologue.

'Roger, Hilary was just looking for you, perhaps you should go and find your wife,' he said, unsmiling.

'She's probably got one of her damn headaches and wants to go home,' he said glumly, 'but we'll have time for one quick dance Ms. Marche, before I get dragged away by my wife.'

'Actually Roger, I was just leaving,' she said.

'Oh, really?' and he did nothing to hide his disappointment.

'Yes, really,' she said a little more firmly.

'Terrible shame. Well in that case Ms. Marche, I shall bid you a good night,' and he bent, kissed her hand and reluctantly turned away. 'Dan, I need to talk to you about the next car wash fundraiser…'

'Felicity, it's been lovely to see you. Hopefully it won't be long until I see you again,' Dan said and bowed slightly, tipping his head towards her.

'Trip, see you for that pint soon' and after shaking his hand, Dan was whisked away by Roger.

Felicity turned towards Trip.

'Thank you for the dance, Mr. Hazard,' a smile reappearing on her lips.

'Are you really leaving?' he said, still struggling to shake off the jealousy he felt towards his friend.

'It's been a very, *very* long day! And I've got an early client tomorrow morning too, so I really do need to go.'

'Come on then, did you bring a coat?'

'Oh, no you don't need to leave too,' she said quickly.

'You think I'm going to let you walk home looking like that!'

'I'll be fine, it's only two minutes down the road. Well, perhaps five in these heels!' she laughed, looking down at her shoes.

'You may well be fine, but I wouldn't be if I let you walk home alone at his time of night.'

'But…,' she tried to protest.

'But nothing. For once, Felicity, let me win this argument.'

'OK.'

He gestured for her to walk ahead, gently placing his hand lightly on her back once more to steer her forward and as usual, her body tensed at his touch. Trip had been using all the restraint possible this evening, but after noting her response yet again, he removed his hand.

'Yes,' she said quietly over her shoulder.

'Yes?' he asked, feeling a strange and long-forgotten sensation deep inside.

She turned to look directly at him. 'Yes, I have a coat.'

He let out the breath he hadn't realised he'd been holding. 'Right, yes, of course.'

At the cloakroom, he asked the attendant for her coat and looked at the long, luxurious cloak that was passed to him.

'Isabella Brock?'

'Of course,' she smiled.

He draped it around her shoulders, her perfume gently wafting towards him once more and he pushed open the door, leading her out into the cold, damp October night.

'Thank you,' she said, pulling her cloak tighter around her shoulders to block out the cold air.

'What is that perfume?' he asked, almost to himself.

'Dolce & Gabbana, Light Blue.'

He swiftly pushed his hands in his pockets, resisting the urge to put his arm around her shoulders.

They walked in silence down the few stone steps and onto the pavement towards her home. Both of them lost in their own thoughts, hearing voices from their inner demons warning them of the dangers that lay ahead.

After a minute, Trip eventually broke the silence.

'I've enjoyed this evening,' and looking down at her, he said, 'and enjoyed seeing this side of you.'

She bristled. 'You mean the make-up and hair?'

He shot her a look. *How had she taken that as an insult?* he thought, feeling stung at her insinuation that he was so one-dimensional and shallow. He bit his tongue.

'I mean at the *relaxed* you,' congratulating himself for not feeding her inference.

'Sorry,' she said quietly, her automatic defences nearly ruining a lovely evening.

They entered her courtyard entrance and slowed to a stop outside her front door. It was taking all of Trip's self-control and loyalty to his memory of Gabby, together with his awareness of her anxiety towards men, that prevented him from kissing her goodnight on the cheek.

His mobile rang, breaking the tension.

'Trip, it's Jack. Thank you for the information the other day,' he said.

'Jack it's the middle of the night mate, couldn't this have waited until the morning?' He felt frustrated and annoyed at the sudden interruption.

'We think your *Clifftop Killer* theory is right.'

'OK?' Trip said questioningly.

'We almost had another victim, but this one escaped. Can you meet me at the farm shop on the Wareham Road, just outside Broadmayne? I need you to contact someone for me.'

Trip glanced down at Felicity, whose eyes were searching his face with questions.

'On my way,' and Trip ended the call. 'That was Jack Wicheloe. There's been another woman, but this one isn't at the bottom of a cliff. She escaped and is thankfully still alive.'

'Go,' she said simply. 'And Trip?'

He looked into her eyes. 'Yes?'

'Be careful.'

'I'll speak to you tomorrow. Lock the door as soon as you get in,' and he began to walk away.

'Wait,' she called.

He stopped, immediately walking back towards her.

'Are you OK to drive?'

He hid his disappointment. 'Yes, I've only had one glass of wine. Never got around to having a second drink, I kept getting distracted,' he winked, then hesitating for a few moments longer, he finally turned and walked away into the night.

***

The dark coloured car was parked in a different position on the road tonight. The figure had been watching and waiting for her to return for many hours.

And when you finally appear, you're with him. So, the problem is going to need sorting after all. Felicity Marche, you have just sealed your fate....and for the journalist too.

The engine started and the car pulled away.

CHAPTER 36

There had been several reasons for Trip's reluctance to leave Felicity after walking her home from the Ball - primarily because of the feeling they were being watched. The car which had raised his suspicions on a number of previous occasions, hadn't been there tonight - or at least not in its usual location. But the uneasy feeling that they weren't alone, had gnawed away at him. Unable to look for the car without alarming Felicity, he had resigned himself to the fact that he may well have become slightly paranoid.

But he didn't think so.

After collecting the Jeep and Bear, he was now driving towards Broadmayne to meet Jack, although his mind was elsewhere. There were other reasons for his reluctance to leave her tonight, but they were far too complicated to think about right now. However, his mind kept thinking back to something earlier that was particularly bothering him – *Flippity*. How intimately did Dan and Felicity know each other? Had something more happened between them, other than him rescuing her from up a tree months ago? - and if that was the case, why did she tense up so much when he himself was near her?

He saw the farm shop ahead, snapping him out of his thoughts and pulled in behind Jack's dark saloon car.

'Jack, good to see you, although I wish it was under better circumstances.'

'Yep, I agree – but you didn't need to get dressed up for our meeting!' Jack laughed looking at Trip's dinner suit.

'Pumpkin Ball.'

'Shit – forgot that was tonight! I was supposed to be going. Did I miss anything exciting?'

Trip cleared his throat. 'Nope, nothing at all mate.'

'Listen, I can't stay long as I've got to get back to the crime scene and then onto the hospital. The victim's name is Grace Jefferies. She's pretty cut up and bruised and in a deep state of shock, but she's alive.'

'What do you know about her so far?'

'She's a solicitor in Dorchester and lives in Broadmayne. We're still trying to find out as much background as we can, but unlike the other two victims, this woman seems to have a good life, husband and a successful business.'

'But you think it's connected to the other two women's deaths?'

'Yes. We haven't interviewed her yet because she'll be too sedated tonight. However, one thing she did tell us as the paramedics wheeled her into the ambulance, was that she was stuffed inside the boot of a dark blue car.'

'Brenda and the blue car she saw in Portland,' Trip said quietly.

'Exactly. My gut's telling me the other two women didn't commit suicide and that they're all somehow connected.'

'So what happened to her?'

'It was a garbled and patchy interview because of the shock, but she was apparently woken up in the night by an intruder in a ski mask. He punched her, carried her out of the house and put her in the boot of his car. When he went to get her out, she managed to kick him in the throat and stomach. He then grabbed her as she started to run away. As she was trying to get free, she saw the car and thinks it was probably blue. She then kicked him in the balls and ran - literally for her life. Her hands were bound in front of her and a wad of material stuffed in her mouth. She was only wearing a night slip and her feet were bare – they're cut to shreds mate. She's lucky there was a house close enough for her to run to for help.'

'Brave lady.'

'She is indeed. I need to find the bastard responsible as soon as possible, before the next victim isn't so lucky.'

'Where did this happen? I'm guessing not here,' Trip said, looking around.

'The cliffs near Stair Hole, west of Lulworth Cove. It's crawling with police and forensics right now and I can't be seen talking to you, which I'm sure you understand.'

'Of course,' Trip nodded. 'You said she's married - where's the husband when all this is going on?'

'He's in Plymouth, on his way back to Dorset now. According to the husband, Peter, they were having a weekend away in Plymouth so he could do some reviews – he's a food critic. He'd gone on ahead early in the morning as she had to finish stuff off at work. On her way home to get changed, she broke down on the A35 near the Wareham turning and had to be towed to a garage. She wasn't getting the car back until the garage opened tomorrow,' Jack paused to look at his watch, '- well, it's today now. Once she'd collected her vehicle, she would have driven on to Plymouth.'

'Have you spoken to the garage?'

'No, not yet. I'll be sending an officer around as soon as they open to ask a few questions. But Trip, anything you can find out about Grace from your sources is going to be crucial to finding this person quickly. Her life, work, any possible connections to the other two women. All the things we aren't going to be able to find out with the resources available to us.'

'OK, leave it with me. Let me know if she say's anything more.'

'Hopefully I'll be able to interview her later today or tomorrow, if the doctors say we can talk to her. But I don't want to wait until then, I need to know we are doing something about it right now.'

'Don't worry, you'll get the bastard Jack.'

'I hope so. Thanks Trip, keep me posted – and we'll grab that pint soon.'

'Sounds good mate. I'll phone you as soon as I have anything.'

As he got back in his Jeep with Bear, he watched Jack drive away in the direction of Lulworth Cove, his dark saloon quickly disappearing into the night. He took his mobile out and made a phone call.

'Don't tell me another woman has fallen off a cliff again?' the voice said, as it answered the phone.

'Unbelievably, yes - well *almost*. Listen Coop, bit of a near miss tonight - but this victim managed to escape. Can you do the usual digging?' Trip asked.

'Shoot.'

'Her name's Grace Jefferies, lives in Broadmayne. Solicitor in Dorchester. Married to a food critic called Peter. That's all I've got for now. Can you see if there's anything she was working on at her company that may be of interest? Also, any connection to Richard Hart or Slasher Stevens.'

'On it.'

'And Coop?'

'Yea?'

'Feel free to phone me in the middle of the night with anything you find out.'

'Got it. Laters.' And Coop once more was gone.

CHAPTER 37

At 3am, Trip finally arrived home from his meeting with Jack at Broadmayne. His mind was too alert for sleep right now, even though his body was pleading with him to go to bed. He poured himself a glass of Aberfeldy whisky, turned off the light and slumped into his armchair, staring down at the ice cube slowly melting into the rich, amber liquid.

He intended to use every contact he knew to stop this killer, for the sake of past and future victims. Jack needed to strike lucky with a piece of forensics evidence to expose the killer – or one of Trip's own associates needed to come up with something quickly. At the moment, both of them had nothing.

Although he was trying to fight it, his mind kept straying back to the Ball - more specifically, to Felicity and the moment when she'd turned and looked up at him on the dance floor. In that instant, it was as though time had briefly paused and realigned for him and he hadn't been prepared for the feelings it stirred up inside.

When he closed his eyes, he was still able to see her in *that* dress, hugging her slender figure. He could remember the feel of her hand in his as they danced, their skin touching for the first time. It was as if something had come alive inside him that had been dead for years.

The whisky now made his thoughts and senses more vivid and he inhaled, remembering the fragrance of Dolce & Gabbana and the coconut scent of her hair...

Slowly, he became aware of an incessant droning noise and tried to open his sleepy eyes. An alarm. Gav's car alarm. Groaning, one eye opened and looked at the clock on the wall; 6am. As his foggy mind cleared, he remembered the dream. *Gabby*. They'd been running on a beach and she'd been wearing a long white dress, flowers twisted around in her hair. She was laughing trying to outrun him, shallow footprints in the sand. He'd kept trying to catch her, but she remained always just out of reach. When he'd looked down at the soft moist sand, he realised that there were only his footprints. She'd left none. Then finally, he'd managed to reach out and grab her hand. It was cold and rigid to his touch and as she turned, tears streamed down her pale face, eyes pleading with him not to leave her. Not to forget her.

And then he'd been woken up by Gav's bloody car alarm.

He sat up in the armchair where he'd fallen asleep, his back aching and head hurting. Still half asleep, he ran his hand through his hair and rubbed his tired bleary eyes. As he stood up, the whisky glass fell to the floor, thankfully onto carpet so it didn't smash.

Bear looked up at the sudden drama and watched as Trip disappeared into the bathroom to wash his face in cold water, hoping it would flush away the painful memories, but it didn't. In desperate need of a distraction and fresh air, he put on his running gear and headed out of the apartment with Bear, certain that the exercise endorphins would act as a reset button.

After thirty minutes of pounding the pavements however, it was clear that wasn't going to help him either. The one thing it did do though, was make him realise that his sleeping mind evidently thought he'd been disloyal to Gabby. The last thing he'd silently promised her, when he'd been forced to officially identify her body, was that he'd remain loyal to her forever.

He now felt ashamed and guilty for the feelings he'd allowed himself to indulge in the previous night, when he'd held Felicity in his arms. This was the first time he'd ever even been remotely interested in believing he could find happiness again, but his mind was clearly not ready. Perhaps it never would be. In the meantime, it wouldn't be fair on Felicity to mislead her and ultimately risk hurting her, when his mind would not, or could not, let go of the past. So he decided it was better to distance himself now, before he ended up hurting or losing another woman in his life.

His mobile rang as he jogged back towards the apartment building.

'Trip, it's Tooga.'

'Good to hear from you mate - how you doing?'

'Yeah, can't complain. Well, I could bloody complain about the mother-in-law playing Des O'Friggin Connor every hour, of every day…bloody woman.'

'Second hypnotherapy session not successful then?' Trip laughed.

'I'm trying to stick with what the hypnotherapist told me - *listen to your subconscious and be tolerant*, but then my conscious mind muscles in, tells me to shut up and arrange for an unfortunate accident to happen,' Tooga sighed, the tension evident in his voice.

'I think you need to escape for a bit before you do something you probably won't regret. Thought any more about coming down to Dorset?'

'Well funnily enough, that's why I'm phoning my friend. It'll be next week some time, if that's OK with you?'

'You're timing couldn't be better mate,' Trip said, in need of a distraction and some good company.

'Maybe you can take me to see that hypnotherapist down there too.'

Trip closed his eyes and winced, exactly the person he didn't want to see, yet fate somehow, kept propelling them into each other's paths.

'Yeah, maybe.'

'Great, I'll call you when I know my plans,' and Tooga hung up.

As Trip jogged up the stairs, he could hear familiar voices ahead and rolled his eyes.

'Scooter, pass me the screwdriver,' Gav said holding his hand out.

'Here ya are.'

'That's a spanner mate.'

'Which one is it then?'

'The one I was just using!'

'I can't remember which one that was,' Scooter said scratching his head.

'It was ten seconds ago!'

Trip stood at the top of the stairs with Bear.

'Is there a particular reason you're taking a motorbike engine to pieces in the hallway Gav?' he asked.

'Yeah, don't want to get the carpet in me flat dirty,' Gav shrugged.

Trip looked at the discarded screwed-up sweatshirt flung to one side.

'And the sweatshirt too?'

'What? Oh, no – I was trying to impress the bird in the top floor flat with me abs.'

Trip raised his eyebrows, surveying the pale skinny torso, inked with random tattoos.

Bear began to growl at Scooter.

'Why…does…h..he…always…do…that…to…me,' Scooter stammered, backing away from the dog.

'You're just lucky I guess,' Trip smiled.

'H…has…he…ever…bitten…anyone?'

'No.'

'Oh…g…good.'

'But he has chewed off a finger.' Trip stepped over the engine to get past to his front door. 'And Gav?'

'Yeah?'

'That tattoo on your back – where did you get it done?'

'Great ain't it – Scooter did it, his mate owns a tattoo shop in Weymouth.'

'That makes total sense then.'

'Why – you want him to do one for you?'

'Absolutely not', Trip said. 'And just so you know - *Noledge is Power* - you don't spell knowledge like that you idiot.'

CHAPTER 38

Felicity woke up screaming, her heart pounding. In that first terrifying second when her eyes opened, she thought it had happened – that he'd found her. Her slumbering mind had been trapped in a dark, bleak world, but then a heartbeat later, her brain thankfully leapt across the abyss from sleep to consciousness, realising it had merely been another nightmare. The logic now slowly trickling into her mind knew he could never find her, it wasn't possible.

Breathless and scared, cold sweat clinging to her neck and chest, she lay for a few minutes staring at the ceiling, waiting for her racing heartbeat to return to normal.

Last night at the Ball, she'd felt happy for the first time in years.

Trip.

The switch he is able to flip which can aggravate her so quickly, making her want to throttle him at times. But last night, when she'd turned around on the dance floor and looked up and seen his face, that switch had instead made her feel something entirely different. His messy hair, the scruffy stubble on his face and the deep brown eyes which crinkle when he smiles. However, the thing which lingered most in her mind, was the feeling of safety as he held her in his arms.

But enough now, she thought. *Those happy-ever-after endings that happen to other people, aren't destined to be mine* - and her daily nightmares served as a reminder of that. As she looked up at the ceiling, she made a decision there and then, that any relationship with Trip, would be purely on a professional basis. She was too broken for any man to put back together and she would never wish her closet full of issues to be a burden to anyone other than herself.

Her two cats, curled up at the bottom of the bed, stretched and slinked up towards her, meowing for breakfast. It felt strange waking up without her dogs sleeping against her. Today she had planned a rare day off from seeing clients, but she was now regretting that decision. Her mind needed to be kept occupied, to revert back to the life she had been leading before the Ball last night. She'd arranged to collect the dogs from Pippa's house at 9am and after that, was going to go for a long walk with her dogs to clear her mind.

***

'You look bloody terrible!' Pippa said as she opened her front door just before 9am.

'Thanks!' Felicity said, unable to feel hurt by the observation, because it was true.

'Someone keep you awake last night did they?' Pippa grinned.

'What do you mean?'

'A certain dashing reporter perhaps?'

'Trip…Mr. Hazard? Absolutely not!' she said feeling flustered.

'Right. Of course not.'

'I…he…we…errr…'

'Did you want your dogs so you can leave and avoid any more awkward probing questions?' Pippa said to end her misery.

'Yes please.'

Pippa laughed and passed her the two dogs leads.

***

Half an hour later, Felicity was sitting on the beach at Weymouth, with a takeaway coffee and her two dogs. It was a cold, but sunny morning and there were only a few other people on the beach. As she tried to focus her attention on anything other than last night's Ball, a voice startled her.

'Flippity?'

She turned to see Ivan the Chinese milkman.

'Ivan,' she smiled, 'what on earth are you doing here?'

'Deliver milk.'

'To the beach?' she asked confused.

'Yes, I milkman, remember? I met you up tree but you not want yoghurt.'

'Yes, I know – but I mean…oh it doesn't matter,' she said knowing it was going to be a pointless and bewildering conversation.

'What you do here?'

She shrugged. 'Just thinking.'

'I sit,' he said plonking down next to her. 'You tell me – I good listener.'

She glanced at him, studying his features. His eyes were warm and kind and she somehow felt they had seen and experienced many things. The lines and wrinkles on his face and his shiny bald head made his age difficult to guess. At first sight she would have said he was in his fifties, but now sitting beside him, she wondered if he was in fact older.

'You are sad person Flippity. Mrs Brumby say you got no friends and no man.'

She was quickly feeling more miserable by the second.

'That's nice of Mrs Brumby to say that,' she smiled weakly, looking out at the sea.

'She old busybum. Confucius say; ignore old ladies with tea cosy on head.'

She turned and smiled.

'Smile good,' he said, 'now you tell me what wrong before all my milk go off.'

'Mrs Brumby is right Ivan, as much as it pains me to admit that she is.'

'Then you make change,' he shrugged.

'It's too complicated.'

'Is it why you always awake when I bring milk?'

'Sometimes. But also, I don't want the milk wee'd on.'

'I not wee on milk. I got empty milk bottle in van in case of emergency.'

She turned her head again towards him wondering if he was being serious, suddenly glad she had milk cartons, rather than bottles.

'I meant a dog weeing up the milk carton outside the door.'

'Oh,' he said, but she wasn't sure he understood what she meant.

'So, what biggest fear, other than dog wee?' he asked.

'Being unable to fight back again.' The words had left her mouth before she realised.

'You want die old maid?'

'That's a bit harsh.'

'Yes or no?' he pushed.

'I…errr…'

'Hesitation mean no. I help.'

'Wait – what? How? I mean – are we even having the same conversation?' she asked puzzled.

'Something happen, make you sad and alone. You want to fight – that mean you scared. I help.'

As confused as she was, he'd somehow managed to sum her life up perfectly.

'How can you help?'

'I Sixth Dan Master in martial arts. I can teach you to kick ass.'

Speechless, she studied him again, wondering if she was dreaming a surreal event on Weymouth beach, where she was talking to her milkman who lived a secret life as a ninja and was going to teach her self-defence.

He reached into his pocket and passed her a card.

'You come this address 6pm tonight and I train you to fight back,' and with that he stood, bowed his head and walked away.

CHAPTER 39

Two days after the Ball, Trip was lying in his bed after yet another bad night's sleep, when his phone started to ring.

'Don't tell me, I woke you again,' Coop said.

'I wish. Sleep isn't going too well for me the last couple of days. What you got?'

'Well, everything you already knew is true. Grace Jefferies had a nice, financially secure life. Husband Peter is a freelance food critic and according to his credit card trail, he's away a lot. She's built her business up from nothing - no partners, just her and six staff. She mainly does conveyancing from what I've found so far, meaning there's nothing to imply that this was work related.'

'Anything on Richard Hart or Slasher Stevens?'

'Nothing. No link or connections anywhere – even looked into anything on her husband's side and zilch there too.'

'There has to be something linking these three women, I'm not buying it that he's just grabbing random women.'

'I'm still waiting on some feelers I've put out, but honestly Trip, I'm not getting anything at the moment.'

'This man has got to be found Coop – and soon. I'm waiting for Jack to phone me with anything forensics may have found at the cliffs, but the weather wasn't great that night, so I'm not holding out much hope.'

'Have the cops spoken to Grace Jefferies yet?'

'Jack's hoping the doctors give him the okay to interview her later this morning as she hasn't been up to it before now.'

'Do you think your hypnotherapist could help if Grace doesn't remember much?'

Trip hesitated. 'I don't think Jack would want that,' is all he could find to say. 'Anyway, thanks Coop. Let me know if you get anything else, no matter how insignificant it might seem.'

'Yeah, 'course. Laters.'

Coop's question about *your hypnotherapist* had thrown him. He hadn't seen or spoken to Felicity since the Ball. There had been several times he'd picked his phone up to call her, usually at night when his defences were lowered. On each occasion, he'd scroll through the contact list on his phone and select her name, but then every time he'd stop himself pressing the green dial button. He wasn't sure what he'd say to her anyway. *Hi Felicity, it's not you, it's me.* A sentence every woman wants to hear. There were no words he could say in a conversation that would make the situation better, so he'd decided the safest and kindest thing to do, was just to stay away from her.

Trip's phone rang again, jolting him from his thoughts.

'Trip, it's Jack.'

'Hey Jack. Any new leads?'

'No forensics from the cliffs, but that would have been a miracle anyway. It's bloody frustrating mate, we're not coming up with anything. You?'

'Nothing. Just got off the phone from my...,' Trip hesitated, not quite sure what Coop's job title was, '*researcher* - and no links or connections between the three women at all so far. Nothing on Grace Jefferies or her husband to raise concerns and no link to Richard Hart or Slasher Stevens either.'

'I went to the garage yesterday who towed her in when she broke down. They actually had her Range Rover up on the ramp putting a new tyre on when I got there,' Jack said.

'Did they say anything helpful?'

'Well, that's my main reason for phoning. A man had stopped to help her on the A35 apparently and given her the number for the garage. When the mechanic asked who'd given the recommendation, she said *a 'tall man with a white beard wearing a baseball cap and sunglasses.'* The mechanic remembered because he'd laughed saying *'it wasn't Santa Claus in disguise, was it?'* and she'd said *'only if he's traded in his sleigh for a blue car.'*

'Shit! Blue car - this can't be a coincidence surely Jack?'

'We've got everyone looking for this mystery man. But I'm hoping you may have means to probe in places we can't.'

'Leave it with me.' Trip ended the call and immediately phoned Coop.

CHAPTER 40

Jack arrived at Dorchester County Hospital to talk to Grace Jefferies, half an hour after the doctors had given him the all clear to interview her. She lay in a side room on her own, with a uniformed officer stationed outside. When Jack walked in, he felt a renewed energy to find the man who'd abducted her.

She wore a loose hospital gown, but the cuts and bruising down her arms were still visible. One side of her face had stitches, her lip and chin both grazed and cut. Her right eye was black and barely able to open, her cheek swollen and bruised. Bandages covered her hands, her left arm was in a sling and two large swathed lumps at the bottom of the bed were protecting her feet, so badly cut from running across the rough terrain.

She looked up at him as he walked towards her bed, a flash of panic at seeing a stranger's face.

'Hello Mrs Jefferies, I'm Detective Inspector Jack Wicheloe from Dorset Police. Are you feeling able to answer a few questions about the other night?'

'Yes…yes, that's fine,' she stuttered, relieved at knowing who the man was.

'Thank you. OK if I sit down?'

'Yes, of course.'

'If you feel at any time that you'd like to stop, just say. OK?'

'I'll be fine – I just want to find who did this,' she said, a tone of resilience in her voice.

'So do we - and soon,' Jack said. 'On the day of the abduction, what can you remember?'

'Peter had gone on ahead to Plymouth early in the morning and I was going to join him after I'd finished work. I left the office about 3pm and started to drive home on the A35. Just before the Wareham turn, I heard a bang and pulled immediately onto the hard shoulder. When I got out, I saw that one of the tyres was split. I phoned the AA but Peter had forgotten to renew the breakdown recovery', she paused and Jack noticed anger flash across her eyes.

'Would that be something your husband would usually remember to do?', he asked, watching for any reaction.

'In the past, definitely – but lately I could easily allow myself to think he'd done it on purpose.'

'On purpose? What makes you think that?' Jack was becoming increasingly interested in Mr Jefferies relationship with his wife.

'Oh, I don't know – just…well…he resents the amount of time I spend at work, but forgets that my business is what funds the lifestyle he enjoys.'

'I see.' Jack made a note to check further into Mr Jefferies background, once he returned to the station. 'So, what happened next when you were on the bypass?'

'I was about to Google local garages, when a man pulled over to see if he could help,' she paused again and took a sip of water through a straw.

'Can you remember what he said to you?'

'He said he'd broken down near here, I can't remember when, but he'd used a garage not far away and they'd been great, so he gave me their number.'

'Which garage was this?'

'Harris Recovery at Troy Town.'

'And can you describe the man who stopped to help?'

'Tall man with a white beard wearing a baseball cap and sunglasses.' She smiled as best as she could with her facial injuries, 'like Santa in disguise.'

'What age would you say he was?'

'Hard to say because of the hat and sunglasses, but I'd guess maybe fifty?'

'What was the hair and beard like?'

'White hair, what I could see of it under the hat - and the beard was trimmed short.'

'Can you remember what he was wearing?'

'I'm not sure, smart though, not scruffy. I think he wore a light-coloured jumper maybe and dark trousers?'

'And what about the car he was driving?'

Grace thought for a few moments. 'Audi I think, but I'm not sure.'

'Colour?'

'Dark…blue, maybe.'

'Did he have an accent or say any words in a way that sounded strange?'

'No,' she said, suddenly feeling panicked. 'You don't think it was him, do you? He was so nice to me…,' and her voice trailed off.

'We're just trying to get a full picture of everyone at the moment,' Jack calmly explained. 'Did he give you his name?'

'No, sorry,' and she looked down at the bed.

'You're doing great Mrs Jefferies,' he reassured her, 'and what do you remember next?'

'I phoned the garage and the mechanic was only a few minutes away – apparently on the way back from another job. The man in the baseball cap said to stay safe while I was waiting for the recovery truck, I suppose in case someone hit the car while it was stationery.'

'So the man didn't wait with you?'

'No, he left then, but he did chat with me for a couple of minutes after I'd phoned the garage. I'd told him I was supposed to be joining my husband on holiday and that it was typical this happened so close to home and…,' she suddenly stopped talking.

'And?' Jack prompted.

Tears began to fill her eyes, 'and I told him I lived in Broadmayne and he said his sister lived there, near the pub…and I said I did too…,' she swallowed back tears, '…the house with the wishing well in the front garden…,' she hung her head down and began to sob. 'I'm such an idiot…I basically told… a complete stranger…where I lived…and that…my husband was away.' Her body started to shake as she sniffed back tears that were threatening to erupt.

'There was no way you could have known that an innocent conversation would have led to what happened,' he said trying to calm her.

A nurse appeared in the doorway, glaring at Jack and tapping her watch. He nodded his understanding.

'Do you think you'd be able to look at some photographs for us and sit with an artist to compile a photofit of this man - when you're able to of course?'

'Yes…yes definitely.'

'And one final question; when you escaped from the boot of the car, can you remember anything else about the vehicle – part of the registration perhaps?'

'It was a saloon because it didn't have one of the shelves in the back, but I don't remember noticing the number plate.'

The nurse started to walk towards them.

'Mrs Jefferies, I'm about to be turfed out now, but here's my card. If you remember anything else at all, please call me straight away.'

'Thank you, I will,' she said, just as the nurse arrived telling him that Mrs Jefferies needed to rest now.

As Jack walked across the car park to his vehicle, he was debating whether the murderer of Roni Porter and Abi

Hart, could perhaps be the good Samaritan who'd stopped to help Grace on the A35.

He was also keen to dig further into Mr Jefferies background, to make sure he wasn't involved in any way.

CHAPTER 41

Tooga was arriving in Dorset today and Trip had arranged to meet him in The Duchess of Cornwall pub in Queen Mother Square at 12noon. He still hadn't seen Felicity since the Ball, now over a week ago - but his mind was feeling heavy and more conflicted with each passing day, so he was glad of the distraction of his friend's timely visit.

After returning from his usual morning run with Bear, he showered, made some breakfast and sat with his laptop, trying to focus on the next edition of the newsletter, when his phone rang.

'Hey Trip.'

'How you doing Jack, any leads yet?'

'Still trying to locate the white-haired man in the Audi. Your contacts found anything?'

'Nothing mate. It's like he never existed, or has vanished into thin air.'

'We've got nothing else. It feels like we're just counting down the clock until the next victim. No murder is perfect, they always make a mistake eventually, but this man is either very lucky, or very meticulous.'

'You'll get him mate; we just need a bit of that luck

ourselves.'

However, they were both having the same thought, that victim number four would be found before the killer was.

'If you get anything, phone me asap,' Jack said.

'Will do mate,' and Trip ended the call.

They had minimal information to go on. All three abductions happened late at night or in the early hours of the morning in rural Dorset. CCTV and road cameras were few and far between, even in the more densely populated areas. Trip couldn't help but think they needed more than a bit of luck to catch this man.

***

Felicity was meeting Pippa for lunch at the Duchess of Cornwall pub today, an overdue thanks for arranging her Ball pampering day. She was due to meet her at 12.30pm, but as always, arrived early at the pub just before noon, as she hated being late for anything. Her last client of the morning had rearranged, leaving Felicity with time on her hands she didn't want. The more time she had to herself, the more opportunity her mind had to wander to places best left unvisited. She hadn't seen Trip for over a week now and this had saved her from a difficult conversation. She needed to keep things on a professional basis, but wasn't prepared to give her reasons why and it was a conversation she'd rehearsed in her head a hundred times.

He hadn't phoned her; she hadn't seen him. This subsequently made it much easier. Why then, did she feel so upset that he hadn't phoned? The answer to that question, she kept screwing up and throwing to the back of her mind.

The pub was still relatively quiet as the lunch time rush hadn't yet started. Felicity tucked herself away in a corner at the front with a coffee and a book, her back to the door.

***

Just before noon, Trip walked down to Queen Mother Square. He entered the pub and went straight to the bar, ordering himself a pint of Fursty Ferret. The young woman behind the bar, glad of a customer to serve in the pre-lunchtime lull, chatted to Trip for a few minutes. She was telling him about her boyfriend's attempt at making a chilli con carne for his mates-night-in.

'…he misread the ingredients and added a tablespoon of chopped up Scotch Bonnet chilli peppers instead of a teaspoon! The idiot is still on the loo now!' she said, squeezing Trip's forearm, trying to stop herself falling over with laughter.

'Put him down love, you don't know where he's been!' boomed a Birmingham accent from across the pub and Trip glanced up and smiled.

'Trip mate, looking as annoyingly bloody handsome as ever!' Tooga laughed and slapped him on the back.

'Jeez, you've just snapped a couple of vertebrae there!' he groaned, forgetting how strong his friend was, from decades spent in a boxing ring.

Felicity had looked over her shoulder at the sound of a woman's raucous laughter - and that's when she saw Trip laughing and flirting with the woman behind the bar. *Typical.* Then she heard a man shout across the pub saying, *'put him down, you don't know where's he's been'. Well, I can guess exactly where Trip Hazard's been*, Felicity thought, feeling suddenly angry at him, although she wasn't sure why.

For a few moments, she watched the man, who was dressed in a three-quarter length black wool coat and smart dark suit, laughing and joking with Trip. His hair was jet black except the slight grey, peppered at his temples and she thought he had a military look about him. She then switched her attention to Trip. He was dressed in jeans and a white shirt, sleeves casually rolled up slightly exposing his tanned arms. She forced herself to look away, trying to refocus on her book, when she became aware of a strong spicy cologne hovering in the air, attacking her senses.

'Good to see you Tooga, notice you packed your Paco Rabanne for your holidays!' Trip smiled; his nostrils immediately assaulted by the bottle of aftershave absorbed into Tooga's skin.

'Distracts the enemies mate!' Tooga laughed.

'Well, hopefully my nose will acclimatise in a minute, either that or I'll pass out. Good drive down?'

'No idea, Tank drove. I had a kip in the back,' he grinned.

'Don't tell me you're making Tank sit out in the car! This isn't your arse end of Birmingham mate where you need an armed guard watching your car. This is sleepy Dorset!'

'Yeah, where you've got women being lobbed off cliffs left, right and bloody centre according to Coop.'

'Yep, that's true,' he said seriously for a moment. 'But get Tank in here, it'll be good to see him again.'

Tooga took his phone out of his inside coat pocket. 'Tank, get yerself in here – Trip wants to say hello. Park the Bentley out the front so you can keep an eye on it.'

A few moments later, the bronze-coloured Bentley glided to a standstill outside the entrance. A man as wide as he was tall, with a head like a bowling ball, walked into the pub. He came over to his boss and Trip reached out and shook his hand.

'Tank, good to see you. How's life?'

'Tidy,' Tank said in a broad Black Country accent. He was not known for being verbose and preferred to save his oxygen for thumping people rather than talking.

'What can I get you to drink Tank?' Trip asked.

'Diet Coke, ta.'

Considering Tank was eighteen stone and square, the diet bit surprised him.

'You got rooms booked in the pub tonight?', Trip asked Tooga.

'We have indeed.'

'Beer instead then Tank?' Trip said.

'Diet Coke, ta.'

'He likes to keep his wits about him when he's working,' Tooga explained.

'Yeah, as I said, sleepy Dorset mate. Unlikely to get anyone wanting to assassinate you here!'

'Always be prepared my old friend. And if you lived by that motto yourself, you might not end up with so many black eyes! How many have you had now in good old sleepy Dorset…?' Tooga winked at him.

'Yeah, point taken.'

The two men chose a table at the back of the pub and Tank retreated with his Diet Coke to the front, keeping a watchful eye on the Bentley and for any would-be assassins.

Felicity had slightly repositioned her chair and watched the huge menacing man walk into the pub and over towards Trip and the man in the black coat. A few minutes later, she saw him take a seat by the entrance. Her book was now long forgotten.

'So, how's life treating you down here?' Tooga asked.

'Yeah good, much calmer pace of life, which is what I needed after…well, you know.'

'Looking a bit like shit, if you don't mind me saying. Sleeping OK?'

'I was, until a few months ago anyway, when women started getting murdered,' *and when he met Felicity*, he thought.

'No leads yet I understand from Coop.'

'Nope. Police have got nothing. They're still trying to find this mysterious man on the bypass. I'm hoping that something pops up soon, before victim number four does.'

'If there's anything to find, Coop will find it.'

'Yeah, I know. I just want the bastard caught sooner

rather than later,' Trip said. 'So, mate, how's the current Mrs Davis?'

'Yeah, still current, although if I'd known a live-in mother-in-law and number one Des O'Connor fan was part of the marital package, then I wouldn't have put a ring on her finger.'

'Not thinking of another divorce, are you!'

'Not yet, this one is a good-un. She makes great lardy cake and she's handy with a gun too.'

The door to the pub opened.

'Tank?' the voice said.

'Mrs Campbell-Lewis,' Tank nodded his greeting, sweat immediately beading on his forehead.

'Where is he? I can smell him from here!'

Tank nodded towards the back of the pub.

'Tooga!' she shouted towards the two men sitting at their table.

'Pippa you old wench! How the bloody hell are you?' Tooga laughed.

'All the better for seeing you!' she said, glancing around the room.

'Get that woman a drink before Interpol finally track her down!' Tooga called over to the girl behind the bar.

Felicity was speechless watching the scene unfold, hoping, no *praying*, that Pippa didn't notice her sitting there and involve her in any interaction with Trip or his friend.

'I'll be there in a mo Tooga…I'm supposed to be meeting…,' Pippa said looking around the pub, '…ah there you are, hiding away!' and she rushed over to a table in the corner.

Too late, thought Felicity, suddenly filled with dread.

Trip watched Pippa disappear around the corner out of sight.

'Kept my visit a secret did you!' Tooga laughed.

'Well, I've been a bit busy with dead bodies. Not exactly had time to announce your upcoming royal visit, have I mate!'

'Sorry I'm late Felicity, had bloody Roger on the phone whingeing about Jeremy being in the photo with him at the Ball,' Pippa laughed.

'I'm sure you managed to wind him up a few more notches though!'

'Maybe one or two', she winked. 'Listen, you have to come and meet Tooga, he's sitting down at the back of the pub with Trip.'

Pippa was already walking away.

Felicity reached out and grabbed her arm. 'I'll just wait here Pippa, you go and…'

'Nonsense! Come on…' and Pippa grabbed her hand, pulling her like a reluctant sulking teenager, away from the sanctuary of her tucked away table.

She walked behind Pippa, hoping that any moment the ground would swallow her or a UFO would beam her up.

Neither happened.

'Tooga! What on earth are you doing down in my neck of the woods!' and Pippa hugged him, leaving a bright pink lipstick kiss on his cheek.

Trip looked up and saw Felicity's anxious eyes staring back at him and yet again, neither one of them spoke.

CHAPTER 42

The man pulled into the multi-story car park on Commercial Road in Weymouth and drove towards the first ramp, leading up to the next level. He carefully glanced from left to right, searching amongst the cars. Unable to find what he was looking for; he drove up to the next level. The frustration was already beginning to build inside him, the voices in his head arising once more from their quiescence.

On the third level, he finally found what he'd been looking for - the silver Lexus driven by the woman with the long dark hair. He'd first seen her only a short while ago, filling her car up with petrol and oblivious to him at the pump alongside, watching her intently; mesmerised by her looks.

He pulled into a space opposite her parked car and switched off his engine. In the rear-view mirror, he watched as she grabbed her coat and handbag from the back seat and walk away towards the exit. Once she was a few metres ahead, he pulled on his baseball cap and sunglasses, got out of his vehicle and followed her. She waited at the lifts, busily typing something on her mobile, so didn't notice him standing near her. His eyes never left her once, absorbing every inch of her from behind the safety of his sunglasses.

The lifts doors opened and she went inside.

A smile twitched at his lips as he walked forwards to join her.

Suddenly, footsteps pounded on the concrete floor.

'Hold the lift!' and a young man slammed the palm of his hand against the door to prevent them from sliding closed.

The woman looked up from her mobile at the sudden drama.

'Hate taking the stairs here – always stink of … well… you know!' he laughed.

From behind his sunglasses, anger was beginning to fizz inside the man from the unexpected intrusion. He looked at the newcomer – baggy jeans and a Nike hoodie, satchel slung across his body. Tinny music bled out from his headphones, head nodding along to the beat.

A few moments later, the lift doors opened and the woman exited first, followed by the young man.

He hung back, hoping the voices would guide him.

Just as the doors were about to close, the voices began, urging him to follow her - so he did.

CHAPTER 43

'Did time just freeze again?' Pippa smirked. 'Tooga, this is Felicity Marche…and this is Tooga Davis.'

Felicity reached to shake Tooga's hand. 'Nice to meet…,' she started to say as Tooga bent forward and kissed her hand.

'A very great pleasure to meet you,' he smiled.

She momentarily froze, but quickly managed to regain her composure.

'What can I get you ladies to drink? Pippa - I'm assuming it's too early for Vodka shots!'

'Oh goodness me, haven't had a drop of Vodka since that night! I still don't know how we didn't end up floating in the bloody South China Sea!'

Trip and Felicity's eyes were still fixed on each other, sharing the same awkwardness of the situation.

'I'll have a G&T thank you. Felicity?' Pippa asked turning to her friend.

She looked away from Trip, breaking the tension.

'Errr…yes…glass of Merlot would be lovely, thank you,' deciding she needed Dutch Courage, yet again.

Tooga shouted over to the bar. 'Glass of Merlot and a

double G&T please, when you can.'

Trip downed his pint. 'I'll get them mate, I need another drink too.' He looked at Felicity again, before standing and heading to the bar.

She watched his back as he walked away.

Tooga, pulled out two spare chairs at the table. 'Pippa, sit down, you look like you're about to ambush someone!', Tooga laughed. 'Poor old Tank still breaks out in a sweat if he hears a posh women's voice!'

Trip waited at the bar, his eyes on Felicity. She wore jeans, brown suede ankle boots and a soft pink jumper. Her hair, as usual, was pulled back into a ponytail, but this time he noticed the blonde streak weaving its way through the mass of brown curls.

The girl behind the bar passed him the drinks, breaking his concentration.

As he walked back towards the table, Trip said quietly, 'Felicity,' and placed her wine in front of her, unable to pull his eyes away once more.

She looked nervously up at him. 'Thank you.'

At that point, Pippa kicked Tooga under the table.

'For the love of god woman,' he mumbled under his breath, reaching down to rub his shin.

'Cheers everyone, to your very good health!' Tooga boomed.

He turned to Felicity. 'How on earth does a lovely young lady such as yourself, know this reprobate?' and he nodded his head towards Pippa.

'Actually, we haven't known each other very long really, have we?'

'Only a few months,' Pippa said, 'but I knew this girl was special the first time I met her, isn't she Trip?'

All eyes focussed on Trip and he suddenly knew what it was like to be a rabbit caught in the headlights.

Pippa continued. 'Can you believe she's been to see The Chipboards! From that moment on, I knew we'd be friends.'

'Bloody Chipboards! Is the restraining order still valid that poor old Barry had to take out on you!' Tooga asked Pippa, worryingly serious.

She shrugged. 'Quite possibly, yes. Anyway, Felicity's a hypnotherapist – she helped my friend Brenda.'

'Oh, *you're* the hypnotherapist! I've heard a lot about you from Trip here!' and he slapped his friend on the back.

All eyes again fell on Trip, so he thought it was best he put a few things straight.

'Tooga's had some hypnotherapy up in Birmingham,' *which is where I bloody wish he was right now,* Trip thought, '- and when he told me, I said I'd recently met one down here.' He realised his explanation sounded as feeble out loud, as it did in his head.

'I may need your assistance at some point soon, not sure my therapist in Birmingham is having much of a positive impact on the issue!'

'How long are you staying?' Pippa asked.

'Couple of days, long enough to cheer this miserable bastard up,' Tooga said.

Again, all eyes looked at Trip, who was getting more paranoid and uncomfortable by the second.

'...and then I've got some business in Plymouth to sort out,' he continued.

'Well, it's good to see you again after - what, two years?' Pippa asked.

'It must be,' Tooga said. 'So, what do you have to do to get fed in here?'

'I'll get you a menu from the bar,' and Trip pushed his chair back, glad of an excuse to escape the constant looks being hurled his way.

While Trip's back was turned, Felicity stood up, 'just nipping to the errrr…,' and nodded towards the toilet sign at the other side of the pub.

After they'd both gone, Tooga turned to Pippa. 'Right

then woman, I'm assuming the kick under the table was for the longing looks and tension you could chop with an axe?'

'Oh my god Tooga, those two are so bloody infuriating! They are up and down more than a fiddler's elbow! One minute they're talking, then they're arguing about bloody melons and then they can't keep their eyes off each other. It's utterly exhausting!'

'Really - that's interesting. Trip never mentioned he'd met someone, other than a hypnotherapist, which, by the way, he only mentioned in passing.' Tooga glanced towards his friend's back. 'Does she know why he moved down here?'

'No and it's not my place to tell her, that's Trip's story to tell. But I'm telling you, these two should be together - I knew that from the first time I met her.'

'Well, she must be special to have had an effect on Trip's emotions. I've never seen him look at anyone the way he does this woman - before or since Gabby.'

Tooga would have argued that he hadn't even looked at Gabby with the flashes of intensity he had witnessed from his friend today.

'I thought his heart had been buried with Gabby to be honest. But you need them to work this out for themselves Pippa, you can't go interfering where Trip's emotions are concerned. He won't thank you for it.'

'Oh, I know, but it's so bloody exasperating! I just want to lock them in a shipping container and send them to Panama, so they have no choice but to sort their issues out!'

'Don't get any ideas about doing that for Christ's sake!' he said, knowing only too well how Pippa's mind worked when she got an itch to do something she shouldn't be doing.

'Yes, yes, you're right I know…but if the opportunity came up and you could just give him a subtle shove in the right direction…,' she winked.

'Shut up now, he's coming back.'

Trip returned with the menus. As much as he was finding the whole situation unbearably awkward, he couldn't control that knot of disappointment that had suddenly twisted in his stomach when he noted Felicity's absence.

Pippa read his thoughts. 'She's just gone to the loo.'

He was going to reply, but decided he would probably muddle his words trying to protest his innocence, so chose to keep his mouth shut instead.

Felicity looked at her reflection in the mirror in the toilets. She wanted to sneak out the pub or pretend she had an urgent call and had to leave. Anything that meant she didn't have to suffer the next hour or so, sitting awkwardly across a table from Trip. A week ago, she had made the decision to keep him very much at arm's length and deal with him only on a professional basis. Yet here she was, hiding in a pub toilet, experiencing every emotion she didn't want to feel after seeing him again.

Right, she said to her reflection, *you can do this, it's an hour out of a lifetime, so put on a mask, smile, be courteous, eat your lunch and leave.*

Mask put in place, she took a deep breath and walked out of the toilets. As she turned the corner, she saw to the right, Pippa and the two men chatting and laughing at the table – to the left, was the exit door to leave. After a few seconds hesitation, she turned right.

'What would you like to eat Felicity - my treat!' Tooga smiled

'Oh no, you don't...,' she started to say.

'No, no, my treat,' he said, putting his hand up to signal an end to negotiations.

She smiled realising refusal would be useless.

'Thank you. Can I have the Chicken Caesar Salad...but could you ask them for the bacon to be crispy, extra parmesan cheese, anchovies if they have them and the dressing on the side?' For once, all eyes fell on Felicity.

'What?' she said baffled by everyone's stunned expressions.

Trip looked away from her, smiling.

'Right come and help me order Pippa, I'll never remember that lot on my own,' and Tooga stood up, with Pippa practically bolting from the table.

As the two conspirators walked towards the bar, Pippa nudged Tooga.

'Bravo,' she winked.

Trip and Felicity were now alone.

She went to speak first, 'I'm sorry we…,' but was spoken over at the same time by Trip.

'Sorry about Too…,' but stopped when he realised she was speaking. 'You go first,' he grinned.

'I'm sorry we seem to have ambushed your lunch.'

'I'm sorry about Tooga ambushing yours,' he smiled. 'How have you been? Sorry I haven't phoned to…,' he wasn't sure how to end that sentence.

'I'm good thank you, busy. How's Bear?' she asked quickly, not wanting to know what the end of his sentence was going to be.

'Sleeping in my bed, breaking all the rules and costing me a fortune to feed,' he sighed.

'But you wouldn't be without him I bet.'

'Absolutely,' he said. 'How's your zoo?'

'Crazy as ever,' she replied. 'Have the police got any further with their investigations on that poor woman who got abducted. I saw your article in The Echo.'

He looked down at his drink and picked up a beer mat, tapping it absentmindedly on the table.

'They've hit a bit of a wall to be honest. I'm worried that there's going to be another victim if they don't get a breakthrough soon,' he paused, 'keep your door locked at night won't you.'

'Don't say that! I'll be fine – I've got two ferocious dogs

to fend anyone off!'

'I mean it Felicity,' and he looked into her eyes. 'Keep your front door locked at night - promise me?'

Sensing the seriousness in his voice, she held his look, 'I promise.'

'Thank you,' and he looked back down at his drink.

Tooga, together with a reluctant looking Pippa following behind, returned to the table having ordered the food.

'So Felicity, are you Dorset born and bred?'

'No, not at all – I've only been here the last eight, maybe nine years.'

'Where are you from originally then?'

'I was born in Oldswinford, Stourbridge.'

'Black Country! Oh, I can see why this pair like you so much my dear! You didn't mention your hypnotherapist was from Oldswinford Trip!'

'That's because I didn't know', he replied, wanting to add that she wasn't *his*, but knowing he'd only make a mess of any explanation.

Tooga continued. 'You have no accent whatsoever?'

'I moved away when I was about five years old.'

'That would explain it. So where did you end up?'

'Oh, lots of places really - Warwickshire, Worcestershire, Devon, Australia…,' she cursed herself, quickly picking up her wine glass and took a large sip, regretting having said the last country.

'Australia? How on earth did you end up over there?' Tooga asked.

She hesitated, wishing it was someone else's turn to speak.

'I wanted to do something different I guess,' she shrugged, forcing a smile.

'And what made you come back to the UK's dreary climate!'

She could find no words to answer that question. Trip looked up at her hesitation, sensing her obvious uneasiness.

Deflecting the attention from Felicity, Trip said, 'hey Pippa, is Roger OK? I haven't had any earache off him for a few days, I'm starting to get worried!'

Felicity looked across the table at him, a silent thank you in her eyes.

Minutes later, the waitress brought their order. She handed out the food and then looked confused with a meal that remained on her tray.

'Ah, that's for the big fella at the front,' Tooga gestured with his head.

The waitress followed Tooga's eyes to where Tank was sitting. She walked over and placed the two burgers, extra chips and onion rings in front of him. Watching this, Trip wondered again why Tank bothered having Diet Coke.

During the course of the meal, Tooga explained the first time he'd met Trip. He was only a boy and was in the process of being knocked about by a gang of bullies after school one day. Tooga, being several years older, had waded in and beaten the crap out of the gang. That's when he began to teach Trip how to fight and look after himself - and Tooga had looked out for him ever since.

It also turns out his real name is actually Tony Davies – but he felt at a very young age that Tooga sounded tougher, so he'd adopted the name. He recounted tales of his years in the Navy and sparse details of Pippa's ever emerging colourful past. It also turns out, they had apparently known each other for several decades.

Felicity quietly sat enjoying their company, revealing no more about herself, which she was grateful for and was now pleased that she hadn't left early.

After coffee, Felicity looked at her watch and said, 'sorry I've got to go. It was lovely to meet you Tooga and thank you for lunch.'

'Not going are you my dear?' he asked.

'Yes, sorry, I have an appointment at the Vets.'

'Well in that case, it's been an absolute pleasure' and he kissed her cheek lightly, whispering, *'don't give up on him.'*

As he pulled away, she looked at him quizzically and he gave a subtle wink.

Before there could be any awkward interaction with Trip, she backed away from the table nervously. 'Trip, nice to see you again,' she said.

He went to get up, but she was retreating too fast.

'Felicity,' he said, nodding his head towards her.

Suddenly, there was a crash behind her and she gasped as icy cold liquid soaked into the back of her jumper. She spun around and saw the waitress crouching down to pick up a tray of drinks, which Felicity had backed into.

'I'm so sorry!' she said, bending down to help.

The waitress went to stand up and their heads cracked into to one another. Felicity rubbed her throbbing forehead looking at the young woman who seemed ready to slap her.

'Let me help you,' she said.

'You've done enough madam,' the waitress smiled through gritted teeth.

Trip went to help, but was stopped by Pippa who gulped down her coffee.

'Felicity, wait I'll come with you - I want to pop in to the printers. I need to make sure they use the photo of Roger glaring at Jeremy Penworthy for the front cover of newsletter. That'll give him heartburn! Tooga, don't leave it so long next time and Trip, I *will* be speaking to you later.'

Trip sighed. If ever there were words Pippa could say to put the fear of god in someone, it was those.

'Tank!' Pippa said as she walked up behind him. He visibly flinched, almost upending the table as he jumped up to turn around. 'Nice to see you again,' she said patting his forearm which was tensed ready in fight or flight mode. 'This is Felicity, Trip's friend – and mine.'

He nodded his head towards her and Felicity smiled at the man as she walked past him, 'bye Tank, nice to meet you.'

Tank immediately liked her as she didn't have a posh voice.

When they were outside, Felicity grabbed her arm. 'Oh god Pippa, I just made a complete fool of myself didn't I.'

'You did my dear – but your actions spoke volumes,' she grinned knowing it confirmed her suspicion that Trip made her nervous and awkward – a sure sign she liked him more than she was admitting.

Felicity sighed and pulled the wet jumper away from her skin as best as she could.

'Pippa, I've got to ask, what did Tooga mean when he said about Interpol tracking you down?'

'What you don't know, you can't be interrogated about my dear,' and she winked, then walked away smiling.

CHAPTER 44

After Felicity's dramatic exit from the pub, Tooga sat back in his chair, looking at his friend.

'So...Felicity?' he said.

'Yep – it was thanks to her gaining the evidence from Pippa's friend Brenda, that initially made me suspect Roni Porter's suicide may have been something more sinister.'

'No,' Tooga said.

'What?'

'Let's try that again. So...*Felicity*?' he repeated.

Trip sighed.

Tooga remained silent.

Eventually Trip spoke. 'She's...,' he thought of the right word, 'complicated.'

'And you're Mr. Straightforward then?'

Trip ran his hand through his hair. 'I can't.'

'Look. I've spent one hour with her and I can see she's got a boot full of baggage hidden away. But I can also see that Pippa clearly adores her - and she's a bloody good judge of character, she's had to be - otherwise her nine lives would have expired years ago!'

'Yeah but...'

'And,' Tooga continued, ignoring the interruption, 'I can

see the effect she has on you. I've never seen anyone do that, other than Gabby.'

Trip flinched and hung his head at the mention of her name.

'And if I'm honest mate, I never thought anyone would have that effect on you again,' he reached over and squeezed Trip's shoulder, 'but Gabby's gone, god rest her soul and there's nothing we can do to bring her back. But we *will* get to the bottom of what happened to her eventually, that's a promise. In the meantime, you're not being disloyal to her by liking someone else. She'd understand. If this was the other way around, would you want Gabby to be alone for the rest of her life, if it was you that had died instead?'

'No of course not,' he said, his head still hanging forward, 'but…'

'But enough Trip. You *are* allowed to be happy. It doesn't have to be today, tomorrow or any time soon, but one day, when the time is right, it is OK to love someone again.' Tooga let go of his shoulder. 'And, just so you know, I think it should be Felicity.'

Trip looked up, ready to protest.

Tooga put his hand up in front of his face to quieten him. 'She's from Oldswinford - that's practically royalty mate!'

Trip couldn't help but laugh.

'Right, you miserable sod, I'm going to get us a couple of pints and then tell you why I'm really down here, apart from to sort out your shit love life of course,' and Tooga disappeared to the bar.

While he was sitting on his own, Trip digested what had been said. How would he feel if it was Gabby mourning his death and insisting on being alone forevermore? He couldn't bear to think that would have happened to her. So why does he think it's acceptable to be alone? He knew the answer to that question, of course, because he blamed himself for Gabby's death.

Tooga returned with their pints.

'Go on then, what's the real reason you're here. I'm going to assume it's something to do with Gabby's death after the whole *it's OK to be happy* speech.'

'I wanted you to hear it from me - Acker Harrison got in touch. He had a red car come in to his scrapyard for crushing. The side was bashed and scraped with white paint and Acker, being Acker, went through the car looking for anything of even the remotest value. Underneath the passenger seat, caught below the floor mat, he found a photo of Gabby - with her car registration written across the back.'

Trip sat completely motionless, holding his breath, trying to process what he'd just heard. He always worried that a story he'd been working on for the Birmingham Evening Mail, had touched some nerves somewhere. He'd shouldered a lot of pain and guilt since the accident – convinced that somehow, *he'd* been responsible for her death. Was it a warning from someone to stay away, stop digging - that he was getting too close to something? And now, those few sentences from Tooga, made him believe he was right.

Tooga leaned forward, 'breathe mate.'

Unaware he was still holding his breath, he quickly released it. 'Have you been to see Acker yet?'

'No, only spoken to him on the phone. After I've finished in Plymouth, I'm going to see him on the way home.'

'Where's his scrapyard?'

'Tipton, so not far from Birmingham.'

'I want to be with you when you go and see him,' Trip said, 'and it's not open for discussion.'

'I thought you'd say that. I'm only planning on being in Plymouth a couple of days, three at the most. Shouldn't take any longer to put a few things right down there. I'll phone you when I'm leaving and you can meet me at the

Broadsword Club. We can then decide when to go see Acker. OK?'

'OK.'

'You can stay in the flat above the club. Of course, you're more than welcome to stay at my house, but I wouldn't wish the mother-in-law on anyone, especially someone I like,' he laughed, trying to lighten the mood.

Trip didn't reply, his mind was now racing with a thousand questions for Acker Harrison.

CHAPTER 45

The man had continued to follow the woman through Weymouth shopping centre and outside onto New Bond Street. He had long ago grown tired of all the clothes shops she insisted on going into and he could feel his irritation growing by the minute, frustrated at trying to casually wait outside for her to exit.

Finally, she went into WHSmith, a shop he could follow her into without looking conspicuous. As she browsed through the magazines, he stood behind her, his back turned, pretending to look at magazines. He inhaled her scent and floral sweetness attacked his senses, too cloying for his liking, but he could forgive her for that because in the end, it wouldn't matter.

She stepped back slightly to let a small boy run past in front of her, the youngster desperate to reach the toy section as quickly as possible, clearly oblivious to any obstacle that got in his way.

She lightly bumped into the man behind and turned.

'I'm so sorry!', she apologised.

He hadn't been expecting her to speak to him, let alone notice him and it momentarily took him aback.

Finally, he spoke. 'No problem at all,' he smiled.

She returned his smile and walked away towards the books.

That one simple smile, unfortunately for her, had sealed her fate. The voices in his head were now relentless, mercilessly taunting and goading him. He knew the only way to silence them, was to silence her.

He watched as she took two books up to the till to pay and he queued behind her. While waiting for her items to be scanned, she flicked her hair over her shoulders, letting it fall down her back like soft dark silk. She paid and began to walk towards the exit, so he quickly placed the exact change on the counter for his magazine and started to follow.

'Sorry sir, I just need to scan the barcode!', the shop assistant called after him.

Angrily he turned and held the magazine towards her while she scanned it, then began his pursuit of the woman once more.

'Do you want your receipt sir?'

He ignored the question and followed the woman outside.

She at last began to make her way back towards the multistorey car park. The clamour in his head was now oppressive, making any other thoughts near impossible and he hit the side of his head with the butt of his hand, two…three times, desperate for a brief reprieve to the noise, but none came.

Eventually, they were back in the car park. She took the lift; he took the stairs aware that if she saw him again, it would be too much of a coincidence. He watched from behind the exit door as she walked towards her silver Lexus. Her mobile began to ring and he took his opportunity while she was distracted, quickly heading to his car.

He started the ignition and removed some bindings from his glove box, then tossed the magazine into the passenger footwell and began to reverse.

As she finished her call and dropped the phone into her handbag, he drove into the vacant space to the left of her car. Glancing quickly around and seeing no other people, he got out of his car, walked to the rear and opened the boot. He pulled the hood of his sweatshirt over his head and tightly gripped the bindings in his hand. A smile spread across his face, but it quickly morphed into a menacing sneer.

The woman dropped her bags into the boot of her car, then leaned over and rummaged inside her handbag.

He made his move and strode towards her.

Suddenly, several metres away, the lift doors opened.

'Sorry I'm so late love!', a man in a smart blue suit shouted and hurried towards the Lexus. 'Meeting ran on far later than I expected.'

'Not to worry – you can take me for a late lunch to apologise!' and she kissed him on the cheek.

The noise of the blood pounding in the man's ears at the interruption was excruciating and debilitating, but he sharply turned, slammed his boot and got back into the driver's seat. Moments later, his tyres squealed as he reversed and sped away towards the exit ramp, incensed and unfulfilled.

What would be a lucky escape for one woman, would be a brutal end for another. The question the voices were screaming in his head now, was *who*.

CHAPTER 46

Gareth Fletcher yawned, rubbed his tired eyes and glanced up in the mirror as he washed his hands. There was a day's worth of stubble on his face and his dark hair was unbrushed and messy. Dark circles shadowed below his eyes, the result of late nights, minimal sleep and high stress levels.

As he opened the consulting room door, the receptionist glanced up at him. She smiled into his deep brown eyes and blushed, quickly looking away.

'Dusty Marche,' he called.

Felicity stood up and smiled as she approached the vet.

'Ah Dusty – how you doing fella?' he said rubbing the dog's head, 'and how are you Felicity? I haven't seen you in a while.'

'I'm OK thanks Gareth.'

'Good,' he said. 'Annual health check and vaccinations today?'

'Yes – great,' and she held onto Dusty while he listened to his heart.

'All sounds good. Any problems?' he asked, opening the cupboard for the syringes, only to find it was empty.

'No problems at all, he's great.'

'Excellent - I'll just get Lucy to bring some more injections through' and he briefly disappeared out of the room to speak to the nurse.

When he returned and to avoid an awkward silence while they waited, Felicity said, 'I've often wondered, is that a New Zealand accent?'

'It is indeed - I'm impressed, most people think I'm an Aussie!'

'Whereabouts in New Zealand?'

'Queenstown.'

'Beautiful.'

'Oh, you've been there?'

'Once - skiing, many years ago now. Do you get back home often?'

'Not since last summer unfortunately,' he said as the nurse brought the syringes through. 'So, not been tempted to go back skiing again?'

'No,' she said too quickly and he glanced up at her. 'I mean, I wouldn't want to leave the dogs for that long – you don't just go to New Zealand for a long weekend!' she laughed, trying to hide her anxiety and wishing she hadn't started the conversation.

Of course, what she really meant, was that it was too close to Australia and that was a place she would never revisit.

'There you go Dusty – all done!' and he gave the dog a biscuit to eat. 'It was good to see you Felicity – and looking so well. If you ever…errr…fancy a drink sometime…?'

She looked up at him, shocked and immediately began feeling even more anxious.

'You don't need to say anything - just think about it. You know where to find me,' he smiled warmly and walked towards the door to open it for her.

She picked Dusty up off the table and forced her legs to move.

'Thanks for…errm…Dusty,' she said, unable to look into his eyes.

'Bye Felicity,' and as he walked back into his room, he briefly glanced back at her.

She was struggling to regain her composure and quickly paid and left. As she hurried around the corner to head home, she collided into someone.

'Oh, sorry,' she said looking up.

The figure dressed in jogging bottoms and a baggy hoodie, ignored her and walked away, head hung low.

CHAPTER 47

When Trip finally arrived home from the pub, it was 11pm. He knew there was little chance of getting any sleep tonight, so he squeezed onto the sofa next to Bear, a glass of Aberfeldy in his hand. His biggest fear had always been that he'd somehow been responsible for Gabby's death and he now believed his paranoia was justified.

He took a large gulp of his whisky and dragged himself up, walking to the wardrobe in his bedroom. His eyes stared at the closed door for a few moments, then pulled it open and reached up for an old brown cardboard box, tucked away on the top shelf. As he sat on the floor, he leant against the bed and looked down at the lid taped shut, closing his eyes for a few moments. An image of Gabby swam into focus - her dark brown hair, deep caring eyes and soft smile...

He opened his eyes and sighed. Once again, he wasn't ready to unseal the box and so returned it to the top shelf, closing the door to his unhealed past.

'Come on Bear,' he shouted through from the bedroom, 'how about we go for a walk.'

The dog trotted in, sitting down in the doorway, while Trip's eyes remained focussed on the closed wardrobe door, his mind still trapped in the past.

Bear walked over and nudged his hand and he looked down into his deep sad eyes. 'We've both lost someone we loved haven't we fella. Come on then, let's get out of here.'

After a few minutes and not really thinking about where he was going, he realised he was on the road approaching Felicity's coach house. He glanced up and saw there were no lights on - she'd clearly already gone to bed, not that he'd planned on knocking her door so late at night anyway.

As he carried on walking past, Bear suddenly started to growl, deeply and quietly. Trip's senses heightened and he glanced around to see what was troubling the dog. He walked to the end of the road, but only three cars were parked there - all of which he'd already established over the last few months, belonged to her neighbours. At the end of the road, he turned right and walked along the pavement until he reached the top entrance into her courtyard. Still nothing unusual and Bear was now no longer growling. Slowly, he walked down through the courtyard until he was standing outside Felicity's house, then looked around. There was nothing unusual or out of place and he reached over and softly tried the front door handle. It was locked and he breathed a sigh of relief.

As he retraced his steps to where his dog had initially started to growl, he heard a car slowly driving away. Instinct told him to run and he chased after the sound, Bear never leaving his side. Breathlessly, fuelled by adrenaline, he came to a stop as he saw a dark blue car turn onto the main road, then accelerate off into the distance, disappearing from sight.

CHAPTER 48

The following morning, Trip met Tooga for breakfast at 8am. After only managing a few fitful hours sleep, which had been filled with disturbing dreams, he was now tired, irritable and distracted.

As he walked down towards the pub, snapshots of the vivid dream still wouldn't clear from his mind.

Gabby was standing crying in a field, the light from the moon illuminating her pale skin. She was in the distance, but he could still make out her features. He tried to reach out towards her, but couldn't move his feet. Then he watched, as she slowly walked towards the edge of the field where it fell away to a cliff. The noise of the raging sea smashing against the rocky precipice, roared in his ears. She reached the edge, turned back to look at him, then silently stepped forward, disappearing into the night. Finally able to move his feet, he ran towards the cliff edge, fell to his knees and looked down into the darkness. Broken and crumpled on the jagged ground below, was the body of a woman. Her brown curls splayed across the wet rocks, a blonde streak glinting in the moonlight - *Felicity*.

Tank was standing next to the Bentley when he finally reached the pub.

'Morning Tank.'

'Trip,' he nodded.

Tooga walked out from the pub. 'Shit mate, bad night?'

'Yeah, not the best,' Trip yawned.

Tooga squeezed his shoulder in acknowledgment and understanding, as Tank opened the rear door for his boss. Wearily, Trip walked around to the other side, letting himself in.

'Want to talk about it?' Tooga asked, straightening his cuffs under his jacket sleeves and adjusting his cufflinks.

'Bad dreams, you know,' he shrugged.

'Where to Boss?' Tank asked.

'Hive Beach Café,' Trip said, handing him a piece of paper with a postcode on it, then turned to his friend. 'I took Bear for a walk last night - past Felicity's house.'

Tooga looked at him, raising an eyebrow.

He ignored the insinuation and continued.

'Bear wasn't happy about something and started to growl. I couldn't see anything out of place - no cars that I wouldn't expect to see there anyway. When I walked up the adjoining street and back around, I heard a car driving off. I tried to catch up with it, but I'm pretty sure I was spotted, because it sped away onto the main road.'

'Did you get the numberplate?'

'No. I only saw the side of the door panel as it disappeared. It was blue though.' He looked down at his hands which were now clenched into fists, knuckles straining white under the skin.

'Blue car as in…?'

'Yep - as in women-being-thrown-off-cliffs blue car.' His voice was strained with tension.

'Contacted Coop?'

'Yeah, as soon as the car had sped off.'

'And Jack Wicheloe?'

'Him too.'

'She'll be OK Trip. Nothing will happen to her.'

'Yeah, but you don't know that for sure. If anything happens to her then it'll be my…'

'Don't finish that sentence,' Tooga interrupted. 'It won't be your fault, just as Gabby's death wasn't and nothing is going to happen to your Felicity. What did Jack say?'

'What could he say? That based on a bad feeling in my gut, he'll use valuable police resources in stationing a car outside her coach house, on the off chance that some psychopath tries to abduct her?'

Tooga shrugged. 'Well, he might have said that, they've got nothing else to go on.'

'Yeah well, he said he'd do what he could. In the meantime, I'm going to be keeping an eye on her house myself.'

'Are you going to tell Felicity that?'

'No, I don't want to worry her.'

'But if she knew, then she'd be more vigilant surely?'

'I've been at the receiving end of many of her rages since I've known her, so I'm feeling pretty confident when I say this - if I told her I was convinced a murdering psychopath had been sitting outside her coach house, on several occasions and from now on I was going to be watching her at night, then she'd bloody punch me,' he said, trying to force a smile.

'Fair point, plus you're not too good at dodging fists are you mate,' Tooga grinned.

'Exactly.'

'I get the feeling Felicity's a survivor though, not a victim and has had to look after herself on more than one occasion in her life.'

Trip nodded, unable to shake the feeling that something bad would be happening soon.

After they arrived at Hive Beach and parked the car, the two men walked up to the café overlooking the sea, leaving Tank to guard the Bentley. Trip went inside and ordered their food, while Tooga stood on the grass at the edge of the seating area looking out at the sea.

Minutes later, Trip joined him and they both glanced down at the water below, gently lapping over the sandy beach. Several fishermen were sitting on the sand, rods cast out into the water and a few dogs ran along catching balls tossed out by their owners. It was an idyllic scene, but both men had the same thoughts. These waters had claimed the souls of two women in recent months - nearly three. It was now apparent that none of the deaths were by their own choosing and they were both concerned there was soon to be another.

An image of Felicity, once again, appeared in Trip's mind.

CHAPTER 49

Tooga left that afternoon for Plymouth, sooner than originally planned, as *something urgent had come up* and Trip still had no desire to know what that was. He hadn't seen or spoken to Felicity since the previous day in the pub and even if he had, he wasn't sure frightening her unnecessarily, was the right thing to do. However, as the afternoon had darkened into early evening, he'd spent several restless hours debating it in his mind – *am I doing the right thing?*

His plan was to sit in his Jeep with Bear and watch Felicity's house for any signs of a suspicious car – blue or any other colour.

Unable to settle, at 10.30pm he began to put items in his rucksack for the night ahead. By 10.45pm, he was pacing his apartment looking for answers he wasn't going to find cooped up inside. At 11pm, he'd had enough, hoping Felicity would now be asleep and therefore oblivious to him watching her house through the night.

He locked his apartment and set off.

As he walked across the car park with Bear, he spotted Gav in the corner talking to his lanky haired friend Scooter again. Having learnt from his previous mistake a while ago, he shouted over, rather than walking up behind him.

'Gav.'

They both turned around. 'Alright Trip. How's things?'

Bear immediately jumped up at Scooter again, pinning his shoulders with his paws, his teeth inches from the man's face.

'Listen Gav, are you around tonight?' Trip asked.

'Can be. Whatssup?'

'Nothing at the moment, but it would be good to know you're not far away if I need some extra help.'

'Errr...d...dog,' Scooter wheezed.

Trip and Gav both glanced briefly towards him.

Looking away, Gav nodded, 'you've got my number if you need me.'

'Cheers Gav,' he looked at his dog, 'Bear, put him down.'

The dog immediately released Scooter and trotted towards the Jeep with Trip.

He threw his rucksack onto the back seat and Bear jumped into the front. The dog looked scary enough in the day, but in the gloom of night he looked like a predatory wolf - a handy asset to have if you were going to be chasing murderers.

Earlier in the day he'd already decided where he was going to park his Jeep - tucked in the shadows of a carport nearby, which had a good view of Felicity's house and the road. The owner of the house, Tony, the printer of the newsletter, was happy for Trip to use it and had asked no questions.

Everywhere seemed quiet as he drove around the streets, but noticed her lights were still on. By the time he'd driven around a few more times and was happy there was nothing unusual in the vicinity, her lights had gone off and he reversed into the car port.

He picked up his phone to make a call.

'Trip,' Jack said, 'are you there now?'

'Yep, just parked up.'

'Listen mate, don't be a hero and do anything stupid. If you see anything, note the numberplate down and phone me straight away. OK?'

'Yeah, understood,' Trip lied.

'I mean it, I don't want a fourth and fifth victim in one night,' Jack said, knowing his best friend only too well.

'I'll be careful, you have my word.'

'That's not what I asked.'

'I know.'

Jack let out a loud sigh. 'For the record, I don't like this. I don't think for one moment Felicity is in any danger tonight or anytime soon. With the lack of anything else to go on, we've been studying a connection between the three women, from a different angle. Rather than assuming something in their past is linking them, we're now wondering if it's their looks.'

'Their looks?'

'Yes - all three women had long dark hair.'

'Is that it?'

'Well, it's all we can find that these women have in common and like you, we don't believe they were taken at random or by an opportunist nutter.'

'Yeah, but hair colour?' Trip said sceptically.

'It's a tenuous link at best I know, but it's one of the reasons I believe Felicity isn't in danger.'

'She's got long dark hair mate.'

'Yes, but the other woman had long, dark *straight* hair.'

Trip laughed, 'so because Felicity's hair's curly, then you think that makes her safe? Oh, come on Jack! Last night, that car saw me and sped off. It was blue. I understand why your chief wouldn't let you have her house watched *officially*, but it is way too much of a coincidence for my liking.'

'Listen, I know Felicity. She's a strong woman and bloody stubborn and definitely not a stereotypical vulnerable woman living on her own. I'm pretty sure she could look after herself and put up a damn good fight if needed.'

Trip immediately felt several emotions explode like a bomb inside him. How the hell did Jack know what sort of woman Felicity was? And perhaps, more importantly, how could he judge whether she'd be able to fend off a murderer if he grabbed her in her sleep?

'Trip, you still there?' Jack said into the silence.

'Yep. I'll phone if I see anything. Night,' and he ended the call, angry, annoyed and although he didn't want to admit it, jealous.

He was aware Jack had been to see her, having seen his car outside her house a couple of months ago. Yesterday, Tooga had said he should get Coop to run a check on Felicity, to find out exactly what was hidden in her past that made her so guarded - most likely from when she was living in Australia. But Trip had said a point blank, *no*. If there was anything in her past that she wanted him to know about, then he'd wait for her to tell him.

A text buzzed on this phone and he looked down at the screen – it was a message from Tooga.

Be careful tonight. Don't be a twat.

Trip couldn't help but smile as he replied.

Noted.

He reclined his seat to make himself as unnoticeable as possible and opened the rucksack, Bear immediately nudging him for his bone. The first thing he saw was the black pouch Tooga had given him before he'd left. He knew exactly what was inside, but he had no intention of using it, if he could help it.

Silence surrounded him as he sat in the dark – watching and waiting. Bear, now bored with his bone, was curled up asleep on the seat beside him, his head hanging over the edge, lightly snoring.

In the distance, he suddenly became aware of a vehicle approaching slowly and his heart rate quickened as his eyes scanned the streets and shadows. The bonnet of a car appeared around the corner and pulled up outside a house, but it was only a taxi. A man got out, tapped the roof of the car which then pulled away and he staggered unsteadily to a front door, fumbling with his keys trying to unlock it. After several aborted attempts, he finally stumbled inside and slammed the door.

Everywhere was quiet again once more.

Just after midnight, Bear looked up and began to growl. Trip sat bolt upright, scanning up and down the street, but there was nothing. He glanced across at Bear who was now standing up on the seat, shoulders hunched down, growling deeply. He tried to follow the dog's line of vision, but he was only staring straight ahead, clearly able to hear something, but not yet see it.

His growls grew deeper and more menacing, just as a blue car slowly drove up the road, passing in front of where Trip was parked. The vehicle crawled past Felicity's house and his gut twisted. It quietly pulled up across the road and switched off the engine and he quickly grabbed a pen and wrote the number plate down on his hand.

Through the cars back windscreen, he could see the shape of a figure behind the steering wheel and Bear suddenly began to bark. Once. Twice - then continually. He tried to silence the dog, but he was too honed in on his prey by then. The figure in the blue car moved its head left to right, clearly trying to see where the muffled barking was coming from.

Suddenly, the engine of the car started up and Trip turned his ignition key, ready to follow.

'Bear, in the back - *now.*'

The dog immediately obeyed and jumped through the gap onto the back seat.

The blue car accelerated away from the kerb, driving towards the top of the street. He pulled out and followed. At the end of the street, it turned left, then immediately right, quickly joining the main road. Trip was right behind and saw the dark form look up into the rear-view mirror. Tyres squealing, it raced away towards a roundabout, taking the second exit. After a hundred yards, it briefly slowed at Monkey Jump roundabout, then sped off again, taking the fourth exit, signposted A37 Yeovil.

The two cars raced down the road, speeding under a bridge and fast approaching another roundabout. The blue car didn't slow, it sped around the roundabout, doubling back on itself and up towards Monkey Jump roundabout once more. Under the bridge again and Trip tried to overtake, but the car accelerated and pulled away.

A lorry was approaching from the opposite direction, causing Trip to swerve back in at the last second and the truck driver blared his horn angrily.

They were now almost back at Monkey Jump roundabout, so once more Trip pulled out to overtake. The blue car suddenly veered across the road, colliding at speed into the side of the Jeep, immediately pushing him across the road. He tried to steer his vehicle back towards the left-hand lane, but it was too late.

He slammed on his brakes, forcing the Jeep to swerve into a layby on the opposite side of the road, crashing through a low wire fence and finally coming to a sudden stop as his front wheel hit a heavy metal fence post, deploying the airbag. The sound of metal crumpling on impact was deafening and his body slammed towards the steering wheel, cushioned by the airbag, then he fell hard against his door. The Jeep dipped, nose down in a shallow ditch at the edge of a field and once again everywhere fell silent.

The blue car had disappeared into the night.

He sat motionless for a minute, heart hammering against

his chest.

'Bear,' he mumbled, breathless with adrenaline.

Silence.

'Bear!' he said louder, turning his head to the left to look for him.

The dog stuck his head through the gap in the seats, nudging his arm to signal he was OK. Trip got out the Jeep to survey the damage, seeing the front left tyre was ripped open and the wheel badly buckled. Other than body paint scratches and some nasty dents, it had survived well, but was definitely not drivable.

He reached inside, wincing at a sudden pain and grabbed his rucksack, then retrieved the phone from the floor of the vehicle and opened the back door. Bear jumped out with his bone and immediately cocked his leg up a bent fence post.

He watched the dog walk for a few steps, to make sure he wasn't injured, then leant against the Jeep to phone Jack.

'Jack, it's Trip,' he said still slightly breathless.

'You OK?'

'Yeah fine. Texting a number plate for you to trace. Dark blue BMW,' and he paused to type the registration into a text.

'Got it. I'll get the team on it straight away. And you're OK mate?'

'I'll live,' and he hung up, still feeling angry about their earlier phone call.

He switched on his torch and walked the short distance to Monkey Jump roundabout, Bear at his side. At the second roundabout, he crossed the road and walked back towards the residential streets, turning the corner at the side of her coach house and paused to glance down the road where the car had been parked.

***

As she opened her front door, a movement caught

Felicity's eye, making her heart rate accelerate.

'Trip? Bear?' she said looking from one to the other, feeling confused.

He looked up. 'Are you OK?'

'Yes, why?'

'Are you going somewhere?' He looked at his watch, 'it's nearly 1am.'

'Milk,' she said.

'You're going to get milk in the middle of the night?'

She bent down in her front door way, picking up a small carton off the doorstep.

'Milk,' she said holding it up for him to see. 'The milkman comes so early and I like to get it in if I'm still awake. I don't like the thought of a dog weeing up it.'

Trip laughed, then grabbed his side wincing again.

'Are you OK?' she asked peering towards him through the gloom.

'Yep, all good,' and he bit down on the pain.

She walked out of her doorway taking a few steps towards him, immediately sensing something wasn't right. 'Are you sure you're OK?'

He glanced down at her clothes. She wore pyjamas with a picture of Snoopy on the front, pink fluffy slippers on her feet.

'Go in, you'll get cold,' he said from across the road.

'Trip something isn't right, what's wrong?'

Bear trotted towards her, wagging his tail and dropped the bone at her feet.

'This for me?' she smiled, crouching down beside the dog rubbing his chest.

He walked towards her to retrieve his dog – keen to get home quickly to make some phone calls. It was then she saw the mud on his boots and jeans.

As she stood up, she gasped. 'You're bleeding!' and pointed to his head, grimacing.

He touched his hairline and looked at his fingers. 'It's just a graze.'

'Let me clean…'

He interrupted. 'Honestly it's just a scratch, I'll sort it when I get home.'

'I'll clean it up,' she said firmly, 'you'll probably spit on a bit of toilet paper and wipe it thinking that's a good job done,' and she walked back towards the front door, Bear immediately trotting inside and running upstairs.

She turned. 'Wait here.'

'What?' he said still walking towards the door.

'Wait here,' she repeated, putting her hand on his chest to stop him coming any closer.

'But…?' he started to say, intensely aware of her hand on his body.

'I don't want you dripping blood everywhere.'

'I haven't severed a limb Felicity, it's just a scratch!'

'It's more than a scratch…and it's trickling. Wait here.'

Too tired and sore to argue, he watched her disappear inside, then slumped down on the doorstep, looking into the courtyard. Upstairs he could hear doors and cupboards opening and closing.

A few minutes later, he heard her opening the stair gate and walk down the stairs.

'OK, you'll have to stand outside in case you drip - then you'll be lower down than me too, so I can reach.'

He stood up, turned around as instructed and couldn't help but smile as he looked down at her.

Her sleeves were rolled up, hands wearing pink latex gloves, holding a tray containing a bowl of water, tissues, cotton wool, alcohol wipes and plasters. Silently he stood and watched as she placed the tray on the stairs and prepared to clean his wound, noticing her face set in a slight grimace.

'I'm guessing you don't like blood,' he smiled.

'It's not the blood I mind, it's just that I associate it with germs. And I don't like germs.'

He wasn't sure whether to laugh or not - but chose not to, erring on the side of caution.

'OK, you're going to have to lean forward a bit more so I can reach.'

She stood on the door step for extra height, then went up on her tiptoes to clean the wound with wet cotton wool, discarding the used pieces into a plastic bag. He watched her biting her bottom lip in concentration, feeling her warm breath on his face. She turned around and opened an alcohol wipe then dabbed it gently on his head making him wince.

'Sorry,' she said, looking down at him.

'Thanks for doing this.'

Her eyes momentarily glanced down at his mouth as he spoke.

'You're welcome,' she said quietly.

Next, she opened a plaster, placing it over the cut and they both looked up at the same moment into each other's eyes. For a few seconds her hand stopped its work and she held her breath, then quickly spoke to break the tension. 'Is there any more blood anywhere while I'm all gloved up?'

He pulled the side of his shirt and jacket up, where the sharp pain had been. Seeing his bare skin at the side of his body, she immediately looked away.

'No bleeding,' she said, her eyes still averted. 'OK, you're done. So, are you going to tell me what happened now?' He noticed the soft tone to her voice was gone, replaced with firmness.

'I bumped my head tripping over Bear in the dark, it's just a scratch,' he shrugged.

Taking a step away from him she placed all the debris off the tray into the bag and pulled off the latex gloves, revealing a second pair underneath. After tying the bag in a knot, she reached inside the office door and squirted sanitiser on her hands from the dispenser on the wall.

'A scratch from a fall,' she muttered, 'why do men do that? Why can't you just say what happened instead of trying to act all macho!'

Oh shit, Trip thought, here we go.

'You have clearly done more than fall over! You've bruised or possibly broken a rib, judging by the pain you felt when you laughed earlier. You're covered in mud and you've got twigs sticking out from your bloody boots!'

He remained silent having learnt the hard way that it was the best course of action.

'Well say something then!', she said, her anger beginning to rapidly rise.

'I didn't want to interrupt,' he smiled, unable to help himself.

'What are you smiling about! I'm being serious, what the hell happened to you?'

'I'm sorry, but it's very difficult having an argument with someone wearing Snoopy pyjamas!' and he continued to smile.

'OH, THIS IS *EXACTLY* WHAT *HE* WOULD HAVE DONE! BLOODY MEN!' her face now turning pink.

'Who?'

'MY BLOODY HUSBAND!'

'Wait - what?' Trip said, feeling as though someone had punched him in his stomach.

'MY BLOODY HUSBAND!', she repeated, hands now firmly on her hips.

'I didn't know you were married?' he said, taken aback at the strength of feeling inside him.

'I'M NOT!'

'OK, can we just rewind a minute, I feel like I've walked into an argument half way through! You…errrr…it's just…well, don't look the sort to be married,' he muttered, confused - or hurt, he wasn't sure.

'AND WHAT'S THAT SUPPOSED TO MEAN!'

Silently staring at each other, like a stand-off scene from a cowboy movie, she finally turned and stomped off up the stairs, opening the stair gate.

'Bear!' she said defiantly.

The dog immediately jumped off the sofa and trotted

towards her, clearly sensing all was not well. She rubbed the top of his head.

'I'm not mad at you,' and Bear wagged his tail in relief and began to trot down the stairs.

'BUT I'M BLOODY MAD AT YOU!' she said glaring at Trip in the doorway.

She stomped back downstairs and bending down, picked up the bag of rubbish.

'AND YOU CAN TAKE THIS WITH YOU!' and flung the bag of bloodied debris towards him.

He caught the bag.

She went to slam the front door in his face, but he grabbed it.

Stunned, she looked at him.

'MY TURN!' he shouted and slammed the door in her face.

He grabbed his rucksack and walked away with his dog, taking the bag of rubbish with him.

CHAPTER 50

The next morning Trip woke up, ribs hurting, head pounding, feeling pissed off and angry. Bear rolled over and licked the side of his face.

'Bear!' he protested, wiping the slobber off.

Last night, after returning home from being patched up and shouted at, he'd phoned Coop with the numberplate of the blue BMW, to see if he could find out any further information. He then left a message on the mechanic's answerphone, whom he'd used once before, explaining where his car was and could he tow it away and fix the tyre as soon as possible.

Eventually Coop phoned back, saying the number plates were fake and moments later, Jack called with the same information.

The news didn't come as a surprise to him.

He dragged himself out of bed, went into the kitchen and switched on the coffee machine. His phone buzzed beside him and he answered it without looking at the display.

'Trip.'

'You stupid bastard, you could have gotten yourself

killed!'

'Morning Tooga. Didn't think it would be long before Coop phoned you.'

'So, last night went great didn't it!' Tooga said sarcastically.

'Yeah, well at least it proved there was someone watching Felicity - and that it *was* a blue BMW.'

'But you're still no closer to finding the *Clifftop Killer*, or even if it's the same person from last night.'

'Have you phoned to just point out the obvious to me and make me feel more shit than I already do?'

'And that you're a stupid bastard, who could have gotten yourself killed last night,' Tooga reiterated.

'Yeah OK, I know.'

'I was also phoning to say I'm heading back up to Birmingham today.'

'OK, well my car's getting towed later, but hopefully if it's just the tyre and minimal damage to the wheel, then I can get it back fairly quick and come up to meet you tomorrow.'

'Have you spoken to Felicity?'

Trip cleared his throat. 'Yep…we exchanged several words last night.'

'So, you told her what you were up to then?'

'Not exactly.'

'Meaning?'

'No.'

'What were the words about then?'

'Fate stuck it's bloody oar in again and she opened her front door to get her milk, just as I was walking back from the smash. She patched me up.'

'Oh, did she now.'

'Don't bloody worry, nothing happened. I wasn't allowed inside in case I dripped blood anywhere! Honest to god Tooga, if you think anything could ever happen with that unbelievably infuriating woman, then you're as crazy as she is!'

'Right, of course.'

'I mean it mate!'

'Yeah, sure, understood,' Tooga said, believing none of it.

'Good. I'll be with you tomorrow morning then.'

'Oh and Trip? Drive carefully mate,' and he hung up, laughing.

Trip threw his phone down on the sofa. How anyone could see him and Felicity together was beyond him. He had never met a woman like her before in his life. *Everything that happened last night, was as a result of me trying to protect her and still she fought with me.*

Tooga's conversation from the previous day came into his mind, suggesting he tell her about the car that had been watching her. *She still would have found something to fight with me about anyway,* he thought angrily.

His phone rang again.

'Trip Hazard,' he answered, tension still in his voice.

'Hello, this is Harris Recovery. Have I phoned at a bad time?'

'No, sorry – it's…ell…bloody women!'

The mechanic laughed. 'Just to let you know, I got your message and I've collected your Jeep and towed it back to the garage.'

'That's great, cheers. How bad is it?'

'I've had a look at the wheel and it's repairable, but you'll need a new tyre obviously. It's only going to take a couple of hours to sort - the paint and bodywork will take longer though.'

'That's great. I'm not so worried about the bodywork at the moment, I just need the car back on the road as soon as possible.'

'I can get the tyre and wheel sorted this morning and have it done by 1pm at the latest.'

'That would be ideal, cheers I owe you one.'

'Great I'll remember that!' the mechanic laughed. 'I'll

phone you when it's ready to collect. Speak to you later,' and he hung up.

Trip looked at the time – it was only 10am. He decided to lay low for today until his car was ready and intended to remain off fate's and Felicity's radar, for the rest of the day.

***

A few hours later, a noise woke him up. He'd fallen asleep on the sofa next to Bear and didn't answer the ringing mobile quickly enough. After listening to the voicemail from the garage to say his vehicle was ready, he splashed some cold water on his face and called a taxi.

Twenty minutes later, he was there. As he got out of the vehicle, his phone rang yet again and he distractedly answered it.

'Trip,' he said walking towards the building.

'It's Felicity Marche.'

He paused before speaking. 'Ms. Marche, how can I help you,' he said sternly.

'I've just had DI Wicheloe in my house who informs me that you crashed your car last night, seemingly moments before you apparently fell over and hit your head.'

He could hear the rising anger in her voice, making the anger flare inside him. *What right did Jack have telling her, when I wasn't even doing anything official!* Anger was quickly joined by another emotion - *and what the hell was he doing in her house anyway?*

'It wasn't his place to say anything.'

'His place?' she said angrily, 'HIS PLACE! He assumed I knew because I'd cleaned you up!'

'And what did he say exactly?'

'Oh, you know, that you thought I had a killer in a blue car sitting watching me at night!' Her voice was fuelled with sarcasm.

'So, you had a good old chat with Jack then by the

sounds of it!' he snapped.

'What's that supposed to mean?'

'Nothing. Was there anything else you wanted?' he asked sharply.

'Yes - I don't need protecting and I CAN LOOK AFTER MY BLOODY SELF!' and she hung up.

Tripped looked down at the screen on his phone. *That woman is absolutely bloody unbelievable!* He took a deep breath and ran his hand through his hair.

The mechanic looked up, 'everything all right there?' he smiled

'Bloody women - again!' Trip laughed, trying to make light of the anger still fired up inside him.

The mechanic nodded his head. 'Jeep's over there,' and he pointed towards the side entrance of the building.

'Thanks. I'm heading up north today, so it's really helped me out getting it driveable so quickly.'

'No problem. Give me a shout when you want the bodywork sorting – I've still got the black paint where I patched it up before!' he laughed.

Trip paid the bill, thanked him again, then walked outside and phoned Tooga.

'I'm coming up to Birmingham this afternoon mate.'

'Everything OK?'

'Yep. Need a change of scenery – *today.*' His voice was still tinged with anger from Felicity's phone call.

'I'll see you later then,' Tooga said knowing that something had clearly happened and he'd bet money on it being in regard to Felicity.

***

After he drove home from the garage, Trip packed a bag and collected Bear. By 3pm he was on the M5 and well on his way to Birmingham. His whole journey so far had been consumed with Felicity. Two hours into his journey, he'd finally decided she was no longer his problem - she was Jack's. After all, *she didn't need protecting* according to the last words she'd shouted at him.

Traffic was heavy on the motorway, but he finally parked behind Tooga's Broadsword Club at 6pm. Grabbing his bag and letting Bear out the back seat, he walked towards the rear entrance, where Tank opened the door before he'd even knocked.

'Cheers Tank.'

'Trip,' he nodded.

'Office?'

Tank nodded again and Bear trotted up to him, wagging his tail.

'Good to see yer again fella,' he said, rubbing the dogs head fondly.

Trip had never heard Tank say so many words in one sentence before.

As he walked towards the back room, he could see Tooga's office door open and he walked inside.

'Trip mate, good drive?'

'Yeah, not bad.'

He looked around the office at the computer screens filling one entire wall. Most of them were CCTV monitors showing the snooker club below and the perimeter outside.

'Gone a bit high tech since I was last here then,' Trip smiled, already feeling more relaxed being in his friends' company and well away from Dorset.

'Gotta move with the times mate,' Tooga grinned.

'Do you even know how to use them?'

'Not one bit. But I got a man who does,' he winked and Trip wondered if he meant Coop, as he'd never actually met him.

'Go on up to the flat and make yourself at home. The Mrs has been making it comfy and fussing around for hours. Don't understand why she's got a soft spot for you - rugged good looks are so 1990's, if you ask me,' Tooga laughed, straightening his silk tie.

***

Later that evening, they ordered a Balti takeaway, one of the many things Trip missed about Birmingham. Tank had taken Bear out for a walk, while the two men sat in the office with a bottle of Aberfeldy.

'Good of Tank to take the dog out,' Trip said.

'Yeah, he prefers talking to dogs rather than people, can't blame him though.'

'What do you mean?'

'His dad was a pawn broker in Sparkhill and a real mean bastard. He tried to rip off the wrong family one day and was given a warning - they torched his shop. Tank was about fifteen at the time and his dad took his anger out on him that night. I happened to be driving through Sparkhill and saw him curled up in a ball outside the laundrette in the pouring rain. His dad had beaten the shit out of him with a baseball bat and there weren't many bones in his body he hadn't broken. I got him to hospital, then when he left after several days in intensive care, he came and worked for me in the club. I taught him how to box and look after himself and he spent every hour he could in the gym getting himself stronger. He's a good lad.'

'I never knew that about Tank. Just assumed he'd come to you the way he is now,' Trip said, respecting his old friend even more.

'Nah he was a skinny little kid when I found him.'

'What happened to his dad?'

'Got a taste of his own medicine and quietly disappeared,' Tooga winked. 'Anyway, come on, out with it.'

'Out with what?'

'What happened to make you come up a day early. I'd wager it had something to do with a certain hypnotherapist.'

'Don't get me started on her Tooga. Seriously, that

woman drives me absolutely bloody insane!' His blood pressure was already starting to rise again.

'Yeah, sure she does,' he smiled.

'She's bloody married too! And seeing Jack Wicheloe! Well, she's *their* problem now!' Trip was getting more wound up by the second.

'Married? Are you sure about that?'

'She told me!'

'And she also told you she's seeing Jack Wicheloe?'

'Yes! Well…no. But he's been around to her house - twice now, that I know of anyway.'

'Oh, well she must be seeing him in that case,' Tooga said sarcastically, watching his friend closely.

'What's that supposed to mean?'

'I'm just wondering why you're so bothered if she is married *or* seeing Jack, you know, considering you're not interested in her and she drives you insane.'

'Well…because…it's just…well…'

'Yes?' Tooga pushed.

'Because she lied about it!' That was the best answer he could come up with.

'Right. And you've been so upfront and honest with her haven't you!'

Trip didn't reply, just stared down into his drink.

Finally, he spoke. 'Can we change the subject please.'

Tooga smiled to himself and said nothing. Pippa was right, he thought, maybe they should be bundled off to Panama in a shipping container together.

'So, what's the plan with Acker Harrison tomorrow?' Trip asked.

'I don't think we're going to get much more than we know already to be honest. But we won't tell him we're coming and we'll take it from there.'

'Do you know him well?'

'I know *of* him, more than I know him - but he'll tell us everything he knows, so don't worry about that.'

Tank came back in the office with Bear, a massive bone

wedged in the dog's mouth.

'Please tell me that's not a human bone!' Trip laughed.

'Nah t'aint,' he said, patting the dogs head.

***

At 9am the next morning, they were on the way to see Acker Harrison, whose scrapyard was located in Tipton and had been since the 1970's. They pulled up outside the portacabin office and Trip immediately tensed.

'Stay with the Bentley,' Tooga said to Tank, who simply nodded.

The two men walked into the grimy office which smelled of stale tobacco and Pot Noodles. Sitting behind a desk in a sheepskin coat and smoking a cigar, was Acker Harrison. His greying hair was slicked back over his rapidly balding head and a beer gut hung over his dark trousers.

'Acker,' Tooga said.

The man looked up.

'Mr. Davis - wasn't expecting you?' he said nervously.

'Didn't see the need to book an appointment Acker.'

'No, of course. How can I help you?'

'This is Trip Hazard. We've come to talk to you about the red car.'

'Red car?' he said, getting more nervous by the second.

'You know the one. We've come to see it,' Tooga said.

Acker swallowed hard. 'Err…right. I err…didn't know you wanted to actually *see* the car.'

Tooga put his hands on the front of Acker's desk and loomed down towards him.

'I'd like to see the car – now, *please.*'

'Right, well, errm…there's been a slight…errr…you know…miscommunication,' Acker said, sweat now forming on his brow.

'Miscommunication?'

'It's well, errm…just…that…well…,' Acker spluttered.

'Show me,' Tooga said.

Acker got up from behind his desk and walked towards the door. Tooga blocked his path and glared at him, then stood aside to let him pass. Acker opened the door and went outside, pausing and swallowing hard when he saw Tank leaning against the Bentley.

They followed him for a few yards, before walking around the back of a rusting tractor, then came to a stop. The scrap dealer nodded his head to the left.

There, sitting on the ground, was a large cube of squashed metal. It's red jagged pieces of bodywork could still be seen amongst the mangled mess.

'You're kidding me, right?'

'Err…no…Mr Davis…like I ummm said…it's a… errr…miscommunication,' he said, nervously rubbing his hand on his head.

Tooga took a step towards Acker and Trip grabbed his arm pulling him back.

'Did you keep anything of any use before you crushed it?' Trip asked.

'Yes, yes - back in the office,' he said, hoping to save the situation and quickly walked back past Tooga, towards the office.

Trip hung back and murmured, 'don't kill him mate.'

'Yeah, the jury's out on that at the moment, let's see what the stupid sod has got first.'

They followed him back into the office and Acker pulled open a dented grey filing cabinet.

'Number plates, VIN off the chassis and the errr…well the…err photo I found,' he said, placing the items on his desk.

Trip's eyes immediately went to the photo and picked it up. A smiling Gabby looked back at him, her dark hair blowing in the wind, walking out of the hospital building where she worked. The picture had clearly been taken by a zoom lens camera and when he turned the photograph over, he saw her car registration written on the back. Every muscle in his body tensed.

'Who bought the vehicle in to be scrapped?' Tooga asked.

'It was dumped in Cannock Chase, vandalised and stripped bare.'

'And how did you end up with it?'

'The bloke who towed it away for the Police is a mate of mine and brought it in here.'

'And the mate is?'

'Billy Turton – got his own recovery business. Do you want his number?'

'No need, I know Billy. Acker, I hope *not* to see you again soon.'

'Yes Mr. Davis. And err…you know…sorry about the …errr…miscommunication,' he said, relief flooding through his body.

Trip picked up the numberplates and the VIN and walked outside with Tooga. He leant against the outside of the portacabin and closed his eyes.

'Come on mate, let's get out of this dump,' and Tooga squeezed his shoulder.

***

Back at the club, Trip went to retreat upstairs to the flat, but Tooga stopped him.

'This isn't a time to be on your own mate.'

They went into the office, closed the door and Tooga picked up two glasses and the bottle of whisky.

'Not for me, thanks,' Trip said, sitting down on the leather sofa, knowing full well he'd get maudlin with alcohol inside him.

'I've texted Coop the plates and VIN, but I'm thinking they are…'

'Fake,' Trip said finishing his sentence.

'Yep.'

'What about this Billy Turton? – do we need a conversation with him?'

'Nah, Billy is as honest as the day's long. If there was anything dodgy, he wouldn't have touched it.'

Tank knocked the office door. 'Boss - trouble.'

Tooga looked at the CCTV monitors, seeing a fight was about to break out at one of the snooker tables.

'Be right back,' he said getting up and left the office.

Trip slumped back on the sofa and closed his eyes, a picture appeared of Gabby in his mind. *I'm so sorry. Whatever I did to cause this, whoever I pissed off or scared, I will find - I promise.*

Several minutes later, Tooga walked back into the office.

'Everything OK? – or are there any bodies to dispose of!'

'Yeah, just Fat Larry and Sammy Roberts getting a bit lairy. Tank's sitting by them, they'll behave now.'

Tooga's mobile rang.

'Coop, what you got?'

Trip looked up, watching his friend's face for answers.

'Right, let me know...yeah, he's with me now, hang on...'

He took the phone away from his ear to pass to Trip. 'Coop says the VIN belonged to a Red Mazda, number plate fake as we thought. He's running traces on the Mazda's history, but it'll take a bit of time. But here...,' and he passed the phone over, 'he wants to speak to you.'

'Coop?'

'Hey Trip. Found a birth certificate for Roni Porter - might be nothing, but I'll let you decide that. She was born in Lynton, North Devon in 1982. I'll email you a copy of it now.'

'OK, thanks Coop. And do whatever you can to find anything on the Mazda, OK?'

'Yeah 'course. Laters,' and the line went dead.

'So, what you going to do now? You can stay here as

long as you like, you know that.'

'Thanks mate. I don't want to go home to Dorset yet - I know that for sure. I think I'm going to head on to North Devon and see if I can find anything else about Roni Porter. It's better than being home on my own thinking,' he shrugged.

'And for what it's worth,' Tooga said, 'my advice is to speak to Felicity. Perhaps you could both try being honest with each other, for once. Novel idea I know,' he smiled.

'No, she's definitely one less problem I need in my life,' and Trip walked out of the office to pack his bag.

***

As the man's eyes flickered open, his heart was pounding in his chest, trying to burst free. His body was slick with sweat and the sheets on the bed were damp and thrown to one side. He stared up at the ceiling, as the voices continued to circle in his head like an edacious vulture, having been left unsatisfied since his recent visit to Weymouth.

His dreams, as usual, had consisted of the women whose souls had already been released. But there was one woman in particular who invaded his dreams more than any other, but she was not one of his victims. It was also her voice that whispered to him in the dark and if he tried to ignore it, she simply spoke louder until it became unbearable.

The voice belonged to his mother.

Her words still lingered in his head from the dream...

'You are your father's son.'

At that point her voice again changed, hearing instead the deep menacing tone of his father.

'May you pour out your fury on them. May your burning anger overtake them.'

He knew exactly *what* he had to do – the question still

312

was, *who*. But he believed in fate and knew that it would help him in his search.

CHAPTER 51

The journey from The Jewellery Quarter in Birmingham, to Lynton in North Devon, took Trip just over three hours. Whenever he drove away from The Midlands, he always felt like he was saying goodbye to Gabby all over again. Birmingham had been their home and that's where his happy memories lay.

For now, there was nothing more he could do. Coop would be doing everything he could to track down the ownership history of the red Mazda, seen following Gabby out of the hospital car park on the night she died. Once he had a list of previous owners of the vehicle, he'd be able to see if any of the names meant anything to him. He could then also check if any had links to articles he'd worked on at the Birmingham Evening Mail.

As he travelled up Castle Hill towards Lynton, he looked for a hotel for the night and saw a sign for The Valley of The Rocks Hotel. He pulled into a car park nearby and left Bear in the Jeep. After a brief conversation with the receptionist, he was told that they didn't allow pets, however, she recommended a pub on Lynmouth Street -

The Village Inn, which was only a short drive away.

Ten minutes later, he'd found the pub and booked a room for a couple of nights, giving him time to find out more information about Roni Porter – if there was anything else to find. It also meant he could keep his distance from Dorset and more importantly, Felicity Marche *with a bloody E*, for a while longer.

The weak winter sun was already setting on a cool November afternoon, as he took Bear for a walk around the village. The small Victorian town had a selection of shops, tea-rooms and cafes and he thought about Roni walking around these streets when she was a little girl, unaware of the horrors that lay ahead in her doomed life.

An hour later, he returned to the room and opened his laptop, pulling up the original information Coop had sent, together with the latest document received - her birth certificate. Trip knew that there may not be anything more to discover in Lynton that would help, but decided he'd spend tomorrow morning asking around the town, on the off chance that someone would remember her.

As he lay back on the bed, he took the photo of Gabby out of his pocket. It seemed hard to imagine all the days he'd lived without her since her death. The birthdays and Christmases that she'd missed; films and technology advances in a world she would never know about. A lot had happened in the eighteen months following her death, yet the one thing he was unable to do, was find out the truth about what happened to her on that night. But he would, no matter how long it took.

***

A couple of hours later, after a fitful sleep, he went downstairs with Bear to the pub's bar for a meal. He asked the barman if he remembered Roni or *Veronica* Porter, but he was only in his early twenties and hadn't even been born when she'd lived in the village. However, he did suggest that he speak to the vicar of St. Peter's Church in the town, as he may remember her.

Distracted by many different thoughts circling in his head, he ate his meal then took Bear for a final walk for the day, eventually heading back up to his room. He slumped down on the bed, his mind unexpectedly wandering to Felicity and the night of the crash when she cleaned his wound. There had been looks he was sure they'd shared, but now wondered if he'd in fact imagined them. The anxiety he saw flash across her eyes when he'd pulled his shirt up to check for blood, was not imagined however. Also, the tension he'd felt in her body when they'd danced together at the Ball, was something he couldn't forget.

So why was it that she felt no obvious discomfort with Jack and why hadn't she mentioned she was seeing him? He knew Jack had been working the night of the Ball, which is why he would have been unable to accompany her. *But why did she dance with me? Because I didn't give her much option*, he thought. *And all of this is going on while she has a husband? Yet I saw no sign of a man living in her coach house when I fixed her towel radiator? Perhaps her husband works away? That would make sense, as she would then be free to see someone else, without the likelihood of her husband catching her. And what happened to her in Australia? And why the hell am I asking myself all these questions about a woman who drives me insane and who clearly despises me!*

He turned off the light in his room, reminding himself once again, that she is now somebody else's problem.

CHAPTER 52

The following morning, Trip walked into the town with Bear and asked around a few of the shops and cafes, but no one knew the name Roni or Veronica Porter. He was quickly beginning to feel even more tired and irritable than he'd felt when he first woke up.

Across the road he saw St. Peter's Church and walked around the grounds, eventually sitting on a bench overlooking the water, Bear at his side. The sun was struggling to generate heat, but closing his eyes he could still feel a gentle warmth on his face.

A voice startled him.

'You look lost, can I help at all?' the man said.

Trip opened his eyes to see at an elderly vicar standing before him.

'I'm not lost thanks Reverend, just enjoying the view.'

'I meant less of lost in *geographical* terms, but more of *life in a general* sense,' the vicar smiled warmly.

Trip laughed, 'you could well be right there!'

'Mind if I…?' the vicar said nodding his head towards the bench.

'Of course,' and Trip moved to make room for him.

'Reverend Ross Clewer,' he said shaking Trip's hand.

'Trip Hazard.'

'Unusual name.'

'My father had a good sense of humour,' he smiled.

'You look as though you have the weight of the world on your shoulders.'

'I certainly feel I've a lot on my mind at the moment.'

'A woman perhaps?'

'Women - plural.'

'Oh!' he said, surprised by his answer.

'No, no! I don't mean like that!' Trip laughed. 'It's… complicated!'

'It always is,' the Reverend grinned.

'She certainly is.' The words had spilled from his mouth without any effort and he was completely taken aback.

'Actually Reverend,' Trip continued, wishing to change the subject and distract himself as quickly as possible, 'I wonder if I could ask you a few questions, about someone who would have lived in the town in the 1980's?'

'And you'd be asking because?'

'Sorry, I should explain. I'm a journalist, well ex-journalist now. I live in Dorset and we've had a couple of suspicious deaths of women over the last few months. They've been made to look like suicides – pushed or thrown off local cliffs. I know the Detective Inspector who's in charge of the case and I have…errr…*contacts* that are useful sometimes…,' Trip was conscious of the fact that he was sounding like a very dubious character. 'Sorry Reverend, I know I'm making this sound very suspicious, but the police have hit a brick wall at the moment and I'm just trying to find anything that may help them find this killer, before he strikes again.'

'What is it that you think I may be able to help you with?'

'The first victim was a woman called Roni, or Veronica, Porter. I believe she was born in Lynton in 1982. Her mother was killed by a hit and run driver when she was eight years old and her father, who was an alcoholic, died not long after. She was taken into care and moved around a lot of foster homes in Devon after that.'

'Well, I moved to Lynton, with my wife Karen, in 1997 and became Reverend of St. Peter's Church. The previous Vicar and his wife used to foster children occasionally, but they weren't here all that long really. It was all very tragic. The wife committed suicide and not long after, the vicarage burnt down in suspicious circumstances and the Reverend was killed in the blaze. I seem to remember being told that the girl they were fostering at the time was blamed. She disappeared a short time before the fire and the rumours were that she had come back to do it. The vicarage was completely rebuilt and that's when I moved here. I don't really remember much more than that. Have you spoken to her brother?'

Trip's head spun around to look at him. 'Brother?'

'The girls' brother – William. Nice lad. I'm assuming it's the same girl, as I know William had a sister who disappeared. He was taken into care from the Reverend and his wife after she left,' he said looking at Trip confused.

'I didn't know she had a brother. That's not come up on any of our searches.'

'He's not called Porter now, that could be why he hasn't shown up perhaps?'

'What's his full name now?'

'William - Billy Mathers. He still lives in Lynton.'

'Do you happen to know where I could find him? I'd like to talk to him about his sister.'

'Best off going to see the harbourmaster in Lynmouth, he'd know where to find him. Billy's a fisherman there.'

'Reverend Clewer, you've been very helpful indeed. I can't thank you enough for your time and information.'

'Two things before you go.'

'Of course, what's that?'

'One, make sure you find this killer…,' he paused.

'And two?' Trip asked.

'Make sure you talk to the woman.'

'The woman?'

'The woman who troubles your thoughts so much,' the Reverend said with a knowing smile.

'Thank you again for your time, Reverend,' Trip said getting up, unable to know what else to say to his last words.

As he walked back to his Jeep with Bear - his journalistic itch was back again, sensing he was close to something. His phone rang as he was about to drive to Lynmouth.

'Trip, it's Jack.'

He immediately felt himself tense up. 'What can I do for you?'

'The man in the baseball cap has been eliminated from our enquiries.'

'How come?'

'He's a pilot from Southampton Airport, John Anderson. He was halfway to Amsterdam International Airport at the time Grace was abducted and he's got flight records giving him alibis for the nights of the other murders too.'

'Right.'

'Everything OK?'

'Yep.'

'I get the feeling I've pissed you off in some way mate, but I'm not quite sure how.'

Trip could quite easily have continued acting childish and said nothing was wrong, but he'd known Jack a long time and felt he owed him more than that.

'You shouldn't have told Felicity about the night I crashed my car,' he said reluctantly.

'What?'

'And that I thought a killer in a blue car was sitting watching her at night. You knew I wasn't telling her because I didn't want to frighten her.'

'I assumed you'd told her because she said that she'd cleaned you up that night. But I clearly *wrongly* assumed.'

'And you said all of this when you went to see her,' Trip said irritably.

'What? I didn't go and see her - I was purposely *not* going to see her, knowing you didn't want to alarm her. I was looking at where the car had been parked on the road outside her house and asking her neighbours if they'd seen anything. She walked past me with her dogs and asked if this was about her patching you up after the bad accident. Therefore, I *assumed* you had told her.'

'I never told her I'd had a *bad* accident. I just said I'd fallen over Bear in the dark.'

'Well, she's not stupid mate - she's pretty switched on you know.'

'And *you* would know,' Trip muttered under his breath, feeling like a hormonal teenager.

'And why would I know? Mate, what the hell is this really about?' Jack asked impatiently.

'You know she's got a husband, right? - the woman you're seeing.' There, it was out. He'd said it. Days of feeling it boiling up inside and now suddenly he felt slightly less burdened.

'Isabella's got a husband?' Jack said confused.

'Isabella? What? No, Felicity!'

'Felicity? I'm not seeing Felicity! What are you bloody going on about?'

'You're not seeing Felicity? But I thought...,' Trip paused, feeling more confused by the second.

'No - I'm - Not - Seeing - Felicity,' Jack enunciated clearly. 'That clear enough for you? I'm dating Isabella Brock and have been for a few months now.'

'The fashion designer?' Trip asked, still struggling to understand what was unravelling.

'Yes! I met her in the Duchess of Cornwall one night when she was up from London visiting her mum who lives in Poundbury.'

'Oh, you never said.'

'Yeah, well it was early days and then all the dead bodies kept appearing – and well, it wasn't really a priority was it, especially with the whole Felicity thing going on in your head. I thought the last thing you'd be interested in was hearing about my love life.'

Trip was trying to rewind the various conversations he'd had with Felicity since he'd thought she was seeing Jack.

'So that day your car was parked outside her coach house was because?' Trip asked.

'Was because of something she should tell you if she wants to, not me.'

'Listen Jack, I owe you an apology.'

'You think!'

'I errr…,' he cleared his throat, 'think I've got the wrong end of the stick somewhere along the line mate.'

'No…really! - and have you *wrongly* accused Felicity too at any point?'

Trip remained silent for a moment, thinking. 'More than likely,' he sighed.

'I thought you were supposed to be some kind of super sleuth Trip, with a knack for sniffing out the truth!' Jack laughed.

'Yeah, clearly not where she's concerned,' he said, unsure of what he actually meant.

'I'm guessing you probably owe her an apology too then?'

'If she'll hear it, without flying into one of her rages again, which on this occasion, she'd be perfectly entitled to do.'

'Rages?'

'Oh yes. I seem to have a knack of winding her up.'

'Perhaps because you keep accusing her of things she hasn't done?'

'Perhaps,' Trip said, feeling foolish and annoyed with himself. *What is it about this woman that always makes me get everything so wrong?*

'And Trip?'

'Yeah?'

'Are you absolutely sure about the husband?'

'A definitely…maybe on that point!'

'I've never known you be so wrong about something mate. Odd that hey,' Jack said amused. 'Listen, I've got to go - another call coming in. Speak to you soon. And apologise to Felicity!' and Jack hung up laughing.

Trip threw his head back against the headrest and rubbed his hand across his forehead. He wasn't sure at which point over the last few months, that pivotal moment had occurred when he'd made a complete and utter dickhead of himself with regards to Felicity. But one thing he did know, he'd apologise to her in person as soon as he returned home – which would now be later today.

He started the engine and drove down the road to the harbour at Lynmouth. When he found the harbourmaster, he was told that Billy was out on a trawler and wouldn't be back until later, unsure of what time that would be. He gave the harbourmaster his card with a message on the back for Billy – asking to call as soon as possible in relation to his sister, then immediately drove back to the hotel to check out. He was now very keen to get back to Poundbury and apologise to Felicity as soon as he could – if she would even listen to him.

Traffic permitting, he hoped to be home by 5pm.

CHAPTER 53

She stumbled, unaware of where she was going as a black hood had been pulled tightly over her head. Suddenly she tripped and fell hard to the ground, landing heavily on her knees, pain ripping through them. She struggled, trying to get up, but it was too difficult with her hands tied behind her back. The kick came hard and sharp into her kidneys, followed by another to her ribs, thrusting her forward so that her head slammed into the ground. The pain was excruciating and she gasped, tears springing from her eyes in fear, but also now in pain. Grit cut into her cheek as her face lay on the cold, damp floor and she wanted to scream for help, but had already learnt that was futile due to the dense wad of material tied around her mouth.

The hood was suddenly grabbed, together with a handful of hair and sharply yanked upwards. She desperately tried to scramble to her feet to relieve the searing pain burning into her scalp, but the more she tried, the more she failed. Finally, after pushing herself up from her shoulder, she managed to stand and her hair was released.

A hand pushed sharply into her back and she lurched forwards, walking towards an unknown destination.

After a short distance, her arm was pulled backwards, forcing her to stop. She instinctively went to turn around, but both shoulders were grabbed roughly to prevent it. Survival instinct suddenly fuelled her and she kicked backwards, colliding with something. A man's voice cursed loudly and he spun her around, slamming his fist into her stomach. She doubled over in pain and bile retched into her throat from the impact, but the material in her mouth prevented it from being regurgitated, so she had no option but to swallow the bitter acid.

The hood was grabbed once more, forcing her head backwards. Her now badly winded body desperately wanted to crumple to the ground, but there was a final assault yet to come.

His fist crashed into the side of her face, snapping her head sharply to the left and she immediately fell to the ground, cracking her head. Blackness quickly descended like a heavy blanket, as she slipped silently into unconsciousness.

After a few moments of trying to control his raging anger towards the woman, he kicked her several more times and once satisfied she was unresponsive, picked up her body and threw her into the boot of the car. *How dare she try to fight back*, he thought. *Perhaps she's a mistake.*

The voices then began to chant their approval, *perhaps not*, he thought.

It was nearly time.

Calmly, he opened the driver's door and got into the vehicle, then quietly recited his already well learnt lines.

'And I looked...and behold a pale horse...and his name that sat on him was Death.....And...'

A landline phone began to ring nearby and he hesitated, unsure whether to answer it. Eventually, deciding he didn't want any loose ends that would need to be dealt with later, he got back out of the car and walked over to the phone.

CHAPTER 54

At just after 5pm, Trip was walking into his apartment when his mobile began to ring.

'Mr. Hazard?'

'Yes, how can I help you?'

'This is Billy Mathers in Lynton. The harbourmaster said you were looking for me today and wanted to talk to me about my sister?'

'Thank you so much for calling me Billy. Can you confirm if you're the brother of Veronica Porter?'

'Yes, Roni. I haven't seen her since I was ten years old. What's this about?'

Trip didn't want to be the one to tell him his sister had been murdered, but he owed it to Roni's memory.

'I'm helping the police in Dorset with an investigation and I'm so sorry to be the one to tell you, but Roni died in June this year. Someone would have been in touch sooner I'm sure, but you didn't show up on any records associated with her.'

'Oh…how did she die?' he asked quietly.

'At first it looked like suicide. I'm a freelance journalist and was asked to write an article on her for the local newspaper, which is why I was looking into her life. But something hasn't been sitting right with me about the whole thing and I then started uncovering small clues that made me believe it wasn't suicide. I'm sorry to say this Billy, but I think she was murdered.'

There was silence at the other end of the phone and he remained quiet letting Billy take his time to process what he'd just been told.

'I always wondered what happened to her. I can still see her face in my mind. Where did it happen?'

'She died off the cliffs in Portland, down here in West Dorset.'

'Portland,' he said hesitating, 'we went on holiday there when I was little, before mum died and before dad lost his job. It was the only family holiday we ever went on,' he said sadly.

'Then I assume she came down here because it was associated with a happy place for her.'

'I guess so.'

'Can you tell me about what you remember of your childhood? I know you were only young, but anything you can recall may help us.'

'I know mum was killed by a hit and run driver, but I don't really remember her. I was only five when she died. Dad was a drunk and never around much and after mum was killed, he couldn't cope with us - he'd forget to buy food and stuff. Roni tried to do what she could, but she was only eight herself. I remember him shouting at me one night that he wasn't even my dad and how he was now stuck with us. Maybe that's why I didn't show up as being related to her, you know, if he wasn't my dad on my birth certificate I mean,' Billy swallowed hard. 'Anyway, our school phoned Social Services in the end, when they caught Roni getting food out of the bins behind the school kitchen. When the social worker came to the house and saw the state of the place, we were taken away and placed in a foster home. We never saw dad again after that. He was found dead a few months later behind a pub. Liver failure I think.'

'Did you always stay together in the foster homes?'

'Yes, always. Roni would kick off if Social Services ever said we'd be going to different places. We moved around a lot of homes; I don't remember most of them. Some of them were OK…,' and his voice went quiet.

'I know this is hard Billy and it must be a horrible shock after all these years. I'm trying to do everything I can to help the police find the person responsible for these deaths, before he does it again.'

'Has he killed more than just Roni then?'

'I believe he has, yes. Can you tell me anything about the last home you were in together?'

'That was the worst one and why Roni decided we were going to run away and find somewhere to live on our own. I was ten at the time and she would have been thirteen I suppose. We were living with a vicar and his wife at the vicarage in Lynton. He was a horrible bloke; terrible temper and always beating his wife. In the day though, he'd be all fake and friendly to the people in the church. She was good at pretending everything was fine in front of people too,' he paused and sighed heavily.

'Take your time Billy.'

'One night, his wife tried to run away, but he found her. I remember looking out the bedroom window and seeing him dragging her back by her hair. He took her into the shed at the bottom of the garden and locked her in there all night. I tried to sneak some food down to her in the morning, but he caught me and beat me with his belt while chanting all these bible verses. He used to hit Roni too, worse than me because she would stand up to him whenever he hit me. Sometimes if I did something wrong like speak when I shouldn't or ask for some food, he'd go to hit me, but Roni would always take the punishment if she could.'

'Did no one know what was happening to you both there?'

'No. We tried to keep quiet and stay out of his way as much as we could.'

'Did his wife never go to the police when he hit her?'

'Not that I ever knew. Like I said, she was good at keeping up a show for all the neighbours and the people at church. He never hit her face and she always wore long sleeves and long skirts, whatever the weather, to hide the bruises I guess,' he paused again, reliving a period from his life he probably never thought he'd have to revisit. 'Eventually, I think his wife just had enough one day and she jumped off the cliffs at the Valley of the Rocks, near Lynton.'

Trip's radar suddenly went into overdrive.

'His wife committed suicide off a cliff?'

'Yes. Roni had stuck up for me one day or been accused of doing something she hadn't, I can't remember what exactly, but the vicar had exploded at her and hit her hard. Roni said that was enough, we were going to leave. So, she packed her rucksack up with the few belongings we had and planned to run away that night. She climbed out the bedroom window onto the porch roof and I was meant to follow her. But I'd forgotten the photo of mum I kept under my pillow. It was the only picture we had of her, so I went back for it. That's when he caught me. We'd already agreed the day before, that if anything went wrong and only one of us got away, we would meet in the trees by the school. But I never saw her again after that night.'

Billy fell silent for a few moments, remembering the last night he ever saw his sister.

'One of the local fishermen who was walking his dog, saw him hitting me that night through the window. He phoned the police and they came out. I lied to them though, saying everything was alright because I knew I would be meeting Roni the next day and we'd run away. But I should have told the truth and left with the police. Social Services came the next morning and I could hear raised voices from the kitchen. They took me away - I don't think the wife could cope with the shame of what people would say. She was paranoid about gossip as it was. I'm pretty sure that's why she killed herself.'

'And what happened to you Billy?'

'I ended up being fostered by the fisherman who called the police. He and his wife couldn't have kids of their own and they ended up adopting me. That's when I became Billy Mathers. They're both dead now, but they were a proper mum and dad to me. They helped me for years to try and find Roni, but we didn't know where to start really. If only she hadn't run away that night, she'd have come with me to the nicest home I ever had,' he said sniffing back tears.

'Oh Billy, I'm so sorry for the life you both had. And I'm sorry Roni isn't alive to see how good you've turned out.' Images of Trip's childhood appeared in his mind, feeling very grateful for the loving parents he had, before their own tragic deaths.

'It wasn't long after the wife's death, that the vicarage burnt down and the vicar was trapped inside. Some of the local gossips reckoned it was Roni who'd come back and done it. But there was no way she would have done something like that, no matter how horrible he was and how much he deserved a bad end.'

'Did they find the person responsible for the fire?'

'No. But I always reckoned it was Matthew.'

'Matthew?'

'Their son. About Roni's age. He was nasty just like his dad.'

Trip felt as though he'd been kicked by a bull.

'Where's the son now Billy?'

'Nobody saw him again after the fire.'

'What was his surname?'

'Louring. Matthew Louring.'

'Billy, I need to go now to make some phone calls, but can I phone you again in a few days to talk some more?'

'Yes of course. And Mr. Hazard?'

'Yes?'

'Please find the person who did this to her - and the others.'

'Oh, I will. Thanks again Billy and I'm so sorry for your loss.'

'Thanks Mr. Hazard for looking into this. I'll speak to you again soon' and Billy hung up.

Trip quickly made a phone call.

'Hey Trip, how was Lynton?' Coop asked.

'Interesting. Listen mate, can you find everything you can on a Matthew Louring. Urgently. He was the son of the vicar in Lynton when Roni and her brother lived there. They were fostered for a short while by the vicar and his wife and Matthew was a similar age to Roni back then, so probably thirteen years old. I need to know where he is now Coop, as I'm pretty sure he's our killer.'

'On it,' and the line went dead.

Trip's mind was buzzing as he paced around his apartment thinking the logic through. *Where is this kid now? He'd have to be in his mid-thirties now I'd guess, or a bit older if Billy got the age wrong?*

He was just about to phone Jack with the name, when his phone rang. Seeing the display, he answered it before it's second ring.

'Coop, did you manage to find anything?'

'Very little. Trail on the name ends the night of the vicarage fire, so he's clearly changed his name. All I've got is his birth certificate so far, Matthew Solomon Louring born 8th January 1980. Will get back to you when I have more,' and Coop hung up.

There was something Trip couldn't quite grasp in his mind, a name, he wasn't sure. But there was definitely something…. he just couldn't pinpoint it.

Suddenly it clicked and he snatched up his phone.

'Trip mate, what do you think I've done now!' Jack laughed.

'What was the name of the garage that towed Grace

Jefferies car away?'

'Errr…let me just check. What's happened?' Jack said, shuffling papers.

'Name please mate!'

'Here it is - Harris Recovery in Troy Town.'

'Shit! Jack it's him – Sol Harris. I bloody know the bloke too!' Trip grabbed his car keys and ran out the apartment, leaving Bear behind this time.

'You know him?'

'Yes! He repaired my car after the crash the other night - and once before after I pranged it. Sol *bloody* Harris. He's changed his name, but it's him, I'm sure of it. Matthew Solomon Louring. Sol and Solomon are not common names mate, it's got to be the same person.'

He jumped into his Jeep and pressed speakerphone on his mobile, throwing it onto the passenger seat.

'Who's Matthew Solomon Louring?', Jack said.

'His dad was a vicar in Lynton, North Devon. Nasty shit apparently. Beat his wife until she threw herself off a cliff. They fostered Roni and her brother for a while. Vicarage burnt down, killing his dad and I think it's very likely Matthew did it and that's when he disappeared - and at some point, turned up in Dorset.'

'Wait, Roni had a brother?'

'Yes – William, now Billy Mathers. He thinks he had a different father to Roni's which is probably why it's not shown up anywhere.'

'Shit. Where are you? I hope you're not going there!'

Trip didn't reply.

'I know you can bloody hear me! We're leaving now. DON'T GO THERE Trip, I mean it!' Jack shouted into the phone.

Trip ended the call. He was already on the A35 now heading towards Puddletown and should be at the garage within ten minutes, five if the traffic was light.

CHAPTER 55

Sol Harris hung up and clenched his fists. The caller had phoned regarding a problem with his car, but had talked continuously. He needed to keep up a pretence and patiently sat through the call, being as helpful and polite as possible. But now he could get back to what needed to be done. It was time.

As he walked back towards his car, he adjusted the dirty grey blanket covering the other vehicle, hidden away. It was unlikely anyone would notice it, as it wasn't visible from the road, but he liked to be thorough and didn't want any loose ends. He went to the rear of his car and waited, carefully listening. It was silent. The one thing he didn't need, was to repeat the mistake he made with Grace Jefferies. To avoid that, he made sure the black hood was secured tightly this time, so even if she regained consciousness when he opened the boot, she wouldn't be able to see him to lash out - and it was going to be a long drive to his old home in North Devon.

He got into his car and closed his eyes and the incantations began.

'And when these signs come to you, see that you take the chance which is offered you.'

And chance and fate had indeed come to him.

Slowly he opened his eyes and smiled. For now, the voices had quietened and he turned the ignition, ready to leave. Glancing around the garage one last time to ensure he had missed nothing, he pulled out onto the quiet secluded road.

His mind began to rewind time as he thought of the destination he was heading towards. Today, 18th November, was his mothers' birthday. The one day each year he would suppress his anger towards her for leaving him in this world, condemning him to his father's evilness. Every other day of the year, he despised his mother for jumping off a cliff to her death. The only reminders he had of her, were an old picture and lock of dark hair tied with red thread, hidden in an old tin box.

As he thought of his father, the voices began once again.

'If by chance my father puts his hand on me, it will seem to him that I am tricking him and he will put a curse on me in place of a blessing.'

The night that his father had beaten him so sadistically and mercilessly with his belt, was to be the last, as he had then sent him to the hell where he belonged.

Patiently, he'd waited in the shadows for his father to fall asleep, exhausted from the exertion of flogging him. Silently creeping around the house, he'd poured petrol from a can kept in the shed. To this day, he could still remember the sound of the match striking and the brief smell of sulphur as he lit the match.

He'd hidden in the bushes, watching with satisfaction as the deep amber flames licked their scorching tongues of fire around the building, eventually entirely engulfing the vicarage. The blaze incinerated the man he despised and transported his soul to a place where all evil resides.

That was the night Sol Harris was born and Matthew Solomon Louring had died. It was also the night his father's curse had taken hold of him. He'd once known how many women had died at his hands, in various coastal counties. But when that number reached double figures, he'd stopped counting. They were all the same to him. The long dark hair of his mother reincarnated onto a different vessel.

He thought back to the woman he'd killed in Portland. He couldn't believe it when he'd seen her walking along the coastal path one morning. At first, he hadn't recognised her as being the young girl his parents had fostered, but the realisation had eventually hit him. As a child, she'd run away from their home one night, leaving him to take extra beatings which normally would have been aimed at her. That was unforgivable, but fate had again rewarded him years later when their paths had crossed once more.

And now today, fate was truly on his side for providing another lamb to slaughter. It seemed only fitting that he should take the offering with him to Lynton and release the poisoned soul into the waters at The Valley of the Rocks - a birthday gift to his mothers' spirit, which was forever entombed there.

He glanced in his rear-view mirror towards the closed boot.

'For thou shalt give him everlasting life and make him glad with the joy of thy countenance.'

***

Trip glanced down at his mobile lying on the passenger seat, Jack's name was flashing again on the screen. He knew he was being reckless driving to the garage in Troy Town, but if there was any chance Sol would be there and could be stopped from abducting a fourth victim, then he decided it was worth the risk.

His phone immediately rang again, but this time he answered.

'Coop, what you got?'

'Hey Trip. All I've found so far are the parents names; father was Reverend Ezekiel Louring, mother Mary Louring, née Harris.'

'Shit – that confirms it then, it's definitely Sol Harris. I'm on my way to his garage now.'

'Be bloody careful mate – because if Sol doesn't kill you, then Tooga most definitely will!'

'Yeah, Jack pretty much said the same. Thanks Coop,' and Trip ended the call.

He was travelling down the A35 as fast as the traffic would allow, which at 6pm on Wednesday evening, wasn't very fast. Swearing under his breath, he slammed his hand on the steering wheel in frustration, willing the traffic to move out of his way.

Finally, the exit sign for Tolpuddle and Troy Town approached and he indicated, veering left to filter off the dual carriageway. After a few yards, he turned left again towards the tiny settlement of Troy Town, which consisted of only half a dozen houses, farm buildings and Sol Harris' Garage.

As he approached the small hamlet, he saw pulling out from the garage in the distance ahead of him, a blue Ford Mondeo. Trip gripped the steering wheel, his body tensing as he neared the garage.

It was closed and he had to make an instant decision; pull into the garage and look around, or follow the blue car on the chance it was Sol. He followed the car, grabbed his phone and called Jack.

'Get to the garage in Troy Town. I've just passed it, but it's locked up.'

'Ok - and where are you now going exactly?' Jack said sharply.

'Following a blue Ford Mondeo.'

'For Christ's sake Trip! Don't be a bloody hero, let the police do their job!'

'I'll just get close enough to get you a numberplate. I can't let this go Jack, it might be Sol and I'm not going to let him slip through our fingers now.'

'I'm NOT happy about this at all,' Jack shouted angrily. 'Be careful and stay well back from him. I don't need the headache or paperwork if you get yourself bloody killed!'

'Understood,' and Trip hung up.

He gripped the steering wheel and accelerated along the narrow road. Trees lined both sides, the leaves now fallen to the ground in a carpet of rich browns and golds. Clusters of wild bracken still remained green and huddled together in the damp November chill. Driving uphill now, the road curved to the left and he briefly lost sight of the blue car. As the road straightened again and started its descent, he was relieved to see it up ahead. He was watching his speed now as the road continued to slope downhill. If it was Sol, what he didn't want to do was gain too much on the car and alert him to his presence.

He passed an agricultural machinery depot on the right and a few yards later, the road stopped at a junction. Trip looked left and right unsure which way the car had turned.

'Shit!' he shouted.

He hit his steering wheel with his hand, angry with himself that he hadn't realised the road came to such an abrupt stop. Listening to his gut, he turned right, hoping that was the way the Mondeo had turned. The road curved again onto a bridge which extended over the A35, then stopped at another junction.

'Shit!'

Left to Dorchester or right to Higher Bockhampton. He hesitated and turned left which led him back onto the A35, assuming the car had opted for a faster road. The traffic was still heavy with evening commuters and he couldn't pull out immediately into the flow. Seconds passed which felt like minutes - valuable minutes where Sol was potentially getting away.

Finally, a small gap appeared in the traffic, enough for him to accelerate away and pull into the stream of vehicles. A car swerved behind him, crashing into plastic roadwork cones at the side of the road. Horns blared, but he didn't look back, too focussed ahead now, frantically searching in the distance for the Mondeo.

The road was too congested to overtake and he still couldn't see the car, so he kept veering across his lane to better see the traffic ahead. A roundabout neared, but trees and overgrown shrubbery prevented his view of the junctions exiting. The left-hand lane had far less vehicles, so he moved across into it.

As he eventually pulled away from the roundabout, he suddenly caught sight of the back of the Mondeo, which was still on the road straight ahead. Trip quickly accelerated, wheels squealing, pulling across in front of a car which had been slowly about to exit onto the road he needed. The driver saw him at the last second and narrowly missed being hit.

Trip sped down the road, trying to gain enough distance so he could read the number plate. Suddenly, the road widened making it possible for him to overtake one of the cars in front. There were now only six vehicles between them.

An exit to Wareham neared on the left, the place where Grace Jefferies had broken down and where Sol had towed her away. Two cars turned off at the exit giving him a valuable gain on the Mondeo.

Trip veered again to the right and finally caught sight of the number plate. He hit the redial button on his mobile and called Jack, shouting the number plate down the phone at him, then immediately hung up before Jack could speak. Another roundabout ahead and the blue car went straight on, heading towards Monkey Jump roundabout and Poundbury. There were now only two cars between them.

The Mondeo took the second exit towards

Winterbourne Abbas and luckily the vehicle directly in front of Trip, turned off left into a layby. One car now separated them.

His mobile rang.

'The plates are fake,' Jack said. 'They belong to a black Peugeot written off six months ago.'

'No surprise there – we're now on the Bridport Road, just before Winterbourne Abbas,' and he again ended the call.

That was all the confirmation Trip needed. Adrenaline released its valve, surging through his veins and he sped up behind the one car remaining between them. The Mondeo swayed right; Trip mirrored his movement and suddenly the car accelerated away. The road was straight and the lanes wide, but there was too much traffic coming towards him to be able to safely overtake. Trip blasted his horn at the car in front, hoping it would move out the way, but it didn't. The Mondeo was rapidly pulling further ahead into the distance now.

A small gap in the oncoming traffic allowed Trip to finally overtake, narrowly missing a white van fast approaching. He slammed the accelerator down, gaining distance at last. As he passed a caravan park on the left, the Jeep was nearing 70mph. The road started winding, the lanes getting narrower and he had no choice but to ease up his speed at the risk of hitting an innocent driver - now a very real danger. The Mondeo sped over the brow of a hill, then the road curved sharply to the left. At the last moment, it veered across the road, taking a narrow single-track lane to the right towards Compton Valence. Trip slammed on his brakes, unable to immediately follow, as two lorries were travelling towards him on the lane he needed to cross.

Road clear, he accelerated onto the narrow single track and could see the blue car ahead. He forced the Jeep to its limit to catch up, any risk to his own life now a non-existent thought. A small white car appeared around a bend towards him and Trip hit his brakes, swerving into a passing place on the left, allowing the car to pass.

Quickly accelerating away again, he could see the Mondeo had been forced to slow because of a Land Rover pulling into a field entrance. He raced towards the car, fishtailing on the damp road and swiftly slammed the Jeep into four-wheel drive.

Ahead the Mondeo ignored a stop sign at a crossroads and pulled straight out, continuing along the road. As Trip approached, he quickly looked left and right at the junction, praying nothing was coming as he sped out to follow the car. The road narrowed, high hedges flanking its sides. He rammed the accelerator down again and was now finally upon him. And that's when he saw Sol briefly glance in his rear-view mirror, looking back at him.

The road eventually widened for a passing place on the right and Trip took his opportunity. He pulled out and swerved his Jeep into the side of the Mondeo, forcing it left into a field and through a gap in the hedge. The car skidded in the mud, its rear end smashing against a telegraph pole, before careering to the right and finally coming to a stop as it slammed, at speed, into a tree. The impact forced the pole to tilt, pulling the base out of the ground. The cables began to strain and stretch before finally breaking its constraints, allowing it to fall heavily towards the Jeep.

Trip threw himself across the front seats as the pole smashed down on his roof. His airbag deployed and he frantically pushed it out of the way as he kicked the driver's door open.

As he dragged himself out, he could see the bonnet of the crumpled Mondeo bent back, smoke seeping from beneath it. Sol staggered out from the car, falling to the ground on his knees and Trip limped up behind him.

He grabbed his collar, yanking him to his feet then slammed his fist hard into Sol's right cheek. There was a crack as his knuckles smashed down on the bone, blood splattering from his mouth. Sol fell to the ground on his hands and knees and Trip kicked him hard in his side. He groaned and fell to the left where he was kicked again in his stomach, completely winding him. Instinctively, Sol curled into a ball to protect himself and Trip knelt over him, throwing a fist into his face once more. Blood ran from his nose and his head lolled to the left; his body now motionless.

Trip fell to the ground, gasping in oxygen, aware of an agonising pain in his shoulder. He heard a noise and looked at Sol, still unconscious on the ground. As he carefully listened for the noise again, there was now only silence.

Suddenly, the noise again. It was muffled, but there was definitely a sound coming from somewhere. He studied the smoking Mondeo, petrol now trickling onto the ground from the crushed engine bay. As the noise sounded again, he realised it was coming from the car and it was getting louder.

He ran to the smoking vehicle and looked inside, but it was empty. Rushing to the boot and skidding in the damp muddy ground, he yanked it open. There was a body inside, a black hood pulled over the head and string tightly fastened around the neck. He pulled the figure towards him and a woman's voice moaned in pain. Reaching behind her, he untied the bindings wrapped around her wrists and grabbed underneath her arms, pulling her towards him as gently as he could. Her trousers caught on something, ripping the material wide open and he bent forward, carefully lifting her out and carrying her quickly away from the vehicle.

As he was about to lay her on the ground, the Mondeo exploded into flames and he threw himself across her body to protect it from any flying debris.

Her chest was heaving against his and he tried to roll away, but his left arm was caught beneath her body. With his free hand, he grabbed one end of the string from around her neck and placed it between his teeth. Biting down, he pulled it undone and spat out the loose fibres. Gently, he pulled the hood up and a mass of curls were released.

He stared down at Felicity's battered and bloodied face, feeling numb and speechless. His heart felt as if it had been grabbed by a fist and twisted.

Quickly pulling the wadding from her mouth, she gasped fresh air into her lungs, coughing and choking. Her eyes blinked open, her brain trying to make sense of her surroundings and she looked up into his eyes.

'Felicity, what hurts?' he asked urgently.

'Everything,' she said breathlessly, lifting her head and trying to sit up.

He pulled his arm from beneath her and gently pushed her shoulders back down.

'No, don't move. You must stay still.'

His eyes scanned her body trying to assess the damage. As he did, he saw deep, healed scarring carved into her thighs through the large rip in her trousers and he removed his jacket, gently laying it over her legs. His throat tightened with emotion.

'Help's coming,' he said quietly and pulled his phone from his back pocket. He called Jack, pressing it on speakerphone to keep his hands free to hold Felicity.

'Where the hell are you Trip?' Jack shouted down the phone.

'Felicity…,' was all he could say.

'Have you got her? Her car was hidden behind Sol's garage.'

'I've got her. Get an ambulance Jack – it's the road to Compton Valance.'

He heard Jack booming out instructions to someone near him. 'And Sol?' he asked.

Trip glanced back over his shoulder; the Mondeo was now engulfed in flames, but Sol Harris was nowhere to be seen.

'He's gone,' Trip said falling back on his heels.

'We'll be there in ten minutes,' and Jack hung up.

He shifted his weight, enabling him to hold her until the ambulance arrived.

'An ambulance is on its way,' he said.

She opened her eyes again, 'Trip?'

'Yes?' he said, softly.

'Do you ever think there will be a time when you don't crash into a vehicle I'm in?' and she smiled weakly.

He laughed and squeezed her tight.

'Ow!'

'Shit! Sorry!'

Gently, he picked up her hand, lightly kissing the back of it before placing it against his face.

'You still haven't shaved I see.'

'Been a bit busy saving your life,' he smiled.

Somehow, they were both oblivious to the cold damp ground they were lying on and the once-blue car, ablaze metres away. He smoothed her unruly curls around her face and again glanced down at the jacket covering her legs.

'How the hell did you end up in the boot of a madman's car?' he asked.

'Well now, that's an interesting story.'

'What do you mean?'

'So, way back in June, a particularly bad driver smashed into my car in a supermarket car park. Two months later, the same person hit my car outside my house. Then, best of all, he gave me the number of a murdering psychopath who repairs cars!' she said, smiling through the pain, 'and on a whim, I drove to the garage on my way home from Poole this afternoon to see if he could book it in to be repaired.'

Trip was speechless as he listened to her, feeling an overwhelming sense of guilt.

'I am so sorry Felicity.'

'Well, I'm assuming you didn't do it on purpose.'

Trip held her even closer and closed his eyes.

***

Sol had ten valuable minutes to escape before the police arrived. He staggered onto the main road, holding the side of his bruised and battered body, then began limping as quickly as he could in the opposite direction.

A dark blue BMW approached, slowing as it drew close and the driver buzzed the window down.

'Do you need a lift?'

'Yeah, I…errr…came off my quad bike – bloody thing's a death trap,' Sol said.

'Of course you did,' the driver smiled. 'I'm on my way to Dorchester – I can give you a lift to the train station if that's any good for you?'

'Perfect.'

As he got into the vehicle, the sound of sirens could be heard in the distance.

EPILOGUE

The helicopter circled overhead, looking for Sol Harris. He was injured and wouldn't be able to get far, or so they thought.

Trip and Jack stood, arms folded, in the field together.

'Think it's a right-off mate,' Jack said nodding towards the Jeep, the telegraph pole still embedded into its roof.

'Needed a new one anyway,' he shrugged.

'Make sure the next one's got hands-free calling will you – I'd hate to arrest you for driving whilst using a mobile,' Jack smiled, but with a hint of seriousness to his voice.

Trips eyes still hadn't left Felicity. The paramedics were tending to her in the back of an ambulance and she was partially sitting up, her hands swatting the medics away as they tried to help her.

Jack followed his eyes. 'Stubborn woman.'

'Sure is.'

'And lucky.'

'I could've killed…'

'Don't even go there, Trip,' Jack interrupted. 'Don't torture yourself on something that didn't happen.'

'Yeah, but…'

'But nothing. You saved her life. Nearly killed yourself doing it, trashed your Jeep and pissed off a lot of drivers on the A35. But miraculously, you're still alive - and so is Felicity. If you had done what I told you to, then she could well be dead by now,' and Jack squeezed his friends shoulder. 'But, if you ever do something so bloody stupid again, I'll kill you myself!'

'Watch the shoulder mate,' Trip winced. 'What about Sol? I can't believe he got away - he was unconscious mate. I hit him hard. Several times. And proper Tooga punches too, the way he taught me to fight,' and he ran his hand wearily through his hair.

'The trouble with psychopaths is that they're resilient bastards. But we'll get him, he'll be hiding in a hedge somewhere and the helicopter will find him.'

Unfortunately, both Jack and Trip were beginning to think, it may not.

The blackened, scorched car now sat dripping with white foam where the fireman had extinguished it. Forensics were searching the ground nearby under the glare of temporary flood lights.

Dan Knight, one of the firemen on call, finished loading up the fire engine ready to return to the station. As he walked towards the ambulance to speak to Felicity, he passed a paramedic.

'How's she doing?'

'Pretty well, considering.'

'OK if I go and speak with her?' Dan asked.

'Sure, make it quick though as we'll be leaving soon.'

Dan walked to the rear of the ambulance.

'You do seem to have a knack of getting yourself into dangerous predicaments don't you,' he smiled.

She looked up, 'certainly feels that way, yes.'

'Seriously though, how are you?'

'Feeling like a herd of buffalos have run over me, but other than that, OK.'

'I'd say you're pretty lucky to be here right now. Good job Trip got to you when he did.'

Felicity glanced across towards Trip, who was looking back at her, 'I know,' she said simply.

The paramedic approached Trip. 'Nasty gash you've got on your head there.'

'I'll live,' he said, eyes still fixed on Felicity.

'We should get it checked out at the hospital. We're just leaving, so…'

'Speak to you later mate,' Jack said pushing him forwards, 'go get yourself cleaned up, you look like shit!'

'You know her?' the paramedic nodded towards the back of the ambulance.

'I do,' Trip said. 'Is she going to be OK?'

'She will be. Few broken ribs and a lot of bruising and cuts, but considering what she's been through tonight, I'd say she's remarkably lucky. Her body is as stubborn as the woman,' he smiled and Trip felt a wave of relief crash over him.

As he reached the ambulance, he wondered what his friend and Felicity had been saying to each other.

'Mate you're a hero! But a bloody foolhardy one according to Jack! He said you could have got yourself killed in the process, but you saved her and that's the main thing,' and Dan patted Trip's shoulder, making the pain scream at him once more.

'Yeah, you know me, always in the wrong place at the wrong time.'

'Look after yourself - both of you. And Felicity?' Dan said,' 'try and keep out of trouble for a bit - we'll have to get a fire engine assigned just to you at this rate!' He tapped the side of the ambulance and walked away smiling.

Trip climbed into the back and sat next to her stretcher. 'Right place, right time I'd argue,' she said looking into his eyes.

He held her gaze, 'and we both know how much you like to argue,' he grinned.

She looked up at the paramedic as he got into the vehicle and closed the rear doors.

'Can you get him his own ambulance please?' she said.

The two men looked at her confused.

'Every time I'm in a vehicle and he's close by, I end up in a bloody crash,' she smiled.

As the ambulance pulled away, she reached over and grabbed Trip's wrist. 'Thank you for saving my life.'

***

Gareth Fletcher turned off the reception lights in the Vets practice, locked the main door and turned the sign to say closed. He slumped down in the chair in his consulting room and pulled the flask of bourbon from his ruck sack, taking a large drink.

He felt the knots in his neck begin to loosen and closed his eyes, stretching his legs out.

His phone beeped with a text.

Open up – I'm outside.

He sighed wearily and walked to the main door, unlocking it.

'You're late,' Gareth snapped.

'I picked up a hitchhiker,' the figure in the hoodie and baggy joggers said.

'You got the money?'

'Of course, here –,' and the envelope was placed on the table.

Gareth unlocked the cabinet in his room and pulled out three phials of ketamine, placing them on the table next to the money.

Their hands reached forward at the same time, retrieving what now belonged to each of them.

The figure turned and walked back towards the door, sliding the phials safely into a pocket.

Gareth picked the envelope of money up off the table and shoved it into his ruck sack. He had no need to count it – he knew who the person was and where to find them – and they knew that too. Both of them had a mutual respect for how much they each stood to lose if anything went wrong.

To be continued in Trip Hazard Book 2...

A BIT ABOUT ME...
...if you're interested!

Firstly, thank you for reading my novel! I have always been passionate about writing and storytelling. From a small child, I became enraptured by stories created in my father's imagination, serialised to us on lazy Sunday mornings. As a teenager I'd write photo romance stories, pretending they were published in magazines (all the rage in the 1980's!)

After emigrating to Australia in 2003, I attempted to write a novel about my adventures. I got to 15,000 words and stopped, having too much fun doing the adventure bit. A trend then continued over the years of novels ending up as short stories. Fast forward to living back in the UK with my own successful business as a Clinical Hypnotherapist. One day, a few years ago, my window cleaner put a yellow A-board outside my house while he was cleaning the windows – and the name I saw on the board inspired the series of novels. That was the day *Trip Hazard* was born.

But he never made it onto paper at that point.

Then two years later, I finally started to write a novel featuring Trip Hazard - determined to complete it. It was only ever supposed to be a stand-alone novel - but I quickly realised all of the characters were coming to life in my mind and I couldn't end those lives after one book. Trip is very much fictional (sadly)…and Felicity Marche? Well, let's just say I have endless adventures to write about in the coming series of Trip Hazard books!

When I'm writing, I become completely immersed in the project - plunging myself into the depths of the world my characters live in, living and breathing the same air as them.

But now it's over to you - so I hope you enjoy reading my books as much as I enjoy writing them!

And if you've enjoyed Book 1 and want to know where the story continues to, then here's a taster for **Trip Hazard Book 2…** *Where Evil Hides…*

WHERE EVIL HIDES
Trip Hazard Book 2

Sometimes you outgrow a town…
…but sometimes you just run out of people you want to kill.

He pulled into the dark car park. There was only one other vehicle there and he parked beside it, undid his seatbelt and took his phone from his pocket to send a text.

I'm here. Where R U?

He waited for a reply.

Bench near the path leading to car park.

He got out of his Porsche, walked to the rear and opened the boot to grab his torch. As he followed the path from the car park, he noticed the first bench and walked towards it.

There was no one waiting there.

Thinking that perhaps he'd misunderstood the text, he made his way towards the next bench, careful not to trip in the gloomy torchlight.

Silence surrounded him and the irritation inside him began to grow. He didn't like playing games and his time was valuable, so he once again sent a text.

I'm not in the mood for games. Where R U?

The torch began to flicker and he hit his palm against it,

forcing it back into temporary life. But that life was short lived and it quickly flickered off for the last time. Stumbling in the dark, he finally reached another bench, but again it was empty. His patience had now disappeared and he turned to retrace his steps to go back to his car.

His phone beeped and he looked down at the text message.

I'm behind you...

* TO BE PUBLISHED IN SPRING 2022 *

TRIP HAZARD NEWS

To receive all the latest news, please visit:

www.janninemillarauthor.com

where you will find a contact form you can complete and social media links too.

Printed in Great Britain
by Amazon